WHY WAS _ _ HIM NATHAN?

That wasn't his name. It was his brother's name! His name was Jake. Yes, that was it: Jake Connor. He was nothing like his brother—at least, he hoped not.

And yet...

His head was throbbing abominably, and through the haze of pain that was dulling his senses he stared at the woman beside him with tormented eyes. He felt a surge of apprehension. She was familiar—yet not familiar. Where was he? And more to the point, what had he done?

Forcing himself not to panic, he quickly glanced around him. He was on a bed, of course, but he had known that. But whose bed was it? He didn't recognize it. Nor the room around him—though he felt he should.

"Are you all right, Nathan?"

There she was again, calling him by his brother's name. He looked at her. His lips parted to tell her she'd made a mistake, that whatever she'd thought, he wasn't Nathan, but that he'd be more than happy to continue to take his place. She was so beautiful. He'd always thought so. Ever since his brother had shown him her picture, right after the wedding.

Their wedding...

He swallowed. He knew who she was.

She was Caitlin.

Caitlin _Wolfe_.

His brother's wife.

Anne MATHER

DANGEROUS
Temptation

MIRA BOOKS

ISBN 1-55166-269-8

DANGEROUS TEMPTATION

Copyright © 1997 by Anne Mather.

MIRA and the star colophon are trademarks of MIRA Books.

Printed in U.S.A.

DANGEROUS
Temptation

Prologue

1955

The afternoon was hot and sultry. A storm had been threatening earlier, but it had moved away, leaving overcast skies and air as thick as cotton wool. It was an effort even to breathe, and most people were taking it easy until the heat of the day had passed.

In the small hospital the maternity ward was quiet now. The babies had been fed and changed, and put down for their rest, and the new mothers were taking a well-earned break, relaxing on their beds. Most of them were dozing, catching up on their sleep, although the heat in the narrow ward was stifling even with all the windows open. But in Blackwater Fork, North Carolina, air-conditioning was still a luxury.

In the end bed, nearest the swing doors, Alice Connor shifted restlessly. Unlike the other mothers, she was not enjoying the chance to get some rest. Being able to rest meant she was able to think, too, and right at this moment Alice didn't want to think at all.

Beside her, in twin bassinets, her two sons slumbered peacefully. Alike as two peas in a pod, the babies knew nothing of their mother's turmoil. They'd been fed, their diapers were clean, and they were content. In their world, they had no worries, not even where their next meal was coming from.

But for Alice, life was not so simple. Having another baby at all was going to mean the rest of them would have to make sacrifices; having *twins* was an eventuality she'd never even considered.

What Fletch would say when he came back from his trip, God alone knew. Persuading him that the child was his had not been easy. Imagining what he'd say when he found out about the twins didn't bear thinking about. He was suspicious of her already, putting the hex on any man he thought might look at her twice. If he ever found out about Jacob—

Her breath caught in her throat, and turning it into a cough, so as not to alert the other women in the ward of her uneasiness, she rolled onto her side. Now she could see her babies, small and vulnerable in the well-worn gowns the hospital had provided. But she'd come into the hospital to deliver *one* baby. The gowns she'd brought for just one baby hadn't been nearly enough for two.

It was just as well Fletch was away, she thought gratefully, delivering another load of lumber to New Mexico. It gave her a few days to come to terms with the situation, even if she still had no idea what was going to happen to them all.

At least the babies didn't look like Jacob. Oh, they were dark-haired, of course, just like him, but their small, pouty features were exactly like the other four babies she had birthed. Unfortunately, as far as she knew, there were no twins in the Connor family tree. No twins in the Hickory family tree, either, she thought, wincing at the pun. Whereas Jacob had told her he'd had a twin brother, who'd died just a few days after they were born.

The thought seeded—and was quickly suppressed—that it might have been easier for her if one of her babies had died. She'd have been upset, of course, but that might have made things easier with Fletch. There was no chance that she could have kept it a secret, though. In a little place like the Fork, there was no way to keep a secret like that.

But at least Fletch wouldn't have had to feed it. And there was always the possibility that he might have become attached to the one that remained. After all, he didn't have any sons, only four daughters. She caught her breath. Which was just another reason why she was so on edge.

It was eight years since Joanne, her youngest daughter, had been born, and she and Fletch had agreed then that they couldn't afford any more children. That was why he'd been so furious when she'd told him she was pregnant; so suspicious, too, that the baby wasn't his.

But, somehow, she'd convinced him that it was, even if she had got a beating for her pains. But that was nothing new. Fletch often beat her when he'd had too much to drink. And at least the fact that he drank too much had given her an excuse. She doubted he knew exactly what he did when he'd swallowed more than a quart of whisky.

Things had gotten harder after she'd had to give up her job at the diner. By the time she was six months pregnant, Ben Garrett had decided she was no longer an asset to his business. The timber bosses and travellers who used the diner wanted a pretty woman to serve their needs. Not one boasting a stomach that stretched the buttons of her overall.

These past three months had been bleak. Fletch grumbled all the time about how they were going to continue paying the rent, and he stayed out later and later, drinking and playing cards with his cronies. The girls were needing new shoes for the coming winter, and the eldest, Lisa, was desperate to go to college. But how could they afford that,

Alice fretted, when they barely had enough to eat? How were they going to feed one baby let alone two?

One of the babies stirred, small lips sucking at some non-existent teat, one star-shaped hand unfolding to expose a milky palm. Oh, God, they were so beautiful, she thought, stretching out her hand to touch a downy head. Dark hair clung to her fingers; a soft scalp shaped itself to her palm.

A hand touched her shoulder. "Alice?"

She started violently, turning to face the man behind her with wide, unguarded eyes. "Jacob!" Her mouth was dry, and she looked anxiously over his shoulder. "Oh, God, Jacob, what are you doing here? Do you want to get me hanged?"

"I just heard." Jacob Wolfe's voice was soft and soothing, his eyes moving beyond her stiffening form to where the two babies lay together, their cribs side by side. "Oh, Alice, they're amazing! Why didn't you tell me you were going to have twins?"

Alice looked around the ward with panic-stricken eyes. But thankfully, most of the women appeared to be asleep. Those she knew, or knew her anyway. The others couldn't know that Jacob wasn't her husband. Or at least she prayed they didn't. But that didn't mean that he could stay.

"You've got to go," she said, her voice low and anguished. "You shouldn't be here. If anyone sees you, if anyone recognises you—"

"They won't." Ignoring her fears, the babies' father hooked his hip onto the bed. He took her resisting hands in his. "How are you? They told me at the diner that you'd been admitted last night."

"At the diner?" Alice was horrified. "Oh, Jacob, you didn't—"

"Hey, there aren't that many twins born around here," he declared softly. "Of course, it's a talking point." He smoothed his thumbs over her knuckles. "I didn't ask any questions. Nobody suspects."

"Fletch will," said Alice unsteadily, drawing her hands out of his grasp. "There are no twins in his family. Mine neither, come to that."

"No." Jacob turned his head and looked almost enviously at the two sons he could never claim as his own. "Are they both strong? Are they healthy?"

Alice stifled a resentful retort, and nodded. "It looks like it," she said, trying not to feel bitter. It was six months since she had laid eyes on him, and she'd hoped she'd never see him again. It wasn't fair, she thought. A man could flirt with a woman indiscriminately; he could tease her and flatter her, and make her feel so good, she didn't know if she was on her head or her heels. Particularly a man like Jacob Wolfe, with his dark good looks and tall, lean figure, and a bankroll to match the flashy car he drove.

He'd come into the diner one day last fall, and from the very beginning he'd let her know he found her attractive. And what the hell, she had been attractive, thought Alice grimly, aware that in a place like Blackwater Fork her red-blond hair and shapely figure had always marked her for attention. It was why Ben Garrett had hired her, for God's sake. He could have had any number of teenage girls to serve his customers coffee and the juicy steaks and luscious cheesecakes his wife cooked up in the kitchen of the diner, but he'd chosen Alice. She might be in her thirties; she might have four children, three of whom were already on the way to growing up. But she was still the best-looking woman he had ever employed, and the increase in his takings since he took her on had justified his confidence in his decision.

Jacob Wolfe was something else. Alice had known that from the start. For all he dressed like the other men in casual shirts and jeans, he was no salesman. Not a trucker like

Fletch, either, with dirty fingernails and calluses on his palms. No, he was a gentleman, she'd known that right away. Which was why she'd been so flustered when he'd shown so much interest in her.

She'd been a fool, she knew it. She'd never been a push-over for any man until Jacob came along. Apart from anything else, she'd known what Fletch would do to her if he ever found her messing with anyone else. And for all her faults, she'd always been a good mother. She loved her kids, and she'd do nothing to threaten their future.

But Jacob had gotten under her skin, and although Ben had told her he owned a mill up north and that he'd only come down here looking for timber, she'd found herself watching for him every time someone opened the diner door.

She hadn't really expected him to come back. After that first time, when he'd taken her home after dark in his fancy car, she'd been sure that was the last she'd see of him. He'd gotten what he wanted. He'd made mad, passionate love to her in the rear seat of his car, parked in the back of Dillon's Grocery, with the fear of Sheriff Peyton finding them and reporting them to Fletch.

But he had come back. All through that winter, when the roads were frozen and treacherous, and anyone with a lick of sense would have stayed home in New Jersey, he'd made the trek to Blackwater Fork. Luckily, he'd been able to strike some deal with Abe Henry out at the lumber yard, giving him a legitimate excuse to stay around. And if Ben had had his suspicions, he wasn't saying anything to Fletch. He'd heard that old story about the king shooting the messenger.

Alice supposed she had been naïve thinking she could get away with it. But the times she was with Jacob were the best times of her life. Fletch had never made her feel like Jacob made her feel. She'd wanted him with an urgency that had defied all reason.

She didn't know what she'd expected would come of it. She never asked Jacob about himself, about his life away from Blackwater Fork, and he never volunteered it. It was as if they were both fooling themselves that this was the only life they knew.

Finding herself pregnant had not been part of the equation. She'd had a coil fitted after Joanne was born, and Jacob always used a rubber. She'd thought she was safe—from that eventuality at least. But accidents happened, and she'd found herself just another victim....

"You knew I'd come," he said now, aware of the wounded censure in her eyes. "I want to help you, Alice. That's why I'm here. I heard Fletch was away and we need to talk."

"Won't your *wife* wonder where you are?" Alice inquired acidly, the resentment jelling into anger and expelling the initial weakness she had felt upon seeing him again. But God, she hadn't even known he had a wife until she'd told him she was expecting his baby. Then, he'd confessed the truth fast enough, before abandoning her to face her shame alone.

"Iris has nothing to do with us," he told her now, his mouth tightening into a thin line. "And before you berate me for leaving you alone all these months, think what would have happened if I'd stayed."

Alice swallowed the bile in her throat. "Don't tell me you stayed away for my sake!"

"No." His eyes darkened. "I admit, I had my reasons. But don't envy Iris, for Christ's sake. I never loved her, and you know it."

"Liar!"

Alice turned her face away from him, but he caught her chin and turned it back. "I mean it," he said. "But I'll never leave her. She gave me what I wanted, and I owe her for that."

"A sawmill," said Alice scathingly, tears stinging her eyes as she remembered at least part of what he'd told her six months ago. He'd married Iris to gain control of her late father's sawmill. However successful he said he'd been, she could despise him for that.

"That was part of it," he agreed. "I'm not proud of it, but I've made her a rich woman. It's a shame we've got no son of our own to leave it to." He looked at the cribs. "Whereas you've got two—" he looked at her again "—that you don't want."

Alice's eyes widened in horror. "*No!*"

"Why not?" Jacob was gaining confidence now. "You've no money. You can't afford two more mouths to feed. Talk is, Fletch beat the living daylights out of you when he found you were pregnant." His fingers dug into her jaw suddenly. "If I'd been here, I'd have killed him for that."

"But you weren't here, were you?" Alice snatched her chin away and rubbed the mark his fingers had made with the back of one shaking hand. "How dare you come here now and suggest I hand my babies over to you?" She took a breath, and then went on defiantly. "They're not your babies anyway. They're mine—mine and Fletch's, do you hear? And there's nothing—*nothing*—you can do about it."

"Hey, calm down." Alice's voice had risen as she spoke, and for the first time Jacob seemed to become aware that there were other people in the ward. "I'm not suggesting you hand both babies over. For God's sake, Alice, what kind of a brute do you think I am?"

Alice sniffed. "But you said—"

"Whatever it was, I said it badly," declared Jacob tersely, realising he was in danger of alienating her altogether. "I just thought we might come to some agreement. It's in everyone's interest to do the best we can."

Alice regarded him suspiciously. "So what do you want?"

Jacob hesitated only briefly. "I think you know."

Alice gasped. "You're mad!"

"They're my sons, Alice." Jacob looked at her unblinkingly. "You know it, and I know it. Why shouldn't I want to help them?"

"Help them?" Alice almost choked on the words. "Like you helped me, you mean?" Her face contorted. "Get out of here, Jacob, before I call a nurse and have you thrown out!"

Jacob didn't move. "Go ahead," he said. "Call a nurse. Call the administrator if you want to. But don't forget, I have some influence around here, too. One word to Abe Henry about that quart of moonshine Fletch keeps in his cab, and he'd be out of a job."

Alice's jaw sagged. "You wouldn't."

"I wouldn't want to," said Jacob, which wasn't quite the same thing. "For Christ's sake, Alice, I care about you. D'you think I want to make life difficult for you with that big ape?"

"Fletch would kill you," said Alice suddenly. "If he ever found out about you and me, he'd kill you." Her lips twisted. "Then he'd kill me."

Jacob sighed. "He's not going to find out about you and me," he assured her. "If you show a little sense."

"And give you one of my babies? What d'you think Fletch is going to think about that?"

"Not—*give*—me one of the babies," amended Jacob steadily. "Let me adopt one." He paused. "Iris—Iris can't have children. We tried—everything we could, but it was just no good. And—adoption isn't easy, even for people like us. We're too old now. We waited too long." He lifted his shoulders dismissively. "I'd make it worth your while."

Alice's mouth curled. "You want to—*buy*—your own son."

"If that's what it takes."

Alice held up her head. "Fletch won't let you do it," she said bravely, but she suspected he would. Jacob had fastened onto the one aspect of Fletch's character she couldn't change. For years, she'd been telling herself he loved his daughters, and perhaps he did, in his own way. But she'd always known, deep down inside her, that he'd marry them off to the devil himself if he made it sufficiently worth his while. And as for these two...

"I'll have to ask him, won't I?" Jacob remarked now, getting up to circle the bed and look down at the twins in their cribs. "My God, they are alike, aren't they? My mother once told me my brother and I were identical when we were born, too."

"Then it's a pity it wasn't you who died instead of your brother," exclaimed Alice recklessly. She flinched at the sudden anger in his eyes, but she pressed on regardless. "I wonder, if he'd lived, would he have married Iris for her money?" She gazed at him contemptuously. "At least Fletch married me because he loved me. And whatever else you say about him, I know he doesn't cheat on his wife!"

She thought he might hit her then. Alice was used to being hit if she voiced her opinion. But she should have known Jacob was far too civilised to do something like that. "I'll overlook your ignorance," he said coldly, "because I know you must be tired. But, please, don't insult my intelligence by pretending the Neanderthal you call a husband has any scruples. I doubt there's anything I couldn't buy from him including you. So I suggest you stop fighting me and take the opportunity I'm offering."

Alice gulped. "Go to hell!"

"I very probably will." Jacob was philosophic. "But before I do, I want to know there's someone I can leave to take my place. A son," he said, looking down at the cribs, a muscle jerking spasmodically in his jaw. "My own son." He lifted his head and looked at her. "Is that really so much to ask?"

1

Jake saw the rental car at once. It was the only half-decent vehicle parked outside Casey's bar at this hour of the afternoon. Which meant Nathan was already inside, waiting for him. Jake grimaced. It must be something serious to bring his brother here. It wasn't as if they were friends. God Almighty, when he'd first found out he had a twin brother, he'd been desperate to see him. But Nathan wasn't like that. Jake was reluctant to admit it, but Nathan always thought first about himself.

When he'd got back to his office, after taking a deposition at the courthouse, Loretta had told him Fletch had been trying to get in touch with him—which was nothing new. Since his mother died, and Fletch had lost his job hauling lumber, he was often on the phone to the man he'd raised as his son. Most times he'd had too much to drink and he'd wanted a sympathetic ear for his troubles. Because he drank so much, his own daughters had given up on him long ago.

But this time Fletch was ringing to complain about the fact that Nathan had come to the house on Jackson Street looking for his brother. "He wants to see you, boy," he wheezed, his gravelly voice revealing the resentment he felt that Jacob Wolfe's son should have come to his house. "I told him you don't live here no more. That you'd got yourself a place out at Pine Bay, but he don't want to come to your office. He says can you meet him in town. The sooner the better, as far as I'm concerned.''

Jake could hear Nathan's voice in the background, but he didn't bother asking to speak to him then. On the rare occasions that Fletch and Nathan had met, their mutual dislike had always coloured the proceedings. Fletch despised Nathan because of his parentage; Nathan thought Fletch was an ignorant old bastard.

Which was ironic really, Jake reflected now, as he got out of the Blazer and locked the door. If anyone was a bastard around here, it was him or Nathan. Only his brother preferred to forget who his real mother had been.

It was dark in the bar, but as his eyes adjusted to the light, Jake saw Nathan slumped in a booth at the far side of the room. There were already a couple of empty bottles in front of him, and Jake reflected that Nathan and Fletch weren't as different from each other as they'd both like to think.

Nathan saw him, and getting to his feet, he gestured for Jake to join him. ''Where the hell have you been?'' he demanded with his usual lack of restraint. ''I've been sitting here for God knows how long. I thought you said you were coming right down.''

''Some of us have work to do,'' remarked Jake mildly, sliding into the booth across from the other man. ''In any case—'' he indicated the empty bottles ''—you look as if you've been busy. You won't forget you're driving a motor vehicle, will you?''

Nathan scowled. ''Don't start shitting me, Jake. I didn't come here for one of your lectures. Okay, I've had a couple of beers, but I'm still sober. Don't treat me like you treat your old man.''

''Fletch isn't my old man,'' Jake corrected him tautly, his fingers flexing on the table between them. The trouble was, he didn't feel as if Jacob Wolfe was his father, either. Somewhere along the way, he'd lost out on both counts.

"Well, okay." Nathan seemed to realise that whatever had brought him here wasn't going to be helped by starting an argument. "But I honestly don't know how you put up with him. It's not as if he ever cared about you. He'd have thrown you out years ago if he could."

Jake arched a dark brow. It was true enough, he supposed. From the moment Fletch had realized that he wasn't the boy's father, Jake's life hadn't been worth living. Not that it had been worth that much before, he reflected ruefully. A man who thought little of beating up on his wife thought less than nothing of beating up on his son.

But, from the time he was old enough to wield a yard brush, Jake had done everything he could to defend his mother. He'd had more than his share of grief, and occasionally the teachers from school formed a delegation to protest about the bruises that regularly appeared on his body. Mostly however, they stayed away. It was well known in Blackwater Fork that Fletch Connor had no respect for authority, and only his friendship with Sheriff Andy Peyton had saved him from certain prosecution.

Yet Jake had known from an early age that Fletch was proud of him in his own strange way. He used to say the boy reminded him of himself at that age, and although it didn't save him, Jake sensed Fletch admired his spirit.

Fletch's attitude had changed when Jake was eleven years old. He'd gashed his knee playing football, severing the main artery, and neither Fletch nor his mother had been able to give him the blood transfusion he needed.

There'd been one hell of a scene, he remembered. His mother had turned up the next day wearing a black eye, and Jake had been as stunned as Fletch to learn that they were not actual father and son. And then to learn that he had a twin brother...

Jake supposed he'd guessed even then there had to be more to it than they told him. Fletch wasn't the type to be philanthropic, and money had to have changed hands for his twin to have been adopted by someone else.

It was only later that his mother had explained that the man who had taken his brother was his real father. And by then, he'd had to come to terms with the fact that his relationship with Fletch could never be the same. Indeed, if it had been left to Fletch, he'd never have come back to the house in Jackson Street. But for once, his mother had put her foot down: either her husband accepted the situation as it was, or she'd take her son and go.

"He's old," said Jake now, as if that explained everything. "So what is it you want to talk about? The last I heard, things were pretty much going your way. Don't tell me you're having marital problems already."

"Doesn't everyone?" Nathan was evidently trying to be sociable. "This humidity is something," he added, changing the subject. "I don't know how you stand it for months on end."

"I was born here," replied Jake drily. "And so were you, little brother. You've gotten too used to being pampered. Juggling figures instead of people has made you soft."

Nathan scowled. "Yeah, well, I wasn't born with a yen to save the world," he remarked shortly. "It's no wonder you're still stuck in this hell-hole. Why don't you give yourself a break and find a decent job?"

"I have a decent job," declared Jake evenly. "Everyone has the right to a defence."

"Even crackheads and losers?" asked Nathan disparagingly, but he offered a conciliatory smile when his brother didn't respond.

Wiping his damp forehead then with a slightly unsteady hand, he unwittingly drew Jake's attention to his flushed face. A face that was amazingly like his own, Jake reflected as he had on many other occasions. How could two men who looked so alike be so different? Even at forty-two, their likeness to one another was still unique.

There were subtle differences, of course, he acknowledged as Nathan pulled out a handkerchief to mop his sweating brow. He guessed his brother was perhaps twenty pounds heavier, and his hair had been cut by an expert hand. It didn't hang straight or show the after-effects of his nails like Jake's did when he had been raking his scalp.

"So—how's Caitlin?" he asked at last, deciding it might be easier if he began the conversation. He'd never met his brother's wife, but he had seen her picture. She'd seemed strangely subdued for a man like Nathan. He'd have expected his brother to want a fashion model for a wife. But, of course, she had had money....

"She's okay," said Nathan offhandedly now, making a careless gesture. "She lives her own life. I live mine. We don't see an awful lot of one another."

Jake stared at him. "Are you kidding?"

"No." Nathan looked resentful. "Anyway, that's another story. D'you want a beer?"

Jake hesitated. "A beer would be fine," he agreed, and his brother left the booth to go and get it. Jake had the feeling he was glad to put off admitting the reasons why he'd come to North Carolina. But unlike Nathan, he didn't have time to waste.

Nathan came back with the two beers and took some time taking a drink before he got to the point. Even then, Jake had to prompt him, and Nathan scowled at his brother for a moment before starting to speak.

"I wanted to talk to you," he said grudgingly. "It's a long time since we talked with one another, man to man." He hunched his shoulders. "How have you been? How's the new apartment? Fletch said it overlooked the ocean, out at Pine Bay."

"You didn't come here to talk about me or my apartment," said Jake quietly. "And I don't know about you, but I've got work to do."

"And you'd rather do that than talk to your own brother," said Nathan peevishly. "It doesn't occur to you that I might need your help."

"And do you?"

"Damn right." Nathan rested his forearms on the table. "Like I said, I need to talk to you. I just—don't know where to begin."

Jake's nostrils flared. "Try the beginning," he suggested drily, and Nathan pursed his mouth.

"I'm in trouble." He expelled a heavy breath. "Deep trouble." He gave an uneasy snort. "Hell, I'll probably end up in jail, if I live that long."

Jake looked disbelieving. "Who?" he said. "Who's going to send you to jail?"

"A guy I know," said Nathan in a low voice, his eyes dark with bitterness. "If I don't do as he says, he'll probably kill me."

Jake frowned and backtracked. "Who is this guy?" he asked crisply, and Nathan shook his head.

"He's someone I owe," he said heavily. "I owe him and he has to be paid." He took another drink of his beer. "One way or the other."

"In blood?" Jake couldn't keep the sardonic note out of his voice, and Nathan gazed at him with angry eyes.

"Oh, yes," he said. "I knew you'd find it amusing. But it's my life that's on the line here. And there's nothing amusing about it."

Jake sobered. "You're exaggerating."

"Am I?" Nathan gazed at him with accusing eyes. "You may think you're tough because you deal with criminals every day, but Carl Walker is a serious menace. He plays for keeps."

"I don't think I'm tough." Jake defended himself mildly. Then, taking a reluctant swallow of his beer, "I take it you owe this Walker some money, am I right?"

"Haven't I just said so?" Nathan's tone was peevish. "That's what I'm trying to tell you. He says if I don't do as he wants, he'll tell Cat's father, Webster, what's been going on."

Jake was growing impatient in spite of himself. "For Christ's sake, Nate, stop talking in clichés. Get a hold of yourself. And why are you short of money? You married a rich woman. Or was that an exaggeration, as well?"

"No!" Nathan was indignant. "She was. She *is*. Her father is anyway. But I can't ask her for money. I can't tell her what I've done. Don't you understand, that's why Walker's got me by the balls. If Cat ever found out about—well, the situation, our marriage would be over."

"And that matters to you?"

"Of course it matters to me." Nathan gave him a resentful look. And then, his expression becoming wary. "What the hell do you mean?"

"I mean, you said you and your wife lived separate lives," Jake reminded him quietly. "It was an innocent question. Do you love your wife, or don't you?"

"What does it matter whether I love my wife or not?" Nathan sounded incredulous. "For Christ's sake, Jake, what's this with the hearts and flowers? I tell you my skin is on the line, and you ask me if I love my wife!"

"I just wondered what we're supposed to be protecting here," remarked Jake idly. "Your marriage—or her money."

Nathan started to speak and then seemed to think better of it. Or perhaps he realised he was in danger of incriminating himself still further. There was silence for a while as he searched for answers in his beer. Then, lifting his eyes, he said passionately, "Of course I love her, dammit. Why do you think I'm here?"

"I thought you were here because this man, Walker, is after your ass," Jake said flatly. "What has Caitlin got to do with it?"

Nathan hesitated. "It's me he's after. I'm not denying that. But don't think Cat'll be safe if I don't do what he says."

Jake sighed. "You still haven't told me what he wants you to do," he pointed out in exasperation. "You say you owe him money. So—what kind of money are we talking about?"

Nathan hesitated. "Half a million—give or take."

"Dollars?"

Nathan grimaced. "Pounds."

"Pounds?" Jake whistled. "You owe this guy half a million *pounds*? For God's sake, Nate, what have you been buying? Coke?"

Nathan started at his brother's words, and the line of red crept slowly up his cheeks. But when he spoke, his answer was resentful. "I don't do drugs," he retorted. "What do you take me for? I'd have thought one dopehead in the family was enough."

Jake coloured now. He could feel the heat in his face, feel it deepening his tan. It was typical of Nathan to throw that at him, typical of him to use any weapon when he was in a corner.

"If you want my help, you'll have to do better than that," he said at last, and even Nathan had the grace to look ashamed.

"Just don't bug me, Jake," he muttered, swallowing a mouthful of his beer. "We're neither of us perfect. We take after our old man."

Wasn't that the truth?

"Okay." Jake heaved a sigh. "So, how come you owe this guy half a million?"

"Well..." Nathan expelled his breath noisily. "Look, Jake, are you going to help me or not? I need to know if I'm wasting my time."

"I don't know what you want yet," Jake declared evenly. "It sounds like you've been embezzling money from the company. I guess that might explain why you can't ask Caitlin for help."

His brother's expression was almost comic. Or it would have been if it hadn't been so serious. "How the hell did you find out?" he demanded jerkily. "Are you psychic or something? How long have you known? Have you told the old man?"

Jake blinked, too stunned for a moment to work out what he meant. "What old man?" he asked blankly, and Nathan gazed at him with suspicious eyes.

"My old man—*our* old man," he exclaimed irritably, and Jake suspected his brother had had more to drink than just a few beers. How the hell could he have told their father anything? He hadn't known there was anything to tell.

"I haven't told Jacob Wolfe a thing," Jake assured him flatly. "How could I? I still don't know what's going on." He took a steadying breath. "For Christ's sake, Nate, what have you done?"

Nathan's hand was gripping his beer so tightly, Jake was amazed the bottle didn't shatter. "I'm trying to tell you, aren't I?" he snarled. "It's all that old man's fault. He should be dead!"

At Jake's look of surprise, Nathan explained, "Matt—Matthew—Matthew Webster. The lying bastard! He's been supposed to be dying for years."

Jake watched him. "You're talking about Caitlin's father? The man you hoped would make you a director of his company when you married his daughter?" He paused. "What happened? Did he change his mind?"

"Hell, yes." Nathan jerked back. "That is, no—no. I am a director. And I deserve it, believe me, after what I've gone through. I've spent the past three years sucking up to that old devil. And what have I got to show for it?" His mouth twisted. "Fuck all!"

Jake shook his head. "What did you expect?"

"I expected to be running the company by now," said Nathan, chewing the inside of his lower lip. "Like I said, the old guy was supposed to be dying. I was supposed to be his successor." His lips curled contemptuously. "Me. Nathan. The son he never had."

"So what went wrong?"

"Nothing." Nathan grunted. "Everything." His fists clenched again, and Jake wondered if he was imagining they were around Matthew Webster's neck. "I'm still no nearer to taking control of the company than I ever was. He's taken on someone else to do the job I was supposed to do."

Jake frowned. "So—you decided he owed you, hmm?"

"I needed the money," said Nathan defensively. "Webster barely pays me enough to live on as it is. Can I help it if I get into difficulties?"

Jake took a deep breath. "How the hell did you get your hands on half a million in the first place?"

"It's a long story." Nathan was evasive. "And I'd have gotten away with it, too, but that bastard's not going to let me."

"Walker?" Jake tried to be patient. "But how does he know?" He paused. "Did you tell him about it?"

"Don't be stupid!" Nathan gave him an aggravated look. "It was his idea, wasn't it? I couldn't have done it at all without his help."

"I thought you said you owed him."

"I did. I do." Nathan emptied his bottle. "Okay. Okay. I was gambling, right? I—got in too deep, and Carl fished me out."

Jake groaned. "A loan shark."

"Sort of."

Jake grunted. "So—okay," he said. "This guy's got you over a barrel. Why don't you do what he says and quit feeling sorry for yourself?"

"Because I can't."

"Why can't you?" Jake stiffened. "What does he want you to do?"

Nathan sighed. "They want me to carry an extra suitcase back from New York."

"Are you crazy?"

Jake's gut was churning now at the sudden realisation of where this was leading. He didn't have to ask what would be in the suitcase; he thought he knew.

"Keep your voice down," said Nathan hastily. "For God's sake, Jake, do you want to see me in jail?"

Jake's jaw clenched. "Maybe I don't care," he said. "If you're even considering smuggling drugs, maybe that's where you belong."

"You sanctimonious bastard!"

Nathan glared at him furiously, and feeling in need of some fresh air, Jake got abruptly to his feet. "Thanks for the character reference," he said. "But I'm not the one who's screwed up my life." He was tempted to shove one of the empty beer bottles down his brother's throat. "Get real, Nate. You're in deep trouble. And you can't blame anyone but yourself."

"I know that." As if realising he had spoken recklessly, Nathan got unsteadily to his feet. "Jake—" he caught his twin's arm "—I'm sorry. But you've got to help me. I'm desperate. If you don't, I'm afraid of what they'll do to Cat."

Jake jerked his arm out of Nathan's grasp, but he didn't move away. Even though all his instincts were urging him to get out of there, some innate sense of loyalty kept him where he was. Maybe it was the memory of that picture of Caitlin that caused him to hesitate. The realisation that whoever she was, whatever she was like, she didn't deserve to suffer because of Nathan's selfishness. Whatever his motivation, he felt himself weakening—ignoring his own misgivings, trying to justify his restraint.

"Go to the cops," he said as Nathan slumped over the table, and his brother gave him a strangled look.

"You're not serious! Carl would kill me."

Nathan's face was streaming with sweat, and with a sinking feeling, Jake sat down again. "Even if I wanted to help you," he said, and as he spoke, he knew it was definitely the wrong thing to say, "there's nothing I could do—"

"There is, there is." Nathan didn't wait for him to finish before breaking in. His eyes blazed now with a frantic light. He grasped his brother's hand. "You could do it. You could go to England on my return ticket. You could use my passport. No one would know you weren't me!"

Jake pulled his hand away and pressed himself back in his seat. He stared at Nathan as if he'd never seen him before, and although they'd never been close, something intangible died inside him. This was what Nathan had really come for. Not to see him, not to talk, not to share anything except this dirty secret. Nathan was prepared to make Jake an accessory to a crime, uncaring that if he was caught, he could go to prison in his place.

His distaste showing in his face, he said simply, "No."

Nathan's eyes narrowed. "You refuse?"

Jake shook his head. "Didn't you expect me to?"

"Frankly, no." Nathan gazed at him with bitter eyes. "After all, it's what you did when you came back from Vietnam, isn't it? I don't recall you having any crisis of conscience because you tried to beat the system then."

Jake bit back the ugly retort that sprang to his lips and made to get up again, but this time Nathan stopped him. "Please," he said imploringly, the veins standing out on his forehead. "Please, you've got to help me. If—if I screw up, they'll involve Cat, and it could kill Pa. I know you don't care about him, but he's not as tough as you think."

Jake's contempt was plain. "You son of a bitch," he said harshly. "You'd do anything, say anything, so long as you saved your own rotten hide! My God, you disgust me. Well, tough, but I won't do it. Find some other nut to screw!"

"What have you got to lose?" cried Nathan, hanging on to his wrist and preventing him from moving away. "I'm not asking you to deal with this guy. Just take the case to London and leave it where I tell you. Then check into a hotel in London. I'll meet you there. I'll be on the next flight."

"No."

"Why not?" Nathan groaned. "It's so simple. You use my ticket, and I follow you. We'll switch passports at the hotel, and you can fly home."

"No."

Jake was adamant, and realising his persuasion wasn't working, Nathan let him go. "All right," he said, dropping his face into his hands. "Go, then. But don't think I don't know why you're doing this." His voice became muffled, but his words were still audible. "You want to get back at me. You've always been jealous of the fact that our father chose me instead of you."

"*Jealous!*"

Jake knew he shouldn't respond to Nathan's desperate accusations, but that one was too close to home. He couldn't deny that there had been times when he'd envied his brother. But it was years since he had thought of it, and he certainly didn't envy him now.

"Yes, jealous," insisted Nathan, sniffing. "You've always resented me. Resented the fact that I had a better life."

"No—"

"Yes. You're not telling me you were happy, being stuck with that moron, Connor? God, it wasn't me who came looking for you, big brother. It wasn't me who used to stand outside of your house, spying on you, wanting for us to be friends! Remember?"

Jake's jaw compressed. "You were glad enough to see me when I pulled those punks off you," he reminded him tightly, recalling their first meeting with an unwilling sense of pain.

It had been just before he left for Vietnam. He'd been in a camp not far from Prescott, and he'd had the crazy notion that he might not be coming back. He'd decided he wanted to speak to Nathan at least once before he embarked for the Far East, so he'd ducked out of camp and hitched a ride to town.

He'd trailed Nathan and one of his pals to a bar in the sleaziest part of town, and then been beaten up for his pains when a couple of thugs had cornered the two rich youths by the jukebox. He'd jumped in to help them, and his uncanny likeness to his brother had caused some confusion. In the ensuing struggle, Nathan and his companion had gotten away.

He knew Nathan had recognised him. He'd found out later that Jacob had never hidden the fact that he had a twin. But Nathan hadn't cared what happened to Jake, so long as he wasn't injured. He'd saved his own skin, and that was all he'd cared about then. Hell, it was all he cared about now.

It was one of those occasions when Jake wondered if he wouldn't have been better off not knowing he had a brother. Although his mother and Fletch had been reconciled before she died, he doubted she'd ever truly forgiven him and Nathan for being born. He'd always reminded her of Jacob—and of the way he'd betrayed her. Her life hadn't been easy before, but it had been a damn sight harder after Fletch found out.

Nathan combed his hand over his hair and looked up at his brother with cold, accusing eyes. "Okay," he said. "Forget it. Forget I ever came here. Forget I ever asked you for help. It was a crazy notion anyway. We're not really brothers. We just share a likeness, that's all."

"That's all it means to you, maybe," muttered Jake harshly.

Right now, he wanted nothing so much as to put this ugly scene behind him. He wasn't totally convinced by Nathan's story, even if his brother's cowardice was plain enough to see. What did Nathan really want, and did he, Jake, really care? It sounded as if his brother's future was as shaky as his marriage.

"What do you mean?" Nathan demanded now, and Jake winced at the sudden hope that had appeared in his brother's face. For once Nathan wanted a brother, so why did it sound so surreal?

"Get the case," said Jake at last, telling himself it was the lingering loyalty to his mother's memory that made him say it. He had plenty of free time due to him; hell, he never took a holiday, and he was making no promises. But perhaps there was something he could do to ensure that Caitlin wasn't hurt....

2

The hospital was teeming with people. Many of the accident victims had been brought to St Anselm's, and the doctors and nurses were working round the clock in an effort to keep up with the load. The lobby resembled nothing so much as a train station, with would-be passengers dashing from desk to desk, desperate for news, desperate for information.

Caitlin wasn't one of them. She didn't feel like one of them; she didn't look like one of them. The anxiety she could see mirrored in their faces was not her anxiety; the fear that some loved one had perished in the crash was not what had brought her here.

Yet, as she pushed her way through the press of bodies, she couldn't help an unwilling twinge of concern. Nathan might be all kinds of a bastard, but he was her husband, and for all her avowed indifference, she would not wish to see him dead.

And he wasn't dead. He was injured, but he wasn't dead. When the authorities had contacted her, to tell her that her husband had been one of the passengers on board the transatlantic flight that had crashed on take-off, they had instantly informed her that Mr Wolfe was one of the survivors. Like many of those who were injured, he had been taken to St Anselm's hospital in New York City, and if she required any further information, Caitlin should contact the hospital direct.

It had come as a complete shock. Caitlin hadn't even known Nathan was flying back on that plane. He'd left for New York over a week ago, ostensibly to visit his father in Prescott, New Jersey. He hadn't told her why he was going, and she hadn't heard from him since.

Not that that was unusual. These days, they rarely discussed personal things at all. It was only because her father expected it that they continued to share the same flat. But they had their own lives, their own friends; they might as well have lived apart.

Caitlin wondered if Nathan had really been to see his father. She knew pathetically little about his background, and what she did know was hardly up to date. She knew his mother was dead and that his father was virtually a recluse—at least, that was the excuse he'd given her for Jacob Wolfe not attending their wedding. And it must have been true, she supposed, or her father wouldn't have encouraged the match.

Weariness descended like a cloud upon her. What was she really doing here? she wondered disconsolately. Why had she let her father persuade her to make this trip? Whatever had happened, Nathan wouldn't want to see her. She should have told her father the truth and made him send someone else.

Marshall O'Brien could have done it. Her father's personal assistant—secretary—*henchman*—would have handled the less attractive details far better than she. He wouldn't have felt as helpless as she did staring round this vast foyer, with no earthly idea where her husband might be. And no helpful nurse to direct her. She sighed heavily. Just a cacophony of voices, and squealing gurneys, and—noise!

Yet it was she who hadn't allowed Marshall to accompany her, even though her father had suggested it. After living a lie for almost three years, she was not about to expose the travesty of their marriage just because Nathan had been involved in a plane crash. Dear God, when she'd first heard the news, for a second—for the minutest, most shameful second of her life—she had actually believed that it was over. In spite of all the guilt and recrimination she had felt later, for that one fleeting second she'd thought she was free. . . .

A harassed receptionist eventually informed her that her husband was in a ward on the twelfth floor. "Just take the elevator, take the elevator," the woman exclaimed when Caitlin asked for directions. Then turned away almost immediately to answer another query.

She could have been a serial killer and she'd have received the same instructions, Caitlin thought wryly. Any security there had ever been had been eclipsed by the very real demands of the situation. It was no one's fault; there simply weren't enough staff to handle it. In circumstances like these, the most you could hope for was a civil tone.

The lifts, when she found them, were jammed with stretchers and still more people. Everyone seemed to be talking at once, and the mix of sounds and dialects was deafening in the ponderous, clanking cubicle. But they ascended, albeit ponderously, to the upper reaches of the hospital, stopping at every floor to disgorge and take on more passengers.

Caitlin inevitably found herself pushed towards the back of the lift, with the iron rails of a gurney crushed against her stomach. She had never felt claustrophobic before, but the panic of confinement rose sharp and unfamiliar inside her. Only the awareness of the injured child on the gurney kept her silent, the bottle of plasma held high by an orderly providing a steadying focus on which to fix her gaze.

They reached the twelfth floor at last, and Caitlin forced herself to step out onto the vinyl landing. The gurney had swished away to her left, and her fellow passengers rushed off to find the nearest nursing station. But Caitlin took a moment to compose herself, as the smells of the hospital washed around her. Nathan would not expect her to rush to his bedside. In the circumstances, her being here at all seemed out of place.

She should never have married him, she thought again, with a sense of vulnerability. It was a feeling she'd had many times before. But it had been what her father had wanted, and after resisting him for so long, it had seemed the most logical thing to do.

How wrong she'd been ...

Another lift stopped beside her, and realising she was causing an obstruction, Caitlin began to walk towards the busy nurses' station. Around her, the tide of humanity continually ebbed and flowed, and listening to the unmistakeable sounds of grief, she wondered how she could be feeling sorry for herself when many of these people had lost friends and loved ones. At least Nathan was alive, and God willing, he'd make a full recovery. She should be glad he'd survived. Not bemoaning her fate ...

She waited her turn silently, relieved that she was not obliged to make trivial conversation. It was a huge hospital, with the corridors stretching away to left and right evidently accommodating many wards. The sign, hanging above their heads, announced Neurosurgery and Neurology, and she was just absorbing the significance of this when the busy nurse asked her name.

"Um..." Caitlin looked at her a little blankly. "I—Wolfe. Caitlin Wolfe."

"We don't have any Caitlin Wolfe on this floor," the nurse declared impatiently.

She was already turning to the next inquirer when Caitlin exclaimed, "It's Nathan. Nathan Wolfe." She flushed unhappily. "I misunderstood. I thought you wanted my name."

She glanced at the couple behind her, hoping for their support, but the woman seemed dull-eyed and lifeless and the man looked right through her. Evidently the news they'd received had left them in a state of shock, and once again Caitlin felt guilty for her lack of grief.

"You're Mrs Wolfe, is that right?" the nurse asked with more compassion, and Caitlin nodded quickly. For the first time, she felt a prickle of alarm. The nurse was eyeing her with some sympathy now. How serious could Nathan's condition be?

"I'm going to have to ask you to take a seat, Mrs Wolfe," the nurse declared at last, compounding her fears. "The doctor would like to speak to you before you see your husband. If you'd just wait over there . . ."

"He's not dead, is he?"

Caitlin blurted the words urgently, and this time even the man and woman behind her in the queue showed some response. But the nurse was professionally reassuring. "He's doing very well," she declared, shuffling the folders on the desk. "The doctor just wants to talk to you. It's nothing too serious." She lifted her hand as if taking an oath. "I promise."

Caitlin wasn't sure how sincere the nurse's promise might be. She was still troubled by those two words: Neurosurgery and Neurology. It must mean that Nathan had injured his head. Oh, God, he wasn't brain damaged, was he? That would be the cruellest blow of all.

But she wouldn't think about things like that, she decided, taking a seat on one of the steel-framed vinyl chairs. She had to be confident, and optimistic. Someone would surely have told her if Nathan was in a coma.

A little girl of perhaps two or three was waiting with her mother a couple of seats away. Although she was obviously too old to do so, she was sucking her thumb, and Caitlin wondered what anxieties she was suffering in her own small way. She had to know something was wrong. Her mother had been crying. Was that why she was seeking comfort in the only way she knew?

Caitlin attempted a smile, but it wasn't returned, and even that effort was too great to sustain. Dear God, she thought, let Nathan be all right. Whatever he'd done, he didn't deserve to be here.

The little girl continued to stare at her, and Caitlin wondered if things would have been different if she and Nathan had had a child of their own. It might not have changed his character, but he might have loved their child.

Her mind drifted back to her own childhood. When had she become aware that her own father had wished *she* had been a son? Was it when he'd realised her mother could have no more children after Caitlin? When he'd learned the dynasty he'd hoped to found was never to be?

To begin with, it hadn't seemed that important—at least not to Caitlin. All through her childhood, all the time she was growing into adolescence, she had never felt she was a disappointment to either of her parents. She had been given everything a child could wish for, and they had had her love in return.

But she had always been a fairly serious child, never happier than when her nose was immersed in a book. She had satisfied every academic hope her parents could have had for her, and following a successful career at school, she had gone on to gain a brilliant degree besides.

Her aim had always been to work for her father's company. Naïvely, she supposed now, she had seen herself taking over from him one day and running Webster Development. It was an ambition she had formed when he had first taken her to visit the Webster Building, and it was not until she'd gained her degree that she'd realised how unrealistic her hopes had been. Her father was from the old school, to whom the idea of a woman in a position of total authority was something of an anathema. He was prepared to make her an associate director, if that was what she really wanted. But as far as taking over when he retired...

A man in a white coat was approaching, and Caitlin felt her mouth go dry. Oh, God, she thought, please let it be good news. But the man didn't even look at her. He just walked by, intent on some objective of his own.

Her thoughts returned to Matthew Webster. Not that she could blame her father for her present predicament, she reflected bleakly. Although his attitude might have caused her to rebel, ultimately she had been the one who'd made the mistakes.

And so, much to her father's dismay and her mother's quiet amusement, she had found herself a flat in London. Instead of commuting to the office from her parents' home in Buckinghamshire, as Matthew Webster had expected, she had abandoned her ideas of working for the company and accepted a temporary position in a friend's art gallery instead.

Of course, from her father's point of view, she couldn't have made a more unsuitable decision. The men she met in the course of her work at the gallery were not the sort of men he admired. Mostly, he regarded artists, of any persuasion, as wimps and losers, and he lost no opportunity to ridicule her chosen career.

But, once her mind was made up, Caitlin had proved to be as obdurate as her father. She liked the idea that people listened to her opinion; that she was treated as an equal instead of being ignored. And the work was easy. She could have done it standing on her head. It was pleasant, it was civilised, and she'd managed to convince herself it was what she wanted to do.

In addition to which, she had a social life at last. Instead of burying her head in a book every evening, she'd started accepting invitations to the theatre, and to parties, and to various exhibitions. She still had no illusions about her popularity, of course. Growing up as Matthew Webster's daughter had made her cynical, and she couldn't throw that cynicism off overnight. She knew she was neither incredibly sexy nor incredibly beautiful, and for all her independence, she was still too willing to accept that her father's wealth was pulling strings.

"Mrs Wolfe?"

A nurse was standing in front of her, and Caitlin jerked her head up so quickly she went dizzy for a moment. "Yes?"

"Dr Harper says he's sorry to keep you waiting, Mrs Wolfe," the nurse explained, urging Caitlin back into her seat when she would have stood up. "He'll be with you very shortly." She paused. "There's a dispenser over there if you'd like to help yourself to some coffee."

Caitlin made a negative gesture, the dizziness receding. Machine-made coffee was usually unpalatable in her experience, and although she'd come to the hospital straight from the airport, her stomach was not yet attuned to the fact that it was only midday here in New York. It was already five o'clock in London, and on any other day she would have been either at the flat, or working.

"It's the pits, waiting," remarked the little girl's mother suddenly, in an accent that Caitlin found harder to understand than that of the nurse. She sniffed. "I guess you're here for the same reason I am. You got someone injured in the crash?"

Caitlin nodded. "My husband." She hesitated. "Did you . . . ?"

"Yeah. Emmy's father was on the same flight," agreed the woman, pulling a used tissue out of her sleeve and blowing her nose hard. "He was on his way to England to see his sick mother. Leastwise, that's what he told me." She grimaced. "Who knows about men?"

Well, not me, thought Caitlin ruefully. She exchanged a wistful smile with the little girl. When David Griffiths had come along, she'd been vulnerable and far too willing to believe what he said.

David was the brother of the friend who'd invited her to work at the gallery, and, for some unknown reason, he had been instantly attracted to her. Had he seen how naïve she was? How inexperienced? Or had he sensed what a pushover she'd be?

Whatever, he had certainly made her feel special. The tall, shy young woman, who had come to help his sister sell her paintings, had been transformed into a glowing creature who believed everything he said. She'd sometimes wondered if he'd ever cared about her. Or if she was the kind of person who only saw what she wanted to see.

His sister, Felicity—Fliss—had approved of the alliance. She'd assured Caitlin that she was good for her brother and that he'd never been so happy before.

Sometimes, Caitlin had found him a little impractical. She was still her father's daughter after all, and his attitude towards money gave her pause. But he taught her that life was not just a series of balance sheets and that personal fulfilment meant more than being a success.

Their affair had not been a passionate one. In lovemaking, as in everything else, David preferred to take it very much at his own pace. Caitlin doubted he had ever felt strongly about anything that didn't directly affect his own wellbeing. He was selfish and self-indulgent—but he was fun.

The only aspect of their relationship that did trouble her was his moodiness. For all his happy-go-lucky ways, there were days when he was not approachable at all. And because in all the time she'd known him he had never had a job, Caitlin had got it into her head that he had financial problems; that although he seemed quite content to borrow money from either her or his sister, secretly he worried about the future.

She remembered she'd even mentioned her fears to Fliss quite early in their relationship. But Fliss had just dismissed them out of hand. David had always had these cranky days, she assured her carelessly. If she had any sense, she'd just leave him alone and he'd come round.

And she had, until that fateful day when she'd entered the small flat he'd occupied above the gallery and discovered him unconscious on the floor....

Looking back now, she could quite see why Fliss had been as angry as she was when Caitlin burst unannounced into her office. She had been dealing with a client at the time, and Caitlin's hysterical belief that David had suffered some kind of stroke had not helped the proceedings. "My God," she'd said later, after David had been carted off to a drug rehabilitation centre, "if you hadn't recognised my brother's little habit for what it was, you must have been living on another planet!"

And Caitlin supposed she had. Or in another world anyway, she conceded ruefully. But afterwards, she'd found it impossible to forgive him, or Fliss, for deceiving her as they had....

"You're English, aren't you?"

Emmy's mother was speaking again, and guessing she needed the comfort of a shared confidence, Caitlin conceded that she was right.

"I flew in from London this morning," she admitted as Emmy left the shelter of her mother's skirt long enough to touch the glossy sable fur that trimmed Caitlin's cashmere coat. "Um—how about you? Do you live in New York?"

"Can't you tell?" The woman was philosophic about her accent. "Yeah, Ted and me, we live on Staten Island. I don't suppose you've ever been there. Believe me, you've missed nothing."

Caitlin smiled. "I'm afraid this is my first trip to New York," she said, grimacing at her ignorance. "I've been to Florida and California, but I've never been to the Big Apple before."

"The Big Apple." The woman repeated the words as if she liked the sound of them. "Yeah, well, I've never been to London. But Ted—he was born there, see."

"He's English, then?"

Caitlin found talking about something other than her own problems was comforting to her, too, and the woman nodded. "Sort of. His father was a G.I., see. His mother's English, of course. But Ted, he always wanted to live in the States."

"Ah."

"His old lady didn't," went on her companion, pulling a wry face. "There was no G.I. bride bit for her. I guess you could say she wasn't much interested in Ted, either. She let his father bring him back to the U.S. That's why him dashing off to see her now she's s'posed to be ill sounds pretty thin, don't you think?''

Caitlin made some reassuring comment about time healing all wounds, but she wondered whom she was kidding. Her first opinion of Nathan had been coloured by the way David had treated her. The assured, confident American had seemed to possess all the attributes the other man hadn't. He was good-looking, well-educated, ambitious; and she was no longer the naïve idealist she had been.

In addition to which, her father had liked him. She'd left the art gallery after her break-up with David, and it was while she was recovering her spirits at home that she'd met Nathan at the party her parents had given for her twenty-sixth birthday. He'd been at Harvard some years before with the son of one of her father's business acquaintances, and because he was staying with the Gordons at the time, he'd accompanied them to the celebrations.

To begin with, she and Nathan had appeared to have so much in common. Like herself, Nathan was a university graduate. He was an older man, of course, but from a business background as she was. He'd told her his father owned a busy sawmill in New Jersey, and that he was visiting England to study British business methods.

His host, Adrian Gordon, had spoken very positively of his interest in the environment. And when Matthew Webster had offered to show him a little of the way he operated, Nathan had been eager to accept. He'd seemed so open, so enthusiastic, so eager to please. So much so, that she'd been completely taken in.

Their marriage was an instant disaster. She'd learned, at the start of her honeymoon, that Nathan had no feelings for her; that he cared for no one but himself. Her hopes, her fears, her needs, were not important. He'd married her because she was Matthew Webster's daughter and because he believed that ultimately her father would give the control of the company to him....

"You come back here, Emmy."

Caitlin came back to the present to find that the little girl had sidled up to her now and was stroking the fur that edged her cuff. "It's all right," she said, almost glad of the diversion. "I expect she's missing her daddy. Just like you."

"You got children, Mrs Wolfe?"

The woman moved into the seat next to her, and Caitlin gave her a rueful glance. "Unfortunately not," she said, the pain of Nathan's betrayal still sharp inside her.

She sighed.

She had certainly had a rude awakening. Until they were married, Nathan had held back from making love to her, and she, poor fool that she was, had imagined it was because he respected her. She winced. How wrong she had been. Nathan hadn't touched her because he'd known his lovemaking would disgust her. She couldn't respond to his violent sexuality, and by the time they came home from Tahiti, she was in a state of shock.

But she was not a quitter, and although she knew she had made a terrible mistake, she was still prepared to give the marriage a chance. She'd known how disappointed her father would be if she said she wanted to divorce Nathan. Particularly when he'd invested so much hope in their union.

She'd discovered Nathan was being unfaithful to her less than three months after their return to London. Seeing him with another woman had shaken her, and she had listened to his excuses with a heavy heart.

She'd learned Lisa Abbott's name just a few weeks later.

The woman was an American, she discovered, and he had known her for years. He had apparently invited her to join him in London, and he had been using the credit card her father had given him to pay for a room at a hotel.

Caitlin had been searching, quite legitimately, for her address book when she'd found the damning statement crumpled at the back of a drawer. She probably shouldn't have looked at it. The very fact that she hadn't seen it before should have warned her it was nothing to do with her. But curiosity got the better of her, and like any normal wife, she'd wanted to know what it was.

The row that had followed had been painfully destructive, the first real indication that any hopes she still might have nurtured for their marriage had been hopelessly naïve. She'd walked out of the flat afterwards, with every intention of seeing a solicitor. She couldn't go on living with a man to whom deceit was second nature.

But it was evening when she left the flat. All solicitors' offices were closed, and rather than go back, she'd taken a room in a hotel. She'd had no knowledge that her father had had a heart attack until she'd arrived at her parents' home the next day to find an ambulance—and Nathan's car—already in the drive.

The sight of her father being carried from the house on a stretcher had sent her running towards the pillared portico. Matthew Webster was clearly unconscious, but her mother was there, with Nathan just behind her, and she'd raised accusing eyes to her daughter's face.

"What is it? What's happened?" cried Caitlin, convinced in those first few minutes that Nathan was responsible for her father's collapse. She was quite prepared to believe he had told some cock-and-bull tale to her parents, blaming her for the rift between them and destroying all her father's hopes for their marriage.

"Where have you been?" retorted her mother tearfully. "If Nathan hadn't come at once, I don't know what I'd have done.'' She glanced round at her son-in-law gratefully. "We've both been trying desperately to find you. If you must continue to go out with your friends, you might at least leave Nathan an address where you can be reached.''

Caitlin's eyes moved to her husband's then, and his smug expression was almost her undoing. But how could she accuse Nathan of anything in the present circumstances? With the guilt successfully transferred to her shoulders, it was doubtful if even her mother would believe her.

Of course, Caitlin could tell from Nathan's expression that he knew she wouldn't say anything now. That half-amused arrogance, quickly disguised when her mother turned to speak to him, was a clear indication of what he was thinking. There was no question now of Caitlin betraying his falseness. Until her father recovered his strength, her hands were tied.

And, unfortunately, since that afternoon, Matthew Webster had never completely regained his strength. He'd recovered from the attack, but his doctor had warned him there was still a weakness in his heart, and he had to avoid any kind of stress.

For her part, Caitlin had eventually resigned herself to the hypocrisy of her marriage. The awful thing was that, as the weeks and months went by, she had actually begun to ask herself what she had to gain by ruining Nathan's reputation. She was grateful that the physical side of their marriage was over, but from an objective point of view, he provided a shield. At least no other man attempted to seduce her. As Nathan's wife, she was protected from men like him.

Gradually, however, she had become aware of a change in her father's attitude towards her husband. He no longer seemed confident that Nathan was the man to succeed him. These days, he never spoke about giving Nathan more au-

thority, and his sudden appointment of Marshall O'Brien as
his second in command had placed a definite strain on their
relationship....

"Mrs Wolfe?"

The unfamiliar masculine voice arrested her uneasy
thoughts, bringing her abruptly back to earth. Whatever
had happened in the past didn't much matter now. Nathan
was injured, maybe seriously, and even her father couldn't
blame him for that.

An elderly man in a white lab coat was looking down at
her, and she forced her brain into action. "Dr—Harper?"

"That's right." Harper looked both harassed and weary.
"Come with me, please, Mrs Wolfe. I'll explain why I
wanted to speak to you before you see your husband."

"Good luck."

Emmy's mother called the words after her as Caitlin followed the stoop-shouldered medic into the corridor, and she
raised a grateful hand. She had the feeling she was going to
need all the luck she could get if Dr Harper's expression was
anything to go by.

The corridors were still busy, with orderlies transferring
patients from one ward to another. Although she tried not
to look at all the gurneys they passed, the need to reassure
herself that Nathan wasn't on one of them was irresistible.
But none of the pale faces she saw even remotely resembled
her husband. Wherever Nathan was, she was not to be allowed to see him until this unsmiling doctor had delivered
his doubtful news.

The office he eventually appropriated was obviously not
his own. A nurse, who had apparently been snatching a
quick cigarette, was unceremoniously despatched, and Dr
Harper opened a window to allow the noxious fumes to
disperse. It allowed a draught of cold air to enter the of-

fice, however, and Caitlin blamed that for the sudden chill that slid down her spine.

"Please—sit down."

Harper gestured to a chair beside the desk, and although Caitlin would have preferred to stand, she obediently complied. The truth was, she felt less helpless when she was standing. As if whatever blow she was going to be expected to weather could be overcome better when she was on her feet.

"Thank you."

Her gratitude was as spurious as the tight smile she bestowed on her companion, and the doctor hesitated only a moment before seating himself behind the desk. It occurred to Caitlin then that he probably welcomed the respite. He wasn't a young man, and he'd obviously been continually on his feet throughout the night.

"You're English, Mrs Wolfe," he remarked at last, unnecessarily, Caitlin felt, but she assumed it was his way of starting the interview. Whatever he had to say, it was probably easier to get the formalities over first. Hospitals had their own form of protocol, even in circumstances like these.

"Yes," she replied now, crossing her legs and making sure the skirt of her coat covered her trembling knees. "I flew over from London this morning."

"This morning?"

Harper arched a quizzical brow, and Caitlin felt obliged to explain. "On the Concorde," she appended quickly. "I was lucky enough to get a cancellation."

"Ah." He inclined his bead. "Your husband's not English, of course."

Caitlin began to understand.

"No," she said evenly. "Nathan was born in this country. As a matter of fact, he was over here visiting his—oh, God!" She broke off as a horrifying thought occurred to her. "Has—has anyone informed Nathan's father? If he knew his son was on the flight, he must be worried sick. And he's not a well man—at least, that's what Nathan said."

"We only inform next of kin," replied Dr Harper flatly. "Right now, I'm more concerned with the after-effects of your husband's injuries. I have to warn you, Mrs Wolfe, there's a problem. He probably won't remember who you are."

Caitlin's jaw sagged. She had barely recovered from the shock of learning that she was going to have to break the news to Nathan's father, a man whom she'd never even met, and Dr Harper's words left her weak.

"I beg your pardon," she began, her mouth dry and taut with tension, and the doctor attempted to explain what he had meant.

"It's quite common, really," he told her, though Caitlin was equally sure it was not common at all. "Your husband is suffering the effects of being involved in a serious—not to say, traumatic—accident. In many cases of this kind, a temporary neurosis can occur."

"You mean—there's some psychological problem?"

"I mean that anyone involved in such a situation can conceivably suffer some kind of mental block."

"Mental block?"

"Mrs Wolfe." He was obviously trying to be patient, but he'd dealt with a lot of anxious relatives already that morning, and he was tired. "Your husband appears—I say, *appears*—to be quite normal. He has one or two minor injuries—cuts and bruises, that sort of thing—and when he was admitted, he was suspected of having a couple of cracked ribs and a dislocated shoulder." He paused. "All of which have been dealt with. He's in a state of shock, of course, and I wouldn't say he was fit to travel. But compared to some of the other—passengers—I've seen, he's in fairly good shape.''

''But . . . ?''

Caitlin sensed there was more, something the doctor wasn't telling her, and Harper gave her a weary look before continuing with his diagnosis.

''But,'' he agreed with a sigh, ''he can't remember anything.''

''About the accident? But surely—''

''Before the accident, and the accident itself,'' Harper interrupted her heavily. ''It may be a temporary condition as I say. It's too soon to tell, and often the victims of car crashes, explosions, that sort of thing, suffer a short-lived amnesia. That may well be all we have to deal with here. But with head injuries, anything is possible.''

Caitlin swallowed. ''You didn't mention he'd injured his head.''

''Because he hasn't,'' declared Harper levelly. ''Unless you count the bruise we found on his temple. We've done a scan, and we've found no internal bleeding. Nothing that might be causing pressure on his brain.''

''Then—''

''Mrs Wolfe, what can I tell you? For the present, there's nothing more to be done. You must be prepared for him not to recognise you, that's all. That's why I wanted to speak to you before you saw him. I don't want you to upset him. I just wanted you to know what to expect.''

3

He had the most God-awful headache. There were times when it felt as if there was an army of blacksmiths hammering away inside his skull. Just moving his head on the pillow sent a spasm of pain spiralling to his brain. A brain, which he had to admit felt like mashed banana, and just about as much use to him besides.

At least he still appeared to be in one piece. He might have a stinking headache, but his brain was still functioning, albeit at half power. Some of the poor devils in the beds around him didn't even know which day it was. And the head injuries one of his fellow patients had sustained made him feel quite weak.

Well, weaker than he did already, he amended wryly, aware that right at this moment, he couldn't have punched his way out of a paper bag. Dammit, even his legs felt like jelly. And although they'd assured him it was just delayed shock, he couldn't seem to stop shaking.

It must have been one hell of a mess, he thought, not envying the fire crews and paramedics who had had to deal with the aftermath of the crash. Bodies everywhere, most of them well beyond the help of anyone in this world. And the screams—oh, God!—he could remember them. He doubted he'd ever get them out of his head.

Which was strange when so much else was gone. He didn't remember getting on the plane. He didn't even remember where he had been going. But most disturbing of all, he didn't remember his name, or any damn thing about himself.

He didn't remember the actual crash, either—just the horror of finding himself on the ground, surrounded by the cries of injured people. Someone had told him, he didn't remember who, that he'd been thrown clear when the plane ploughed into the end of the runway. By some uncanny quirk of fate, the fuselage had fractured near his seat, and he'd been pitched onto the grass verge that edged the tarmac.

He remembered the smell—a sickening odour of kerosene—and the searing heat of the ball of fire that had consumed what was left of the aircraft. He knew that more people had died, engulfed by the flames, while he'd lain there unable to do anything.

They said he'd been knocked unconscious, which accounted for his memory loss now. He just wished he could have forgotten the aftermath of the crash. At present, it was the only thing on his mind.

Yet, if he concentrated, he could remember superficial things. It caused the throbbing in his head to increase, but he knew the name of the president who was presently occupying the White House, and he was pretty sure he could still read and write. For instance, those blacksmiths who were taking his skull apart had to come from somewhere. And no one had had to tell him where he was.

Or was that strictly true? Had he really known he was in a hospital in *New York*? He frowned. So, okay, someone had told him that, but he'd known what a hospital was, and he'd known what was happening after the crash.

The hammering was worse, much worse, and his mouth felt as dry as a dust bowl. Probably tasted like one, as well, he thought ruefully, wishing he could call a nurse. The injection they had given him earlier to relieve the pain must have worn off.

He closed his eyes for a moment, and when he opened them again, a face swam into view. A female face, oval shaped and somehow vulnerable, it was gazing at him rather uncertainly. As if the woman didn't quite believe he was alive, he mused, forcing himself to concentrate on who she was. She was nothing like the nurse who'd attended him earlier, who'd scolded him for trying to get out of bed. Just because he'd wanted to go to the bathroom instead of using one of their damn bedpans. Dammit, he might have lost his memory, but he still had some pride.

He wondered briefly if he'd died and gone to heaven. The way his head had been hammering earlier, there was always a chance. And surely only an angel could have eyes that vivid shade of sapphire. Or were they violet? he pondered dazedly as a sooty fringe of lashes swept her cheeks.

He licked his lips, but whatever romantic words had formed in his mind, his outburst was hopelessly prosaic. "A drink," he whispered, giving in to the urgent needs of the moment. "I need a drink. I'm parched."

Every word caused the pain in his skull to expand, and her timid "What?" had him groaning for relief. Dammit, what was the matter with her? Was he speaking a foreign language? Why was she gazing at him with those big blue eyes, as if he'd scared her half to death?

"Oh—water," she eventually stuttered faintly. And now he heard the unfamiliar inflection in her voice. "I didn't think—I didn't realise—you want a drink?" She glanced around. "I'll get the nurse. Just hang on a minute."

"No," he began as she would have moved away, and although he sensed her reluctance to obey him, she stayed where she was. "There," he croaked, "on the cupboard." And she turned to look at the carafe of water and the glass.

It was her accent, he realised as she poured a little of the water into the glass, dropped in a straw, and slid a slim arm beneath his shoulders. It was different, unfamiliar—*English*? Yes, that was it. He would almost swear it was English So—he knew her accent, but he didn't know who she was.

A drifting cloud of fragrance enveloped him as she lifted him. And her breath, as she murmured, "Are you sure this is all right?" was just as sweet. Perfume, he breathed; nurses didn't usually use expensive perfume. Or wear fur-trimmed overcoats besides, he thought as the softness of her sleeve brushed his neck.

He was so bemused by what his senses were telling him that when she brought the straw to his lips, he felt some of the water go sliding down his chin. Oh, great, he thought, he was dribbling like a baby. What an impression he was going to make.

Nevertheless, the drop of water that made it past his lips was refreshing. The straw was only plastic like the glass, and the liquid had a faint metallic taste, but it felt like liquid honey on his tongue. It eased the awful dryness that was almost choking him, and although his head was still throbbing, the woman's appearance had distracted him from his woes.

When she lowered him back to the pillow, he groped blindly for her hand. "Who are you?" he demanded, hearing his voice, hoarse and anxious in his panic. He gripped her wrist, feeling the narrow bones taut, and somehow fragile, beneath his fingers. "You're not a nurse," he stated with more conviction. "Nurses don't dress—or smell—the way you do."

She hesitated. "Don't they?"

"No." He frowned. "I guess I should know you, right? We have—we have met before?"

"You don't remember?"

"If I did, I wouldn't be asking."

He sighed. That was stupid. He had to calm down. Getting angry with her wasn't going to achieve anything. She was here because she was concerned about him, not to listen to his griping. It wasn't her fault that the damn plane had crashed.

"If—if they let you in to see me, you must be a relation," he ventured steadily. He expelled his breath in frustration. "I can't remember."

She licked her lips now, her tongue appearing almost hypnotically to lave her upper lip. Its tip, pink and provocative, was mesmerising. It reminded him that his emotions hadn't been paralysed by the crash, and he let go of her wrist, not wanting her to recognise his reaction. For God's sake, the woman could be his sister, though he sensed with a kind of gut feeling that she wasn't.

"You don't remember—anything?" she asked at last, clearly as dismayed by the circumstances as he was himself. And, although he had no reason to think so, he sensed that it alarmed her. So their relationship was not as simple as he'd like to think.

Yet why wouldn't she be alarmed to hear he was virtually a stranger? He was someone who couldn't even tell her why she was here. It must have been a shock. Hell! It was something more than that to him. But he still had the feeling there was something she was trying to hide.

"Nothing—personal," he replied at last, his headache rapidly overtaking his will to speak to her. He was too weak to play word games, and he half wished she would go. That surge of sexual attraction had all but dissipated, and he just felt tired. Deathly tired, actually. He could hardly keep his eyes open.

She was still watching him, warily, he thought, his imagination refusing to give in. He guessed she was trying to decide whether she believed him or not, and that was strange. Why would she think he might lie? What might he have done to make his answer seem so untenable? In the present circumstances, she must surely realise his limitations. For Christ's sake, he was lucky to be alive.

Or not...

"You don't remember going to see your father?" she ventured, and it was a great temptation to yell that he didn't know who the hell his father was. But at least she'd supplied another piece of the jigsaw. He had a father, if no one else. He wasn't completely alone.

"No," he sighed, finding the strength to answer her somehow. "Believe it or not, I didn't know I had a father until you said so. Or—a girlfriend, either," he added weakly. "Perhaps if you told me your name...?"

Her lips parted. "I'm not your girlfriend!"

Her denial was absolute, and his hands curled helplessly into fists. For God's sake, she couldn't be his sister! He recoiled from that solution with a tortured breath.

"Then who...?" he began, but the effort defeated him. Behind his eyes, the darkness was rising, albeit against his will. With a sense of shame, he felt his senses slipping. The woman, whoever she was, dissolved.

When he opened his eyes again, it was evening. He knew it was evening because the long blinds had been lowered over the windows in the wall opposite, and there were lamps glowing all about the ward. It was strange how in such a short time the place had become familiar. But—God!—it was the only point of contact that he had.

His head wasn't aching quite so badly now. Even when he moved his head on the pillow, he didn't get the awful ham-

mering he'd had before. The shaking in his limbs had re-
ceded to an occasional spasm, and he actually felt as if he
might be able to sit up.

He could smell food and he wondered what time it was.
Early evening, he surmised, judging by the muted activity
in the ward. They'd be serving supper soon, and then they'd
allow the patients to have visitors. At least, that's what he
seemed to remember had happened the night before.

His lips twisted at the word: *remember*. It was ironic, really, how some things seemed so clear. Like the night before, when he'd been transferred to this bed, and they'd
been serving chicken soup for supper. He wondered what it
would be tonight and if he'd be allowed to eat.

He closed his eyes for a moment as if to test his powers of
perception. Yes, opening them again was definitely not the
effort it had been. Last night, he'd felt as helpless as a baby.
Which was silly, really, when he hadn't been badly hurt.

He closed his eyes again, and this time the image of the
woman he had seen earlier that day swam into his vision.
Her vivid gaze seemed so real that he opened his eyes once
more, half-convinced he'd find her sitting beside his bed.
But there was no one near him; the activity of the ward went
on around him. Had she really existed? he wondered, or had
he dreamt the whole thing?

He shifted restlessly, and a drift of perfume brushed his
consciousness. She'd been wearing perfume, he remembered. He'd noticed it when she'd put her arm around him
and lifted the glass of water to his lips. The scent of her must
have lingered on his pillow. So, she hadn't been a dream;
she'd actually been there.

Such a distinctive fragrance, he reflected, luxuriating in
the memory. Cool and somehow innocent, yet purely sensual in its appeal. He knew instinctively it was the kind of

perfume he liked to smell on a woman, and he briefly entertained the thought that she'd worn it just for him.

Yet when he'd suggested she might be his girlfriend, she'd been so affronted. As if the idea was too ridiculous to be borne. So—what? If not his sister, could she be his—wife? Dear God, he thought, if that were so, surely he would have known.

Or would he? Excitement stirred. The idea that he might be married to the beautiful creature who'd leant so confidently over his bed was tantalising. And it was an idea that, once having taken root, was hard to shift. Was that why she'd hurried to his bedside? And was she nervous because they'd had some altercation before he left?

But he'd been going to England, he reminded himself uneasily. And she hadn't been with him, so far as he knew. No, she couldn't have, to be so calm and collected. So had he been going to see her? Did they live apart?

She was English. He remembered that. Or if not English, then she'd lived there for some considerable time. God, if only he knew what had caused their separation. He knew so very little about himself.

As another thought struck him, he lifted his left hand and examined his third finger. But there was no ring—not even a sign that one had been there. But that meant nothing, he told himself fiercely. Not all men wore wedding rings. He frowned. Had she?

Refusing to let the insidious waves of panic scramble his already tortured senses, he made an intense effort to remember everything he knew about her. As if she were part of some imagined identity parade, he summoned up her image. Blue eyes simply weren't enough. He needed to recall her face in intimate detail.

But the features he forced back into focus were no more familiar now than they had ever been, and the knowledge that he could meet someone from his past without feeling any sense of identification almost frightened him to death. She'd known his father, he reminded himself desperately, which meant she had a part in his life. But what part? And for how long? And where was his father? The questions scared him more each time he struck out.

Panic almost overwhelmed him. He could smell the cold sweat that had broken out all over his useless body. Fighting it back, he struggled to find something to hold on to. But terror had him firmly in its grip.

Christ, what would he do if he never regained his memory? If the black hole he called a brain refused to work? What did people do in circumstances like this? Did they all feel so helpless? God, he thought, he'd have given anything for a shot of a single malt.

He blinked rapidly, feeling the incipient twinges of the headache he seemed to have had forever gnawing at his temple. It seemed as if whatever way he turned there was no relief. Dammit, he wasn't a chicken; he had to overcome this. But for someone who seldom got headaches in the normal way, it was draining his strength.

He swallowed. Now, how had he known that? he wondered shakily, clinging to the thought like the proverbial drowning man. How did he know he wasn't a slave to migraines, or suffer hangovers whenever he drank? And he did enjoy a drink; he was fairly certain. Oh, Lord, was his memory slowly coming back into life?

Afraid to explore something that still seemed so fragile, he turned his attention to what he had been trying to do before. With a determined effort, he forced the woman's face back into his consciousness. She must hold the key, if he could only remember what it was.

Her face seemed familiar now, but he knew that was just an aberration. Because he'd been concentrating on her image for so long, it had acquired a recognisable shape. But he didn't doubt that she was real; that she existed. He knew her, and that had to be a plus.

He breathed heavily. She'd had light brown hair, he decided, recalling the silky strands that had brushed his collar. Sort of toffee-coloured, he amended, and streaked with butter. Like caramel and cream or corn and coffee. He delighted in the comparisons. And just as smooth.

As far as her face was concerned, that was harder. It was oval, yet she'd had quite a determined chin. Her cheekbones had been high, her cheeks streaked with colour; and she'd had a mouth that he'd badly wanted to kiss.

Ridiculous!

He dispatched the thought instantly, drawing in another unsteady breath. It was no use speculating about their relationship. Until she told him who she was, it was far too dangerous to permit.

Once again he forced back the frightening void that loomed in front of him. He had to stop being so negative about his condition. That doctor—Harper—had said there was no easy answer. It would take days or weeks or months to recover completely.

Or never . . .

Of course, it was easy for a doctor to say. He didn't have to live with this terrible emptiness, this lack of knowledge that threatened to drive him mad. He didn't have to wake up to an awareness that was only partial. He didn't know his name, his age, his identity. He didn't have a life.

The brief spurt of optimism he'd been feeling while he was recalling the woman's image faded. There was no point in pretending he was getting anywhere with that. She was just as much a stranger now as she had ever been. Beautiful, yes, but anonymous just the same.

Which surely proved that their relationship couldn't be an intimate one, he decided wearily. And, looking back, she had shown little joy in finding he was alive. If his opinion meant anything, she'd seemed to look at him almost critically. As if she was searching for some recognition she hadn't found.

But that way lay danger. He refused to allow himself to approach the abyss again. She had to know who he was. Why else had she come here? The name—his name—Nathan Wolfe, had meant something to her.

A draught of air cooled his throbbing temples, but when he opened his eyes it was to find a nurse lifting the clipboard from the end of his bed. On it, he knew, were all the details of his present condition. They kept a note of his temperature, his blood pressure and his pulse.

And what else? he wondered. Judging by the way he was sweating at the moment, his temperature was probably way over par. He had only to think of how helpless he was, and his heart started pounding. The symptoms might be physical, but he knew it was mostly due to nerves.

"How are we feeling?" the nurse asked cheerfully, treating him to a gap-toothed smile. Haynes, he thought, frowning. Her name was Nurse Haynes. She'd been on duty last night when he was admitted. Only then he'd barely acknowledged she was there.

"I don't know about you, but I'm feeling terrific," he said, the cynicism in his tone barely disguised. He forced a grin to his dry lips to mitigate his sarcasm. "Say, who was that woman who visited earlier today? I did have a visitor, didn't I? She wasn't just a vision brought on by all those drugs you've been pumping into me?"

Nurse Haynes looked at him over the rim of the clipboard. She had nice eyes, thought Nathan objectively, though not as nice as some others he recalled. Nevertheless, she was his best hope for enlightenment. He didn't think old man Harper would be making any ward calls tonight.

The nurse lowered the clipboard to rest against her ample bosom. "She didn't tell you?" she inquired, and his impatience flared anew. Why was it that everyone seemed to think it was necessary to respond to his questions with other questions? Did they think he'd be asking if he knew?

"No," he replied at last, tersely, seeing no virtue in admitting some half truth. "So who was she? I have a right to know, don't I? Or is this some guessing game I have to play?"

The nurse's blonde brows elevated to somewhere near her hairline, and he realised he might have gone too far. He was in no state to make demands on anyone. Least of all some innocent nurse, who was only doing her job.

But Nurse Haynes was evidently disposed to be generous. "Why, Mr Wolfe," she said, in what he knew instinctively was a Southern accent, "that—woman—as you describe her, is your wife."

His stomach clenched. "My wife?"

"That's right." The nurse smiled. "A Mrs Caitlin Wolfe, from London. England, of course. What did you say to her? I hear she was quite upset when she left."

He couldn't believe it. My God, if she'd been his wife, he'd have recognised her, wouldn't he? She'd been so close; she'd helped him to a drink of water, for Christ's sake. He'd have identified something about her, even if it was only her perfume.

"I guess it's come as quite a shock to y'all?" the nurse ventured, suddenly anxious. Was she afraid she'd get into trouble for letting the cat out of the bag? But, dammit, if the woman was his wife, he deserved to know about it. If only so that when she came back he'd have something to say.

And then, as the rest of what she'd said struck him, he stared up at her. "She's left?" he exclaimed, gulping for air. "Dammit, where's she gone?"

"Why, to check in to a hotel, I imagine," responded Nurse Haynes soothingly. She hooked the clipboard back onto the rail and came to take his pulse. "I guess she'll come back tomorrow. Particularly as she's come such a long way."

"Pigs might fly," he muttered, resenting her suddenly for disrupting his pensive mood. How the hell was he supposed to relax when he supposedly had a wife he didn't recognise? And why hadn't she identified herself to him?

"She'll be here," declared Nurse Haynes confidently. She released his wrist and slipped her watch back into her breast pocket. "There now, you've got something to look forward to. Not everyone's so lucky, believe me."

His jaw clamped. He knew that was true. The aftermath of the accident was still horrifyingly fresh in his mind. After all, he was alive, and apart from his loss of memory, apparently not seriously injured. If he could only be patient, he had every chance of making a full recovery.

So why was he feeling so apprehensive? Why did the memory of his—*wife*—stick painfully in his gut? He had no reason to doubt she cared about him, yet he'd sensed a certain ambivalence in her gaze.

He spent the following day in a state of wary anticipation. Despite the depressed feeling he'd had the night before, he'd slept reasonably well and he'd awakened feeling infinitely brighter. At least he knew who he was, he told himself firmly. And from that basis, he would eventually rebuild his life.

So far as his marriage was concerned, he was determined to be optimistic. If it had been going through a rocky patch—and he had only his instincts to go on—then the accident could work in its favour. If he and—dammit, what had Nurse Haynes said her name was?—Caitlin? That's right, Caitlin. If he and *Caitlin* were having problems, they'd have a chance to solve them. They were being given a new start, whether they wanted it or not.

Before lunch, Dr Harper appeared, trailing his usual pack of interns. Evidently, his case had warranted some excitement in the medical school, and he was forced to lie there saying nothing, while every detail of his condition was brought out and discussed in embarrassing detail.

Not that any conclusions were reached. Despite the fact that they all seemed to have an opinion on the matter, he knew there was no real treatment available. Harper had already broken the news that physicians were still largely uninformed about the way to treat amnesia, and his primary brief, so far as Nathan was concerned, was to ensure that his vital signs remained good and his prognosis positive.

His determined optimism took a dive when afternoon visiting came and went with no sign of the woman they said was his wife. So far as his fellow patients were concerned, it was no big deal. Several of them didn't get any visitors, either, but he had been banking on her coming back and answering some of the questions that were now tormenting his brain. Who was he? What did he do? Where had he come from? And why had he been on the flight that had come to such an unhappy end?

Even so, he refused to be too downhearted. Perhaps she had other things to do. What other things, he didn't care to speculate. The possibility that she hadn't travelled to New York alone was becoming a source of anxiety he refused to face.

He barely touched his supper, earning a reproof from the ubiquitous Nurse Haynes. "Y'all should be thankful you're alive, Mr Wolfe," she declared, taking his pulse with impatient fingers. "If you're worried about losing your memory, just think how you'd have felt if you'd lost a limb!"

He agreed that he wouldn't have been too happy, though in his present state of mind he felt as if it might have been the lesser of the two evils. At least a man who'd lost a leg or an arm knew what was happening. He didn't need a doctor to tell him his name.

When his wife didn't appear for evening visiting, he knew he couldn't go on keeping his panic at bay. He couldn't think without resurrecting the ache in his temples, and although he was allowed to get out of bed to go to the washroom, his legs were so shaky he was practically in a state of collapse when he returned.

Where was she? Who was she? What if she wasn't his wife at all, but some sicko who enjoyed making other people sweat? No, they'd said her name was Wolfe—Caitlin Wolfe—and that was his name. He had his passport to prove it, if nothing else.

He slept badly in spite of the medication they insisted he swallow. And although his sleep was shallow, it was tormented by dreams. He had some crazy notion that he was looking in a mirror, but the man looking back at him wasn't himself.

He tried to shave the next morning. Designer stubble might look good on some hunk with a Miami tan, but on his pale face it just looked dirty. The trouble was, his hands shook so badly he ended up with a string of cuts, and his pallor wasn't improved by so much blood.

Still, what the hell, he thought, crawling back into bed, it wasn't as if anyone cared how he looked. This morning he had no expectations of a visit from his "wife." Whoever she was, she was keeping out of his way.

Yet, lying there, he couldn't help wondering what it was
he'd seen in her face. He was convinced now he had seen
something, and the thought occurred to him that she might
have been afraid. But afraid of what? Of him? Of his condition? What kind of man had he been before the crash?

He looked at his hands, examining them, as if the answer
might be found within their trembling grasp. What if he was
a violent man? A wife beater? Dear God, was that the reason she'd looked so—strained?

Once again, the old fears threatened to overwhelm him.
And once again, he managed to fight them back. Yet his
sanity was in danger; he felt it. Even if he believed he wasn't
a violent man.

He caught the man in the next bed watching him warily,
and he realised he must look strange, staring at his hands.
Thrusting them under the bedclothes, he offered the man a
wry grimace. If he wasn't careful, he'd prove what he was
trying so hard to refute.

Even so, another thought had occurred to him. His hands
might not tell him what manner of man he was, but they did
hold clues to the kind of work he'd done. His hands were
hard, but he didn't remember seeing any calluses, and his
nails were free of oil and grease. Which pointed to the fact
that he wasn't a manual worker. Was it possible if he
thought about an occupation he might have some success?

He made a salutary effort to swallow the stew and greens
they served at lunchtime. But the meat was tough, and the
greens were floating in their own juice. He seemed to remember that hospital food was always unappetizing. Could
that mean he'd been in hospital before?

An hour later, he'd achieved no conclusions, either about
his occupation or about whether he'd been in hospital before. It was like butting his head against a brick wall, which,

come to think of it, was what it felt like had happened. His brain felt thick and mushy, just like soup.

He elbowed himself into a sitting position. It was almost visiting time again. The man in the next bed hadn't had a visitor the day before. In fact, he didn't think he'd had any visitors at all. He turned to him, preparing some friendly remark of commiseration. And then saw the woman walking toward him down the ward.

It was her.

Caitlin.

His wife!

He swallowed convulsively and immediately wanted to go to the washroom again. Christ, he was like a kid, getting excited just because she was here. It wasn't as if she was doing him any favours. For God's sake, she was twenty-four hours late!

But immediately on the heels of this came the awareness of his own shortcomings. He should have made an effort to improve his appearance while he had the chance. The nightshirt he was wearing was hospital issue. But what the hell! He usually slept in the raw.

The question of how he knew that was overwhelmed by his delight at seeing her. For almost forty-eight hours, he'd lived in anticipation of this moment, and for all his brave attempts to motivate himself, he admitted he needed her now, probably more than ever before.

4

Lisa Abbott stood at the sitting-room window of her fourth-floor apartment, watching the rain dancing on the balcony outside. The plastic table and chairs that furnished the small balcony were dripping with water, and it was hard to imagine now that she'd actually sunbathed from that very spot.

Of course, that had been months ago, she acknowledged dourly. Since then, she had had plenty of time to complain about the English weather. Why didn't it snow, for God's sake, instead of this interminable rain? The dampness seemed to have invaded the apartment and seeped into her bones.

Still, the weather mirrored her mood, she thought grimly, crossing her arms over her slim body. Was it really only weeks ago she had felt so optimistic about the future? She'd been so happy; so sure nothing could go wrong.

Tears pricked at the back of her eyes. She should have known she was tempting fate. Oh, yes, she knew she should be grateful that Nathan was still alive, but why the hell hadn't he phoned? His secretary had said he had been admitted to a New York hospital; no one knew when he'd be back, but for God's sake, there had to be telephones there. Why hadn't he gotten hold of one and rung her? Didn't he care how she was feeling?

She sniffed, shivering a little in the sheer satin teddy that was all she was wearing. She'd bought the garment just a week ago, anticipating Nathan's reaction when he saw her in it. Now, it seemed it would be weeks before she was likely to find out. She didn't even know how badly he'd been hurt.

She'd worn the teddy today in an attempt to raise her spirits. It hadn't worked, even though she had gained some satisfaction from the knowledge that she still looked remarkably good for her age. The close-fitting satin accentuated the full swell of her breasts and hugged the narrow contours of her hips. For a woman of thirty-nine, she was remarkably well-preserved.

She sighed. If only there was something she could do, but her job at the casino meant she was virtually tied to staying put. Besides, it wouldn't do for Carl to think they were trying to cheat him. If she went flying off to the States, he was bound to think the worst.

Her teeth ground together at the thought of the hundreds of thousands of dollars that had literally gone up in smoke. She couldn't be certain, of course, but it seemed highly unlikely that Nathan's suitcase could have survived unscathed. He wouldn't have carried it on board as hand luggage. The last thing he'd want to do was draw attention to it. No, like everyone else's baggage in the hold, it would have been destroyed.

Still, at least Nathan had survived. And Carl could hardly blame him because the plane had crashed. It was an accident, pure and simple. She just wished she could convince herself that he'd understand.

That was why she'd called Carl and invited him to come over. She knew Nathan wouldn't like it, but dammit, he didn't have to know. He hadn't bothered to try and reach her, and she was restless. She ran slightly unsteady fingers over her stomach and down to the moist cleft between her legs, shivering in anticipation. She was horny. Oh, God, was she horny! She needed a man—any man—tonight.

If only Nathan's secretary had been more friendly when she'd gotten up the courage to call his office. She'd suggested she contact Mrs Wolfe if she wanted any further information. Close-mouthed cow! Lisa wondered if she knew Nathan had a mistress. One thing was certain—she'd never get anything out of her.

In the meantime, she had needs; she had priorities. Not the least of which was finding some more cash. Unfortunately, she'd speculated a little on Nathan's expectations. Maybe Carl would be generous. He used to like her not so long ago.

Lisa's lips tightened. It wasn't fair. It just wasn't fair. There was that bitch—Caitlin—who'd never had to fight for anything in her life, and here she was, with her only chance of happiness slipping away. What if Nathan was paralysed or disabled? Would she still feel the same way about him if he was?

But that was only morbid speculation. She couldn't afford to be negative about the future. Nathan would get better; he would be all right. She was convinced of it. And when he did, she was going to make sure he got a divorce. Caitlin didn't satisfy him; if it wasn't for her daddy's money, Nathan would never have looked at her. She had to remember that when things were looking black.

She sighed. If only Nathan's original scheme had been successful. If Matthew Webster had retired and given his son-in-law control of the company, they'd have been together by now. Once the shareholders had seen what a good job Nathan was doing, they'd have supported him whether he was married to Caitlin or not. It was what they'd planned when she'd followed him to England three years ago.

But it hadn't worked out that way. Somehow, Caitlin had discovered they were having an affair. If the old man hadn't had a heart attack, she'd have spilled the beans to her father, and then Nathan would have lost any chance of making good.

The final straw had been when Webster had employed that creep, O'Brien. They hadn't accused Nathan of anything, but it was obvious they didn't trust him. Caitlin must have said something or why else had Nathan been sidetracked? Lisa didn't blame him for using any means he could to screw the bastards.

She shivered again. It was getting dark. Across the square, lights were appearing in the windows of other apartments, reminding her that Carl was coming at six. She still hadn't fixed her make-up, but that didn't matter. She didn't intend to get dressed until after he'd arrived.

Was she being reckless, getting involved with a man like Carl Walker just because she was feeling peeved? If Nathan found out she'd cheated on him, would he throw her out? She scowled. He wouldn't find out. Carl wouldn't tell him. His wife ensured there'd be no complications of that kind.

Marshall O'Brien entered Matthew Webster's office with the ease of long familiarity. He'd only been Matthew's personal assistant for the past two years, but his relationship with the older man went back much further than that. Even so, it was Matthew's illness that had precipitated their association. Until then, it had remained virtually undisclosed.

Even now, there were only a favoured few who knew of—or suspected—its inception. And most of them would have thought twice before putting it into words. Matthew Webster had never been the kind of man to encourage confidences, and he treated his staff in much the same way he had treated his daughter—with consideration and respect, but little affection.

Nonetheless, his heart attack had changed many things. Not least, his plans for retirement. Despite what his doctors might have said at the time, Matthew had not handed over the reins of command as had been expected. On the contrary, after the attack his retirement had been indefinitely deferred.

And only he knew his sudden seizure had not been unwarranted. For months before the attack, he'd been living on his nerves. He hadn't wanted to accept it, but it hadn't taken him long to discover that Nathan was not the man he'd first believed him, and his suspicions had left him sick at heart.

Physically as well as mentally, as it had turned out. The husband he'd chosen for his daughter had proved to have feet of clay, and although Matthew had never had much time for emotion, especially not in business, having to consider his daughter's feelings had frustrated him beyond belief.

After all, only months before, he'd been congratulating himself on his success. After years of having to live with the fact of Caitlin's rejection of his plans for her, he'd been given a second chance. That wimp she'd been living with had blotted his copybook, and Caitlin had come running home with her tail between her legs.

He remembered how hard it had been not to say "I told you so" and he thought he'd been rewarded when Nathan Wolfe appeared on his horizon. Even then, he hadn't been able to believe his luck when Caitlin had showed she was attracted to him, too, and when they'd announced their engagement, he'd thought he was the luckiest man alive.

He should have known better.

In fact, he thought now, he should have been suspicious of any man Caitlin was attracted to. Her record, so far as emotional relationships was concerned, was abysmal, and she'd proved time and time again how sensible he had been not to take her ambitions seriously. In his opinion, women were hopelessly impetuous and far too easily led.

Even so, Nathan had appeared to embody everything he'd hoped for in a future son-in-law. He was older than Caitlin, which was a distinct advantage. It meant he had experience, and although he hadn't been married before, he'd had plenty of time to sow his wild oats. In addition to which, he'd insisted he was willing to learn, which meant that Matthew would be able to teach him his own methods and consequently keep one hand on the reins even after his retirement.

The only doubt he had had concerned the Wolfes' own operation, but Nathan had admitted—modestly, Matthew had felt—that his father's sawmill was having problems due to a slump in the market, and consequently there'd be no conflict of interest should Matthew choose to take him on.

To trust him . . .

Matthew felt the familiar flutter in his heart at the remembrance of how gullible he'd been. Dear God, after all those years of trusting no one but himself, he'd been pathetically easy to deceive.

Well, initially anyway, he conceded, his lips twisting. But Nathan had not only *not* been as clever as Matthew thought him to be, he hadn't been as clever as he'd believed himself, and within months of his tenure, Matthew had been receiving reports that proved beyond doubt that Nathan's judgment was sadly flawed.

His heart attack could not have come at a worse time. For weeks afterwards, he'd been forced to lie helpless while Nathan systematically took the company down. Only his lack of experience of a large organisation had worked against him, and his efforts to award tenders for contracts on the basis of favours granted had eventually been noticed in accounts.

Nevertheless, the half-yearly figures had been appalling, and by the time Matthew dragged himself back into his office, the shareholders were lusting for his blood. They were threatening to hit him with a vote of no confidence in the company's management, and with competitors breathing down his neck, something drastic had to be done.

But he hadn't fired Nathan. He'd known that by admitting his son-in-law's incompetence, he'd be indirectly blaming himself, and any hint of a lack of judgment on his part could trigger an instant collapse of Webster shares. Instead, without actually making any overt reference to his mismanagement, he had systematically stripped Nathan of all responsibility in the company. And, just as inevitably, Matthew had resumed his former position, against medical advice and at the risk of his own health.

He didn't know what Caitlin had made of her husband's obvious change of status. She seemed content, and he had never allowed himself to entertain the thought that Nathan might have been a failure as a husband, too. He still refused to admit he could have been so totally wrong about the man, and in consequence he'd kept Nathan's mistakes to himself.

Well, almost . . .

That was when he'd asked Marshall to join the company. He'd been prepared to pay him anything if he'd come to work for him. He needed someone he could trust in a position of authority. Someone who could be his eyes and ears, without alerting the other members of his board—or Nathan—what was going on.

Now, as he watched the younger man cross the thick carpet towards him, he was aware of his own mortality as never before. One day soon, he was going to have to make a decision about Marshall, and the knowledge filled him with defeat. He'd fought against it for so long, but fate was catching up with him. He couldn't go on running Webster's. Already, he had had intimations that his health was deteriorating more rapidly than even his doctors had expected, and despite his misgivings, he had to choose someone to be his successor. Obviously, it couldn't be Nathan. Whatever happened, he couldn't allow that. But Marshall... Marshall was still largely an unknown quantity. Despite their enforced intimacy, Matthew knew he was only here under duress.

He sighed. If only the boy could understand. But he'd never forgotten that once Matthew had forbidden him the privilege of working for the company. Never forgiven him, either. And if Marshall's mother wasn't still alive—and vulnerable—the young man would never have agreed to his request.

"Caitlin called," he said now, lounging into the chair across the desk from Matthew and regarding him with cool blue eyes. He hooked his heel across his knees. "I thought you'd like to know."

Matthew kept his temper with an effort. But he couldn't suppress the indignant flutter in his chest. God, was his wife right? Had he made another foolish error? Marshall appeared to hate him as much as he admired him; he certainly showed him no respect.

"Didn't she want to speak to me?" he demanded, his tone just short of an accusation. "You knew I wanted to talk to her if she called."

Marshall shrugged. He was a man of middle height, stocky but muscular, and Matthew knew he worked out several times a week. He had short brown hair and he wore wire-rimmed spectacles, but his appearance was deceptive. He was as strong as an ox and just as stubborn when he chose. Like Caitlin...

"She wouldn't wait," Marshall said carelessly, flicking a speck of lint from his sleeve. He hesitated, and then added reluctantly, "I got the impression she was—nervous. I guess finding your husband doesn't know you is quite a strain."

"If he doesn't," muttered Matthew sceptically, tapping a pen somewhat agitatedly against his blotter. "What do you think? Is he lying, or has he really lost it? How the hell are we going to handle it if it's true?"

Marshall's face was annoyingly blank. "You're talking about the discrepancies in the South American contract."

"Well, I'm not bloody interested in his health, if you're in any doubt." Matthew scowled. "How in God's name did we let him get away with it? Does nobody do their jobs around here but me?"

Marshall's expression hardened. "It was you who insisted on keeping him on," he pointed out evenly.

"Only because it would have been a damn sight more dangerous to let him go," snarled his employer harshly. "Besides, I didn't think he'd be reckless enough to attempt to defraud the company again. After bringing us to the brink of bankruptcy the last time, I thought he'd have learned more sense. Christ, the man's a complete shit, and I want him out!"

"So you weren't thinking of Caitlin's feelings, then?" Marshall was sardonic, and Matthew gave him a brooding look.

"That, too," he said defensively. "Hell, she's married to him, isn't she? How could I tell her what a bastard he was? Credit me with some feelings, Marshall. I'm not totally without discrimination."

"But you've changed your mind now."

"Situations alter cases," said Matthew pedantically. He shook his head. "We have to think of the company. God, if this present fiasco were made public, I can just imagine what that would do for our shares."

Marshall considered. "Well, I don't think there's anything we can do until he's back in England. Then you can have your own physician check him over without causing too much fuss. But—" he paused "—if it's true, it's going to be difficult to prove his guilt. You can't accuse a man who doesn't remember what you're accusing him of."

Matthew flung the pen across the desk in frustration. "The truth is, it's going to be hard to prove whatever the prognosis. If he's fooled the doctors in the States, why shouldn't he fool them here? And how am I going to tell Caitlin her husband's a criminal? Thank God there aren't any children to complicate things even more."

Marshall's lip curled. "Thank God," he echoed harshly, and Matthew gave him a remorseful stare.

"You're a lot of help, I must say," he muttered. "And don't pretend you don't know what I mean. I've made mistakes in my time, I admit it. But dammit all, Nathan was the worst."

Marshall sighed as if expelling his impatience on the breath, and then drew his brows together. "Well—there's always the chance that his condition will be temporary. If he has lost his memory, it may be he'll recover it when he gets home. Familiar things, familiar places, familiar people. I've heard there are no hard-and-fast rules where amnesia is concerned."

"Which doesn't do a lot for us," declared Matthew wearily, lines of strain appearing beside his mouth. "Whatever happens, it's going to be weeks, maybe even months, before we can nail him. Which means I'm going to have to make good the damage myself.''

Marshall's brows elevated. ''There is the woman—Lisa Abbott. She may know something about it. I could go and see her.''

''And warn him that we're onto him? Not likely.'' Matthew shook his head. ''No, for the moment, our hands are tied. I just hope he hasn't spent all the money. Half a million, Marshall! God, I can't believe he had the brains to do it. He must have the luck of the devil!''

''I wouldn't call being involved in a major air disaster particularly lucky,'' observed Marshall sardonically. ''And if he has really forgotten everything, I'd guess he's feeling pretty low. Okay, you want your money back, but spare the man some pity. No name, no identity, no nothing! I'll be interested to see how he handles it. It can't be easy.''

''Hmm.''

Matthew was noncommittal. Right at the moment, he couldn't find it in his heart to feel any compassion for Nathan at all. For all he knew, there might be other scams not yet discovered. For a man as unscrupulous as his son-in-law, there were always loopholes he could breach.

''Think about Caitlin,'' said Marshall now, aware of the other man's brooding countenance. ''And you're not going to do yourself any favours if you can't put this out of your mind. I've told you, when he's recovered I'll handle it. Think of your daughter and what this might do to her.''

''I'm not without sensitivity as far as my daughter's feelings are concerned,'' retorted Matthew defensively. ''I know you think I'm totally selfish, but it isn't true.'' He met the younger man's accusing eyes and dropped his gaze abruptly. ''All right. I'll do as you say. That's what I employed you for after all. You don't have to keep reminding me you'd rather not be here.''

5

Caitlin turned onto her left side, trying to find a comfortable spot, and then remembered why she'd turned the other way in the first place. Now she had an uninterrupted view of her husband's reclining body. And although his eyes were closed, he was no less disturbing to her peace of mind.

All around them, the other occupants of the first-class cabin of the aircraft were unaware of her distraction. Apart from the comforting drone of the engines and an occasional snort from a sleeping passenger, all was quiet. Even the cabin staff had disappeared to enjoy their meal next to the kitchens. Now and then, the tantalising smell of the prime sirloin Caitlin had been offered earlier drifted her way.

It was ironic that she was wishing now that they'd taken the following morning's Concorde. If she hadn't been so eager to get back to England, it would have made more sense. But she'd seen the overnight flight as a chance to avoid conversation. She usually slept on the aircraft without any problem.

But the selfishness of her decision had dawned on her at the airport. When she'd glimpsed Nathan's taut face, she'd immediately realised her mistake. The prospect of the overnight flight must have brought back horrific images for him. And although he didn't remember boarding the plane, he remembered the aftermath of the crash.

But when she'd booked the flight, it hadn't been his feelings she'd been concerned about. And although she'd offered to change their reservations, Nathan had shaken his head. He appeared to be asleep now, so she didn't know what she was worrying about. With characteristic insensitivity, he'd left her at the mercy of her fears.

She shifted again, turning her head so that he was no longer in her line of vision. She didn't want to look at him. She didn't even want to think about him, but she knew from recent experience that that was not so easily achieved. From the minute she'd walked into the hospital ward and seen him lying there, she'd been in a state of panic. He was in her thoughts; he was in her mind; there seemed to be no escape.

Which was stupid considering the circumstances of their previous relationship. Dear God, they'd been virtually estranged. She'd only come here at all because it was what her father had expected her to do. She didn't want to get involved, however hard that sounded. It wasn't her fault that there'd been an accident and Nathan was hurt.

Yet . . .

She moistened her lips. What had she really felt when he'd opened his eyes and seen her hovering over him? It had certainly not been indifference, she had to acknowledge that. Such dark eyes he had; had they always been so expressive? He'd looked thinner somehow, as if the accident had drained him. And she hadn't noticed before that he'd let his hair get over-long.

But it was the way he'd looked at her that had set her knees trembling. If she hadn't known better, she'd have said there was sudden desire in his gaze. God, he'd told her so often in the past that she repelled him. Yet when he'd looked at her, there'd been hunger in his eyes.

Her lips twisted in sudden self-denial. It had been the aftermath of the accident, that was all. In his position, discovering he was still alive after such an event must have been traumatic. But his reactions had unnerved her. It was not what she had expected—or *wanted*, she reminded herself again.

Since then, she'd done her best to convince him that they didn't have that kind of marriage. Any attempt he'd made to touch her—to stroke her cheek or hold her hand—had been met with obvious reluctance. She didn't want him touching her; she didn't want him creating a relationship for them when none was there. And most of all, she didn't want him stirring up emotions that she'd believed were dead and buried; that had never been real emotions from the beginning and were nothing more than pity now.

It hadn't been easy, and even now she didn't know if she'd achieved her objective. She'd caught him watching her sometimes with a curious mix of doubt and speculation, and her skin had feathered at the thwarted intimacy in his eyes. But whatever he was thinking, he didn't voice it. Was he waiting until they were completely alone before he made his move?

For the present, she thought he had enough to do, trying to absorb the restrictions that his amnesia had thrust upon him. Caitlin had done her best to deliver the bare facts of his life to him, but she knew he was finding it difficult to put it all together. It would have been easier if she'd been able to arouse some latent point of contact for him to cling to. If there'd been something that had rung a chord in his memory. But there wasn't. So far as his previous life was concerned, it was as if a blanket had descended and covered it. Even his father's visit had meant nothing to him.

Caitlin frowned. Her first encounter with Nathan's father had been something of an anticlimax. She'd decided not to shock the old man by delivering the news of his son's accident by telephone, and the day after she'd first visited Nathan at the hospital, she'd flown to see him.

After taking a cab from the airport in Atlantic City to Prescott, she'd had no difficulty in locating the Wolfes' sawmill. It was a well-known landmark on the outskirts of the small town, and she'd felt a certain eagerness to see it. After all, Nathan had never brought her here before.

But the dilapidated state of the timber yard depressed her. Whatever previous success it had enjoyed, it was obviously neglected now. In fact, if she hadn't seen a plume of smoke issuing from the house next door, she might have asked the driver to turn around and take her back to the airport. As it was, she'd asked him to wait in case Jacob Wolfe wasn't there.

But he was there. He'd answered the door himself, and Caitlin had been horrified at his skeletal appearance. Of course, she'd reminded herself, Nathan had told her his father had been ill. For God's sake, that was why he'd been in the United States in the first place.

But she'd soon discovered her mistake. Although Nathan's father had seemed pleased to meet his daughter-in-law at last, he insisted he hadn't seen his son for over a year. Which had prompted the question of why Nathan had been in the United States and why he should have lied about it to her.

Jacob Wolfe couldn't give her any answers. However, his concern for his son was obviously genuine, and he'd insisted on accompanying her back to New York. Caitlin was sure he had been eager to see his son himself; to ensure that his injuries were not serious, as she'd said. For her part, she'd prayed that seeing his father again might spark some chord in Nathan's memory. It was clear that her husband didn't recognise her.

But, in the event, it was Jacob Wolfe who seemed most affected by the encounter. After visiting his son, he'd seemed bewildered and distrait. Although he'd actually said little to Caitlin, she'd sensed his confusion. Then he'd made some excuse about needing his medication, and left.

He hadn't come back and Nathan's comments about the old man's visit had hardly been satisfactory. He said the old man had seemed strangely bewildered, but Caitlin guessed he'd been shocked to find his son didn't recognise him.

Caitlin had tried to ring him before they left to tell him they were going back to England, but there'd been no reply. Either Jacob Wolfe wasn't at home, or he wasn't answering the telephone. Short of visiting him again, there was nothing more she could do.

Besides, her conclusion that amnesia could affect other people as well as its immediate victim was relevant. Sometimes, when she was talking to Nathan herself, she'd had the feeling she was losing her own mind. It was hard to relate to someone who didn't share your memories—though some of those memories she'd have liked to lose herself.

Naturally, there were things she hadn't chosen to tell him. Although he might very well suspect that their relationship was not all it should be, she hadn't actually told him they lived separate lives. Nor did she intend to do so for the present. Dr Harper had warned her not to say anything that might upset him; that his recovery could be a long and painful process, and controversy could only obstruct those ends.

But there had been occasions when Caitlin had wondered who she was fooling. Whether it wasn't as much to her advantage as to Nathan's that she keep their troubled association to herself. It was pride, she thought, that made the choice so easy. But she sensed another reason that she preferred not to name.

Why? she asked herself now, feeling him move beside her. It wasn't as if she wanted him back, husband or not. She didn't love him. She had never loved him, she assured herself firmly. And just because she was feeling sorry for him was no reason to confuse the issue now.

But the awareness that he could disturb her emotions was hard to swallow. When she'd flown to New York, she'd been so sure she knew how she felt. Yet, seeing him again in that vulnerable state had jarred her defences. If she didn't know better, she'd have said the man she'd married was not the man in the hospital bed.

But he was....

Shifting again, Caitlin wished she could stop thinking; that she could put all her doubts and misgivings to the back of her mind. What she was going to do when they got back to England she had yet to consider. Nathan was going to need constant attention, and she couldn't see herself in the role of a nurse.

The idea of giving up her job and looking after him herself was not an option. And she resented the feelings that had put the thought into her mind. What would Janie, her business partner, think if she suggested it? After the way Nathan had always treated her, she'd say she was mad.

Besides, she enjoyed her work at the antique shop and she saw no reason why she should give it up. Let Lisa Abbott look after him, she thought maliciously. Except that he didn't remember the other woman, and she had no intention of telling him about her yet.

The flickering glow of a video screen attracted her attention. Across the aisle, one of the other passengers was evidently finding it hard to sleep and had switched on his personal monitor. Caitlin wished she'd had the foresight to ask for a video. Anything to fill the empty hours before it was light.

"Am I disturbing you?"

Nathan's voice in her ear startled her. She hadn't been aware he was awake and she hoped he couldn't read her thoughts. It wouldn't do for him to know how much he disturbed her, or how easy it would be to deceive herself into thinking he wasn't the man he was.

Trying to be objective, she was struck all at once by his accent. In the quiet surrounds of the aircraft, his lazy drawl was suddenly unfamiliar, too. Had it always had that softness, that almost Southern intonation? It must have had, but why hadn't she noticed it before?

"Um—no," she responded at last, wishing it were true. Of course he disturbed her. Though perhaps not in that way he expected. She forced a smile. "I probably woke you. I haven't been to sleep."

"Nor have I," he confessed, and to her dismay, he shifted onto his side to face her. "To be honest, I was thinking about the accident." He grimaced. "Fate can really fu— mess up your life."

Caitlin bit her lip. "Yes, I was thinking about the accident, too," she said, not altogether untruthfully. "I should never have booked us on this flight. I'm sorry. It was totally thoughtless." She paused. "Would you like to talk about it? If you think it might help—"

"There's nothing to talk about," replied Nathan flatly. The muted lights in the cabin cast most of his face into shadow, but they couldn't hide the sudden anguish in his eyes. "All I remember is lying at the edge of the runway. That, and the horror of hearing people screaming for help."

Caitlin knew the increasingly familiar desire to comfort him. "There was nothing you could do," she said softly. "The emergency services were there almost at once. It's getting on the plane that's aroused all these apprehensions.

As I said before, we should have taken the morning flight.
Or even sailed home on the *QE2*.''

''The ship,'' murmured Nathan wryly, proving once again
that his brain was still functioning normally when it came to
external matters. Then, ''No. It's better to face your fears,
don't you think?''

Caitlin shrugged a little ruefully. ''At least you haven't
forgotten everything. Dr Harper told me that some people
have to learn to read and write all over again.''

''God!'' Nathan was appalled. ''And I was feeling pretty
sorry for myself just now. Imagine being as helpless as a
baby. I think my brain's like a cabbage, but at least I know
my left foot from my right.''

''Your brain's not like a cabbage,'' Caitlin assured him
firmly. ''A person's memory can be selective even without
losing your memory. I know that.''

''Do you?'' He slanted a lazy glance her way, and she was
uneasily aware of his attraction. ''So, tell me, Mrs Wolfe,
what have you forgotten? Or don't you remember?''

''Me?'' Caitlin's ungrammatical use of the personal pronoun owed as much to her own disconcerted state as to any
surprise at the question. The realisation that this man was
her husband suddenly had a deeper meaning. How might
their relationship develop without the chains that had bound
her to him in the past?

''Oh—things,'' she replied at last, when it became obvious he was waiting for a response, and his dark brows
quirked disbelievingly. ''It's true,'' she went on doggedly,
striving desperately for an illustration. ''Like—when I fell
in the stream at Fairings. I didn't remember that.''

''Fairings?''

Nathan frowned, and Caitlin hastily explained that that
was the name of her parents' house. ''In Buckingham-

shire," she added. "About forty miles from London. You'll see it, I expect, when we get back."

Nathan inclined his head. "And how old were you when you fell in the stream?" he inquired sceptically.

Caitlin hesitated. "Four—I think."

"Four?" He gave her a retiring look. "Oh, yeah, right. That makes me feel a whole lot better. I don't know why I've been so worried. It's obvious it's just a childish prank."

Caitlin pursed her lips. "Don't be so cynical. Shock can cause all kinds of problems. You have to work it through. That's what Dr Harper said anyway."

"Mmm." He didn't sound convinced. "Do you really think telling me about some ducking you took when you were four—and which, incidentally, you'd forgotten—is a positive thing to do?"

"I thought so." Caitlin looked dejected. "I suppose I didn't—didn't—"

"Think?" he prompted drily. "Yeah, that about covers it. Oh, Kate, you're not the most tactful counsellor I've known."

Caitlin shifted a little uncomfortably at his words. It was the first time he had called her Kate, and it troubled her more than she wanted to admit. If Nathan had ever shortened her name, he'd made it Cat, not Kate. A word he'd used with malevolent pleasure on occasion.

Nathan's warm breath was on her temple, and she could smell the faint aroma of the wine he'd drunk earlier. She'd been doubtful about him drinking it all, but she hadn't voiced her objections. And at this moment, she could have done with a little Dutch courage herself.

She was uneasily reminded of the problems she still had to face when they got back to England. How would he react when he discovered they slept in different rooms? His attitude towards her was so unguarded at the moment. For all her reticence at the hospital, he'd made it clear he had no problem with regarding her as his wife.

Needing to say something, anything, to dispel the sudden intimacy that had developed between them, Caitlin chose the first words that came into her head. "It's probably because I wasn't trained to be a counsellor. My father wanted an obedient daughter, but I'm afraid I disappointed him, as well."

"Did I say you'd disappointed me?" Nathan asked, his voice softer than she'd ever heard it, and she felt the wave of heat that swept up her throat. "From where I'm sitting, I've got no complaints about your upbringing. I just wish I could remember where we met."

"It was at a party, my birthday party, I told you," said Caitlin hurriedly, feeling the need to loosen the collar of her shirt to get some air. "How—how about you? Don't you remember anything about your childhood? What kind of school you went to? What you did?"

"Mmm..."

He seemed to be considering the question, and she was grateful that his eyes had dropped from her face. But the coolness that brushed her throat alerted her to another explanation. In her haste to cool her face, she'd gone too far.

The realisation that, instead of thinking of an answer, he was seemingly entranced by the swell of her small breasts above the satin camisole horrified her. With shaking fingers, she dragged the two sides of her shirt together and refastened the buttons. But not before he had glimpsed her unwilling arousal and the pertness of her nipples against the cloth.

Instead of cooling down, she was now burning with embarrassment. She just hoped Nathan didn't think it had been a deliberate attempt to tease. Dear God, this was proving to be far more arduous than she'd imagined. She must get her emotions under control.

"Don't worry," he said, his words achieving exactly the opposite effect. "No one else could see what I could see. And, believe me, I enjoyed the view."

Which was precisely what she was afraid of, she thought anxiously. He may once have had the right to touch her, but no more. And just because he had aroused her sympathy was no reason to humiliate herself again.

"You were asking about my childhood," he said eventually, perhaps sensing her discomfort, and Caitlin breathed an unsteady sigh of relief. All she needed to do was get things into perspective. She was overreacting and reading things into his behaviour that probably weren't even there.

"Yes," she murmured, grateful for the diversion, and he sighed.

"Unfortunately, I don't remember anything. Except..." He frowned. "You know, I do seem to recall getting a beating. Yeah, my pa used to beat me." He gasped. "How about that?"

His voice had risen as he spoke, and Caitlin put a warning finger to her lips, regarding him with wary eyes. He seemed delighted with his success, but she had the suspicion he wasn't being totally honest. How could he remember a beating and nothing else?

Besides, from what little she knew of Jacob Wolfe, she couldn't imagine him beating his son. He hadn't struck her as being a violent man. He'd seemed far too gentle for that.

"You don't believe me," he said flatly before she could put her thoughts into words, and Caitlin made an awkward gesture.

"I don't disbelieve you," she said, which wasn't what he wanted to hear, and his lips twisted.

"Well, we know where my father is. Why don't we ask him? Better that than you think me a liar. I assure you, I'm not making it up. I distinctly remember him taking his belt to me—on more than one occasion."

"If you say so." Caitlin was noncommittal. "But how can you be so sure? It could be a memory of something you once read about—or saw. Why are you so convinced? Do you have any proof?"

"Not unless I've still got the stripes across my butt," responded Nathan tersely. "Hey, can I help it if you don't like what you hear?"

Caitlin sighed. "But your father seemed such a—a gentle man. He didn't strike me as someone who'd abuse his son."

Nathan shrugged. "And that's proof that he didn't?"

"No. No—but, for heaven's sake! When he found out you'd been injured, he had to come and see that you were all right."

"Correction," retorted Nathan sourly. "The old guy's half-senile. You've got no idea what he used to be like when he was my age."

Caitlin pressed her lips together. "I admit—he did seem confused."

"Didn't he just?"

Caitlin frowned. "I don't really know him well enough to judge."

"Why not?"

"Why not?" Caitlin looked perplexed for a moment, and then comprehension dawned. "Oh—well, because that was the first time I'd met him."

Nathan stared at her. "Run that by me again."

"What?"

"That bit about your not knowing my father." He scowled. "Are you kidding me?"

"No." Caitlin sighed. "He—didn't come to our wedding because he wasn't well. Or so you said," she added a little resentfully. "In any case, we never met until I saw him the other day."

"And we've been married how long?"

Caitlin swallowed. "Three years."

"Three years?" He was evidently amazed. "Are you sure about this?" He shook his head. "Are you sure you're my wife?"

Caitlin flushed. "What do you mean by that?"

"Well, hell..." Nathan made a frustrated gesture. "You must admit this gets more and more bizarre. I've only your word you are who you say you are, and now you tell me you never even met my family. Why didn't we go to see him after we were married?"

"I don't know." Caitlin had no intention of going into that. "We—just didn't, that's all."

"Any minute now, you're going to tell me that Prescott is a long way from London."

"Well, it is."

"But you didn't think twice about getting on a plane when you found out I'd been injured, did you?"

"No..."

"So, you have to admit, it's pretty strange that you didn't ever meet my father, isn't it?"

"All right." Caitlin spread her hands. "I—I've been negligent, okay? Does it matter?"

Nathan shook his head. "It might. We've only this old guy's word that he was my father, haven't we?"

"No." Caitlin frowned. "I told you. I went to Prescott. I visited his house. The house you grew up in. He—he has pictures of you all over the place."

"Huh." Nathan grunted, but it seemed her explanation had gone some way to reassuring him on that score at least.

However, his next words proved he hadn't totally abandoned the topic. "And, based on what, less than twenty-
four hours experience, you're telling me my old man wasn't
the kind of man to take his belt to his son?"

"I—I think so."

"So where does that leave me?" She was alarmed to see
how drawn his face had become. "Something's not right
about this, Kate. I can feel it. I just wish to hell I knew what
it was."

He moved then, shifting onto his back again and staring
at the roof of the cabin as if he hoped he might find some
inspiration there. It was obvious her insistence that Jacob
Wolfe was not as he remembered him had driven a rift between them, and conversely now, Caitlin regretted her re-
calcitrance. After all, as he'd said, what did she really know
about his father? Her half-formed impressions were hardly
reliable. The whole situation was far too uncertain for that.

And she'd never expected he might question her identity.
Yet, when she thought about it, it was exactly the kind of
thing he would do. Nothing made sense to him: not her ignorance as to why he should have been visiting the United
States without her, nor her reluctance to allow him to get
close to her. He wanted answers she either couldn't—or
wouldn't—give him, and the future had never looked as
bleak as it did at that moment.

6

The apartment was in Knightsbridge, which he knew—with one of those strange quirks of his condition—was a rather select part of London. It was quite spacious—comfortable, without being overly luxurious. Two bedrooms, two bathrooms, and a large living room, with a tiny dining alcove overlooking the square below. The kitchen was high-tech and spotlessly clean, which indicated that Caitlin employed someone to keep it that way. It was on the top floor of the building, ten levels up from the street, so that any traffic noise was negligible.

He had hoped he would remember their apartment. Caitlin had described it to him during one of their stiff conversations in the hospital, and although he was fairly sure he'd never seen it before, he did know his way around.

But Caitlin had told him a lot of things while he was still confined to bed, none of them arousing any element of recognition in his memory. She might have been a complete stranger were it not for that instantaneous attraction he'd felt towards her. That, he knew, was not imagined, and her insistence in talking about impersonal things had only heightened his desire to breach the very definite barriers she had erected between them.

Well, he reflected somewhat wearily, he was a comparative stranger to her, as well. For all his disturbing attraction to her, he didn't remember her at all. Sometimes, when he was lying sleepless in his bed, he'd tried to remember making love to her. But, although he'd usually gotten hard and frustrated, he had no memory of their lovemaking, either.

He'd blamed it on the fact that she'd remained so aloof from him. Although she'd kissed his cheek when she was leaving, she'd never ever kissed his mouth. It was as if she was afraid of getting too close to him. But, whatever his mental state, he knew his body craved hers.

What had he done to turn her against him? Because he sensed he had done something, no matter what she said. And if she didn't love him, if she wished she hadn't married him, why hadn't they divorced? If it seemed that simple to him, why didn't it seem so to her?

Yet, that thought, coming on top of the conversation they had had on the plane, was definitely depressing. He had thought they were making some progress until she'd told him about his father. It was obvious there was a problem, but she didn't want to discuss it with him. Just as he seemed to be reaching the real Caitlin Wolfe, she pulled away.

And he needed her, he thought, looking bleakly around the strange apartment. He needed her friendship; he needed her trust; he needed her support. If only she'd let him get near her, he felt sure he'd find what he was seeking. She couldn't mean to keep him at arm's length until he remembered who he was, could she?

Once, during their conversations at the hospital, he'd asked her if he could have gone to New York seeking employment. It had seemed to offer a legitimate reason why he might have gone alone. But Caitlin said he worked for her father, and once again he'd been baulked of any success.

"D'you like it?"

Caitlin breezed into the living room behind him with all the impersonal charm of a real-estate broker, and set her suitcase down on the Persian carpet. Nathan had left her downstairs, settling up with the cab driver who had brought them from the airport. After ascertaining which apartment was theirs, he'd come up alone.

He had hoped that seeing the place where he had lived would arouse some familiarity, but in the event, all it had aroused was a feeling of sick dismay. And Caitlin had looked at him strangely when he'd asked for her keys and the number of the apartment. He suspected she still harboured doubts about what he might, or might not, know.

"It's very—comfortable," he replied now, the words as inadequate as the way he was feeling at present. And looking at her, he sensed she was just as apprehensive. She'd been getting increasingly more agitated all the way from Heathrow. "Do we—own it? Or is it on a lease?"

"My father bought it for us," Caitlin responded quickly. "It was his wedding present to us." She glanced around. "I expect you're tired."

"No," he denied, although in truth he was feeling incredibly weary. But he resented her making him feel like an invalid. He'd lost his memory, for God's sake! He wasn't recovering from the plague!

"Oh, well..." She licked her lips, looking at him as if he were a rather irritating child she'd been left in charge of. "It's probably just as well. Mrs Spriggs will be here directly."

"Mrs Spriggs?"

"My—*our* housekeeper. She usually arrives about half past nine, and it's almost that now."

"Ah." Nathan was relieved to find he'd been right about something.

"She's a daily woman, actually," went on Caitlin, clearly glad of the distraction. "Mrs Spriggs comes in every morning while I'm at the shop. She's very nice. She keeps the place beautifully, and she generally prepares an evening meal for—''

"The shop?" he interrupted her abruptly. "You work in a shop?" It didn't seem to fit the image somehow.

"The antique shop," Caitlin reminded him pleasantly. "I believe I told you about it while you were in hospital. I share the running of it with a friend, Janie Spencer. You must remember. We've had the shop for over two years."

"I don't remember anything," he reminded her bitterly, wishing she would stop treating him like some mentally retarded child. Then, realising she was probably finding this as difficult as he was, he relented. "Is there any chance of having a shower?" He ran his hand over his roughening jawline. "I could do with a shave."

"Of course."

She was almost too eager to accommodate him, and he guessed she'd be glad to be rid of him for a while. It couldn't be easy coping with his moods and attitudes. He should stop feeling so sorry for himself and think about her instead.

The trouble was, that was all he thought about, he chided himself tersely. Either they normally had a very active sex life, or the two weeks he'd spent in the hospital in New York had left him desperate for a fuck. Just looking at her, he could feel himself hardening. He wondered what she'd say if he invited her to join him.

"Where—where is our room?" he asked, eager to dispel such feelings, and was inordinately pleased with himself when he guessed which door led into the inner hallway of the apartment. Then, confronted with several more doors, he conceded the choice to her, following her into a bedroom that seemed far too luxurious to be his.

"Um—this is your room," she said, emphasising the personal pronoun. And then, before he could object, she hurried across the room and opened another door. "And this is your dressing room through here, with your bathroom beyond it. You'll find all your clothes in the closets, and your socks and underwear are in the drawers—"

"Wait a minute." He didn't let her go any further, closing the bedroom door behind him and leaning purposefully back against it. Then, ignoring her alarmed expression, he folded his arms and regarded her coldly. "Are you saying we don't share a bedroom?" He glanced distastefully about him. "That this—room—is all mine?"

She licked her lips. "Of course."

"Why 'of course'?"

"Well, because it is."

"So I ask again, why?"

She was obviously disconcerted now. "It—it seemed the most—sensible arrangement at the time."

"At what time?" His dark eyes bored into her. "When we got married? When we had our first fight? When I *beat* you? Goddammit, Kate, I want to know."

"I—well—you didn't beat me," she mumbled, and he was amazed at how relieved he felt.

"Okay. So what did I do?"

Her eyes darted anxiously about her, and he guessed she was desperate to escape. But so long as he was blocking the door, that way was closed to her, and he was determined to have an answer, however painful it might prove. "I don't remember," she said at last, falling back on the oldest excuse in the book, and he regarded her disbelievingly. "I don't," she persisted doggedly. And then, "You've never complained before."

He winced at the deliberate reminder. But he refused to let her get the better of him now. "Tell me what I've done," he said, his expression hard and accusing. "You've been keeping me at arm's length ever since you came to the hospital.

There must be a reason for that and for why we chose to sleep apart.''

"I—you—" Caitlin faltered. "You haven't done anything," she protested, but her voice was sadly lacking in conviction. Then, before he could press her further, the doorbell rang. "Oh—that must be Mrs Spriggs," she exclaimed with the air of one being given a reprieve. "I'd better let her in. She must have forgotten her key."

Her relief as she came across the thickly piled carpet towards him was almost palpable. Though the tension still showed in her face as she waited for him to step aside. He was tempted to detain her; to let the housekeeper wait until he was good and ready to admit her. But the doorbell pealed again, and he reluctantly moved away.

The door slammed behind her, deliberately, he thought, signalling her resentment at his audacity. But dammit, she was his wife; and he deserved to have his questions answered. If she hated him so much, why did she stay with him?

Putting such negative thoughts aside, he forced himself to examine the bedroom more closely. Not that by doing so he felt any more strongly that it was his. The opulent four-poster, the heavy satin drapes at the windows that matched the fringed bedspread, were curiously repulsive. It reminded him of a brothel. Yet he didn't even know if he'd ever visited one.

It occurred to him that perhaps their sleeping in separate rooms had been a recent innovation, which resurrected the question of whether he had done something for which Caitlin couldn't forgive him. But what? Could there conceivably have been another woman? He didn't think so, but what did he know? Just because he had a hard-on every time Caitlin came near him didn't mean he was necessarily immune to the rest of her sex.

But it did seem unlikely, he had to admit. And it was always possible he was exaggerating the reason for their separation. Perhaps Caitlin didn't want to get into bed with a man who didn't even recognise her. Perhaps she'd rung this Mrs Spriggs and had her make up the spare bed. It would be easier to accept than believing he had had anything to do with decorating this revolting room.

He wished she hadn't done it just the same. He only felt half-sane when she was in his vicinity, but it was better than the panic he experienced when she wasn't around. He needed her—more with every day that passed—and he wondered again if it was only her fear of the unknown that was keeping them apart.

The bedroom windows were set high in the wall to allow for complete privacy. There was no possibility here of being overlooked from any angle. A person could walk around nude, without fear of observation. Something he could appreciate after a spell in a public hospital.

And because he'd told Caitlin he wanted a shower, he decided to take advantage of the fact. He had no fears that she might return and find him in a state of undress, however appealing that image might be to him. She would stay with the daily woman until he emerged, confident that he wouldn't do anything to embarrass her in someone else's presence.

The room seemed suddenly gloomy, and abandoning any further introspection, he switched on the stylish lamps beside the bed. Of all the furnishings in the room, he thought the lamps looked the least tacky, and their bronze shades cast a warm glow over furniture and drapes alike. Then, ignoring any lingering sense of alienation, he sauntered into the dressing room.

The clothes he found in the long wall of closets seemed reasonably normal, but had he really bought so many suits and pants and jackets? His growing awareness of the affluence around him was beginning to disturb him. It was something else he hadn't expected to have to deal with.

He supposed he should have guessed their financial situation sooner. After all, they had travelled back from New York in the first-class cabin of the plane, and his previous assumption that it had been arranged for his comfort seemed rather hollow now. He was obviously used to spending money without any apparent restraint.

Which led, naturally enough, to thoughts of his employment. He wasn't sure he liked the idea of working for Caitlin's father, but obviously that was something he wouldn't have to deal with immediately. Dr Harper had advised him not to rush into situations he wouldn't be able to handle, and right now, the idea of sitting at a desk all day struck him as being totally unappealing.

He sighed, wishing these first few days were over. Surely, when he'd had the time to familiarise himself with his surroundings, he'd begin to feel more optimistic. Things could only get better. He had to remember that. And sooner or later, something—some small thing—would trigger his memory.

Recalling his intention to take a shower, he tossed off his shirt and jacket, and peeled his jeans down his legs. Even these things were unfamiliar to him, he reflected, once again fighting the panic that overtook him. Caitlin had bought them, on his instructions, in New York, and he was not unaware of their dissimilarity to the expensive clothes hanging in the closets.

But he wouldn't think of that now, he determined, running exploring fingers over the roughened skin of his jawline. He needed a shave. That was his first priority. He wouldn't think about how anonymous his face still looked to him. That way lay danger, and he'd had just about as much of that as he could take.

Pulling on the white towelling bathrobe he found hanging on the back of the bathroom door, he surveyed the remainder of his domain with a positive eye. At least the bathroom was familiar, although creamy white marble tiles and a wall of mirrors took some getting used to. The sunken bath was big enough for half a dozen people, and all the taps were gold-plated and shining. There was a separate shower cubicle, also big enough for more than one person, and twin washbasins set into a marble console.

None of it struck a personal chord, but he refused to be downhearted. At least he knew who he was, he reminded himself again. If he hadn't been carrying some identity, it might have been a different story, and he'd had no desire to stay in the hospital any longer than was absolutely necessary.

All the same, he couldn't help wondering if he'd have felt any better about himself if Caitlin had had to identify him. There had been something so impersonal about Dr Harper reading his name out of his passport. Like when he was a soldier and he'd been identified by his dog tags . . .

He expelled an uneven breath. Now where the hell had that come from? he wondered, his mouth drying at the thought that it might be a genuine memory. Had he been in the army? Caitlin would know, and he wanted to rush right out and ask her. But the daily woman would be there, and he had no desire to arouse her curiosity, as well. It would wait, he told himself, controlling his impatience. There'd be plenty of time when she'd gone.

He felt a lot better after his shower. Even the unsettling sight of his own features as he shaved wasn't enough to daunt his rising spirits, and he determined to be more positive about the future. Believing that he had been in the army was just the start. Pretty soon, he'd remember everything, and when he did, he'd know why the hell Caitlin was so determined to keep him out of her life.

Later, dressed in a pair of dark trousers and a black knit shirt, he surveyed himself in the mirror. The waistband of the pants was a little loose, even with the belt on its final hole, but the shirt didn't look at all bad. He'd probably lost weight while he was in the hospital, though that didn't account for the fact that his loafers felt way too tight.

He heard the sound of a vacuum as he emerged from the bedroom. It was coming from the living room, and he guessed Mrs Spriggs was earning her keep. Deciding he might as well get the encounter over with, he opened the door. A woman of middle years, with greying blonde hair, Mrs Spriggs started in some surprise when she saw him, and immediately turned the cleaner off.

"Hi," he greeted her lightly, and then converted it to "Good morning." Dammit, he wondered, why was she looking at him so anxiously? Did he terrify every woman he came into contact with?

Mrs Spriggs gathered herself. "Er—good morning, Mr Wolfe," she stammered hurriedly. "I—er—I'll be finished in here in just a minute, if that's all right."

"Take your time," he said, wondering what Caitlin had told her about him. Either his condition had made him psychotic, or Mrs Spriggs really was nervous of him.

"How—how are you?"

The woman had evidently decided it was politic to show some concern about his health now, and he managed a creditable smile. "I'm much better, thanks," he assured her, pushing his hands into his trouser pockets. "Um—where's my wife? I'd like to speak to her."

"Oh—she's gone to Harrods," exclaimed the woman quickly, which he thought might explain her nervousness with him. "That's the department store, you know. Mrs Wolfe likes their food hall." She hesitated. "Do you know what I'm talking about?"

His expression relaxed. "I have heard of Harrods, Mrs Spriggs," he remarked drily. "So—do you know when she'll be back?"

"She won't be long," the woman replied with rather more confidence. "It's just round the corner. She said she needed one or two things."

He nodded, and then realising the daily woman was waiting to start vacuuming again, he walked out of the living room and into the kitchen. He decided he might as well familiarise himself with its contents before Caitlin got back. But he soon found why she'd gone dashing out for food. There were only tins and packets in the cupboards, and the fridge was almost empty.

Yet he felt strangely at ease in the kitchen. He had the distinct feeling he had cooked here at some other time. Or was it just the kitchen and its appliances that were familiar? No, he must believe he remembered something that couldn't be explained away.

Accepting this as further proof of his returning memory, he waited eagerly for Caitlin's return. But when she came into the apartment, he was once again struck by her withdrawal, and although he'd been flicking through a newspaper he'd found on the bureau, he followed her when she went to put her purchases away.

Her attitude made it difficult for him to speak casually to her, and he was at once reminded of their contretemps before Mrs Spriggs arrived. Dammit, he thought, they couldn't go on circling one another like two wrestlers in a ring. There had to be a point when politeness gave way to honesty.

He could tell she was nervous as she thrust cartons of milk and eggs into the fridge and stowed frozen foods in the freezer. But refusing to be deterred, he took a packet of coffee beans from the cupboard and tipped a couple of handfuls into the grinder. Working with her, surely he could breach the wall of antipathy she'd erected around herself.

His familiarity with the food processor obviously surprised her, and he guessed she was wondering how he knew where the coffee beans were. But he didn't explain. Let her think it was a subliminal memory, he thought irritably, instead of the result of his earlier explorations.

With the ground beans transferred to the filter, and a jug of fresh water poured into the dispenser, he felt ready to bestow his news. "Um—when was I in the army?" he asked. "Was that before or after I went to college?"

Caitlin turned to face him, her brow furrowing with obvious anxiety, and his stomach lurched. "As—as far as I know, you've never been in the army," she declared, instantly destroying all his hopes. "And—and Mrs Spriggs doesn't drink coffee," she added, observing the three ceramic mugs he'd set beside the coffee maker. "She prefers tea."

7

Nathan's look of disappointment almost made her wish she'd been able to lie to him. He'd apparently remembered something while she was out, and he'd imagined it was a fragment of his past. But she remembered too well her husband's boast of how he had avoided the draft, and whatever hopes he'd had on that score could not be allowed to proceed.

"You're sure about that?" he asked now, thrusting one of the mugs back into the cupboard and pulling out a china teacup and saucer. His lips twisted. "Shit, I was certain I'd remembered something positive. So how the hell did I know about dog tags? Can you tell me that?"

"I think most people would know what dog tags are," replied Caitlin quietly, finishing putting the perishable foods into the fridge. "They're identification discs, aren't they?" She glanced his way. "You haven't found some, have you?"

Nathan gave her a retiring look. "Now, would I?" he exclaimed with a sigh. "No. I just—oh, I don't know. It doesn't even seem very convincing to me right now. I guess it was just wishful thinking." He paused. "Did you get what you wanted?"

"Yes, thanks."

Caitlin realised that once again he was between her and the door, but with the sound of Mrs Sprigg's vacuum drifting through from the bedroom, there didn't seem any need to be alarmed. Besides, sooner or later they had to talk; she knew that. He wasn't going to be put off by her prevarications for much longer.

She forced a smile. "I see you took a shower." With his hair still damp and clinging to his neck, that seemed a safe comment to make. "I—I should have told you. There's a hair dryer in one of the drawers in your dressing room."

"A hair dryer, eh?" Nathan's mouth compressed a little sardonically. "Well, what do you know? I don't remember ever using one. Seems like my hair's used to drying naturally. Though I guess it is getting over-long."

"Oh, no, I . . ."

The protest spilled automatically from her lips, and Caitlin felt the wave of heat sweep up her neck. For God's sake, what had possessed her to say that? How he wore his hair was nothing to do with her. It was just that its length added to his alienation—a circumstance she was quite prepared to admit she preferred.

He was waiting for her to finish, and with an awkward shake of her head, she said offhandedly, "I rather like it as it is."

"Do you?"

The words were spoken very softly, and his narrowing gaze held a depth of emotion she didn't ever remember seeing before. Those moments in the bedroom when she'd been so aware of him came back to haunt her, and she wondered why she was so drawn to him now, when she'd never felt this way in the past.

Whatever, when he lifted his hand and brushed his thumb almost sensuously across her parted lips, her tongue crept forward instinctively. She wanted to taste the pad that had touched her and she savoured the faint aroma of coffee on his skin.

His indrawn breath showed he was not unaware of the intimacy, and long muscles, taut and masculine, flexed beneath the short sleeves of his black knit shirt. Dark eyes, as soft and smooth as velvet, impaled her nervous gaze, reminding her, if any reminder were needed, of his strength and her vulnerability to it.

Struggling to escape the trance he was laying on her, she found refuge in an unusual way. It was so long since she had been this close to Nathan, and a sudden awareness of how brown his skin looked—how healthy—brought the unwelcome thought of Lisa Abbott to mind. He must have been attending a health spa, she decided. Had he taken his mistress along?

A pain knifed through her stomach, banishing her weakness and replacing it with cold resentment. Why was she even contemplating his appearance? Whatever he did, it didn't matter to her.

So, when he moved closer and bent his head towards her, Caitlin recoiled in revulsion. He was not going to make a convenience of her. If he'd forgotten about the other woman, she hadn't, and she shouldn't allow her sympathy to get in the way of common sense.

His reaction was not unexpected. When she drew back before his mouth could connect with hers, he uttered a muffled oath. And with a feeling that mingled an unwilling regret with triumph, she put the width of the kitchen between them, bending to take a carton of cream from the fridge to avoid his eyes.

"What is it with you?" he demanded angrily, long fingers combing back the heavy hair that had fallen over his forehead. "For Christ's sake, Kate, I'm your husband! How long are you planning on keeping up this crazy charade?"

Caitlin set the cream on the drainer and made a play of removing its plastic cover. "It's too soon," she said, realising she didn't have a satisfactory answer. So long as he didn't mention Lisa Abbott, neither would she.

"Too soon?" He stared at her impatiently now, and she offered him a wary look. "Too soon for what? For kissing my wife? For welcoming me home? For letting me make love to you? Dammit, what's wrong with us? Don't we communicate any more?"

Caitlin swallowed. "Of course we do."

"On what level?"

"I don't know what you mean."

"I mean, why are you acting like we never slept together? You'll be telling me next you're a virgin! Hell, you surely know what that can do to a man."

Caitlin held up her head. "There's no need to be rude."

"Isn't there?" He regarded her scathingly. "Seems to me it's the only way to get a reaction around here."

"That's not true." Caitlin sighed. "I just need a little—time, that's all. We have to get to know one another—again."

"Bullshit!"

Nathan's response was predictable, and Caitlin wondered why she had expected anything else. And at least his outburst was familiar. He had never been any good at guarding his tongue.

Deciding there was no point in trying to reason with him in this mood, she turned away to check on the coffee, but his next words were not predictable at all. "Can't you see?" he implored. "I'm just trying to make some sense of my existence. And it seems to me that our relationship should be the most important aspect of that."

Caitlin swallowed. "Well—"

"You don't get it, do you?" he demanded suddenly. "You have no earthly idea what I'm saying." His lips twisted. "Why should you? I'm the one who's all screwed up. Oh, shit, what I need is a drink."

"You're going to have a drink. The coffee's almost ready," said Caitlin, deliberately misunderstanding him. But she didn't like it when he appealed to her sympathies, particularly when she so badly wanted to respond. "I—I bought some pastries. I thought you might be hungry. You didn't have any breakfast on the plane."

"At three o'clock in the morning? Give me a break," he countered, reminding her of the five-hour time change between New York and London. "Anyway," he added wearily, "I'm not hungry. I guess I lost my appetite along with all the rest."

"Nathan—"

Caitlin started to speak, but before she could say anything she might have regretted later, Mrs Spriggs appeared in the open doorway. "That's it, Mrs Wolfe," she said, offering Nathan a nervous smile. "I've finished the bedrooms. I'll come back tomorrow and do the laundry."

"Thanks."

Caitlin was grateful. She had never had any cause to doubt Mrs Sprigg's word. From time to time, Nathan had complained that she got in his way, or that she didn't iron his shirts as well as he was used to, but most of the time they kept out of each other's way.

Aware of this, she glanced somewhat awkwardly towards Nathan, and as if sensing his presence was surplus to requirements, he brushed past the daily woman and left the room. He didn't even take the cup of coffee she'd poured for him, and presently she heard the outer door of the flat slam.

Immediately, she wanted to go after him. She was terrified of what might happen to him out in the street. But although her hands clenched tightly on the marble worktop, she forced herself to remain where she was.

"Gone out, has he?" inquired Mrs Spriggs in a return to her usual garrulous fashion. Caitlin's father had always said that his daughter allowed the daily woman too many liberties, but there'd been times when she'd welcomed her friendly chatter.

"It looks like it," Caitlin answered now, pushing the newly made pot of tea towards her. And then, because she needed any reassurance, however specious, she added, "D'you think he'll remember where he lives, or ought I to follow him, Mrs Spriggs?"

"Well..." Mrs Spriggs evidently welcomed the opportunity to offer an opinion. "I dare say he can ask somebody else if he gets lost. I shouldn't worry about him, Mrs Wolfe. He's not a baby." She pulled a wry face. "As a matter of fact, he seemed—well, rather competent to me."

"Mmm."

Caitlin wished she felt more confident about his actions, but at least it seemed that Nathan had been civil to Mrs Spriggs. He had been known to swear at her on occasion, particularly if he had a hangover and she started hoovering the floor.

"How—er—how long is it likely to take?" the woman was asking now, and Caitlin didn't pretend not to understand what she meant.

"I wish I knew," she said. "Apparently, there are no hard-and-fast rules about amnesia. No one seems to know exactly how long it may last." She shrugged. "We can only hope for the best."

"I see." Mrs Spriggs nodded. "The best being that—er—Mr Wolfe recovers his memory?" she added curiously, and Caitlin frowned.

"Of course."

"Of course." Mrs Spriggs looked a little discomforted. "But I have to say, he seems—very nice as he is."

Caitlin couldn't prevent a rueful smile. She knew exactly what Mrs Spriggs meant. It would be nice to think that Nathan wouldn't change when he recovered his memory, but she was realistic enough to know that miracles didn't happen.

"I suppose he's just trying to find his feet," she offered neutrally, wondering how much Mrs Spriggs really knew. She had to have her own opinion as to why they had separate bedrooms. And Nathan had been known to speak carelessly in the past.

The sudden ringing of the phone gave her a welcome excuse to abandon their conversation. Excusing herself to the daily woman, she went to answer the call in the other room. But when she picked up the receiver, no one answered. It was obviously a wrong number, she thought, because when she gave her name, the call was immediately disconnected.

She sighed, wishing Nathan hadn't left the flat without telling her where he was going. How dependable was his independence if he didn't recognise the flat? It was just as well the call hadn't been from her father, she mused ruefully. She could imagine his impatience if he called and Nathan wasn't there.

As if the thought was father to the deed, the phone rang again right beside her. And this time when she picked it up, it was her father. The bell had jangled her nerves, and she collapsed into the chair beside the phone rather wearily. She could have done without Matthew Webster's intervention right at this moment.

"Cat?" he demanded, as if her voice wasn't perfectly familiar to him. "Where've you been?"

"Well, I have just got back from New York," she replied tersely, aware of the deliberate irony. "And yes, I had a good journey, before you ask."

"Don't be clever with me, Cat." Her father had never had much of a sense of humour, and she could tell by his tone that he was not in the mood for whimsy now. "I know where you've been and I know what time your flight landed. What I want to know is why you haven't rung me before this."

Why, indeed?

Caitlin rested her head back against the soft velour of the chair's headrest and closed her eyes. "I haven't had the chance," she said at last, recognising that for the prevarication it was. "We haven't been back that long, and I had things to do—"

"Yes, you did," said Matthew Webster sternly. "You had to ring me. You must have known I'd be concerned about you, Cat." He paused. "So—how is the invalid? Has he remembered who he is yet?"

"No."

Caitlin opened her eyes, finding herself resentful of that particular tone in her father's voice. Whilst she might have had her doubts, she found she objected to anyone else being suspicious of her husband. Besides, why should her father think he might be lying? So far as she was aware, he had supported Nathan in everything he'd done.

"I see." Matthew Webster sounded thoughtful now. "Well—why don't you put him on the line? Perhaps I can jog his memory. I know what women are like. They avoid plain speaking if they can."

How would you know? thought Caitlin indignantly, aware suddenly that the amicability of her present relationship with her father was just a veneer. Oh, she still loved him and she had no doubt he loved her in his own way. But she hadn't forgotten his disparagement of her abilities, and at times like this, the cracks began to show.

Now she felt a certain amount of satisfaction in saying, "He's not here." She knew, better than anyone, how much her father liked to get his own way. But in this instance, he was bound to be disappointed. She could even have said that Nathan didn't care.

"What do you mean, he's not there?"

Her father's response was just as aggravated as she had expected, and having a belated care for his blood pressure, she attempted to calm him down. "He's gone for a walk," she said, although she didn't honestly know what Nathan was doing. "This has been a difficult time for him, Dad. Just give him a little breathing space."

The silence that followed was decidedly hostile. She could hear her father's laboured breathing and knew he was having quite a job controlling his temper. Whatever sympathy he might have had for Nathan's condition was being sorely tested, and knowing him as she did, she guessed he was resenting putting his faith in a man who had let him down.

"When will he be back?" he demanded at last, and Caitlin considered before answering.

"I don't know," she said. "Probably not long."

"Well, where's he gone?" exclaimed her father, losing his personal battle. "For God's sake, Cat, I thought the fellow was sick!"

"Not sick—just suffering from amnesia." Caitlin wondered why she was bothering to defend Nathan. It wasn't as if he would thank her for it. "And I'm afraid I don't know where he's gone. He didn't give me an itinerary before he left."

Her father snorted. "I've told you, don't take that tone with me, young woman. I'm not the one who's allowed someone who apparently can't even remember his own name to go wandering all over London." He bit off an expletive. "Have you no sense? What if he gets lost?"

Caitlin sighed. "He's not stupid, Daddy." She straightened her spine. "And if you must know, I didn't 'allow' him to do anything. He doesn't need my permission to go out. I doubt if I could have stopped him, even if I'd wanted to."

"What do you mean by that?" Matthew Webster sounded suspicious now. "Have you two been having a row? If you have, I want to know about it."

"Oh, no." Caitlin knew she couldn't allow him to think that. "He's just—upset, that's all. Impatient. I expect he finds the situation frustrating. He can't even remember the flat."

"Hmm, well…" Her father seemed to be considering her answer. "Well, I don't know how he feels, do I? I haven't had a chance to find out. But I suppose I can wait until later, if I have to. And we'll be seeing you on Friday at the house."

Caitlin's throat dried. "Will you?"

"Of course." Her father gave a peevish exclamation. "Naturally, your mother and I are expecting you and Nathan to join us for the weekend. It's been far too long since you both spent any time at Fairings. And it will give me a chance to assess Nathan's condition for myself."

To see if he's lying, thought Caitlin drily, but she didn't say it. "Oh—Daddy," she said instead, wishing she had a reasonable excuse to give him. "I don't think Nathan will want to go away again. He's just got home."

"Don't you think you're being rather selfish, Cat?" her father asked abruptly. "Surely you can understand our feelings just this once. You're our daughter, for heaven's sake, and Nathan's our son-in-law. Naturally, we feel we have the right to welcome him back."

Caitlin stifled a groan. "All right," she said resignedly. "I'll—see what he says." She bit her lip. "But I don't intend to browbeat him into accepting. He needs to take things slowly. That's what his American doctor said."

"Did he?" The sarcasm in her father's voice resurfaced. "And I suppose that's why he's gone out without an escort, is it?"

"No."

Caitlin wondered if it was only her imagination, or was the criticism being levelled at Nathan as well as herself? After all, her father had never had much patience with illness. In his own case, he'd been desperate to get back to work.

"So—providing he finds his way home again, we can expect you on Friday afternoon, can we?" her father continued when it became obvious that Caitlin had nothing more to add, and she lifted her hand in a gesture of defeat only she could see.

"Why not?" she agreed tersely. "I'm sure Janie won't mind covering for me again." That was a deliberate provocation. She had no real idea when she'd be returning to the antique shop. She pressed her lips together. "Is that all?"

"Not quite." Her father snapped out the words. "You know very well you can't consider going back to work while—while Nathan is in his present state. Why—why anything could happen. And I'm not paying for a full-time nurse to take care of him."

"No one's asking you to," retorted Caitlin indignantly. "And I've told you—Nathan's not answerable to me. He's proved that by—" She broke off, and then continued rather more evenly. "I can't be expected to mollycoddle him, Daddy. He does have a mind of his own."

"Does he?"

Her father didn't sound convinced, but Caitlin eventually made some excuse about Mrs Spriggs calling her and hung up. She knew if she stayed on the line any longer, she might be tempted to reveal the truth about her marriage, and that would never do. Besides, they seldom talked about personal things, which generally suited her very well. It was only now, with the whole fabric of her world in tatters, that she wished she had someone she could talk to.

If only she and her mother had had a close relationship. But from the very beginning, Caitlin had wanted to follow in her father's footsteps, and by the time she was married to Nathan, it was too late to change her ways. Besides, Daisy Webster had always had a soft spot for her son-in-law, and Caitlin had known she couldn't confide her problems to her.

She was still sitting dejectedly by the phone, her mug of coffee cooling in her hand, when Mrs Spriggs came to tell her she was leaving. ''I've left the coffee on the hob,'' she said, ''just in case Mr Wolfe wants a cup when he gets back.'' She hesitated. ''I—I shouldn't worry about him, if I was you, dear. He'll find his way back. And our Wayne could always go and look for him. He's got nothing better to do.''

Caitlin doubted Wayne Spriggs would appreciate being volunteered so arbitrarily. In her opinion, the daily woman's son seemed quite happy doing nothing at all. If he wasn't down at the dog track, he was in the pub or sprawled in front of the telly playing computer games.

But she thanked Mrs Spriggs for the offer, and after the woman had gone, she went to pour the rest of her coffee into the sink. Alone now, she was becoming increasingly anxious. Her father was right: she shouldn't have let Nathan go out alone.

Yet, she had to admit that in the past she'd been happiest when he was out of the flat. She'd been glad when he'd just used it as a place to shower and change his clothes. He'd spent most of his time with Lisa Abbott, she reflected, trying to drum up her usual resentment. But unless the other woman had been waiting outside, he couldn't be with her now.

Which is what made the present situation so disturbing. If only Mrs Spriggs hadn't interrupted them, they might have made some headway after all. Though she'd been grateful enough for the daily woman's arrival when he'd had her imprisoned in the bedroom, and the frustration he'd exhibited later had hardly augured well for a breakthrough in their relationship.

She decided to ring Janie Spencer. She'd only spoken to her friend once since she'd left for the States, and that was over two weeks ago. Janie deserved to know what was happening and when she might expect some assistance at the shop.

The phone rang for some time before Janie answered, and when she discovered who was calling, her relief was at once evident. "Hey, am I glad to hear from you," she exclaimed as soon as she had assured herself that Caitlin was back in England. "You don't know how much I've missed you. When are you coming back to work?"

Caitlin sighed. "I'm not sure."

"You're not sure?" Janie uttered a little gasp. "But I thought you told me Nathan wasn't seriously hurt. I assumed, now that you're back in London, that there wasn't any problem. Don't tell me he needs nursing. I need you at the shop."

Caitlin hesitated. "It's not that simple." She wished now she'd been more forthcoming when she'd spoken to Janie from her hotel in New York. "Nathan—Nathan's not ill exactly, but he—well, he's lost his memory. He doesn't remember anything that happened before the crash."

Janie's breath gushed out in a low whistle. "You're kidding!"

"No, I'm not." Caitlin wished she were. "I didn't tell you before, because it could have been a temporary condition.

Well, we hope it will be a temporary condition," she added swiftly. "But he hasn't recovered his memory yet."

"Are you sure?"

"What do you mean, am I sure?"

"Well..." Janie was sardonic. "How do you really know he's amnesiac? It could be just an act."

"And what would he have to gain by it?" protested Caitlin, realising that once again she was defending him. "Janie, believe me, he's not acting. He hates the uncertainty as much as I do."

"Huh." Janie didn't sound convinced, but she quickly got the underlying message. "So—you're saying you can't leave him on his own, is that it? Oh, Cat! What are you going to do?"

"I don't know." That was the truth. "It—it may be that I'll be able to come back soon. It—depends what Nathan wants to do."

"That sleaze!" Janie had no time for Caitlin's husband. "Don't tell me you're feeling sorry for him. If you ask me, it serves him right. And maybe if he stays that way, you'll find it an advantage. Your father can't expect you to stay married to someone who doesn't remember who you are."

"Janie!"

"Well..." Janie snorted. "He's made your life a misery long enough. It's time you finished with him and started having some fun. You're nearly thirty, Cat. The old biological clock is still ticking."

"I know." Caitlin was defensive for herself now. "But I can't walk out on him just like that. Besides, he's changed, Janie. I can't explain, but he's different. He'd not half as—well, disagreeable—as he used to be before."

"Oh, please!" Janie's voice rose an octave. "You're not telling me you're having second thoughts about leaving him, Cat, surely? Oh, I can see he needs you right at the moment. But he's just using you, for all that. God knows, if I had the things on my conscience that he has on his, I'd probably wish I could lose my memory, too."

"*Janie!*"

"Don't *Janie* me, Cat. Characters are formed in childhood, you know that. People don't change. They can't."

"All the same—"

"You know that old saying about a leopard not being able to change his spots. Well, it's true. Once a sleaze, always a sleaze, Caitlin. You'll regret it if you forget it now."

"All right."

Caitlin wished they were not having this conversation, but Janie wasn't finished yet. "What about Lisa Abbott?" she asked. "Or was she just a figment of your imagination? Have you forgotten how he hurt you? Don't let him hurt you again."

"I won't." Caitlin caught her lip between her teeth, wondering whether there was any point in saying anything more. Janie was a good friend and she meant well, but she didn't understand the situation. "He doesn't remember anything," she reminded her. "And I'm certainly not going to bring it up."

"There'll be someone else," declared Janie indifferently. "Sooner or later, we'll have this conversation again. I'm just thinking of you, Cat. I'm very fond of you. I don't want you making a fool of yourself over a man who doesn't care."

Caitlin shook her head. "Just because I'm feeling sorry for him doesn't mean I'm going to fall into bed with him," she exclaimed irritably, ignoring the sudden quiver that shook her stomach. "But you must see how it is. He—he's depending on me. Until he knows what he's doing, I can't abandon him."

"Oh, he knows what he's doing," replied Janie unsympathetically. "Whether he's lost his memory or not, men know exactly how to behave to get what they want. He needs you—ergo, he's playing the nice guy. But as soon as he finds his feet, you'll see I'm right.''

"Well, I'll deal with that when—*if*—it happens," said Caitlin, eager now to get off the line. Janie's warnings had struck far too close to home for comfort, and the truth of the matter was, she didn't want to know.

8

Fletch sat alone in a corner booth in Casey's bar and stared broodingly at the row of empty beer bottles lined up on the table in front of him. He hadn't intended to drink so much. He'd just called in for a beer on his way home from the pool hall, but his mood was blacker than a witch's tit, and he'd needed some consolation. Dammit, he deserved some creature comforts, he told himself indignantly. Outside of getting drunk, he didn't have much in his life.

The trouble was, nobody cared about him. Four daughters, he brooded, and not one of them gave a shit for their old man. If it wasn't for his grandchildren, he wouldn't know what they were up to. And the kids just came around when they were broke.

This bar and the pool hall were his only means of entertainment, and he couldn't afford to come down here more than a couple of times a week. In a town like Blackwater Fork, the recession had dug deep and lasting, and most of the menfolk lived on welfare like himself.

It was ironic, really, he thought, but the only person who felt any responsibility for him was Jake. For all he'd treated the boy so bad, he still came around most every week. And he wasn't afraid to put his hand in his pocket. Not like his daughters' husbands, all of whom made sure they were looking the other way when it was their turn to buy the old man a beer.

Thinking of Jake reminded him that it had been the better part of two weeks since he'd seen him. Dammit, he'd forgotten that, and now he felt a rising sense of indignation. He hadn't spoken to him since that afternoon when that punk of a brother of his had turned up to see him. Supercilious jerk, Fletch thought contemptuously. It was amazing how two brothers could turn out so different from one another.

Yeah, he mused, but that was his doing. He felt an unaccustomed glow of self-congratulation at the thought. Okay, so maybe he had been hard on the boy, but that was what he'd needed. His brother had been treated like a prince, and look how he'd turned out.

'Course, Jake's running away to join the army when he was sixteen might have had something to do with it. He remembered when he'd been in the military, they'd taught him to have respect. But all that bootblacking and saluting and sucking up to officers hadn't done anything for his career. And Jake had been in a God-awful mess when he'd gotten back from 'Nam.

He shoved his hand into his trouser pocket and pulled out a handful of small bills and some coins. Enough for one more beer, he figured, grunting, if he could get by without buying any more cigarettes for the rest of the week. He pushed himself up, ambled over to the bar, and ordered a Budweiser. What the hell, the doc was always telling him to cut out smoking, and in spite of the cool fall afternoon beyond the leaded windows, his throat still felt as scratchy as hell.

With a fresh bottle clutched in his hand, he resumed his seat at the table, his mind returning to Jake and his unfamiliar absence. He couldn't believe anything he'd said to Nathan could have caused a rift between them. Dammit, the boy knew what his brother was like, and he had no time for him.

Jake was the only one who cared if he was alive, he brooded lugubriously. It'd probably be a lot easier on all the rest if he was dead. Ever since Andy Peyton passed away, he'd been waiting his call to join him. And if he drank any more of that 'shine he brewed in his back yard, it wouldn't be long.

Bitterness soured his tongue at the thought of what was facing him, with no one to shed a tear over his coffin now that Alice was gone. Would she be waiting for him like she was supposed to have waited for him all those years ago? Or had she found someone else—just like she'd done before.

He'd blamed Jake for that, he recalled ruefully. He'd beat the shit out of the boy because his mother had spread her legs for someone else. Of course, it hadn't been the boy's fault, but dammit, he'd had to take his grief out on someone. He'd trusted Alice, trusted her completely, and she'd treated him like a fool.

And they'd been happy before Jacob Wolfe and his money had come along, he thought, growing maudlin. Oh, there'd been times when he'd let his temper get the better of him, when he'd had too many beers, and his fists had begun to fly. But that was the way it was. A man needed to feel the master in his own home, and when he wasn't home, he was travelling, trying to earn enough to feed his brood.

Including the cuckoo in his nest, he conceded harshly. God, he'd been so proud of his "son." He'd even neglected his daughters because of it, giving Jake all his love and attention. And when he'd found out Alice had been lying to him, he'd wanted to kill them both.

It had been the knowledge that the whole town had known what was happening and had been laughing at him behind his back that had really crippled him. He'd threatened to throw the boy out, and he would have, too, if Alice hadn't said that if he went she'd go, as well. In the event, his anger couldn't sustain the thought of her desertion. For all she'd let him down, he couldn't let her go.

And he'd still rather have Jake than all his daughters put together. He'd never gotten married, and although there were always women around, Jake seemed to find his stimulation in his work. He'd never said so, but Fletch suspected he saw his defence of young drug offenders as a kind of vocation; a chance to pay back something of the debt he'd taken out. There was no doubt those shrinks at the psychiatric unit had had their work cut out with him when he got home from the service.

God, it was over twenty years, but he could still hear the boy screaming, waking up nights, soaked in his own sweat. And babbling on—hell! If half of what Jake had talked about during those attacks was kosher, then Fletch didn't know how he'd kept sane.

The things he'd experienced, the horrors he'd seen, probably still haunted him. But Jake didn't talk about it any more. Instead, he expunged his own fears by confronting the problem in others. And there was no doubt he was well-respected at the public defender's office.

One of these days, Fletch was sure, Jake would be hanging out his own shingle. Not bad for a truck driver's son. 'Course, whatever anyone said, Jake was his son. He might have Jacob Wolfe's blood in his veins, but he was a Connor through and through.

Still, remembering how sick Jake had been, Fletch couldn't help thinking about Alice. They'd been closer then, caring for the boy, than at any other time he could recall. They'd both been to blame for him running away to join the army, and when he'd come back all fucked up, there was nothing they wouldn't have done for him.

It had taken three long years for Jake to come back from whatever hell he'd been inhabiting. Three years of nursing and therapy and plain old tender loving care. And by the time Jake was well, Alice had developed the tumour. The doctors said they couldn't operate; that there was nothing they could do.

For a while, he and Jake had been inconsolable. Maybe that was when their strange alliance had begun. Whatever differences they'd had in the past, they'd both loved Jake's mother, and Fletch had felt he'd owed it to Alice's memory not to let the boy down.

But with the bottom falling out of the lumber market, and the haulage company he'd worked for going to the wall, it hadn't been easy, and when Jake announced that he was going back to college, he'd felt pretty sorry for himself. Yet, when Jake graduated, there wasn't a prouder man on the college campus. The first Connor in the family to get a degree.

He lifted the bottle in his hand, only to discover it was empty. While he'd been reliving the past, he'd swallowed every drop. And dammit, his throat was still as dry as a desert. Was it something to do with the fact that his eyes were damp?

That was when he looked across the room and saw Jacob Wolfe.

Blinking in disbelief, he saw his old enemy standing by the door. Jacob was squinting in the smoky atmosphere of the bar. He hadn't seen Fletch yet, and his expression was hard to read.

Fletch lurched to his feet. Even after all these years, he had no difficulty in recognising his nemesis. And as much as he hated to admit it, he was still the spitting image of his son. Of both his sons, Fletch thought with angry resentment. What the hell was he doing here in Blackwater Fork?

Before he could do more than stand there, swaying on his feet, Jacob saw him. Then, after a brief word with the bartender, he headed for Fletch's booth. Jacob had evidently lost weight and he looked pale, but Fletch had no sympathy for him. This was the man who had ruined his life, he thought savagely. If it hadn't been for Alice, he'd have gone after him years ago.

"Connor," said Jacob politely, apparently unaware of Fletch's fury, "I know I'm the last man you want to see, but I have to talk to you. Now. It's urgent. May I sit down?"

Fletch's outrage brought the hectic colour surging into his stubbled cheeks, and his hands curled into two tight fists. But before he could speak the words that were fulminating inside him, he saw Casey approaching with a tray on which resided a bottle of Scotch whisky and two glasses. The reason for the other man's conversation with the bartender was suddenly obvious, and although he despised himself for his weakness, he sank back into his seat.

Jacob took the grunt he uttered as he sat down again as a gesture of consent, and gripping the edges of the table, he lowered his lean frame onto the opposite bench. Pulling a hundred-dollar bill from his pocket, he dropped it on the tray after Casey had unloaded the bottle and glasses. "I'll get the change later," he said, nodding at the man. "We don't want to be disturbed."

"Yessir."

Casey could be irritatingly servile when he chose, and Fletch fixed him with a glowering look. The barkeep went away showing no signs of having been intimidated by Fletch's stare, and he was left to look broodingly at the other man.

Still, first things first, he thought as Jacob picked up the bottle and half filled the two glasses. He could already taste the smoothness of the malt. The whisky slid down his throat like the softest kind of velvet, and his fingers itched to pour himself another.

"Oh, that's good," said Jacob now, savouring the taste of the whisky, and Fletch thought contemptuously that he drank like a woman. Men didn't sip at it like that. Goddammit, he hadn't swallowed enough to clean his palate. Whisky was meant to be thrown to the back of the throat. In his case, it usually went down without touching the sides.

"What do you want?" he asked abruptly, deciding he had had enough of this. His fingers curled into a fist beside his glass. "We got nothing to say to one another."

"Don't we?" Surprisingly, for such a frail man, Jacob was obviously not intimidated, either. Shit, thought Fletcher in anger. Was he losing his touch?

"No, we don't," he said, emptying his glass with his second gulp. "I suggest you get outta here, while you still can."

Jacob sighed as if in resignation and pushed the whisky towards him. "Help yourself," he said wearily, not moving. "While I decide where to begin."

Fletch resisted the pull of the bottle and pointed a finger that he couldn't prevent from trembling slightly at the other man. "I should beat your fucking brains out. I've been wanting to push your fucking teeth down your throat ever since you came through that door!"

"Charming," said Jacob sardonically, without any of the alarm Fletch had expected. But somehow, over the years, he'd lost that cutting edge, and Fletch wondered what had happened to pull him down.

And because there was no point in looking a gift horse in the mouth, Fletch grabbed the bottle and filled his glass. What the hell, he thought, he might as well enjoy it. If Jacob wanted to reminisce that was up to him.

"How long is it since you've seen Jake?" Jacob asked suddenly, and Fletch, who was considering the dregs in his glass, felt a sobering shot of fear invade his loins. Dammit, Jacob hardly knew Jake. The boy never bothered with him. But he was reminded that his son hadn't been around.

"What's it to you?" he demanded, exhibiting a defiance he didn't truly feel, and Jacob took a shuddering gulp of air.

"Humour me," he said. "How long is it since you've seen him? Or don't you keep in touch with him any more?"

"'Course we keep in touch." Fletch was indignant. "As a matter of fact, I see Jake at least once every week. He doesn't forget his old man. It wasn't you that cared for him when he got home from 'Nam."

Jacob exhaled wearily. "I'm not interested in the past, Connor. Nor am I here to dispute the fact that you've been a better father to him than I could ever be. But—" he moved his thin shoulders in a dismissive gesture "—I want to know when you last saw him." He paused. "Tell me, has he ever tried to pass himself off as Nathan?"

"What?" Fletch's indignation was so great, he spluttered whisky all over the table, causing Jacob to draw back in distaste. "There ain't no way *my* boy would want to imitate that bastard! Believe me, he despises the both of you almost as much as me."

Jacob moistened his lips. "D'you think so?"

"I don't think it, jerk. I know it." Fletch swept the half-empty bottle of whisky and all the beer bottles from the table as he got unsteadily to his feet. "Like I said before, you and me got no damn thing in common. Now get the hell outta here! Before I break your neck."

Jacob sighed. "Sit down," he said, barely raising his voice, and Fletch glared at him with bloodshot eyes.

"You can't give me orders," he snarled. "I'm still not too old to beat the shit outta you. Just ask anyone around here. They know old Fletch still has what it takes."

Jacob gave him a pitying look. "Sit down," he said again. "You've just wasted twenty dollars' worth of fine malt whisky. How about if I call the sheriff to sort this out?"

"Wouldn't do you no good," retorted Fletch, but his defiance was less convincing. He knew the new sheriff, Ellis Hutchinson, wouldn't hesitate to throw him in jail. Since Andy Peyton died, things in Blackwater Fork had gone from bad to worse.

Jacob was waiting, and with a feeling of frustration, Fletch subsided into his seat again. He should have dealt with Wolfe when he was younger, he thought bitterly. These days, his threats were hollow things at best.

His spirits lifted a little when Jacob signalled Casey to bring another bottle, and after his glass was full again, he looked squarely at the other man. "What's all this about?" he demanded. "Why are you asking all these questions about Jake?"

"You'll find out." Jacob cradled his own glass between his hands. "So you don't think he envies his brother at all?"

Fletch scowled. "Jake? Envy that ponce?" He grimaced. "If you asked me if Nathan envied Jake, I might agree with you. He was pretty desperate to see him a couple weeks ago."

Jacob stared at him. "Nathan came to see Jake?" he echoed. "When?"

"I've just told you. A couple weeks ago," replied Fletch carelessly. "Made me call him from the house. Said he didn't want to go to Jake's office."

Jacob looked disturbed. "So what did he want? Did he tell you?"

Fletch gave the other man a scornful look. "Oh, sure. He'd do that, wouldn't he?" He sneered. "Nathan wouldn't piss on me if I was on fire."

Jacob ignored the provocation, and then asked shortly, "So did he speak to Jake? How long did he stay?"

"I don't know how long he stayed, do I?" Fletch was resentful. "He arranged to meet Jake in town, and I ain't set eyes on either of them since."

Jacob's face turned even paler. "You don't think—"

"What?" Fletch stared at him. "What don't I think?" Then, as if realising what Jacob might be insinuating, his face turned red. "You ain't suggesting Jake's gotten rid of his brother, so's he can take his place, are you?" His eyes darkened angrily. "Now see here..."

He started to get up out of his seat again, his swaying bulk threatening to overturn the table, but this time Jacob's hand placed squarely between his sagging pectorals drove him back onto the bench. "I'm not suggesting anything," he said with a warning note of caution. "But I'd like to know why Jake was on that flight."

"Flight?" Fletch blinked. "What flight?"

"The one that crashed on take-off in New York," replied Jacob heavily. "Christ, don't you read the papers? A jumbo ploughed into the runway at JFK."

Fletch quivered. "Jake's—dead?" A sour wave of bile filled his throat. "God—why didn't you say so?" Tears pricked his eyes. "Oh, Lord, I loved that boy!"

"No." Jacob was impatient now. "Jake's alive. Didn't I just say so? And he's supposed to have lost his memory in the crash. But the reservation must have been made in Nathan's name because that's what they're calling him. Do you hear what I'm saying? But I went to see him in the hospital, and it was Jake!"

9

"**D**'you wanna refill?"

He started, his thoughts far away from the dingy diner where he had come to try and sort out what he was going to do. Hunching his shoulders, he had the uneasy suspicion that the woman was staring at him, but he guessed she was only impatient because he hadn't given her a tip.

Besides, no one knew he was here, and even if they did, he wasn't doing anything wrong. Well, not yet, he amended broodingly. He was just sitting here, nursing a half-empty cup of cold coffee, and wondering what in hell he should do next.

He'd been so clear in his mind at the beginning. Getting his brother to help him had seemed an inspiration. He'd always resented the fact that despite the differences in their backgrounds, the other man had made more of a success of his life than he had. And it shouldn't be true, for Christ's sake. He had had all the advantages. Why did everything he attempted go so wrong?

This time, he'd been sure that nothing could stop him. With his brother on board the plane to England, all he'd intended to do was phone the Heathrow authorities and warn them that a certain passenger from New York was carrying drugs. A small amount, true, but enough to put his brother away for a little while.

But before he'd had time to make the call, he'd heard about the accident on the car radio. God, he remembered the elation he'd felt when he'd heard that news. For a full twenty-four hours he'd been convinced his troubles were over. What had the chances been of his brother surviving?

But like every other time in his goddamned life, he'd drawn a loser. The initial reports of a total disaster had been revised, and by the time he'd reached here, the rescue services were being praised for their bravery in saving so many. A call—anonymously, of course—to the hospital had confirmed his fears. His brother was one of the "lucky" survivors, and instead of that putting him out of danger, it had created problems he hadn't even thought of before the crash.

He grimaced. He'd even considered going to the hospital and finishing the job himself. What would it take to make a man who was already suffering from shock and concussion to stop breathing? But he had been heading for the border with Canada by that time, and in any case, he knew he didn't have the guts to do it. He could tell himself that even with a disguise someone might recognise him, but the truth was, he was too scared to kill his brother in cold blood.

He scowled, and the waitress, imagining the scowl was for her, gave him a surly look. "Hey, you've been nursing that cuppa coffee for over an hour," she exclaimed defensively. "Can I help it if the boss thinks you oughta vacate the table. This is a diner, not a waiting room."

He hid the scowl behind a rueful grimace. He had enough problems without creating more. The woman was only doing her job. She wasn't to know what he was thinking, thank God!

"I'm sorry," he said. "I wasn't listening. I've not been sleeping well lately." Wasn't that the truth? "I guess I must have dozed off."

The waitress seemed mollified by his apology. He guessed apologies weren't thick on the ground around here. "You live local?" she asked, pouring the coffee and gesturing at the neon lights beyond the grubby windows. He thanked her and fumbled for a convincing response.

He could hardly tell her he'd only been in town a couple of days. That this small town, on the U.S. side of the Canadian border had never been intended to be his destination. It reminded him too much of Prescott in any case. All small-town folk were the same: they wanted to know far too much about you for your own good.

"Just passing through," he offered at last, stirring some more sugar into his cup. It was the only thing that made the stuff palatable, though he had to admit it filled a corner. At present, he was finding it difficult to swallow any food.

"You going north?" she asked, propping a hand on her hip and evidently deciding she had time to chat. And why not? The diner was virtually empty. No one could accuse him of stopping a would-be customer from finding a seat.

"Maybe," he responded, regretting the impulse that had made him open up to her in the first place. "I—as a matter of fact—I'm looking for work. My last job folded and my girlfriend threw me out."

That was good, he complimented himself. Enough information to satisfy her curiosity and just a bit of pathos to gain her sympathy. Hell, if he'd been in the mood, he guessed he could have persuaded her to take him home with her. But getting involved with another woman was not in the cards right now.

Besides, he thought, giving the woman a critical glance, he could do better than this. Okay, his relationship with Lisa had been going nowhere, but at least she still had her looks. His lips curled. It was the only thing she had to offer, and she was going to find out soon enough it wasn't enough.

"I could ask Eddie if he needs someone," the waitress offered, indicating the pock-marked proprietor, who was scowling at them from behind the bar. "He knows most people in town. If he doesn't have anything himself, he might know someone who does."

"I don't think so."

He tried to sound regretful, but he could tell by her expression that she knew she was being given the brush-off. "Suit yourself," she said, and tossing her head, she sashayed back to the bar. Bending forward, she exchanged a few words with the burly proprietor, and when they both turned and looked in his direction, he decided it was time to call it a day.

Tossing a couple of dollar bills onto the table, he picked up his bag and hurried out into the parking lot. It was getting dark, the overcast sky bringing a premature twilight in its wake. It was time he got back to his hotel. He had no desire to be mugged on top of everything else.

He climbed into the rental car, stowing the bag beside him, but he didn't immediately start the engine. He was in no hurry to get back to the dump where he was staying. That was why he'd been spending time in the diner—because the room he was occupying was such a wreck. He'd never stayed in such a fleapit, but it was cheap and convenient, even if he had slept on the only armchair rather than climb between those grubby sheets.

He sighed. If only he knew what was going on in New York. Okay, his brother was in the hospital, but what had he told them about himself? What might he have told Carl Walker's henchmen, for God's sake? Had the other guy sent someone over to check out he was really there?

Yet why should he? he argued, trying to convince himself. The crash had been public enough, and no one could doubt that the plane had gone up in smoke. And all the baggage with it, he reminded himself grimly. Whatever happened, Carl must believe the cocaine had been destroyed.

He licked lips that had suddenly dried. He couldn't dismiss the thought that Carl was too clever to let him get away with it. What if he'd already been to see his brother and found out from him that he had been going to double-cross him? He caught his breath. What if they were waiting for him when he tried to cross the border? God, it might be simpler to go back and face the music.

And face going to prison, he amended bitterly. Whatever happened, Matthew Webster would demand his pound of flesh. Even if Carl was mollified by getting his property back—which he doubted—there was still the problem of the South American contract. He could expect no help from Carl. He'd tried to defraud the man, and Carl Walker didn't forgive that sort of thing. If he got away with his life, he'd consider himself lucky. A life sentence was probably more than he deserved.

So, was he committed to going on with this? He shook his head. What alternatives did he have? If only he knew what his brother was saying. There was only one person who might help him find out.

10

They left for Fairings on Friday afternoon.

Caitlin was driving—her own hatchback, not the flashy Cosworth that Nathan had left parked in the underground garage. She'd half expected him to object when she drove the Corrado out into the watery autumn sunshine, but of course he didn't know what he usually drove.

Besides, they were hardly speaking to one another. Since he'd arrived back at the flat on Wednesday afternoon, their relationship seemed to have gone from bad to worse. But Caitlin had been nearly out of her mind with worry, and it didn't help when Nathan behaved as if nothing was wrong.

When he hadn't returned by three o'clock, she'd even considered contacting her father again and asking him if he thought she should call the police. After all, Nathan was missing. And he probably shouldn't have been allowed to go out on his own in the first place.

But the knowledge that her father would blame her for Nathan's disappearance had prevented her from asking for his help. And, in the event, her husband had arrived back, apparently none the worse for wear. He'd merely offered an excuse about forgetting the time, and his assertion that he remembered the city was little compensation in the circumstances.

Consequently, she hadn't been entirely able to prevent her anger at his thoughtlessness from showing, and their stilted exchange had swiftly deteriorated into an uneasy silence. She'd justified her anxiety by the fact that Nathan was still on medication, and as far as she knew, he'd had nothing to eat all day.

She couldn't help it if he had been disappointed when she'd dashed his hopes about the army. It wasn't her fault that he'd got it wrong. For heaven's sake, if he didn't want to hear the truth, he shouldn't ask her. It was no use telling him lies just to make him feel good.

An uneasy supper had followed. Mrs Spriggs had prepared a chicken casserole before she left, and Caitlin had served it with pasta. But Nathan had only picked at his food, despite her careful admonitions, and he'd eventually admitted he'd bought a burger with a ten-pound note he'd found in his jacket pocket.

The news had infuriated Caitlin. The knowledge that while she had been frantic with worry, he'd been sitting in some fast-food restaurant, stuffing himself with cholesterol, brought a resentful lump to her throat. Though why had she expected anything different? she wondered, digging her fork with some fury into her food. Nathan had never considered her feelings. Ever. Losing his memory was unlikely to alter that.

He left her alone after supper. He made some remark about needing the bathroom, and Caitlin spent another fretful couple of hours waiting for him to come back. When he didn't return, and despite her better judgment, she felt obliged to go and check on him, she discovered he was fast asleep on his bed, still fully clothed.

Exhaustion had evidently got the better of him, and she'd stood there for some time, wondering if she ought to try and take off his clothes. But the fear that he might awake while she was doing it made her cautious. Although she couldn't deny the unwilling tug of compassion he aroused in her, she had no desire for him to get the wrong idea.

She contented herself with removing his shoes and throwing a blanket over him. At least she could be sure he wouldn't take a chill. He didn't stir; he seemed to be sleeping like a baby. And in spite of everything that had gone before, she was relieved.

On Thursday morning, Caitlin received a phone call from a neurologist whom her father had apparently asked to take over Nathan's treatment. He wanted to arrange an appointment for her husband at his clinic, and although her father had said nothing about it to her, Caitlin made a provisional booking for the following week.

But she resented the fact that once again her father should have chosen to interfere in her life. All right, so Henrik Neilson was a friend of his, and the man had contacted her himself instead of leaving his secretary to do it; nevertheless, it was an intrusion. Her father had no right to try and run their lives. Besides, Nathan had his own doctor. And as he apparently didn't need any further treatment, what did Neilson hope to do?

Nathan himself hadn't been around when she took the call. It was still fairly early, and so far as she knew, he was still in bed. She got something of a shock, therefore, when she heard someone coming into the flat. It was too early for Mrs Spriggs, and the sight of her husband in a dark blue jogging outfit brought an unwelcome awareness to her bones. His dark hair was damp and sweaty, and he exuded a distinctive aroma of cool air, heated skin and raw masculinity. A cocktail she was not as capable of dismissing as she should, she thought tensely.

In consequence, her voice was sharp as she challenged him. "Where have you been?" she demanded, forgetting that the night before she had determined not to get involved in what he did. He obviously didn't need her concern, and she could do without the hassle. If he chose to take risks with his health, it was nothing to do with her.

"Running," he replied after a moment, and she guessed he'd been tempted to mock her words. "Do I need your permission to leave the apartment? I borrowed your keys and locked the door. You'd left them lying on the table."

Caitlin didn't trust herself to answer him. Right now, he seemed too aggressive to provoke. But she couldn't help wondering when he'd decided to take up physical exercise. Was that why she'd thought he'd lost some weight?

He said nothing about her entering his room the night before, and neither did she. Instead, he went to take a shower, and Caitlin went into the kitchen to prepare breakfast. She was glad now that she'd chosen to dress before leaving her room. She didn't know why, but she suddenly felt vulnerable when Nathan was around.

It was over breakfast that she mentioned Henrik Neilson's phone call. She had been reluctant to do so, but in the event, Nathan seemed undisturbed. "I guess your old man doesn't trust me, either," he remarked, helping himself to another cup of coffee. "What's the old guy afraid of? Does he think I might make off with his hard-earned loot?"

"Of course not." Caitlin didn't like remarks like that, even if they were justified. "Dr Harper himself said you should check in with a doctor."

"He said he'd send all my medical records to my own doctor," Nathan corrected her drily. "He didn't say anything about needing a specialist on my case." He shrugged. "Hey—if that's what your old man wants, then so be it. If anyone can do anything to help me, then I'm game."

Caitlin pressed her lips together. "My father is very—protective."

"Yeah. Right." Nathan regarded her with a studied gaze. "Did he tell you not to go to bed with me until he'd checked me out?"

"No." Caitlin was horrified, and she looked it. "I—think—we just need—"

"Some more time," finished Nathan sardonically. "Yeah, I've heard that one before. I just wish you'd tell me what's going on."

There was no answer to that, and Caitlin made an excuse of going to refill the coffeepot to leave the table. The trouble was, she was having difficulty in dealing with the present situation herself. Despite all that she knew of him, she was attracted to him. She was afraid of herself, afraid it would be fatally easy to succumb.

The morning had passed fairly uneventfully, with Mrs Spriggs providing a welcome buffer between them. It wasn't until Caitlin's father rang in the early afternoon that she remembered she hadn't given Nathan his message, and by then, her husband was resting on his bed.

"You'll see him tomorrow, Daddy," she protested when Matthew Webster exhorted her to go and wake him up. "Besides, I don't know what you expect him to say to you. So far as he's concerned, he doesn't even remember your name."

"We'll see," responded her father enigmatically, revealing that Nathan hadn't been far wrong in his estimate of why the older man had chosen to contact the Harley Street physician. But at least it had enabled her to turn the tables on him. He'd rung off with her resentment ringing in his ears.

This morning, she'd made sure Nathan was still in bed when she'd left the flat. Deciding there was no point in trying to wet-nurse him, she'd left a message for Mrs Spriggs that she had gone to the shop. It was running away, and she knew it, but she needed an objective viewpoint. At least Janie understood what was going on.

And it was so good to see her friend again. After exchanging hugs, the two young women had sat down to share a mug of coffee together, Janie turning the sign on the door to Closed so they wouldn't be disturbed.

"So—what's happening?" she asked when Caitlin showed no inclination to offer an explanation. "Aren't you going to Fairings for the weekend after all?"

"No. That is—yes, yes, we are," said Caitlin confusingly, cradling her mug of coffee between her palms. "But—I just felt like coming to see you." She bit her lip. "It seems ages since I was here."

"Don't I know it?" Janie's response was fervent. "But I thought you couldn't leave Nathan on his own."

"I—I didn't say that exactly." Caitlin wasn't sure how far to take this. "Oh—if you must know, he has been out on his own."

"Out?" Janie stared at her. "You mean—as in driving his car? Oh, Cat, is that wise? Are you sure he still understands the rules of the road? He is an American, when all's said and done."

Caitlin regarded her dourly. "Did I say in his car?" she protested. "No—I mean he's been out walking. And running, too, yesterday morning."

"Running!" Janie stared at her. "Since when did Nathan exercise his bulk?"

"Since—I don't know." Caitlin was discomforted. "But it's obvious he's not unused to doing it. And—and he's lost some weight, as well. He looks quite—thin."

"Thin?" Patently, Janie didn't believe her. "Are you sure we're talking about the same person, Cat? Your husband likes his liquid lunches too well to ever be called—*thin.*"

Caitlin could feel her colour rising. "Well, I can't help that. It's happened. He's—changed. I told you that." And at Janie's arching brows, "He has!"

Janie frowned. "If I didn't know better, I'd say you sounded as if you admired him for it. Why have you really come here, Cat? Are you trying to tell me you've changed your mind about the divorce?"

"No." Caitlin was indignant, but her colour didn't subside. "I just wish that you could see him for yourself."

"Why?"

"Why?" Caitlin found it difficult to say. "I don't know. He's just so—different, as I say."

"Different?" Janie regarded her speculatively. "Okay. So you say he's lost weight, and he's not abused you like he used to do, and you're feeling sorry for him, right?"

"Right." Caitlin could live with that.

"But you're not attracted to him, are you?"

"No. That is..." Caitlin could feel Janie's eyes upon her. "It's not that simple, Janie. Sometimes I don't know what I feel myself."

"Oh, this is ridiculous!" Janie exploded. "Must I remind you that this is the man who brutalised you on your honeymoon and has been keeping another woman for the past God knows how many years? The man's a parasite, Caitlin. I thought you understood that. Just because he's feeling sorry for himself now, don't let him make a fool of you again."

"I don't intend to," exclaimed Caitlin defensively, but the truth was, she'd never felt so unsure. She was overwhelmingly grateful when a customer tapped on the door with an inquiry, and Janie was forced to assume her business face.

The woman asked about a nineteenth-century Tiffany lamp that was displayed in the window, and Janie was too professional a dealer not to treat the inquiry seriously. It gave Caitlin the time she needed to finish off her coffee, and by the time the woman was ready to leave, so was she.

She knew Janie wasn't pleased with her, but there wasn't time to say much more than, "Have a good weekend." But their conversation wasn't over; Janie's wry expression promised that, and Caitlin fretted about what she hadn't said all the way home.

Lunch was an omelette and salad, prepared without too much effort and eaten in much the same way. Nathan acknowledged her reappearance, but he didn't ask about her morning, and after the meal was over, Caitlin went to pack.

She used two suitcases, one for herself and one for Nathan. If she'd been concerned that he might come into his bedroom while she was organising his clothes, she needn't have worried. He was lounging on the sofa in the living room when she emerged, one ankle propped across his knee.

"Ready?" she asked, attempting to behave naturally, and Nathan gave a careless shrug of his shoulders.

"As I'll ever be, I guess," he responded, getting sinuously to his feet, and she was unhappily aware that her emotions were still not under control. The trouble was, she couldn't remember ever being so aware of him before, and his lean, powerful body made her feel weak.

It crossed her mind, as they set off, that her father would find a difference in him, and he was unlikely to approve of the jeans and the bulky sweater he was wearing today. In fact, she doubted her father had seen Nathan in anything other than a suit or well-cut casual trousers and a cashmere jacket. Until recently, she'd have said the same of herself.

His hair, too, would be another source of irritation. Although it was clean, her father would think it was far too long. A swift glance reminded her of how sleekly and smoothly it lay against his scalp, but the urge to run her fingers through its silky darkness was swiftly suppressed.

Besides, as they passed the Paddington Basin, heading towards the junction of the M40, she realised there were more important things to worry about than Nathan's appearance. What would he do if his memory never returned, for instance? How could he work for Webster Development if he couldn't even remember what he did?

Obviously, her father was going to find it very hard to cope with. Never a patient man, in recent years Matthew Webster had become irascible at best. In one of their few conversations in recent months, Nathan had implied that he was being made a scapegoat by her father. Ever since Marshall O'Brien had joined the firm, Nathan's authority was constantly being challenged.

And, in this instance, Caitlin had had to agree with him. Never a fan of Marshall's herself, she could quite see how his attitude might aggravate the other man. It aggravated her, for heaven's sake, reminding her of what she had once aspired to. Marshall was always there at her father's side, like some Machiavellian skeleton at the feast.

It had got to such a point that even she had begun to feel resentful. It was as if her father couldn't make his own decisions any more. What power did Marshall hold that her father should always defer to him? It wasn't as if he'd worked for the company that long.

Sometimes, Caitlin had wondered if there was something her father was keeping from them. Just occasionally, when she'd caught Marshall watching her, she'd wondered if his role wasn't mainly that of a spy. Certainly, his familiarity with her father was suspicious; Matthew Webster had never let anyone get that close before.

Whatever, Marshall's appointment, just a few months after her father's heart attack, had infuriated Nathan. She knew her husband had been expecting her father to retire, but instead, he'd installed a stranger in his place. The wonder was that no one else had voiced their disapproval. After all, Marshall had had little experience in that field.

Of course, he didn't run the company single-handedly. Even before he'd returned to his desk, Matthew Webster had been the guiding force behind any decisions he had made. For all her father had been warned to take things easier in the future, he had gradually resumed his authority, with Marshall at his side—in Nathan's place....

"How far is it?"

Nathan's question interrupted her troubled thoughts, and she turned to him with some relief. The idea that her father might use Nathan's disability to get him out of the company should have pleased her. If he was becoming disillusioned with her husband, she might soon be free.

"Um—not too far," she answered now, her hands tightening on the wheel. "The house is in Buckinghamshire. Not far from High Wycombe. We should be there in a little less than an hour."

Nathan frowned. "Buckinghamshire," he said, pronouncing every syllable. "That's what you call a county, is that right?"

"Right." Caitlin caught her lower lip between her teeth. "It's good to know you haven't forgotten your geography. Do you remember Brook's End?"

"Brook's End?"

Clearly, he didn't, and forcing herself to speak casually, Caitlin explained. "That's the name of the village where my parents' house is situated. I told you about Fairings, didn't I? That's the—"

"Name of the house," he finished drily. "Yes, I remember that. Despite what you think, I'm not totally goofy. I remember most of what you've told me since that accident. If only I could remember what came before."

Caitlin sighed. "You will," she said comfortingly, and sensed the frustrated look he cast her way.

"Will I?" he countered sardonically. "Well, hey, that's reassuring. But, you know, I get the feeling you don't really care."

"That's not true!"

Caitlin was indignant, but Nathan merely slumped farther into his seat. "You have no idea what it's like," he said, pressing the heel of his hand against his forehead. "I seem to have an enormous void where my memory used to be."

Caitlin swallowed. "I know it must be hard—"

"Oh, it is. Bloody hard," he told her harshly. "And it's a damn sight harder when you've got no one to support you." His lips twisted. "I wouldn't want to upset you, but I'm gradually getting the feeling that you'd have been happier if I hadn't made it back."

"That's not true."

Caitlin was horrified now, but Nathan didn't appear convinced by her denial. "No?" he taunted softly. "When we don't appear to have a life together? For Christ's sake, Kate, we even sleep in separate rooms."

"Lots of people sleep in separate rooms," responded Caitlin defensively. "And in the circumstances, I really think it's for the best."

"The best for whom?" asked Nathan scornfully. "For you—because you don't trust me? Or because you'll do any damn thing to ensure we're never alone?"

Caitlin caught her breath. "We're often alone," she protested. "We're alone now."

"In a car? On a busy road?" Nathan gave her an impatient stare. "I meant in intimate circumstances. You know what I mean."

Caitlin licked her lips. "I don't know what you mean," she said.

"Don't you?" His expression mocked her. "Would you like me to draw you a picture instead?" His fingers brushed her arm. "You might enjoy it. Or shall I just tell you what I think we'd do in bed?"

A wave of heat swept over her body, moistening her palms and causing little rivulets of awareness to spread to every extremity. If she'd been standing, she was sure her knees would have shaken. As it was, her foot pressed a little jerkily on the pedal.

"Watch it!" he snapped suddenly, and she realised she'd been accelerating up to the back of a furniture lorry instead of moving into the overtaking lane.

But dammit, she thought, she wasn't used to anyone making those kinds of insinuations to her, and her nerves were already stretched beyond belief.

There was silence for a while after that, and she was beginning to hope he had forgotten their conversation until he spoke again. "I guess it was easy to fool me while I was in the hospital," he ventured wryly, "when you didn't have to prove the way you felt. But since we got back to England, you've avoided any explanation, and you run a mile every time I get too close."

Caitlin took a steadying breath. "I think you're exaggerating."

"Am I?" He regarded her disparagingly. "So it's not because of our—disagreement, shall we say—that you conceived this idea of spending the weekend with your folks?"

"No." Caitlin endeavoured to concentrate on the road. "It was my father's idea, actually. Naturally—naturally, he and my mother want to—to assure themselves that you're—all right."

"Not lying, you mean?" he said, disconcerting her intentionally. "I guess you had to think of something to tell your father when I wasn't available. What excuse did you give, just so I know the score?''

Caitlin pressed her lips together. ''I didn't give any excuse,'' she replied tersely, realising that once again he had assumed the upper hand. ''I'm not a child, you know. I don't have to report all my actions to him. But I could hardly tell him where you were, because I didn't know.''

''True.'' Nathan was laconic now. His lips twisted. ''I doubt if I'd have had an answer for you if you'd asked. London is—familiar, but not Knightsbridge. At least—I've heard of Harrods, of course, but not Wellsley Square.''

Which was where the flat was situated, as Caitlin well knew, and for a few moments she sensed his feelings of despair. But the junction for Wendover and Princes Risborough distracted her attention, and putting all negative thoughts aside, she turned the car off the motorway and joined the minor road that eventually led to Brook's End.

She did notice that Nathan was studying the signposts, too. But he made no comment, and she guessed they meant nothing to him. Evidently, the villages of Bledlow and Owlswick were as unfamiliar as their flat, and she felt a sense of pity for his loss.

Still, Caitlin couldn't deny a certain lifting of her spirits. Despite the fact that she'd lived in London since she was twenty-one, she had always preferred the country, and Brook's End was one of those sleepy villages that seemed rooted in a previous century. Situated off the beaten track, with no main road to divide it, and a pond where a handful of ducks had taken up residence, it was delightfully rural. Even the atmosphere was decidedly Victorian, with little traffic to disturb its calm civility.

A row of pretty cottages faced the green, with a general store-cum-post office at one end and a tearoom at the other.

St Aiden's and its adjoining vicarage provided for its spiritual needs, while The Bay Horse accommodated the rest.

Fairings was situated at the far end of the village, with wrought-iron gates that stood open beside a single-storied lodge. Beyond the gates, a stretch of parkland surrounded a mellow building, and the tyres clanked noisily over a metal grid.

"Very feudal," remarked Nathan drily, his tone intimating that so far as he was concerned, their previous discussion was at an end. "Tell me, are your parents the lord and lady of the manor? Don't tell me you're an Honourable, as well."

"No."

Caitlin decided not to start anything else she couldn't finish, and as they came off the cattle grid, Ted Follett, who lived at the lodge, appeared from around the side of the house.

"Afternoon, Mrs Wolfe," he greeted her warmly, doffing his tweed cap. Then, his eyes darting inquisitively to the man beside her, "Mr Wolfe," he appended politely. "Nice to see you up and about again, sir."

Nathan exchanged a swift glance with Caitlin, and then forced a thin smile. "Thank you," he said stiffly. "Um—it's good to be back."

"The hedges are looking pretty, Mr Follett," Caitlin put in quickly, realising Nathan hadn't recognised the man. She gave her husband a sideways glance, and then continued, "There are so many berries. Are we going to have a hard winter?"

"That's what they say," agreed the old man, but his attention was clearly fixed on Nathan. "What do you say, Mr Wolfe? I reckon you'll be looking forward to a few days' rest."

"Maybe."

Nathan's response was wary, and as if sensing this, Mr Follett scratched his bald pate before replacing his cap. "We was sorry to hear about the accident," he added. "I said to Ellie, I said, it must have been terrible for you."

"Indeed."

Nathan's tone had hardened almost imperceptibly, and Caitlin guessed he was well aware of Ted Follett's efforts to pry. But for all that, she prayed he wouldn't say anything outrageous. The last thing she wanted was for him to offend the old man.

However, "It's good to see you again, Mr Follett" was all Nathan offered. "Perhaps we'll meet again before I leave. Please give your wife my good wishes, won't you?"

Fortunately, Caitlin had anticipated what was coming and had put the car into gear and pulled away before her husband could finish what he was saying. Looking back through the rear-view mirror, she could see the old man staring after them with some bewilderment, but she was fairly sure he'd missed Nathan's final words.

"There is no *Mrs* Follett," she said in answer to her husband's silent indignation, and he uttered a muffled oath beneath his breath. "Mr Follett's a bachelor. He always has been. Ellie is his niece. I should have explained."

Nathan grimaced. "Oh, well—I don't suppose it matters. He'll probably think I'm drunk or on drugs—something like that." He gave her a rueful smile. "You'll have to give me some tuition. I'd hate to make the same mistake again."

"You won't."

Caitlin tried to sound confident, but she was afraid it came out rather differently than she'd hoped. The trouble was, when Nathan smiled at her like that, she found it incredibly difficult to concentrate on anything but him, and the knowledge brought a sudden tension to her words.

11

He sprawled indolently on the cushioned window seat, one leg outstretched on the carpet, the other drawn up on the seat beside him, a resting place for his chin. He was supposed to be relaxing, looking out at the darkening garden beyond the windows, but half his attention was on Caitlin as she moved about the bedroom behind him.

She was nervous. He knew that. Even though his view of her was only a reflection in the glass, it was obvious from the agitated speed of her movements that she was constantly on edge. She was unpacking their suitcases. She was removing skirts and dresses from one, jackets and trousers from the other and hanging them away in the massive closets to be found in the dressing room next door.

He didn't know what she was doing with their underwear. From time to time, she'd bustle out of the room with something held closely against her chest. He didn't kid himself it was his boxer shorts that were receiving such special attention. Rather that she didn't want him to glimpse her lingerie.

She was behaving as if he was about to jump on her, he thought idly. And perhaps she had some justification for that. She knew he'd made no objections when her mother had explained the sleeping arrangements. But it was obvious they made no sense to her.

It was ironic, really. Despite what she'd said in the car, he knew she'd been eager to leave the apartment. He supposed she'd thought that at Fairings she'd be safe. But that was before her mother had told her that someone called Marshall O'Brien was spending the weekend with them and that she'd given him Caitlin's old room while he was there.

Of course, Caitlin had made some objection. But she'd couched it in terms that wouldn't reveal to anyone but him exactly what she meant. He didn't believe she really thought O'Brien was invading her privacy. No, he was fairly sure she'd planned on occupying that room herself.

But her plans were thwarted, and he couldn't help feeling slightly amused by it. Particularly as she'd gone to great pains to assure her mother there was nothing amiss. Her excuse—that he would rest more easily without her tossing and turning beside him—had met with little sympathy. On the contrary, Mrs Webster had been of the opinion that she should be there in case he needed her through the night.

He was sure there must be other rooms—other suites, even—but these days, without an army of servants to run the place, they were evidently not prepared. And why shouldn't Caitlin share a bedroom with her husband? In his opinion, that was what marriage was all about.

All the same, judging from the look she'd given him as Mrs Goddard, the housekeeper, escorted them upstairs, he knew he had no reason to feel optimistic about the situation. He felt sure that if his wife had anything to do with it, she'd prefer to spend the night on the floor rather than share the generously sized double bed with him.

He just wished he knew what had gone wrong with their relationship. It wasn't that Caitlin lacked passion; he was fairly sure of that. She should have been indifferent, but she wasn't; she was powerfully aware of him. Whenever he came near her, he could sense the raw emotions she was trying to hide.

But why? Why was she afraid of her feelings? Why was she so nervous? What had he done to make her fight the attraction between them? Because he sensed it wasn't his choice that they remained apart.

There seemed to be only one solution. One of them must have had an affair with someone else. And as Caitlin clearly treated him as the usurper, he could only assume that he had been to blame.

Briefly, he explored this new consideration. But for all he allowed the thought to germinate, he wasn't convinced. For all he couldn't remember their wedding, he was sure he must have been in love with her when he married her. Was in love with her still, he mused. So why would he turn to someone else?

Conversely, the alternative to this was no less unpalatable. The idea of Caitlin with someone else filled him with an anger he could barely control. She was his, he thought violently, and he'd do anything to keep her. Including taking her against her will, if he was forced.

The lid of an empty case banged behind him, and he swore as the unexpected noise caused him to start. The lamps in the room and the darkening sky beyond the windows revealed the irritation Caitlin was feeling, and his nerves tightened impatiently at the sight.

Dammit, what was wrong with her? he wondered harshly. It wasn't as if she could blame him for what had happened, and her mother had treated him without any censure as far as he was aware. On the contrary, she had spoken to him affably, almost with affection. So whatever he had done, Caitlin had kept it to herself.

He had yet to meet her father, of course, and he had to admit that that prospect was more daunting. Caitlin had described Matthew Webster as a committed workaholic, who cared little for his health and expected a similar commitment from his staff. The man had survived a serious heart attack and had been warned not to continue running the company, but in spite of that, he still retained control.

It had crossed his mind that he might have been being groomed to be Matthew Webster's successor, but again, according to Caitlin, that was not in the cards. The other man, Marshall O'Brien—he was proud he remembered his name—was now acting as Webster's deputy, so he apparently had what was needed to take his place.

Which, unwillingly enough, brought him back to the present situation. Was it possible that it was this that had caused the rift between him and his wife? He refused to consider a connection between the two alternatives. Matthew Webster could not have found out that *he* was having an affair....

"Are you going to get changed for supper?"

Caitlin's inquiry was delivered in a cool, dispassionate voice, and he guessed she had decided to act as if nothing was wrong. How she really felt was anyone's guess, but she was prepared to be civil. Even if there was an edge to her voice that hadn't been there before.

"Are you?" he countered, turning to run his eyes over her dark-suited figure, and Caitlin seemed to recoil from his appraisal. She had worn the three-piece outfit to go out this morning, and she hadn't bothered to change when she returned.

"Of course," she responded now. "My father always expects us to observe the formalities." But it was his guess that she'd wear something just as prim. It wasn't her intention to provoke his interest, whatever her father's wishes, and his eyes moved half-mockingly to her face.

"Then you should know I wouldn't do anything to offend your father," he countered. "Or were you hoping to make me look a fool?"

"Not at all," she said defensively, but her cheeks were bright with colour. "And as you apparently prefer casual clothes these days, I couldn't be sure."

His eyes narrowed. "Are you saying I normally wear a suit?"

"It has been known." Caitlin moved a little uncomfortably now. "Not all the time, of course. But you didn't used to like jeans until—until the crash."

His stomach hollowed. "I can't believe it."

"Nevertheless, it's true." Caitlin glanced behind her. "Look—you can use the bathroom first. I'll—er—finish my unpacking while you change."

He got to his feet. "I thought you'd finished the unpacking," he said tersely, aware of the void yawning at his feet again. He remembered telling her to buy jeans. He remembered it distinctly. God, what was wrong with him? The implication was that his brain had been impaired.

"Oh…" she murmured now, turning away, as if even the sight of him disturbed her. "I've still got one or two things to sort out. You go ahead. I've—er—I've put your shaving gear on the shelf, and there are plenty of towels. If you tell me which suit you want to wear this evening, I'll lay it out for you."

He scowled. For all his raw uncertainty, his strongest impulse at this moment was to grab hold of her and take her in his arms. He badly needed reassurance, and she was the only one who could give it to him, but he sensed she wouldn't appreciate being mauled.

"Any suit will do," he muttered now, tugging the thick sweater he had been wearing over his head. He was unaware of any impropriety until he saw her staring at him, but her startled eyes were wide with shock, not contempt.

If he hadn't known better, he'd have said she was gazing at him with unguarded fascination. He could feel his muscles tensing beneath her wide-eyed stare. His nipples reacted correspondingly; he could feel them. They were button hard in their fine nest of hair.

He wanted to do something, anything, to capitalise on the suddenly potent intimacy between them, but as soon as she realised what she was doing, she looked away. With the silken weight of her hair hiding her expression from him, she put a little more space between them, and he felt his heavy arousal start to subside.

"Are you scared of me, Kate?" he demanded, needing some reason for her withdrawal, and the memory of what he had considered in the hospital came back to taunt him. But dammit, he'd thought he was used to wearing jeans, and he'd been wrong about that, so how did he know if he'd ever treated her like a beast?

"No," she denied now, flicking a glance towards him. And then, "Aren't you going for your shower? It's getting late."

"To hell with the shower," he muttered harshly. "We need to talk, Kate. And I don't mean about trivialities. When are you going to tell me what I've done?"

She sighed, allowing the sound to escape her lips lightly, though he sensed she wasn't feeling that way at all. But he couldn't go on behaving as if it would all turn out all right tomorrow. Who knew but what tomorrow might never come?

"I don't think this is the time to have any kind of meaningful discussion," she declared after a few moments, and he noticed how she avoided looking at his bare chest. If she wasn't scared of him, she was scared of something. Clearly, his uninhibitedness had shocked her, and he wondered what she'd do if he got completely undressed.

Putting his thoughts into action, he snapped open the button at the waist of his trousers and lazily hooked his thumb around the tab of his zip. He was wearing silk underpants, for heaven's sake, he assured his reluctant conscience, though his reviving arousal made a mockery of that defence.

Her reaction was swift and predictable, but although he had expected her to express some objection, he was not prepared for the horror in her eyes. "I'll leave you to it," she said tightly, heading unmistakeably for the door. "I'm sure you would prefer to be alone."

"Shit!" He swore angrily, but somehow, perhaps because of his longer legs, he reached the door when she did and slammed his fist against it, keeping it shut. "Just a minute," he said roughly. "Do I really disgust you that much? Or can I believe you've never seen me naked before?"

"Don't be ridiculous!"

Her denial was automatic, but somehow he wasn't totally convinced by her words. He was beginning to wonder if they'd ever consummated their marriage. Dear God, he couldn't believe that! He doubted he could have kept his hands off her for three days, let alone three years!

"Then what's wrong?" he persisted, aware that when her eyes dropped nervously to his gaping zip, his body responded accordingly. He could feel his hard arousal forcing the zip to part, and the pain was quite exquisitely intense.

"Must we go into this again?" she said unevenly, looking away, and he felt the urge to bury his face in the scented hollow of her neck. And not just his face, he thought bitterly. He wanted to bury himself inside her, to find his own heaven in the sweetness of her sheath.

But he couldn't do it. He couldn't force her to have sex with him—even though he sensed she wouldn't stop him if he tried. With her mother within earshot, and her father and his cohort probably equally as accessible, whatever he did, she wouldn't run the risk of embarrassing anyone else.

And he found that knowledge a distinct turn-off. As far as he knew, he'd never had to force a woman in his life. He didn't want her that way; he didn't want to make love to a martyr. But there was more to her resistance than she'd admitted so far.

"All right," he said at last, moving away, aware that she remained where she was, frozen against the door. "If I'm wrong, there has to be another explanation. Is what you're not admitting the fact that there's someone else?"

Her silence was unnatural, charged, and when he swung round to face her, he found her pressing the back of one hand to her lips. Until that moment, he hadn't believed it. Even though he'd made the accusation, he'd been boxing in the dark. But the consternation in her face was unmistakeable. She looked—guilty, and he felt gutted at the thought of what it meant.

"You don't know what you're talking about," she declared at last, and he felt a sudden surge of anger at his impotence. Dammit, what did she think he was? Some idiot colonial who wouldn't care if she was unfaithful? Some hick country boy she could dupe without remorse?

"I think you do," he snarled angrily, thrusting his face into hers. "There's another man. Isn't there? Goddammit, is it someone I should know?"

Caitlin caught her breath. "There's no other man," she protested, her face a picture of bewilderment now, and if he hadn't been so incensed, he'd have realised she was telling the truth. "Honestly, Nathan, I'm not that kind of woman. You've always said I was..."

What?

He stared at her in raw frustration when she didn't finish the sentence, but whatever she had been going to say, she had evidently decided she had gone far enough. Pressing herself back against the door, she took her lower lip between her teeth, and no amount of silent prompting on his behalf could persuade her to go on.

He wanted to shake her then, was tempted to shake her, only he was afraid that if he touched her, he wouldn't be able to stop. Her tension had made her vulnerable, and he was intensely aware of her femininity. Beneath her cream silk blouse and the ridiculously formal waistcoat, her breasts were heaving anxiously against the cloth.

The sight of the dusky hollow, just visible above the vee of the blouse was electrifying. Just a glimpse of her flesh and he was again at the mercy of his sex. He wanted her; he didn't care if she'd been unfaithful, he just wanted her. She was his wife, and she had no right to keep him at arm's length.

"If—if you think threatening me is going to prove anything, forget it," she got out eventually, and he realised she had completely misread the way he felt. Across her throat, he could see a fine vibration, and there was a feathering of goose bumps up her neck.

"Dammit, Kate," he groaned as guilt made him run restless fingers into his hair. He could feel the same covert trembling within himself. "I'm your husband. I'm not a monster. I'm not going to hurt you. If you're afraid of me, for God's sake, tell me why."

His words, obviously as unexpected to her as they'd been to him, seemed to disarm her. No doubt she'd anticipated another angry outburst, and his hoarse plea for understanding seemed to neutralise her response.

"I'm—not—afraid of you," she protested, though her eyes were still wary. "And I want to help you, if I can. But you can't expect to absorb everything at once."

He drew in a breath. "And what I said?" he asked, unable to leave it be. "About there being someone else. You swear it's not true?"

"I swear—I've not—I've never been unfaithful to you," she said. "Now, do you think we could talk about something else?"

He gave in because it was easier, and because, quite frankly, he didn't feel as if he had the strength to go on. All this emotion was exhausting. He could feel his temples throbbing. God, what he'd really like to do was go to bed.

"Are you all right?"

Caitlin's voice seemed to come from a great distance, and he realised he was wearier than he'd thought. Actually, he was feeling rather dizzy, and he sought the edge of the bed behind him, sinking down onto the mattress and burying his face in his hands.

"Nathan!"

She was really concerned now, kneeling down beside him and pressing the back of her hand against his neck. Why couldn't she have done that earlier, he thought, when he might have had the strength to do something about it? Right now, he couldn't have made love to her if she begged him to do it.

"I'm okay," he said, forcing his head up. "But—look, do I have to go down to supper? If you don't mind, I'd rather go straight to bed."

Caitlin got to her feet. "Well…" She glanced towards the door, gnawing on her lower lip as she did so, and he decided that whatever she decided, he was staying here. "I suppose I could explain you're tired," she added. "I know Mummy will understand. It has been the most strenuous day you've had so far."

"Hasn't it?"

He was sardonic, and as if coming to a decision, Caitlin nodded. "All right," she said. "I'll do it. Of course, Daddy will be disappointed. But there's really nothing spoiling, is there?"

"You tell me," he said, flopping back against the pillows. "But—you're your father's daughter, aren't you? I'm sure you'll handle it with tact."

Caitlin stiffened. "Is that a criticism?"

"No. Just a statement of the obvious," he answered wearily. "Now, be a good girl and help me get undressed."

"Help you get . . ."

Caitlin's lips parted as once again she failed to complete her sentence. Clearly, she had not anticipated that requirement, and he could see her unwillingness to touch him warring with the concern in her flushed face.

"If you'd take off my boots," he amended gently, taking pity on her confusion, and he saw, through narrowed eyes, the sudden relief that filled her eyes. "That's great," he added gratefully, when she obeyed his instruction. "Why don't you go and have your shower? I'll use the bathroom after you've gone downstairs."

He awakened to the awareness of a warm body beside his in the bed.

For a moment, the feeling was so pleasant, he didn't attempt to understand where he was. He just lay there and let himself enjoy it. He didn't even try to comprehend what it implied.

But on this occasion, his memory was all too capable. The reason why the ceiling looked unfamiliar, why the walls with their subtle shading of cream and gold roses didn't arouse any sense of recognition, was obvious. He was at Fairings, his father-in-law's country house in Buckinghamshire. And, ergo, the woman lying beside him was his wife.

The thought was startling, hinting as it did at an intimacy she had hitherto denied. Half-disbelievingly, he turned his head on the pillow. But he wasn't mistaken. It was Caitlin curled beside him in the bed.

She was still asleep, and his breath escaped him on a low sigh. After last night's altercation, he'd been sure she'd find somewhere else to sleep. What had happened? he wondered. Had her mother forced her to accept her responsibilities? Or had his own weakness aroused her compassion? Because he was still recovering from his injuries, did she believe herself immune from any unwelcome approach?

As he looked at her, he couldn't deny a sense of incredulity. He still found it amazing that this beautiful creature was his wife. For all he felt a strong attraction to her, she seemed such a stranger. But a stranger he desired, more with every passing day.

She was lying half on her back, with one arm extended above her head. She was breathing deeply. Not snoring exactly, but her breath sighed softly between her teeth. Her lips were ever so slightly parted, and there was an appealing lack of tension in her face.

And then he noticed something else, something he'd have noticed right away if he hadn't been so entranced by her vulnerability. But, without make-up of any kind, she was so deliciously natural, and he had had the most ridiculous urge to wake her with a kiss.

Ridiculous, because he was no Prince Charming, and he doubted Caitlin would welcome his efforts if he did so. And now, as common sense reasserted itself, he took in what she was wearing, and his yielding sense of beneficence melted away.

He wondered if she could have borrowed the garment from her mother, though from what he had seen of Mrs Webster thus far, he would not have believed she would have such an item in her wardrobe. Mrs Goddard, then, he thought, his resentment increasing at the thought of Caitlin asking the housekeeper to help her out. Surely no one else would own a flannelette nightgown with a high, round collar and long sleeves buttoned at the wrist.

Fury gripped him. The idea that his wife should have chosen to wrap herself up in such ugly nightwear in the hope of spiking his interest would be laughable, if it didn't anger him so. Didn't she realise that a man liked nothing better than a challenge? That no amount of protection would put him off?

He scowled. His fingers itched to tear the offending garment from her sleeping figure. He wondered if she was still wearing her underwear, as well. He knew he'd get a great deal of pleasure out of exploding the myth she'd created, and he'd like to see her face when she realised she'd made a mistake.

Then he became aware of something else, something he'd also overlooked upon wakening. He was still wearing the trousers he'd been wearing the night before when he flopped down upon the bed. He must have fallen asleep while Caitlin was taking her shower. And all she'd done was bundle him under the quilt when she came out.

He now understood his own feelings of discomfort. He'd been aware of the constriction ever since he opened his eyes. But he'd been so excited to find his wife sharing the bed with him, he hadn't thought about what he was wearing. As he hadn't worn any pyjamas at the apartment, he hadn't given his own nightwear a thought.

It was unbelievable that in this day and age a woman of Caitlin's experience should behave so—childishly. Couldn't she at least have pulled off his trousers before rolling him into bed? Of course, she'd have been afraid that if she did that, he might wake up and get the wrong impression. She was scared to death he'd take advantage of her weakness.

Being careful not to wake her, he turned onto his side and propped his chin on the palm of his hand. Was she really his wife? he wondered, feeling again that sense of alienation he'd hoped would have subsided by now. God, she looked more like Mama Walton at the moment. But her appearance of innocence didn't please him. He didn't want to feel sorry for her. He wanted to sustain his anger until she awoke.

Yet his feelings towards her were as complex as the rest of this situation. If only he knew what had happened to cause the rift between them. Because, whatever she said, however she denied it, she was not comfortable with him. God, his lips twisted bitterly, this latest development was proof enough of that.

A strand of her hair lay on the pillow beside him, and giving in to an urge as primitive as time, he carried the silken tendril to his lips. It smelt of warmth, and cleanness, and a faintly citrus essence, which he guessed she'd used to wash it. When he touched it, when he tasted it, it was every bit as appealing as he'd expected.

Taking the strand into his mouth, he bit into its fine texture, enjoying doing something so intimate to her without her being aware of it. He wondered how she would feel at the thought that he had been making subtle love to her. It was a tantalising thought in the present circumstances.

But when he spread the strand of her hair between his fingers again and saw how damp his tongue had made it, he realised that playing with her like this was causing havoc with his own sexuality. Beneath the confining tightness of his trousers, his erection strained the seams of his silk briefs, and with a feeling of resignation, he put his hand beneath the covers and released his taut arousal from its restraint.

His relief was swift and soothing, although it in no way assuaged his needs, his body's craving. Nevertheless, he was satisfied that he could pervert her efforts so easily. He could imagine how shocked she'd feel if her hand brushed against his throbbing flesh.

So much for the best laid plans, he mused sardonically. She should have made sure she was out of bed before he awoke. He couldn't believe she didn't know that something like this might happen. It wasn't the first time he'd had a morning erection, he was sure.

Dismissing that kind of speculation because of its obvious dangers, he resumed his contemplation of her sleeping form. He wondered how she'd react if he unbuttoned her nightgown. It apparently fastened down the front, and he mused that if he opened the buttons, its appearance would be much improved.

Ignoring any twinge of conscience—any warning that he knew exactly how she'd react—he put out his hand and touched the first pearl button. By carefully widening the buttonhole, it easily popped through. The garment wasn't new and the fabric was soft and yielding. Without a great deal of effort, it was no problem to repeat his success.

He had to draw the quilt away to continue his investigation, and he saw to his regret that the buttons only opened as far as her waist. But, what the hell, it was perfect for his purposes. And it would prove how silly she had been to play this game.

And, in many ways, the nightgown was more of a temptation than some of its scanty contemporaries, he thought ruefully. It wasn't always the most obvious item that attracted a man's attention. And Caitlin, in her modest chemise, was a temptation. He didn't need his memory to tell him that.

As witness the sudden unsteadiness of his hands.

She stirred suddenly, as if the cooler air invading the neckline of the nightgown was disturbing her rest. Perhaps she'd sensed his excitement; perhaps his shaking hands had accidently nudged her awake. Whatever, he was gripped by an overwhelming desire to continue even though he knew she was bound to find out.

But she was deeply unconscious, and it took some time for her to rise through the layers of sleep and realise what was going on. As she stirred, she made appealing sounds that were half submissive, half in protest, as if she knew exactly what he wanted and was urging him to go on.

His inflamed senses reacted instantly to this provocation. Besides, he was eager to capitalise on his success. He knew he didn't have much time before she opened her eyes and realised what was happening, and although he chided his ruthless need, he allowed his hand to move over the soft cloth and touch her breasts.

The hardening in his groin became almost unbearable. The sight of her taut nipples, puckering in the cool air, made him long to take them into his mouth. Ignoring the fact that he was risking more than her indignation, he bent his head towards her, taking one hot little bud gently between his teeth.

God, it was heaven!

Even though he knew she was an unwilling party to his ministrations, he couldn't deny the sweetness of her arousal against his tongue. He suckled hungrily, like a man who's been denied his life's sustenance for far too long, changing to her other breast with a fervour that fired his blood.

Then, two things happened almost simultaneously. Despite his intention not to go any further, his hand moved almost of its own volition to caress her flat stomach. And Caitlin's eyes opened.

He couldn't honestly have said who was the most shocked by her sudden awareness of what was happening. For all his resentment at the way she had treated him, he felt almost embarrassed to be caught out behaving in such a way. And he didn't try to stop her when she uttered a cry and rolled away from him. He was already regretting his actions and anticipating how depressing the remainder of the day was going to be....

12

It was late when he reached Prescott. But that suited him. He didn't want anyone questioning his arrival, noting the strange vehicle in the vicinity of Varley's Mill. With a bit of luck, the old man would still be up. Jacob didn't sleep well these days, and his son knew he often watched television until the early hours of the morning.

The old house that abutted the now-unused lumber yard looked deserted, but he wasn't worried. His father had always been a mean old skinflint and he was unlikely to leave any lights burning that weren't needed. God knew, anyone else would have sold the lot for development years ago, but Jacob clung to the old place as if he was afraid his son might get his hands on the proceeds if he sold out.

Still, the house's isolation at the edge of town, among a handful of run-down factories and warehouses, suited his purposes tonight. It would be easy enough to stow the rental car in one of the empty woodsheds, and the fewer people who knew he was here the better. He even left the suitcase in the car. He had no wish for his father to get his hands on it, and Prescott wasn't New York after all.

Deciding it wouldn't be wise to go poking round for a place to store the car until he'd spoken to his father, he parked in the yard and walked across to the house. His key still fit the lock, but it didn't gain him admission. Evidently, the old man had become more security conscious in recent years.

He had no choice but to press the bell and wait for his father to answer. But although he listened intently, he couldn't hear any movement inside the house. He looked up at the blank windows with raw frustration. Where was the old devil? He never left the premises.

He had rung the bell three times before he heard a sound beyond the heavy panels. Was it a footstep? He didn't think his father kept a dog, but he couldn't be sure. Whoever it was, he was breathing heavily. The skin on the back of his neck prickled. It had to be his father. There was no one else.

"Who is it? Who's there?"

There was no mistaking his father's querulous tone, and he pressed his face to the door. "It's me," he hissed. "Come on, Pa. Open up. It's freezing my balls off out here."

There was a pregnant silence, and belatedly he wondered what his father had been told about the crash. He might even think he had come here straight from the hospital. Oh, shit, this was going to be harder than he'd thought.

"Pa," he said again, adopting a wheedling tone, "aren't you gonna let me in?"

There was another pause, a shorter one this time, and then, to his relief, he heard the sound of a chain being lifted and bolts withdrawn from both the top and the bottom of the door. At last, it swung inwards onto the dark passageway beyond, and without waiting for an invitation, he stepped inside.

The door closed, and in the dim light from a dusty bulb, he surveyed his father. "Hi there," he greeted him with forced cordiality. "Well, here I am. The prodigal has returned."

Jacob Wolfe secured the bolts again and replaced the chain, while his son glanced distastefully about him. Damn, he thought, this place was filthy. If the old man thought so much about it, why didn't he keep it clean?

He turned from his appraisal of his surroundings to find his father watching him with wary eyes. "Nathan?" he said. "It is Nathan, isn't it?"

He was tempted to say, "Who did you expect?" but it wasn't the time for levity. "Who else?" he asked instead, sauntering down the hall towards his father's study. "God, it's bloody cold in here. Don't you ever heat this place?"

His father said nothing, just followed him down the hall, and by the time he'd tossed a couple more logs on the smouldering embers in the hearth, the old man had resumed his seat. He'd also turned off the television, which he'd noticed had been tuned to some old black-and-white movie from the forties. Now he was regarding his son with narrowed, assessing eyes.

The room hadn't changed much. The ceiling might look a little more grimy, but the leather volumes on the book-lined shelves seemed resistant to the passage of time. Not that the heavy tomes had ever been removed in his memory. Jacob had never been a reader. They'd belonged to his wife's father, when he was alive.

"Where have you been?"

Jacob's first words startled him. He had at least expected him to ask about the accident, but evidently his father had other things on his mind. "I've been in New York," he said, the lie coming naturally to him. "I guess the—er—authorities got in touch with you about the crash?"

"I heard about it," replied Jacob eventually. "It was quite a shock to begin with. And then I found out you weren't on that plane."

His son scowled. Shit, he thought frustratedly. He should have known. The old man had spoken to his brother since it happened. So where was Jake now? What had he been telling their father about the reason for his trip?

"How did you find out?" he demanded, not stupid enough to try and deny it. "I guess Jake told you. Right?"

"Your wife came to see me," replied his father, and he felt a twinge of panic. God, had Jake told the authorities who he really was?

"Caitlin came here?" he said, trying to sound casual, and his father gave him a scornful look.

"That's what I said," the old man replied, nodding. "She was concerned about me. She didn't want me to worry about you being hurt."

"Me being hurt?" His brows descended. "But I thought you just said she told you I wasn't on the flight."

"No." His father's smile was mocking. "She told me you were. She thinks Jake is you. Why wouldn't she? You'd never told her you had a twin."

"What?"

He was confused, bewildered. Of course he'd never told Caitlin he had a twin. It wasn't a story he'd want to brag about to anyone, and when Jake had first given him all the sordid details, he'd wanted to puke. His father had always let him think his mother had had some genuine reason not to keep both children, and learning that she'd been some cheap waitress his father had seduced on one of his trips south had really screwed him up.

All the same, that didn't explain why Jake hadn't told Caitlin who he was; why his father hadn't told Caitlin who Jake was....

He tried to make sense of what his father was saying. "You're telling me that Caitlin identified Jake as me?"

"Why not?" His father shrugged. "The seat was booked in your name, he was carrying your passport. If I hadn't seen him in the flesh, so to speak, I'd probably have believed it myself.''

Nathan swallowed, and seeking refuge behind the old man's desk, he sank into his worn leather chair. "You went to New York?"

"That's right."

"And you saw Jake?"

"In the hospital," agreed his father.

"But why?" he ventured tightly as the grandfather clock ticked relentlessly at his back. "I mean, why would you let him get away with it? Is this some way to get back at me for neglecting you? Why didn't you tell Caitlin the truth?"

"I would have." Jacob was infuriatingly offhand. "But I was pretty skewed myself at the time. I couldn't believe what I'd seen, and I guess I was shocked, too. In any event, I needed time to think."

"But what did he say?" demanded his son. "Did you confront him with your suspicions? What did he do?"

"He didn't do anything," replied Jacob evenly. "I think he thought I was senile. Like I said, I couldn't wait to get out of there."

"I don't believe this!" The younger man was getting angry. "I can't believe you didn't call his bluff. I know we've had our differences in the past, but dammit, you raised me. If you don't like what you've created, it's not my fault."

"No." At last, Jacob seemed to agree with him. "Okay. I'll accept that your faults are partly mine. But I want to know what's going on. Why was Jake on that plane pretending to be you? It wasn't his idea. I'm sure of that."

His son's lips twisted. "Why not? I'm not pretending to be him."

His father merely looked at him, and aware that he was in danger of losing all sympathy, he bent his head. Until he knew what was going on, he was stuck with the old man. It wouldn't do to antagonise him, not when he needed his help.

"Okay," he said in a low voice, wondering if he could repeat the story he had given Jake. He hunched his shoulders. "Jake was helping me, as you suspect. I'd asked him to go to London in my place."

"Why?"

"Does it matter?"

"I think so." Jacob's mouth compressed in distaste. "I want to know what dirty business you've got him mixed up in. I assume it involves money. That is your god."

Nathan ground his teeth together. Whatever he said, the old man could always make him feel small.

"That is why you married that sweet, innocent girl, isn't it?" his father appended. "You should have invited me to the wedding. I'd have warned her what to expect."

"Which is exactly why you weren't invited!" exclaimed his son angrily. "And Caitlin's no innocent. Don't be fooled by those doe-eyed looks."

"Not now, perhaps." His father shook his head. "She's lived with you for three years, hasn't she? Oh, go on, boy. You're beginning to irritate me."

His son looked as if he would have liked to respond in kind, but instead, he hauled open a drawer in his father's desk and pulled out a bottle of whisky. "You don't mind, do you, Pa?" he asked carelessly, unscrewing the cap. "It's not as if you ever touch the stuff yourself."

Jacob's expression grew daunting. Big as he was, his son could still be intimidated by his father's moods, and with an exclamation of disgust, he returned the whisky to the drawer. Then he got restlessly to his feet to pace about the room, trying to compose his words into a believable story.

"Jake—Jake offered to take something to England for me," he declared at last. "He knew I'd never get away with it myself."

Jacob's eyes never flickered. "What—something—are we talking about? Cash?" His gaze narrowed. "Drugs?"

"That's not your concern."

"It is my concern." Jacob swore. "Christ Almighty, Nathan, if it's what I think it is, I should kill you for involving Jake in your reckless schemes."

"What makes you think I had to twist his arm?" retorted his son resentfully. "Look—I may have mentioned the idea to Jake, but he didn't need much persuading to take part. God!" He almost began to believe his own reasoning. "He seems to like being me better than being himself."

"Get real, Nathan." His father regarded him contemptuously. "You're not only corrupt, you're stupid with it. Do I have to remind you, the plane crashed? Hasn't it occurred to you that Jake might be badly injured?"

His son grimaced. "He's not."

"How do you know?" Jacob's hands clenched. "Oh—I suppose you phoned the hospital to find out." He slammed his fist against the chair arm and his son jumped; he couldn't stop himself. It was obvious Jacob wished it was his head.

"Are you saying that's why he hasn't been in touch with me?" the younger man demanded. "Why he's letting my own wife believe he's me? You can't answer that one, can you? Admit it, he's just as corrupt as I am."

Jacob arched a scathing brow. "You wish."

"What do you mean?" His son stared at him. "What haven't you told me?"

Jacob shrugged. "The resemblance is uncanny," he remarked obliquely, and his son gave him a frustrated look. "He's not as—well-fed as you are, and his hair's a bit longer, but the features are identical. His accent's slightly different, but if you weren't looking for any differences, I doubt you'd notice it. It's no wonder Caitlin was deceived. I almost was myself.''

"What are you saying?'' For all it should be what he wanted to hear, the other man felt strangely bereft. "Do you accept the fact that Jake has stolen my identity? For God's sake, Pa, what are you trying to do?''

"Jake hasn't stolen anything,'' said Jacob flatly.

"Then he's a liar. You can't deny that.''

"I can. I do.'' His father regarded him contemptuously. "Jake's not lying, boy. He really thinks he's you.'' He paused. "He's got amnesia. That's why he and Caitlin have gone back to England. For the present, he's incapable of deceit.''

13

"Why don't you take Nathan for a walk this afternoon, darling?" Mrs Webster suggested pleasantly, apparently prepared to overlook the fact that her daughter was pacing rather restlessly about the room. "You never know, he may find something familiar to strike a chord in his memory." She poured herself another cup of coffee and pushed Caitlin's untouched cup and saucer to the edge of the table. "If this weather improves, of course," she added. Then, "Drink this up, dear. I'm sure it must be getting cold."

Caitlin turned, pushing her hands into the pockets of her baggy cardigan, causing it to dip to mid-thigh. Worn with black leggings, the amber-coloured jacket was supposed to disguise what shape she had, and she could tell from the wince her mother gave that she considered the outfit fatally flawed. Her own neatly pleated skirt and cream silk blouse were in the best of taste, impeccably tailored to match her svelte appearance.

Picking up the cup of coffee, Caitlin carried it back to the long windows. Beyond the wood-framed conservatory, the formal gardens that surrounded the house were draped with mist. Although the forecast had been good, the dampness was lingering, its vague oppressiveness reflecting Caitlin's mood.

"I hope your father and Nathan won't be much longer," her mother continued, determined to behave as if nothing untoward had happened. "And Marshall, too, of course," she appended, her lips tightening. "That young man is becoming quite a fixture."

Caitlin leant her shoulder against the window frame and looked back at Daisy Webster. It was easier to consider her mother's problems than to contemplate her own. After what had happened that morning, she'd just as soon not think about Nathan at all, and Marshall was the ideal target for her frustrations.

"So why did you invite him?" she asked, arching a brow interrogatively. "I'm sure if Daddy knew you didn't care for him, he'd confine their consultations to the office."

"I wouldn't bank on it." Her mother was uncharacteristically terse. And then, as if like Caitlin she'd rather not dwell on her own difficulties, she went on, "You didn't mind sharing a room with Nathan, did you? I'm afraid you caught us unprepared."

Caitlin looked down into her cup, where the cream her mother had added to the coffee was congealing round the rim. "I suppose not," she conceded, trying to sound indifferent. "Um—Daddy's invitation was unexpected for us, too."

Mrs Webster frowned. "Your father invited you?"

Caitlin nodded. "Yes. Didn't you know?"

"No." Her mother pulled a face, and then moved her shoulders impatiently. "He just said you and Nathan were coming down for the weekend, and I'm afraid I assumed it had been your idea."

Caitlin expelled her breath a little quickly. Her idea, she thought ironically. To invite herself and Nathan here, where it was obviously going to be harder to maintain the fiction of their relationship? Hardly. Though even she had had no idea how dangerous it might prove.

"I'm sorry," she said now. "I'm afraid I thought it had actually been your idea. In recent months—well, Nathan and Daddy haven't exactly been—close, have they? Since Marshall joined the company, the gulf between them seems to be getting wider by the day."

"I know." Her mother grimaced. "I knew it would happen as soon as Marshall became his second in command. But your father says he isn't ready yet to surrender the reins of the company, and I suppose he believes that Marshall doesn't have an axe to grind."

"But why not?" Caitlin stared at her mother curiously. "Why should he trust Marshall when he doesn't trust anyone else?" She paused, and then continued carefully, "You know, I've sometimes wondered, how did Daddy find Marshall in the first place? I mean, he hadn't worked for Webster's or anything. And it's such a confidential position."

She thought she saw a faint trace of colour enter her mother's cheeks at her words, but it disappeared again so rapidly that she decided she must have been mistaken. Nevertheless, when Mrs Webster spoke again, there was a thread of anxiety in her voice.

"I believe—I believe he knew the boy's mother many years ago," she declared, putting her cup back onto the tray. "Oh, look. The mist appears to be clearing. You'll be able to take Nathan out for some air."

"He's not a dog, Mummy," observed Caitlin drily, aware that she had been deliberately diverted from asking any more awkward questions. "Besides, he doesn't like walking. Surely you remember that?"

Daisy Webster shrugged. "At this moment, I doubt if he remembers what he likes or dislikes," she declared rather callously. "Oh, thank goodness, here they come. You'll be able to ask him yourself."

Caitlin turned back to the window as the three men came into the conservatory. She needed a moment to compose herself before she met her husband's knowing gaze again. Just because she had awakened in time to prevent him from taking any further liberties with her body, the memory of the incident still caused her pulse to race.

God, she thought incredulously, what would have happened if she hadn't opened her eyes at that moment? How much further would he have been prepared to go? What more could he have done, short of actually invading her body, for God's sake? He'd been suckling her breasts. They were still throbbing from the hungry tug of his teeth.

She shivered. She'd been vaguely aware of what was happening before she acknowledged it. But in that mindless state between sleeping and waking, she'd welcomed his touch. It had been like a dream; she hadn't been in control of her emotions. The sensual response her body had offered was an instinctive reaction to her psychological state.

It was disturbing all the same, because Nathan had never been so considerate of her before. When he'd bitten her breasts while they were on their honeymoon, he'd hurt her badly. But this time, she'd been totally relaxed, totally uninhibited. Her body had been pleasured, and she'd wanted the experience to go on...

"Missed me?"

Nathan's lips against the side of her neck were unbearably seductive. Lost in the blind world of introspection, she'd been totally unaware of his approach. But now, his mocking salutation brought her swiftly to her senses. She must not allow him to see how vulnerable she'd become.

All the same, her initial response had been to turn her head and let those knowing lips consume her. But the awareness of where she was—and who was watching—prevented her from making that mistake. Nevertheless, it took all her self-control to resist him, and the knowledge that he was aware of it, too, sent her backing out of his reach.

Straight into the coffee table.

"Careful, darling!"

Her mother's anxious cry saved the day, but not before Caitlin had been made to feel a fool for the second time that morning. Her reaction had been warranted, she defended herself, conscious of being the cynosure of all eyes. But she had drawn attention to herself—unwillingly—and even Marshall O'Brien was giving her a curious look.

"Oops," she said, pretending it had been a genuine mistake, and turning, she set her cup down on the tray. But she sensed no one was deceived by her play-acting. Least of all her husband, she realised in some dismay.

Her father, too, was watching her rather suspiciously. But what could he deduce from such an obvious non-event? And, judging by his expression, he wasn't altogether happy with the situation, either. They were all being compelled to deal with a virtual stranger in their midst.

Nathan had now assumed her position, propping his shoulder against the hardwood frame of the window and gazing out at the view. What was he thinking? she wondered. Did amnesiacs experience normal thought processes? There was so much she wanted to ask, but she didn't know how.

As if becoming aware of her scrutiny, he turned now to look at them all with a sardonic gaze. In cream trousers, a navy shirt, and a linen waistcoat, his clothes looked more familiar this morning. But his lazy gaze impaled her and left her feeling weak.

"Sit down—all of you," exclaimed her mother with determined brightness, and as her husband's assistant took the chair nearest to her, she made an effort to be polite. "Did you sleep well, Marshall?" she inquired, handing him a cup of coffee. "I know it isn't always easy when you're in a strange bed."

"I slept very well, thank you, Mrs Webster," he responded, pushing his wire-rimmed glasses farther up his rather prominent nose.

Caitlin frowned suddenly as his profile seemed unexpectedly familiar. But then, he spoke again, and the feeling slipped away.

"I want to thank you once again for inviting me," he continued. "It's been quite an experience visiting—Matthew—in his home. I know it must be quite an imposition while you're entertaining your family. I hope you'll tell me if I get in your way."

"I'm sure you couldn't do that, my dear," replied Mrs Webster crisply. And Caitlin, meeting her husband's eyes, realised she wasn't the only one who had noticed the hidden barb. All the same, her smiling courtesy was in direct contrast with the way she had spoken earlier, and her daughter could only assume she'd decided to bite the bullet.

Waiting until Nathan had hooked a tall, rattan stool and straddled it before choosing her position, Caitlin sank gratefully onto the sofa beside her father. There was no way Nathan could take advantage of her there, she assured herself. Though his constant observation was unnerving all the same.

Mrs Webster handed Nathan and her husband each a cup of coffee, refilling the jug from a Thermos off the tray. Then she turned to the older man with a brittle air of inquiry. "So—don't keep us in suspense. Was Nathan any help in your urgent consultations?"

Matthew was still considering his response when his son-in-law broke in. "I'm afraid not," he answered disarmingly. "I was a complete waste of time. I don't even remember the countries we deal with."

Caitlin, obliged to look in his direction while he was talking, found herself watching his hands. Unlike Marshall, who used the handle of his cup to drink with, Nathan's palm practically encased the cup. The fine china almost disappeared within the embrace of his long brown fingers, and the realisation that earlier that morning that same hand had been cupping her breast sent a fiery tingle of awareness along her veins.

She tried to distract herself by summoning her memory in an effort to recall if she'd seen Nathan hold a cup that way before, but it was difficult to concentrate with the images before her, and for once she was relieved when her father spoke.

"I suppose the question you should have asked was whether we had been of any help to him," Matthew remarked satirically, though he was showing more tolerance than she'd been led to expect. And with some relief, she abandoned her attempt to ignore her husband, hoping her father would attribute her quickened breathing to the humour in his words.

"And did you?" she asked, more to prolong the conversation than anything else, but unfortunately, her father shook his head.

"I think not," he said ruefully. "Nathan has no knowledge of me or Marshall. He has no conception of his life before the crash."

"No."

It was the expected response, and because the magnetism was still there, she looked at Nathan again. But now his eyes were guarded, and she guessed that for all his air of inconsequence, the restrictions of his condition were a constant drain.

"I have to admit, Nathan," her father remarked suddenly, "that until we talked, I had had my doubts about your—well—amnesia. I'd never met anyone who'd actually lost their memory before, and it just seemed a—convenient way to—to escape—your problems."

Nathan frowned. "Any problem in particular?" he inquired, his eyes narrowing, and Caitlin saw how Matthew Webster was struggling to find a response. Whatever her father had on his mind, he'd overstepped his brief, and it was left to his assistant to repair the damage.

"What Matthew means is, we're experiencing some confusion over a contract that was placed in Colombia," said Marshall evenly. "I know Matthew was hoping you might be able to help us out." He made a dismissive gesture. "It's not important. I can handle it. It just might take a little longer than we thought."

Nathan stared at him. "This—contract. It was for a job?"

Marshall moved a little uncomfortably, as if he, too, realised he was in danger of saying too much. "For a dam, actually," he conceded with an almost imperceptible shrug towards her father. "As I say, it's not important. We can cope."

Nathan didn't let him off the hook. "A dam," he echoed. "That sounds fairly important to me."

"But not insuperable," Marshall assured him with a thin smile, and Daisy Webster gave an impatient flap of her hand.

"Really, Matt," she said, though Caitlin knew very well her complaint was addressed more accurately to his assistant, "must we discuss business matters morning, noon, and night? It's Saturday, and I shouldn't have to remind you that Nathan has just left hospital. I wasn't happy with you cornering him the minute he came down this morning, and I wish you'd consider other people's feelings sometimes, as well as your own."

"It's all right, Mrs Webster."

Nathan was quick to defend his superior, and Caitlin wondered rather uneasily what had been going on. If Marshall hadn't been around, she might have persuaded her father to take her into his confidence, but in the present circumstances, she didn't stand a chance.

"It's not all right, Nathan." Caitlin remembered her mother used to have quite a soft spot for him years ago. It hadn't been so evident recently. But then, Nathan seldom came to Fairings these days. "And you used to call me Daisy," Mrs Webster added, dimpling almost girlishly. "And you were not invited here to undergo an interrogation. You must forgive Caitlin's father. He thinks of nothing but work."

Nathan smiled, but Caitlin sensed it was a thin veneer, put on for her mother's benefit. "I'm sure—your husband is just frustrated—Daisy," he assured her gently. Then, with a rueful glance at Caitlin, "Have we kept you waiting long?"

Not long enough, thought Caitlin tensely, but her mother had turned to Matthew now and was continuing her tirade. "I suggest you and—your assistant—confine your discussions to the office in future. Caitlin wants to take Nathan for a walk this afternoon, don't you, darling? And she doesn't want to spend the time worrying about what you're going to do when they get back."

Caitlin's jaw dropped, and Nathan, who had obviously still been considering what Marshall and her father had said, now gave her a mocking look. "What a good idea," he said, seizing the opportunity as she'd been afraid he would. "I could do with some exercise. I'm used to working out at least a couple of times a week."

"Working out?"

"Where do you work out?"

Caitlin and her father spoke simultaneously, and Nathan's brow darkened with the effort he was making to answer them. Then, "I don't know," he groaned at last. "I just—feel that's what I used to do." He frowned. "I know I enjoy running, but did I belong to a gym, as well? Surely you can tell me that, Kate."

His diminutive of her name did not go unnoticed, but Caitlin was too busy trying to think of a way of answering him to care what the others might think. And, in the event, her father took the initiative from her.

"You may have belonged to a health club," he conceded, using his own interpretation of the question. "Many of your colleagues do." He exchanged a look with Marshall. "Though I have to say you never mentioned it to me."

"Nor to me," added Marshall with infuriating candour, and Caitlin wondered anew what role he really fulfilled in her father's organisation. After all, he and Nathan had never been friends. Quite the opposite. So why would her father expect him to offer any insight into her husband's life?

Feeling compelled to say something positive, however small, she took a steadying breath. "I'm sure Marshall doesn't—*didn't*—follow Nathan around, Daddy. And you know, I think he did belong to a sports club. I remember him playing squash on occasion."

Nathan gave her a grateful look, but Caitlin didn't want his thanks. She could have added that, as far as she'd been aware—until this week—he'd never enjoyed exercise for its own sake. He had played squash in the early days of their marriage—or said he had anyway—but she suspected it had just been a front for the affair he was having with Lisa Abbott.

And at least her mother welcomed her explanation. "There you are, Matt," she said impatiently. "It's obvious it's only going to be a matter of time before Nathan remembers everything. I suggest you learn a little tolerance. It wouldn't hurt you to feel some sympathy sometimes, instead of always thinking about yourself. You're beginning to allow that damn company to mean more than your own family!"

14

The smell of wood smoke was in the air. Now that the mist had finally dispersed, the sun was clearing away the remaining clouds, and the woods beyond Fairings were displaying all the many colours of autumn. Underfoot, the woodland paths were slippery. It had rained the night before, and the dampness had turned much of the vegetation into mulch. But at the edges of the path, it was still possible to feel the crispness of the fallen leaves, and Mrs Webster's old spaniel, Flora, crunched happily beside them as they walked.

The scent in the woods was quite distinctive. It was an earthy mixture of wood, and foliage, and gentle decay. Where water was dripping from the bare branches, it sounded almost hollow—a haunting evocation of the season, of nature's grief that summer was gone.

Caitlin walked a little ahead of Nathan, ostensibly to show him the way. But, in truth, it was to avoid any intimate conversation. She was seriously wishing the walk was over. Her mother had had no right to force this situation on her, and for all his apparent enthusiasm, she was sure her husband wasn't enjoying the outing, either.

Apart from a casual remark about the weather, Nathan hadn't spoken since they left the house. She was sure he was still concerned about the contract her father and Marshall had mentioned that morning, and for all she had determined not to get involved with him, she guessed it didn't get any easier not knowing who he was. But at the same time, she could appreciate her father's position. If there was some problem for which Nathan had been responsible, his amnesia must be causing some delay. But at least he believed Nathan's condition wasn't fabricated now. Until he'd spoken to her husband himself, he hadn't been convinced.

As for Marshall...

Glancing surreptitiously behind her, she found Nathan bending to pick up a twig to throw for Flora. The spaniel loped away to collect its booty, and Nathan straightened before she could look away.

"Something wrong?" he asked, quirking a dark eyebrow, and Caitlin wished he hadn't caught her watching him. She had no desire for him to think she was even mildly interested in his welfare, and it annoyed her that he could provoke her without any obvious effort.

"No."

Her answer, short and curt, was hardly convincing, but she turned about anyway and advanced along the path. If only she didn't find him so disturbing, she thought uneasily. Why now, when he'd only aroused her revulsion before?

Despite the apparent changes in his behaviour, she was too cynical to believe he'd been transformed by the accident. Characters didn't change; they only revealed different facets. As soon as his memory returned—and with it, all the unpleasant aspects of their history—he'd be just as objectionable as before.

Yet...

"Why don't I believe you?"

Once again, the warmth of his breath on her neck alerted her to the fact that he had closed the space between them. While she had been pondering the inconsistencies of human nature, Nathan had quickened his stride and was now immediately behind her on the path. The solid strength of his body was providing a welcome shield to the breeze that curled a little chillingly through the bare branches, and her skin tingled in anticipation of the threat his nearness evoked.

"Because you enjoy creating problems?" she suggested crisply, determined not to be intimidated by his mood. She schooled her features into neutrality before casting a careless look over her shoulder. "Are you sure this isn't too tiring for you? We can go back."

"And miss seeing the view from the top of the hill?" he countered innocently, and Caitlin couldn't be sure if he was making fun of her or not. It was true. The woods did slope up towards the distant plateau, and Mrs Webster had mentioned the panorama of three counties, which could be seen from the top of Keeper's Hill.

"It's not compulsory," Caitlin said now, aware that her father's old parka had never suited him so well. Once, she would have said that Nathan in anything other than his expensive designer suits would look totally out of place. But suddenly, the shabby purple jacket gave him a ruggedness she'd never noticed before.

"Aren't you enjoying the walk?" he asked, continuing his deliberate appeal to her sympathies, and her gloved hands curled into fists. "I am," he added, coming abreast of her on the path and slinging an arm across her shoulders. "These woods remind me of the woods back home."

"Back home?" Caitlin was too shocked by his words to displace the unwelcome familiarity of his arm.

"Yeah, back home," he repeated, his expression vaguely ironic. "But don't ask me where that is, 'cause I don't know."

Caitlin's breath escaped on a sound of aggravation. "Are you sure you don't say these things deliberately?" she demanded. "You must have known how that would sound to me. Or are you really so naïve you don't even think of it? I should be careful if I were you. People might get suspicious."

Nathan's lips tightened. "Are you?"

"Am I what?"

"Suspicious." He paused. "I'd like to know what you think I have to gain." His eyes dipped to her mouth, and she felt an inward shiver. "I thought you were on my side, but I guess I was wrong."

"Oh, don't be silly." Caitlin's response was coloured as much by her own unwilling attraction to him as by any sudden confidence in his cause. "I just don't want—anyone—thinking you're making a fool of them. And—and these sudden spurts of memory don't even make sense."

"Anyone?" Nathan's mouth twisted. "I guess you mean your father, don't you? And that robot clone, O'Brien. What's he to you?"

"To me?" Caitlin was astounded. "Marshall means nothing to me. He's just Daddy's assistant, that's all."

"Mmm."

Nathan was thoughtful, and in his present mood, Caitlin didn't like to draw away. Yet the weight of his arm was absurdly physical, and she stood there stiffly, waiting for him to go on.

"I thought his attitude towards your father was—well, rather familiar," he said at last. "Has he been his assistant for long?"

"No." Caitlin didn't like his inference, and this time she didn't hesitate about putting some distance between them, and his arm fell to his side. "I don't know what you're implying. But you never liked him, so I suppose I can't expect anything else."

"I didn't?" Nathan's grimace was mildly humorous as he ambled after her. "So I haven't changed that much, wouldn't you say? I can't honestly say I disliked the guy, but he does appear to call the shots. If I didn't know better, I'd say he was in charge."

"That's ridiculous!"

Caitlin's response was predictable, but it was unnerving to hear her husband echoing her own doubts. If she and Nathan had talked more in the past, might they have reached an understanding? she wondered. But, no. Nathan had never been so approachable before.

Or so dangerous...

"Anyway," she went on, changing the subject, "you have to admit it's odd how you keep getting these flashes of memory."

"Yeah, right." Nathan gave her a wry look. "But I don't know any more about it than you do. I wish I did. How do I know if it's a real memory or just something I once read in a book?"

Caitlin shrugged. Again, she could feel herself responding to the weight of his frustration, and because she didn't want him to know it, she hurried on. It wasn't her problem, she told herself repeatedly. He'd deceived her too often in the past to expect her to support him now.

"You don't believe me, do you?"

He'd caught up with her again, and she felt the disturbing twinge of sensuality in her bones. "It's not that," she said. "I'm simply trying to make some sense of what you've told me. It doesn't achieve anything to keep going round in circles. I'm just trying to help you, that's all."

"Tell me about it." There was anger in his voice now, and she realised he'd completely misread her mood. "It's a pity you didn't think of that this morning. When I tried to make love to you, you were shaking in your shoes. Okay, before you say it, you weren't wearing shoes at that moment. But what kind of a marriage do we have, Kate? Tell me, have I ever raped you in the past?"

"No." Caitlin's breath caught in her throat. "I never said—oh, you're exaggerating—"

"Am I?" His ungloved hand fastened about her upper arm. "So what is it? Why are you so afraid of me? Dammit, I'm not some monster, am I? Can't you see I need to know?"

Caitlin could feel the heat of those hard fingers clear through the fine wool of her sleeve. There was frustration in his grasp, yes, but also an unknowing feeling of possession. Whether he was aware of it or not, he was demonstrating how powerless she could be.

She shivered in spite of the warmth of her long duster. She had wrapped the thick coat about her in an effort to augment her almost amorphous attire. She hadn't wanted him to think she was doing anything to provoke his interest, unaware that its dusky folds accentuated the pure clarity of her face.

"No," she said again, forcing herself to stay still within his grasp. As she turned her head to look at him, strands of honey-blonde hair caught against her black velvet collar, and she realised when she saw his gaze move to them that any wrong move on her part could precipitate a crisis. "Of course I'm not—afraid of you," she added. *Afraid of herself, maybe.* "But you are—unfamiliar. If you'd let me get to know you, it would help."

"Get to know me?" His eyes, dark and impenetrable, moved over her pale face. "How the hell am I supposed to let you do that if you won't give me a chance?" His thumb moved against her sleeve in a circling motion. "Help me, Kate. You're the only one who can."

"I will." But Caitlin's heart was in her throat, and although she was trying to steel herself against him, she could feel his heat invading her, melting her resistance, destroying her reserve. "Look," she appended hastily, "this isn't the place to have this kind of discussion. You're cold. I'm cold. I think we should turn back."

"You don't feel cold to me," said Nathan, his voice softer now, gentler, imitating the sensuality she could see in his eyes. Oh, God, she thought, how would she feel if he kissed her? How far was she going to allow this to go?

His breath fanned her cheek, warm and pleasantly flavoured with the coffee he had drunk after lunch, and it was becoming increasingly difficult to appear unaffected by his nearness. The Nathan she remembered had usually smelt of alcohol, and she struggled to keep that thought foremost in her mind.

The sound of Flora, scuffling through the leaves at their feet, was a welcome distraction. Glancing down at the dog, she said, "Look, even Flora's ready to go home."

"I'm not," said Nathan, startling her, and lifting his free hand, he brushed back the silky curtain of her hair. "This is my home," he added simply, and cupping his hand round her neck, he brought her lips to his.

Weakness, hot and debilitating, flooded over her. His mouth on hers had a sweetness it had never had before. The fear he'd once evoked was absent. She felt dizzy, but it was a pleasant sensation, as his moist tongue learned the contours of her mouth.

And because she was curious to find out what he intended, she let him prolong that intimate invasion. After all, she told herself, in the tiny corner of her brain that was still functioning, she had nothing to fear from him here. With the damp leaves beneath their feet, and the mist slowly reappearing, it was hardly an ideal situation. He could surely not attempt a seduction in the woods.

She was wrong.

As the kiss lengthened and deepened, she knew she'd made another miscalculation. Before she could even drag her gloved hands out of her pockets, he had backed her against the tree behind her and imprisoned her within the barrier of his hands. His mouth possessed hers; there was no other way to describe it. His warmth, his weight, his whole body threatened her very existence.

Yet, in all honesty, it was not a threat that alarmed her. For all she still offered some resistance, her senses were imploring her to give in. Almost against her will, her body was responding to the muscled power she sensed he was still controlling, and deep in her stomach a flame began to burn.

The memory of how he had treated her on their honeymoon returned to taunt her. But the fears she had had of him then no longer seemed to apply. As crazy as it was, she sensed he wouldn't hurt her. Had time—and his relationship with Lisa Abbott—taught him constraint?

She didn't know; she didn't care. She particularly didn't want to think of the woman who had to take some of the blame for Nathan's behaviour.

His lips were devouring hers now, eating away at any opposition she might make. His tongue, wet and forceful, was filling her mouth with the taste of him, almost stopping her breathing. Her head was swimming as she was mindlessly caught in the web of his fascination. He was consuming her, and she was rapidly losing the will to care.

He kissed her nose, the delicate curve of her cheek, her eyelids; they fluttered closed beneath the sensuous touch of his caress. Now he filled her senses as well as her vision, and as if aware of her crumbling defences, he allowed his heavy body to rest on hers.

Caitlin felt as if they were moulded together. She couldn't think, she couldn't act, she could only feel. Her whole being was suffused with a wholly unfamiliar hunger. His muttered words—sensuous, sensual, sometimes even erotic words—only added to the unreality of his embrace.

And part of that unreality was the knowledge that Nathan had never made love to her as he was doing now. Even in the earliest days of their relationship, when she had foolishly believed he respected her, he had never kissed her in such a sensuous way. She had never felt this tingling, this awareness, this anticipation of what might come after. She'd always wanted to pull away before they got that far.

But nothing could prevent the wild delight she was experiencing at this moment. Awakening feelings she'd never even known she possessed. With the growing pressure of Nathan's arousal against her stomach, she was incapable of coherent reasoning. And when he wedged his leg between her thighs, she had no fear.

His mouth found hers again, teasing and biting at her lower lip, sucking the tip of her tongue into his mouth. With every sensual touch of his lips, he was inciting her desire, and tearing off her gloves, she cupped his face.

His response was to pull one of her hands against his mouth and press a moist kiss into her palm. She felt as if she could feel that urgent caress through every nerve of her being, and when he licked the dampness from her palm, she felt a matching dampness pooling between her legs.

Did he know how she was feeling? she wondered anxiously. Could she feel the heat that throbbed against his thigh? Did he know how much she wanted to rub herself against him? To ease her aching need against his leg?

"Do it," he said against the hollow of her ear, and for a shattering moment she thought he had read her mind.

"Do what?" she asked, dry-mouthed, and he used the moment to draw the sides of her coat apart and fill his hands with the swollen fullness of her breasts.

"Touch me," he breathed, and when she hesitated, he took her hands and drew them to his groin.

He pressed her quivering fingers along the hard shaft that strained his zip, and then left them there while he opened her woollen jacket to continue his exploration of her body. Beneath the bodysuit she was wearing, she could feel her own arousal, and the abrasion of his palms caused the tender buds of her nipples to thrust against his hands.

The sensation caused a sharp pain of longing to spiral down into her thighs. It was impossible not to be aware of what he was doing to her, and where before she had been an unwilling spectator, now she was a willing participant. Almost without her volition, her hands moved to his buckle. She wanted to touch him; she wanted to wrap her hands around him, and his sudden intake of breath proved that he wanted it, too.

And then Flora barked.

The spaniel had evidently detected the presence of someone else in the woods, and Caitlin barely had time to drag her coat about her before Ted Follett and his two retrievers came strolling out of the trees. Flora's barking increased in volume as she went to investigate the intruders, and Caitlin took advantage of the dogs' frenzied reunion to slide out from between Nathan and the tree.

She probably wouldn't have been able to escape so easily if Nathan hadn't taken rather longer than she did to pull himself together. As it was, she noticed rather worriedly that he slumped weakly against the trunk when she pulled away. But his groan of frustration seemed to reassure the elderly gardener. He evidently thought the walk had tired him out.

"I say," he exclaimed, ignoring the dogs in his haste to offer his assistance, "is Mr Wolfe all right? If you need any help to get him back to the house, just say, Mrs Wolfe. It's pretty chilly at the moment, and Mrs Goddard was just telling me your husband wasn't even well enough to come down to supper yesterday evening."

"I'm fine."

As if he was resentful of the other man talking to her about him as if he couldn't answer for himself, Nathan turned and braced himself against the tree. He didn't look fine, Caitlin thought guiltily. In fact, he looked exhausted. But he forced a smile to reinforce his claim.

"Thanks for the offer," he added, directing his remark to Ted Follett. "But perhaps you're right. I think I have had enough." His eyes were guarded as they flickered over Caitlin. "However, I'm sure my wife can manage. We'll have to miss out on the view for today, Kate. Come on. I'm ready to go back to the house."

15

Supper that evening was a fairly formal affair.

There were six of them at the table: Matthew and Daisy Webster, Marshall O'Brien, himself and Caitlin, and Nancy Kendall, a young schoolteacher from the village, invited, he was sure, to even the numbers.

Or to keep Marshall from monopolising Matthew's attention, he pondered, still sure there was something not quite right about their relationship, no matter what Caitlin said. The conclusion might have been obvious, but for all his doubts, they didn't act like lovers. But they sure as hell didn't act like employer and employee.

Then there was Mrs Webster's attitude towards Marshall to consider. It was apparent she had no love for the young man. Yet, if that was so, what was he doing here? Surely she had the right to say who came into her house.

It was curious, he reflected, that he should feel so certain about some things, and yet totally unsure about something else. He had the feeling Daisy Webster was not unaware of the connection between her husband and Marshall, but did she know what it really was?

Caitlin didn't, he decided, thoughts of his wife too easily conjuring up memories of the afternoon. It was ironic that what had happened between them in the past should have vanished so completely, yet every new encounter was emblazoned on his mind.

And on his loins, he appended dourly, remembering how he'd felt when Flora had warned them of the gardener's approach. It didn't really surprise him that since they'd gotten back Caitlin had done her best to avoid him. Her response had blown her previous complaint of needing to get to know him again to ribbons.

She'd wanted him; he was sure of it. And if Ted Follett hadn't come blundering out of the woods, God alone knew what might have happened. He could still feel her soft fingers fumbling with his belt, and his reaction to that was better left unseen.

He was glad he was sitting at the table, glad that the lower half of his body was safely hidden by the heavy damask cloth. He could torment himself by watching her, by anticipating what would eventually happen; for whatever she said—or did—he was going to have his way.

He'd never imagined it would turn out the way it had after their altercation this morning. When she'd awakened to find him making love to her, she'd almost convinced him he disgusted her as much as she said. She hadn't wanted to touch him then—or if she had, she'd hidden it very successfully. When she'd discovered how he'd loosened his trousers, she'd practically jackknifed out of the bed.

Still, he mused, it was her own fault for wrapping herself up like a mummy. Had she really thought that ugly nightgown would put him off? But he'd never yet had to force himself on a woman. Which was another little certainty he couldn't explain.

This afternoon, though, he'd had to revise his opinion of her reasons for acting the way she had. If it didn't sound so unlikely, he'd say she was only pretending she didn't care about him. Perhaps the stranger she feared most was herself.

It was all very Freudian, and he suspected he didn't know everything that was going on. But the memory of how she'd made him feel was totally believable, and he couldn't wait for an opportunity to rekindle the fire.

Yet, glancing at her now as she spoke to Marshall, he wondered if it would prove as easy as he hoped. In spite of the way she had responded, in spite of the way she had yielded to him, arching herself against him, tonight she'd resumed that almost-untouchable pose.

Whatever had happened in the woods, he'd be a fool if he didn't realise that she would just as soon forget it. Just because he'd broken down the barriers once was no reason to believe he could break them down again. In fact, because of what had happened, she'd be that much more on her guard against him. He may have been proved victorious in a skirmish, but the real battle was still to be won.

Her mother had seated her daughter diagonally across from him at the table, and so far she'd barely glanced his way. When she wasn't eating, or talking to Marshall or her father, she was hiding behind her wineglass. And for all she appeared to be at ease, he sensed she wasn't enjoying it at all.

His lips twisted at the memory of waking and finding her already dressed for supper. When they got back from the walk, he'd needed no persuasion to take a rest, and he'd been unconscious for a couple of hours. Evidently, he'd used up what small amount of stamina he'd accumulated. But whether it was the walk—or his tortured emotions—that had exhausted him, he didn't know.

Anyway, by the time he lifted his head from the pillow, she'd been dressed in the ivory silk jersey tunic she was wearing this evening. He guessed she'd arranged it that way, making sure she didn't disturb him until she was safely ready to go downstairs. Her excuse, that he had needed the rest, was one with which he couldn't argue. Though he'd promised himself he wouldn't be quite such a pushover again.

And there was no doubt that in one way Follett's intervention that afternoon had proved beneficial. He had been frozen, and his legs had felt like jelly by the time he got back to the house. It would have been embarrassing if he hadn't been able to finish what his raging hormones had started. It was easy to be confident after the event.

And, after all, the doctor had told him it would take him some time to recover completely. Apparently, shock could do that to you. Shock, and the blow he'd taken to his head. Just because there was nothing to see, the damage was no less debilitating. He was still considered convalescent, but if he was patient, he'd eventually recover his strength.

And his memory...

But he didn't want to think about that, and there was no doubt his weakness had proved beneficial to his wife. He'd given her the perfect chance to regain her composure and that annoying air of vulnerability that she wore around her like a shield.

He wondered what she'd been doing while he was sleeping. Socialising with Marshall? He found he didn't like that idea at all. And she certainly seemed to be getting on well with him this evening. He'd noticed her mother kept giving them a thoughtful look.

As for Matthew Webster, he guessed the events of the day had tired him, too. What had Caitlin said? That he wasn't supposed to suffer any stress? Well, that was a joke, if this morning's interview was anything to go by. Despite the fact that O'Brien had asked most of the questions, the older man was still the guiding force.

"Mrs Goddard is a marvellous cook, isn't she?"

Beside him, the young schoolteacher had evidently decided he'd been silent long enough. And although he wasn't really in the mood to indulge in pleasantries, it would have been rude not to acknowledge her words.

"Are you an expert, Miss Kendall?" he inquired, and was gratified to see his smile had found its mark. It was a relief to find that she welcomed his attention. After the way Caitlin behaved, he was getting quite a complex where his amnesia was concerned.

"Who, me?" she exclaimed now, her eyes full of humour. "Heavens, no. I've been known to burn water. But I do appreciate good food. Particularly Mrs Goddard's. I've tasted the cakes she sometimes makes for the church's coffee mornings. They're sold out in no time, believe me. And they're delicious."

"Oh, I see." He pulled a wry face. "So I suppose you couldn't resist an invitation to Fairings. Even if you've been stuck with the oddball of the bunch."

Nancy Kendall looked surprised. "The oddball?" she echoed, a trace of embarrassment staining her cheeks. "I don't think I understand what you mean."

"Oh, I'm sure you do," he replied feelingly, and then realised he was using her to expunge the frustration he felt towards Caitlin. "At least, you should. You must have heard what's been going on."

Nancy frowned. "What has been going on?"

He gave her a bleak look. "Don't tell me you don't know about my condition."

"Well, I know you were on that plane that crashed on take-off in New York." Nancy shrugged. "I heard that you weren't seriously injured. But that you've had some temporary loss of memory since it happened."

His smile was ironic now. "Some temporary loss of memory." He repeated her words. "You make it sound almost normal."

"Well, it's not uncommon, is it?" she exclaimed. "And the accident must have been a terrible shock to your system. I once went over the handlebars of my bike, and I couldn't even remember where I lived for about an hour. I know that isn't really comparable, but it shows that sort of thing can happen. You just have to be patient."

His smile widened. "Is that so?" he said mockingly. "All I have to do is get on with my life, and my memory will come back?"

"Well, it's better than feeling sorry for yourself, isn't it?" she countered. "At least you're not paralysed, or anything like that."

"No." He nodded. "You know, you've made me feel a whole lot better. The amnesia is only temporary. I've got to remember that." He grimaced. "It's just going to take a little time. I guess I'm not a freak after all."

"Who said you were?" Nancy was horrified, but he found he couldn't blame anyone else for that. It was his own hypersensitivity to any criticism that was really the problem. And Caitlin's unwillingness to share her fears with him.

"I guess I did," he said now, as the maid Mrs Goddard had hired for the evening came to clear their soup plates away, and Nancy relaxed as she realised he had made a joke.

"So long as I haven't upset you," she murmured. "I'm not always the most tactful person around."

"On the contrary." He was finding it was easy to talk to her. It was a relief to speak to someone who didn't have a stake in him getting well. "As a matter of fact, I'm very glad you came."

Nancy smiled, and aware that they were attracting his wife's attention now, he deliberately sought a way to prolong the conversation. "Tell me," he said, "how long have you known the Websters?"

"Not long." Nancy pulled a face. "And I don't know them that well, really. But I run the junior Scout pack in the village, and Mrs Webster is a patron of the church."

"Ah." He nodded. "Is—Mrs Webster involved with the Scouts, too?"

"Oh, no." Nancy shook her head. "She just lets us hold our jamborees in the grounds here at Fairings. And fêtes, too—to raise money for the church."

"I see." He paused. "So I suppose you're quite a regular visitor here."

"Oh, I wouldn't say that." She was appealingly candid. "I've never been invited to supper before."

Which meant his earlier supposition was probably correct. She had been invited to even the numbers. It seemed Matthew Webster would go to great lengths to make his "assistant" feel at home.

But why?

The solution when it came was so obvious, he was amazed he hadn't thought of it before. And he knew in some distant corner of his mind that he wasn't yet privy to, he had encountered such a situation in the past. He didn't know what the situation was, or how it might connect with himself. But he was firmly convinced he'd hit the jackpot. Marshall wasn't just Matthew Webster's assistant. He was his *son*!

But not his legitimate son, he guessed, or surely Caitlin would have mentioned it. Which begged the obvious question: did she know about it? His guess was that she didn't. But Mrs Webster—she was a different matter. Judging by the way she'd treated Marshall earlier, he was fairly sure she wasn't in the dark.

He shook his head a little ruefully. No wonder he'd felt so tense when they'd been giving him the third degree that morning. He'd been convinced then that there was more to their relationship, but he'd been following a different train of thought. Now, however, he was stunned by the resemblances between them. If Marshall hadn't always worn his glasses, surely Caitlin would have noticed, as well.

"Does your doctor have any idea how long the amnesia is likely to last?" Nancy asked suddenly, diverting him, and he forced himself to offer a reply.

"Not as far as I know," he said. "It's one of those imponderables. As a matter of fact, Caitlin's father has made arrangements for me to see another specialist next week."

Nancy nodded, and then the maid's reappearance with the main course prevented her from going on. A delicious rack of lamb was on offer, along with a selection of vegetables, but because he was more used to hospital fare, he took very little.

Caitlin was still watching them, he noticed. It was a surreptitious appraisal, interspersed with the conversation she was having with Marshall, but vaguely hostile just the same. He guessed she was wondering what he was saying to Nancy. If it wasn't so absurd, he'd have said she was jealous.

"It must be frustrating," his companion added, after the maid had passed along the table, and he acknowledged that that emotion was his constant tribulation.

"It would be nice if I could remember my own family," he conceded. "Until then, I'll just blunder on, I suppose."

"Well, if you ever need someone to talk to, I hope you won't hesitate to call on me," she averred firmly, and to his astonishment, she placed her hand on top of his as it rested beside his plate. She squeezed his knuckles as he looked at her disbelievingly. "I mean it, Nathan. I'd be happy to be of help."

He sucked in his breath. "Thanks," he said, but as soon as he was able, he drew his hand away from that intimate clasp. It appeared that Nancy Kendall was not as shy—or as innocent—as he'd imagined. And, although there was nothing in her eyes to alter his original opinion of her, he sensed she felt some justification for her behaviour.

But what? For God's sake, he thought impatiently, he'd thought she was talking as his friend. But now it appeared she'd received entirely different signals. And she wasn't averse to taking advantage of her chance.

As well as angering him, it also resurrected all his earlier fears about himself and the kind of man he really was. Was this why Caitlin refused to let him near her? Was he the kind of guy who came on to every available female in sight?

He couldn't believe it. He wouldn't believe it. He had never been that interested in the opposite sex. Oh, he liked women, and there was no doubt about his sexuality. But he wasn't the kind of man who'd cheat on his wife.

Or would he . . . ?

Although he made an effort to enjoy the meal, he hardly tasted the meat or the mouth-watering fruit compote that followed. His efforts to avoid any further embarrassing incidents were giving him a headache, and he couldn't wait for supper to be over so he could leave the table. If Nancy thought he was being rude, he didn't care.

Coffee was served in the drawing room. It was another area of the house he wasn't yet acquainted with—or was it reacquainted? he wondered broodingly. At any rate, it was new to him. In an effort to distract his thoughts, he tried to find some point of recognition. But nothing would stimulate his absent brain.

It was a beautiful room. He didn't need any spurt of memory to acknowledge that reality. With delicately striped walls, a veined marble mantel, and an enormous Chinese carpet covering the polished floor, it couldn't help but elicit some response. The appointments had obviously been chosen with care and elegant simplicity, but it was no more familiar than anything else had been.

Still, at least since leaving the table, he'd been able to avoid any further involvement with Nancy Kendall. Declining her invitation to join her on one of a pair of matching Regency sofas, he had taken up a position by the hearth, where a real log fire crackled in the grate. The warmth was welcome, too, helping to thaw the anxious core of nerves inside him. And, as he stared into the leaping flames, he felt a faint glimmer of perception stir his mood.

The phone rang at that moment, shattering any trace of recognition he had nurtured. And Caitlin, who had just entered the room behind her father, said, "I'll get it," and disappeared along the hall.

"If it's for me, tell whoever it is I'll get back to them later," called Matthew Webster diplomatically, taking note of his wife's expression. He offered an apologetic grimace. "People always ring at the most inconvenient times."

"Your friends do, certainly," agreed his wife crisply, seating herself beside the low table where Mrs Goddard had set the coffee tray. She looked across at the young schoolteacher. "Cream and sugar for you, Nancy?"

Mrs Webster was serving Marshall when Caitlin returned, but although she arched a quizzical brow at her daughter, the younger woman barely spared her mother a glance. "It's for you," she said, directing her attention to her husband. "You can take it in the study," she added coldly. Then, without waiting for his response, she went to collect her cup from the tray.

"For me?"

He knew his voice shook a little, and he could feel the sudden wave of curiosity that swept the room. Christ, he thought sickly, who could be calling him here? And what had he done to deserve those hostile looks?

Caitlin nodded, looking at him over the rim of her cup with narrowed eyes. "For you," she repeated, without enlarging on the statement. And because they were all waiting for him to go and answer the call, he set his own coffee cup down.

He wanted to ask who it was that was calling him, but his pride forbade an inquiry of that sort. In any case, as soon as he left the room, Caitlin would probably tell them. And it wasn't as if he wasn't eager to hear a friendly voice.

With a murmur of apology to Mrs Webster, he walked somewhat stiffly across the room. He wouldn't give Caitlin the satisfaction of asking why she looked so scornful. And at least he knew where the study was.

The room looked slightly less intimidating in the lamplight. That morning, it had had a decidedly businesslike air. Or perhaps it was just the questions Matthew Webster and his cohort had levelled at him that had made him feel so uncomfortable. Although he'd answered them as honestly as he could, it was obvious he hadn't been of any help.

His hand shook as he reached for the phone. Despite the fact that he kept telling himself that he must have friends in England, he pulled his hand back once, feeling his fingers curling into a fist. But he couldn't hang up, not without finding out who was calling. Drying his damp palm against his thigh, he finally forced himself to lift the receiver off the desk.

"Hello?"

His throat was dry, and the word came out barely audibly. But whoever it was seemed to recognise his voice. "Nathan?" someone said. "Is that you, Nathan?"

Ridiculously, his first reaction was to deny it. The name sounded more unfamiliar than ever. Nathan? he thought. Was that really his name? Nathan. Dear God, it should mean something—but it didn't.

But he had to answer, and acknowledging the fact that it was a woman's voice, he said carefully, "Who is this? Do I know you?"

"Do you know me?" Her shrill response warned him she knew nothing of his loss of memory. "Quit shitting me, Nathan. I don't know what game you think you're playing. I've been waiting for you to call me. Where have you been?"

"Where have I been?"

He was stunned by the accusation, and as if realising she had been a little unfeeling, she moderated her tone. "I know, I know," she said. "You've been in the hospital. But, dammit, you must have known how I'd be feeling when I heard about the crash."

"Well, I—"

His uncertainty was evident, and before he could even begin to explain what had happened and ask her her name, she drew a breath. "Oh, I get it," she said. "There's someone there with you. Is it your wife?" She paused, but not long enough for him to make a denial, before continuing, "I didn't mean to make things difficult for you. But I was getting desperate. Ring me. Ring me tomorrow. You know where I'll be."

16

He hadn't expected to find Caitlin in the bedroom when he finally found his way upstairs.

Since the embarrassing incident of the phone call, she hadn't even spoken to him, and he was well aware she hadn't believed him when he'd told the others he didn't know who the caller was. Of course, no one had actually asked him. It had been left to him to explain. And he'd done so to the best of his ability, hoping the Websters might know the woman's identity.

But no one had professed to have any knowledge of her at all. Although, judging from his wife's expression, he suspected she was not deceived. It was obvious she thought the woman was his mistress. Who else would have the nerve to ask for him after his wife had answered the phone?

Which could explain Caitlin's attitude towards him. If— however unlikely it seemed at the moment—he did have a mistress, then their marriage was probably on the rocks. Yet her parents had invited him here, so they apparently knew nothing about it. And Caitlin was still living with him, whatever he had done.

Nevertheless, the call had ruined the remains of a fairly unsatisfactory evening, and he couldn't help feeling slightly resentful at the thought. His feelings towards the woman, whoever she was, were decidedly unfriendly, however, and he wondered if all amnesiacs suffered such a lack of self-respect.

Caitlin was standing by the window.

She had said she was going up to bed earlier, straight after Nancy Kendall had left, and he had not anticipated that he would find her here. On the contrary, after what had happened, he'd been quite prepared to find that her belongings had been removed. Even before that call this evening, she hadn't trusted him.

He had shared a rather strained glass of brandy with her father and Marshall after both the women had gone to bed. They'd apparently suspended hostilities—at least until the morning—but he'd been glad when he could plead tiredness and escape.

It had been an exhausting day—in more ways than one—and finding his wife waiting for him wasn't exactly to his taste. In other circumstances, of course, that would not have been his reaction, but he doubted her intentions were charitable.

However, if she was expecting an explanation, she was going to be disappointed. He simply didn't have one to give. Somehow the woman had known this number. For some reason, she'd expected him to ring her. But whatever Caitlin believed, she meant nothing to him.

Caitlin turned when she heard the door open, and he saw she was still dressed in the slim-fitting tunic she'd worn for supper. It was short—its hem ended a good two inches above her shapely knees—with a modestly scooped neckline and long sleeves. The ivory silk jersey hugged her upper body before flaring into a wealth of pleats from the hip. It was simple, yet effective; unpretentious, yet stylishly elegant, and was not designed to keep his blood pressure at rest. But her expression wasn't sexy; it was downright disapproving, and he wished she'd saved her resentment for the morning.

Still, there was no reason why their conversation should be overheard by the rest of the household, and closing the door, he leant back against the panels. He felt incredibly weary, and his head was swimming slightly, due no doubt to all the alcohol he'd consumed.

"Are you all right?"

Her first words disconcerted him. He'd been expecting an accusation from her, or worse. To discover she was apparently concerned about him didn't fit the image. He didn't want her pity, whatever she might think.

"I'm tired," he replied at last, relieved to hear he sounded less muddled than he felt. He flexed his spine experimentally, wondering if it would continue to support him. Then, evenly, "I thought you'd gone to bed."

"Not yet."

Her response was unnecessary in the circumstances, but he guessed it gave her time to think. He wished he knew why she'd chosen to wait up for him. To inform him she was sleeping someplace else?

"You don't look very steady," she observed, and he wondered if she was enjoying his confusion. "You shouldn't have drunk so much wine at supper. I'm not sure you should be drinking alcohol at all."

He expelled his breath on a sigh. "Is this what you've waited up to tell me?" he asked. "Your concern is duly noted, if not appreciated at this time." His lips twisted. "You know, I was expecting a verbal lashing. Or perhaps a continuation of the icy silence you treated me to downstairs."

Her lips tightened. "What did you expect?"

"I make it a point not to expect anything," he countered, regarding her with a weary contempt. "And whatever you say, I know this isn't a friendly visit. So why don't you tell me what you really want?"

Caitlin drew in her breath. "I don't know what you mean."

"Yes, you do." He loosened the top button of his grey silk shirt and pulled his tie away from his collar with a heavy hand. "I know it's not going to help to repeat the fact that I don't know who the hell she is. You were in a black mood before she phoned."

"I was not in a black mood," she contradicted him angrily. "You can't possibly know what kind of mood I was in when you slept until it was time to go down for supper. And this evening, you've done your best to humiliate me. Tell me, what did you think you were doing, holding hands with the pushy woman from the village?"

"We were not holding hands." He was annoyed now. "For Christ's sake, what was I supposed to do? The woman was coming on to me, dammit. You should get your facts straight before you start throwing accusations like that around."

"Coming on to you?" Caitlin was flushed. "I'm not surprised. After you'd spent practically the whole meal flirting with her. At least—" she paused "—until your— mistress—interrupted you."

"My mistress?" He frowned. "How do you know who she was? Did she tell you?"

"No." Caitlin had the grace to colour. "But who else would ring you here. My God, I don't know how she had the nerve to do it. You gave her the number, I suppose."

He shrugged. He could do without this, but it was obvious Caitlin was spoiling for a fight. "I must have, I suppose," he said wearily. "Do you have any proof to substantiate your claim?"

Caitlin gasped. "Why should I offer you proof? My God, you used to have the decency—or should I say the good sense?—to keep your conquests out of my father's house. If you expect me to tell you about the way you've humiliated me, forget it." She snorted. "I think you've lost your mind as well as your memory!"

He came up off the door with an aggressive lurch. "Take that back."

"No. Why should I?" Caitlin was unrepentant. "Why should I let you make a fool of me again? I have some rights, you know."

"And so do I," he snarled, coming to a halt in front of her. "I'll say it again. I don't know who the woman who called me is. You maintain that she's my mistress. But what I want to know is--how do you know?"

Caitlin's features froze. "I'd rather not discuss it."

"I'll bet you wouldn't. There are too many unanswered questions that you're desperate to avoid. If she is—*was*—my mistress, and the jury's still out on that one, then tell me why I needed another woman if I was happy with my wife?"

Caitlin turned her head away. "I don't know."

"Don't you?" He didn't believe her, but the effort of continuing the argument was sapping what little strength he had. "It couldn't be because my dear wife was looking somewhere else as well."

"No."

Her denial was almost believable, but it did nothing to reassure him. "Well," he said heavily, "I'm going to find out why, sweetheart. That's one thing about which you don't need to have any doubts."

Caitlin's lips twitched. "Don't call me sweetheart."

"Why not?"

"Because I don't like it."

"Like you don't like me?" he suggested. "Or like you don't like sex? Like you didn't like me touching you in the woods, when we both know that was a lie, as well?"

Caitlin caught her breath. "I've told you, I don't want to talk about—personal—things tonight." She fixed her gaze at some point beyond his shoulder, as if she was afraid to meet his gaze. "I'm sure you should sit down. You're swaying on your feet."

"Don't pretend you care." His voice was harsh and frustrated. "If it was left to you, I wouldn't be here at all."

"That's not true."

"So help me," he said heavily, leaning to rest his forearms on her shoulders. "If you really don't despise me, why don't you act like a wife for a change?"

His weight caused her shoulders to dip slightly, but it was his words that had caught her attention. "I am acting like a wife," she protested. "If I wasn't, I'd have thrown you out. Now why don't you sit down on the bed before we both end up on the floor?"

His lips twisted. "Y'know, that doesn't sound half bad," he told her huskily, and he saw the wary look that entered her eyes at his words. "But I agree with you, the bed does sound more inviting. Are you going to tuck me in?"

Caitlin would have pulled away then, but finding a strength he'd hardly known he possessed, he fastened his hands on the slim bones that had held his weight. Then, ignoring her resistance, he bent his head to hers, and his mouth found the sweet temptation of her lips.

Desire, hot and strong, revived his flailing senses. Like a man who'd lost all hope of redemption, he found a fiery sustenance in the kiss. Her mouth was soft and gentle, and hopelessly unprepared, but her response promised all the nourishment he craved.

Her bones felt so fragile beneath his hands, but when he gathered her close, her body possessed an unexpected strength. Her hands, caught between them, were balled like fists against his chest, and for all her mouth was vulnerable, she seemed determined to escape a closer embrace.

But the taste of her was heaven, and the feel of her slim body brushing his stirred him like no other woman could have done. He wanted her, he acknowledged; he wanted her so badly it almost hurt. He couldn't think of anything he wanted more.

She had kept her lips tightly clenched at first, but the necessity of breathing was her undoing. When her lips parted to gulp some air, his tongue brushed past her teeth, and his head swam with the honeyed taste of her hot mouth.

With a groan, his hands slid over her shoulders and down to the delicate hollow of her spine. The fabric of her dress was no softer than her skin beneath his caressing fingers, and her narrow hips shook slightly as he cupped her rounded bottom.

He was shaking, too, so badly that he was sure she must he able to feel it, but he was half-afraid he'd lose the initiative if he gave in. And the softness of her stomach, and the slender legs beneath her skirt, were a delight he'd waited for too long to share.

"Kiss me," he ordered thickly. "Kiss me, and then tell me we don't feel anything for one another any more." He caught her chin in one hand and tipped her face up to his. "Look at me, and deny you want this, too."

Caitlin tilted her head as if trying to remove her chin from his grasp, but the effort was too much for her, and her nervous gaze swept anxiously over his face. Her eyes were dark and troubled, but there was a certain softness in them, too, and her fingers stretched and flexed against his chest.

He could feel his own arousal pushing hard against her stomach, and he cursed himself for his obvious lack of control. It was not the way to play it; he didn't want her to think it was just sex. His feelings were much more complex than that.

But then, as if giving in to some need inside herself, he felt her hands sliding up his shirt. She looped a finger in the buttonhole he had unfastened earlier, and then reaching up, she brushed his mouth with her tongue.

It was sweet, and it was sensuous, and it almost brought him to his knees. When her small teeth bit his tongue, and her mouth shaped itself to his startled lips, he could only draw her closer, and he found to his delight that she no longer pulled away.

"Christ!"

His response now was swift and satisfying. As his mouth covered her face with hot, hungry kisses, his arousal found its home in the cradle of her hips. Feeling himself against her inspired an almost painful pleasure, and his need became an all-consuming flame.

For the moment, the weakness that had plagued him since the accident was forgotten. The weakness he was feeling at the moment could only be cured by burying his aching flesh inside her. With trembling fingers, he drew up her skirt and felt the brush of pure silk against his fingers. She was wearing stockings, not tights, and the sensation was unbelievable, as he curled his eager hand about her thigh.

But for all the urgency he was experiencing, he realised that if he didn't take the weight off his legs soon, he knew his knees would give out on him. There was only so much a man could stand, he thought dizzily, and kissing Caitlin was draining every ounce of strength he had.

All the same, he had no intention of letting her go. Somehow, some way, he was going to make it, and covering her mouth with his, he backed her towards the bed.

His head swam at the change of status. When he collapsed on top of Caitlin on the bed, the room spun sickeningly about him, and for a moment he thought he was going to black out. But he didn't. Within seconds, the room righted itself again, but now he had what felt like a blacksmith's hammer beating away inside his head.

He couldn't help it. Sweat beaded on his forehead, and the groan he uttered was an unwilling admission of his feeble state. Like a beached whale, all he could do was roll off her, raising a hand to his head as he waited for the hammering to subside.

"Nathan?"

He'd half expected her to leave him; to scramble off the bed while she had the chance and make good her escape. After all, the situation hadn't been of her making, and after what had happened that afternoon, he had every reason to suppose she was already regretting what she'd done.

But she didn't do any of those things. Instead, she scrambled onto her knees and leant anxiously over him. He felt her hands, soft and deliciously cool, smoothing his damp forehead, and there was a genuine look of concern in her eyes.

"Nathan," she said again, "Nathan, what's wrong? Are you feeling ill? Do you need a doctor? Was it something I did?" She caught her lower lip between her teeth. "Can I get you a drink?"

He tried a rueful grin and failed abysmally. Although the hammering in his head was beginning to ease, he still had a roiling sensation in his gut. It appeared all he'd achieved was a grimace, and she applied herself to pulling his tie free of his collar and loosening a couple more buttons on his shirt.

The cool air against his hot skin was revitalising, and he attempted to breathe deeply and slowly, as he seemed to remember hearing one should do in cases like this. But the awareness of her there beside him was a constant distraction, and for all he had made a complete fool of himself, he was glad she was there.

"I guess—I guess I'm not the stud I used to be," he declared at last, and then gave an inward groan at the recklessness of his words. The last thing he should be doing was reminding her of the way this had started. He closed his eyes against the censure he was sure he would see in hers.

But, whatever she had thought of his loose comment, Caitlin seemed indifferent to it. As he lay there, fighting his own demons, she continued to loosen his clothes. She unbuckled his belt, undid the waistband of his trousers, and tugged his shirt free of any constriction. She didn't touch his zip, but she didn't have to, he thought drily. If she continued to brush against his over-sensitised skin, his rapidly hardening erection would undo it for her.

Realising he had to say something, he opened his eyes and met her startled gaze. "What are you planning to do?" he inquired huskily. "I thought you had an aversion to my nudity."

"No—I..."

She moved her head in a nervous, awkward gesture. She was staring down at him now, as if she'd never seen him before. Even as he made his protest, the tips of her fingers drifted over his pectoral muscles, snagging the fine covering of dark hair that arrowed down to his navel and beyond.

"You're so brown," she said at last, as if that was any excuse for what she was doing to him. Already his flesh was responsive to every move she made. Only the fear of rekindling the pain in his head prevented him from doing something about it. "I don't remember you being this brown before."

His stomach contracted. Now was not the time for her to start worrying about his identity. "Does it matter?" he asked, praying she wouldn't pull away.

"I don't suppose so," she answered, lifting her eyes to his almost defensively. "As a matter of fact, I like it. I just don't remember—noticing before."

God, did she know what she was doing to him? As he gazed into those shimmering depths, he hardly knew. But, as if realising she was being provocative, she did something about it. Pulling her hands away, she imprisoned them between her thighs.

His bruised senses stirred, and consigning his swimming brain to the hell it had put him through, he reached for her. And perhaps because he wasn't standing this time, his body didn't let him down. Even though he linked his hands behind her head before reversing their positions and imprisoning her beneath him, he only felt a trace of the imbalance that had troubled him before.

Desire, pure and simple, displaced all other emotions. And for all Caitlin had been startled by his sudden reaction, he saw a similar feeling mirrored in her eyes. Her arms, so doubtful in the beginning, now linked around his neck, and her fingers twined into the tumbled darkness of his hair.

And, oh, Lord! she felt so good beneath him. He could feel every sweet curve and angle against his skin. Her breasts, confined by the ivory silk of her bodice pushed against his chest, and he couldn't wait to feel her, flesh to flesh.

All the fantasies he'd had about her while he was lying in the hospital bed were no wilder than the reality. She was every bit as responsive as he'd dreamed she'd be. Her waist, her hips, her legs—every inch of her enchanted him. He wanted to tear the dress aside and see all of her for himself.

But he had to be gentle. Something told him that if he rushed this—rushed her—he was in danger of destroying everything he had. His body ached, it was true, and he was forced to suffer a painful anticipation. But it would all be worth it in the end.

So he kissed her and caressed her, allowing his tongue to ravish her mouth in a fair imitation of what he hoped to do to another part of her anatomy. But he had to steel himself not to grind his hips against her. Even if he knew it was the only way to ease his throbbing sex.

Taking his life into his own hands, he rolled onto his side, but once again, his balance didn't let him down. Then, with unsteady fingers, he eased her skirt up to her hips and explored the tempting flesh that he'd exposed.

Her response was unexpected. He'd been half-afraid she might object that he was moving too fast, but instead, she wriggled closer and attempted to release the zip that ran down the back of her dress. With exquisite pleasure, he did it for her and eased the dress down to her waist, discovering to his delight that she wasn't wearing a bra.

He already knew her breasts were round and slightly tilted, but the nipples had never looked so swollen before. The areolas were dark and throbbing against his palms, and he couldn't wait to taste the eager buds.

He managed to contain himself until he'd disposed of the dress, however, and then he bent his head and rolled one glorious nipple against his tongue. She caught her breath as he did so, emitting little sounds of pleasure, and he wondered how much more he could stand before seeking his own release.

He withdrew long enough to tear off his shirt and jacket, his eyes tortured by the sight of her long, sexy legs. The briefs she was wearing were made of lace, and they left little to the imagination, and unable to prevent himself, he hooked an unsteady finger under the hem.

Her legs clenched around him, and then steadied, and he wasn't surprised to find that she was wet. As her trembling knees parted, he tugged the briefs away and replaced his searching finger with his tongue.

She went wild then, arching up against him, clutching his shoulders and saying, "Yes, yes, yes," in a strangled voice. If he hadn't known better, he'd have said she'd never had an orgasm before, and her urgency was almost more than he could take.

He knew if he didn't get out of his trousers soon, he'd go mad, and he released the zip and pushed them down his legs. His boots proved a temporary barrier, but at last he managed to kick them off, and his trousers joined his jacket on the floor.

And it was so good to ease himself between her legs, to feel his arousal pulsating against her thigh. It took every ounce of will-power not to finish what he'd started, but he had no intention of hurrying something so unique.

He didn't attempt to remove her garterless stockings. He liked the way they drew attention to her legs. Besides, there was no doubt that as her only attire, they were infinitely sexy, even if he didn't need that kind of stimulation right now.

Her skin was so soft, so smooth; creamy white where his was brown; a perfect foil for the darkness of his flesh. He liked the fine distinction; he liked to see his hands on her. And he couldn't believe he'd given her up for someone else.

His own needs were becoming uncontrollable, and gliding over her body, he abandoned any thought of delaying any longer. He'd reached the limit of his endurance, and there was no doubt that she was ready for him, as she clutched his shoulders and brought his mouth to hers.

Nudging her legs wider, he rubbed his thumb against the swollen nub, and once again she arched against his hand. Dear God, she was so responsive, he thought as he eased himself inside her, and he groaned as he felt himself enfolded in her flesh.

Her intake of breath was barely audible. For one awful moment, he thought he'd hurt her, but although she sighed, it was not a sound of pain. But she was so tight around him, tight and slick and hot. It was as if some superior being had designed them to form two halves of a perfect whole.

She had been made for him; they had been made for each other, a concept, he realised, he'd never considered before. Well, not in living memory, he conceded, aware that this all felt new to him. She hadn't been a virgin, it was true, but he felt sure he must have neglected her in the past.

The idea was inconceivable; he couldn't understand it. Unless he had been impotent with her. Was that why he'd sought a mistress, if indeed that accusation was true? Was that the secret Caitlin had been trying to hide?

But if that had been true, it was true no longer. Indeed, it was an effort to control his raging needs. It was only his determination to make this the most memorable night of her life that was forcing him to steel his hormones now.

Her trembling sob was his undoing. "Oh, Nathan," she breathed, winding her arms about his neck. "Love me—please."

He needed no second bidding. The blood was already pounding through his veins, pooling in that throbbing place between his legs. It was magic, he thought dizzily, his senses reeling pleasurably this time. In shedding all her inhibitions, she'd truly become his wife.

He began to move, slowly at first, not trusting his own intoxicated senses, but even that small withdrawal brought a remonstrance from her. "Don't go," she begged urgently, and he cupped her small buttocks and brought her fully to him. "I won't, I promise," he answered thickly, before burying himself deeper than before.

His passion flared ever stronger, and with it came an awareness of how much he loved this woman he was holding in his arms. What might have begun as a reaction to the limits she'd put upon him, as a need to exert his rights as her husband, had blossomed into a complete submersion of his soul.

He must have loved her before. Dear God, he'd married her, hadn't he? He refused to consider any other reason why he might have done such a thing. Even if it was implicit in Matthew Webster's attitude that there'd been more to it than a love match, he was convinced that the attraction between them must have been there from the beginning. Yet, this feeling felt new—this sense of falling *in love* completely. She was his wife, his *woman*; and he was determined that this time he'd make her happy, no matter what.

Her slim hands were clutching him now, digging into his shoulders, her nails raking his flesh, as she sought her own release. He loved the feel of her hands on him, he loved the feel of her all around him, and he loved being so deep inside her, he felt as if he were touching her soul.

He was certain no other woman had ever made him feel like this. For all he had no reason for trusting his instincts, he was convinced that the pleasure he was experiencing was a first. But how could that be, when their marriage wasn't new? Oh, God, he didn't want to think of that now.

He wanted to tell her how he felt. He wanted to share his charged emotions with her, and lifting his head, he looked into drowned indigo eyes. "I love you," he said simply.

"Whatever I've done in the past, you have to believe me. I may have hurt you before, but I'll never hurt you again."

Caitlin gazed at him tremulously. "Do—do you mean that?" she ventured, and he drew her hand down to where their bodies joined.

"Believe it," he said hoarsely. "This is our new beginning. And I'll never let you go again."

She cupped his face with her hands, and the touch of those soft fingers stroking the roughened skin of his jawline, brushing across his mouth, was more than he could stand.

"Oh, God," he groaned, feeling his body convulsing, and her choking cry sent him hurtling over the brink.

He was half-afraid he had climaxed too soon, but her shuddering body reassured him on that score. He could feel her own convulsions rippling through her muscles as his body spilled its bounty into her womb....

The awareness that she was crying came to him from a great distance.

He hadn't had a female cry over him in years—not since he was fourteen and he'd made out with Marcie Kenyon behind the courthouse. Of course, he'd known it hadn't been Marcie's first time, however much she'd tried to tell him it was. She'd been putting out for years, but he let her think that he believed her because it had suited him to do so. It had saved him having to admit it was his first time, as well.

But this was different. This wasn't Marcie's ugly sobbing. He wouldn't have known she was crying at all, if it wasn't for the dampness against his neck. Of course, he thought uneasily. He should have worn a rubber. Were those tremulous sighs an indication that she wasn't on the pill?

"Hey," he said, lifting his head, wondering if it was something more fundamental, and she gave a half-apologetic sniff.

"I'm sorry," she said. "I don't know what's the matter with me. Except—except I never knew it could be so—so good." She offered him a half-tearful smile, and then hid behind the heel of the hand she scrubbed across her swollen eyelids. "Thank you," she said unsteadily. "Thank you, Nathan."

Nathan?

He blinked. Why the hell was she calling him Nathan? That wasn't his name. It was his brother's name, for God's sake! But how did she know that? Did she know Nathan, as well? He scowled. His name was Jake. Yes, that was it: Jake Connor. He was nothing like his brother—well, he hoped not anyway.

And yet . . .

His head was throbbing abominably, and through the haze of pain that was dulling his senses, he stared at the woman beside him with tormented eyes. He felt a surge of apprehension. She was familiar—yet not familiar. Goddammit, where was he? And more to the point, what had he done?

Forcing himself not to panic, he quickly glanced around him. He was on a bed, of course, but he had known that. But whose bed was it? He didn't recognise it. Nor the room around him—though he felt he should.

"Are you all right, Nathan?"

There she went again, calling him by his brother's name, her soft hands like silk against his jaw. Her body was still moulded to his; God, he was still *joined* to her. And if the way he was feeling was anything to go by, the sex had been good.

Oh, yes. He closed his eyes for a moment, as the images his thoughts evoked caused him to harden inside her. It had been good; better than good, it had been bloody fantastic. Hot and strong and exciting, and achingly sweet.

He opened his eyes and looked at her again. His lips parted to tell her she'd made a mistake, that whatever she'd thought, he wasn't Nathan, but that he'd be more than happy to continue to take his place. Despite the fact that her nose was red and those drop-dead blue eyes were still rimmed with tears, she was so beautiful. He thought so anyway. He'd always thought so. Ever since his brother had shown him her picture, right after the wedding.

Their wedding . . .

He swallowed.

He knew who she was.

She was Caitlin.

Caitlin *Wolfe*.

His brother's wife.

17

What the hell was he going to do now?

Studying the remains of the whisky in his glass, Nathan's eyes were dark with anger and resentment. He should never have come back to Prescott; he should never have allowed his curiosity to get the better of him. He had played right into the old man's hands, and whichever way he turned, he had the ignominy of knowing that Jacob was watching him.

It wasn't as if he and his father had ever been the best of friends. From the time he was old enough to understand, he'd had a certain contempt for him, but it wasn't until his brother had spilled the beans about their parentage that his feelings had been given some focus.

And now Jacob had him exactly where he wanted him. By revealing what he had planned to do, he had made his father an unwilling accessory after the fact. And there was no way Jacob was going to let him get away with it. Between his father's contempt and Carl's anger, he'd be lucky if he got out of this alive.

He scowled. It was all Lisa's fault, he decided resentfully. If she'd never introduced him to Carl Walker, he wouldn't now be in this mess. It was her fault that he'd started gambling again; her fault that he'd gotten in over his head.

He hadn't intended it to be that way. Okay, so he'd had some losses in the past, but in those days his father had always been there to bail him out. Only when he married Caitlin, his father had washed his hands of him. He couldn't condone his son marrying Matthew Webster's daughter just so he could get his hands on Webster's company.

Which was a laugh when you considered that that was exactly what Jacob himself had done. He hadn't thought twice about marrying Iris Varley to get control of her father's mill. He had a bloody nerve complaining about his behaviour. He'd only been following Daddy's example, after all.

But that was all water under the bridge now, and when he'd first met Carl Walker, he'd never imagined that one day he'd have anything to fear. On the contrary, Carl could be courtesy itself when he chose to, and he'd assumed Carl was being friendly because of his association with Lisa.

How naïve could you get?

He acknowledged now that he had been pretty stupid right from the start. Men like Walker didn't do people favours unless you had something they wanted. But he'd been itching to get even with Matthew Webster and his sidekick, and when Carl had come up with the South American deal, it had seemed like manna from heaven.

Of course, he'd known Carl was into drugs—selling them, that is, not snorting them. But until Carl had broached the subject, he hadn't given a lot of thought as to his suppliers. It wasn't until later, when he'd mentioned that Webster's had won the contract for a dam to be built on the Magdalena River in Colombia, the question he'd never asked had been answered.

The plan was so simple, he'd been amazed no one else had ever thought of it. Or perhaps they had, but they hadn't had the means or the contacts to pull it off. Carl had everything: an organisation already set up and running in Bogotá, and contacts who would do anything for the right price.

It was Carl who had suggested the deal. Matthew Webster might have thought he was clever, stopping his son-in-law from having any involvement in the financial dealings of the company, but with his help, Carl was able to ensure that the cement company, who got the contract for supplying the dam project, submitted invoices for hundreds of tons of raw materials that were never supplied. Instead of which, the money received went into a numbered bank account in Bogotá.

The original idea had been to split the profits, only when it came right down to it, Carl had proved to be less scrupulous than Nathan had thought. Instead of getting a healthy boost to the crappy salary Webster paid him, he'd found himself faced with exposure. If he didn't do what Carl told him, he'd arrange for his father-in-law to find out what was going on.

That was why he'd agreed to carry the stuff into the country. He'd been shit-scared that first time, and only the thought of what would happen if his luck ran out kept him going. But he didn't have the nerve to go on doing it, and he'd also known that Carl was never going to let him off the hook. God knew what else he might be compelled to do to save his reputation. With the threat of a prison sentence hanging over his head, he was vulnerable.

When he'd come up with the idea of switching places with Jake, it had seemed impossible. But the more he'd thought about it, the more feasible the idea had become. He had nothing left to keep him in England. His job was on the line, and his relationship with his wife was just a sham. On top of that, Lisa was beginning to bug him. She'd never lost sight of the idea that he'd promised her marriage once his use for Caitlin was over.

As if.

For a moment, the memory of the satisfaction he'd felt at the thought of duping Lisa, too, swept over him. She thought he was a loser. She'd never said as much, but he'd known, and he'd derived a great deal of pleasure from imagining how she was going to feel when she found out the truth. Of course, he'd expected it to take a little time before she'd discovered what had happened. But he knew better than to think that Jake would fool her for long.

If he even tried.

He hunched his shoulders, his good mood soon giving way to melancholy. Trust Jake to fuck everything up by losing his memory. For Christ's sake, why hadn't he died in the crash?

But he hadn't, and he was left to try and rescue the situation. The only person he'd really succeeded in fooling was Jake himself. Of course, if Jake had carried that case to London, Nathan would have made sure the Customs knew about it. Jake might be a hotshot defender, but he'd have had a hard time explaining why he was carrying drugs in his bag, particularly with his history. And they'd been hidden so cleverly, he doubted anyone would have noticed without fair warning. If Jake had decided to open the case, there would have been nothing for him to see.

Which was exactly what he'd planned; that and the fact that Jake was carrying his passport instead of his own. He'd known that sooner or later Jake would have managed to prove his identity, but that didn't give him an excuse for carrying cocaine.

With a bit of luck, Jake would have been tied up in London for some considerable time, and by then, Nathan had intended to be long gone. And he would have been, too, if he hadn't been so bloody nosy. It was partly the fear that

Carl might too quickly have found out what had happened that had brought him back.

Of course, he could board the next plane to England with Jake's passport, and trust Carl would believe him if he could think of some reason for the delay. But he'd be back where he started, always supposing that Carl did buy his story. And if he didn't, they'd probably fish his body out of the Thames.

And to cap it all, he had his father on his back, asking awkward questions, wanting to know the truth. If he left now, there was no guarantee that the old bastard wouldn't put the authorities onto him. As soon as he'd found out that Jake was innocent of any crime, he'd been urging him to go and put things straight.

He poured himself another slug of whisky, feeling his mood darkening with the day. Why did his father always take Jake's side against him? It wasn't as if his brother had shown any love for the old man.

But ever since Jake came back from Vietnam, Jacob had made him out to be some kind of hero. And why? He hadn't done anything particularly heroic that he could see. Lots of guys had come back from 'Nam without the habit, but Jake had come back so fucked up he'd fallen apart.

Jacob liked to pretend that in Jake's position, he'd have deserted. He wouldn't believe that his younger son might just have handled it without resorting to dope. All that stuff about bodies decomposing in swamps, and kids with their heads blown away, had to be an exaggeration. Hell, how bad could it be? He was alive.

Still, it had annoyed him when he'd heard that Jake had gone cold turkey and kicked the habit. It had given his father another reason to admire him, and he was mad as hell when Jacob offered to pay for him going back to school. But in the event, Jake wouldn't take the old man's money—another reason for his father to bug him—and when he'd gotten his law degree, Jacob had been as proud as if he'd taught the guy himself.

It wasn't as if Jake had done anything startling since he left college. Nathan had laughed his head off when he'd discovered Jake was working for the public defender's office. All that education, and all he was doing was defending punks and freaks. In his place, he'd have taken off for California. Lawyers there earned million-dollar salaries just for helping some poor little rich kid to get a divorce.

Maybe he should have gone in for law himself, but at the time, the old man had had some notion of him staying here and running the lumber yard when he retired. What a joke! As if he'd have been content to stay in Prescott. As far as he was concerned, the sawmill was just a millstone round his father's neck.

In the event, it had all been academic anyway. What with a shortage of investment and a slump in the manufacturing industry, Varley's Mill had become just another statistic. Like the rest of the town, it had folded beneath the weight of its own debts.

He was still brooding over the past when his father appeared in the doorway. Nathan had thought he had gone to bed, which was why he'd felt at liberty to help himself to a drink. He knew the old man was unlikely to miss it. Since Jacob had given up hitting the bottle himself, it was just there for medicinal purposes.

"I should have known I couldn't trust you," Jacob muttered now, coming heavily into the room and snatching the bottle out of his son's hand. "How long do you expect to stay here, hiding out like some petty criminal? Why don't you find something useful to do, like telling the Websters Jake's not you?"

Nathan's mouth compressed. "Get real, old man. And don't pretend you can't afford to buy whisky. You're not spending your money on anything else."

"I'm feeding you, aren't I?" Jacob thrust the bottle back into the drawer of his desk. "And what I choose to spend my money on is no concern of yours. I suggest you find another bolt-hole. Before those lowlife friends of yours come to flush you out."

Nathan started. "What the hell do you mean? Has someone been in touch with you about me?"

"And if they had, do you think I wouldn't have told them where you are?" Jacob sneered. "No, you can relax. There haven't been any funny phone calls. But you must have gotten the stuff from somewhere, and my guess is, they won't give up just because the plane went down."

He had been afraid of that himself. Afraid that when Carl found out Jake was in London, he might decide to collect his dues. It didn't worry him that Jake might be in trouble. But what if Carl sent Lisa to deliver the news? She would recognise, where Caitlin obviously hadn't, that the man still in shock from the crash was not Nathan Wolfe.

He swallowed now, and as if sensing his son's uncertainty, Jacob frowned. "You know what I'm talking about, don't you? You don't think they'll forget who was carrying the stuff."

He tried to bluff it out. "It's not my problem."

"It's not Jake's, either," said Jacob harshly. "I suggest you think about this seriously. I wouldn't want to have to call the cops."

Nathan snorted. "Oh, yeah. I should have known. It's not my hide you're worried about, it's my sainted brother's. What did Jake ever do to earn his halo? Except escape being brought up by you!"

"Why, you—"

"What? What?" His son goaded him. "What's to stop me taking off right now? I've got Jake's passport. I could go to Pine Bay. It would serve him right if I pretended to be him."

"Well, I wouldn't fancy your chances if Fletch Connor came around," said Jacob contemptuously. "Face it, boy, you haven't got a hope of pulling it off."

"So what do you suggest?"

"You know what I suggest."

"And what will that achieve, short of getting us both arrested?"

Jacob stared at him. "What do you mean?"

"If I go to the police, Jake will still be in deep trouble." Nathan sneered. "Particularly if I tell them what I believe he had in that case."

18

When Caitlin awakened, she was alone.

It was morning. A watery sun was already streaming through the cracks in the curtains, and although she didn't know exactly what time it was, she suspected it was quite late.

But for a moment, she was perfectly content to lie there and contemplate the day. She didn't want to get out of bed. She didn't want to do anything to spoil the delicious sense of wellbeing that she was experiencing. She felt relaxed and vaguely lethargic, and although her limbs felt weak and languid, it was not a sensation she had any wish to change.

She knew why she was feeling that way, of course. The moment she'd opened her eyes, the memories of the night before had come flooding back to her. A faint warmth invaded her cheeks at the remembrance. Dear God, she thought, after three years of marriage, she was finally Nathan's wife.

But that was melodramatic, and she knew it. For heaven's sake, it wasn't as if he had never made love to her before. In the early days of their marriage, he had abused her body all too frequently, appalling her with his brutal possession and with the sordid things he had expected her to do.

She caught her breath uneasily.

So why wasn't she appalled now? Why wasn't she stricken by the memory of allowing a man like that to take possession of her again? He was the same man—she had to believe that. Or run the risk of losing what little sense she had.

Her breath escaped in a wisp of sound, and thrusting any doubts to the back of her mind, she turned onto her side and surveyed the unoccupied half of the bed. The pillow was faintly dented, and the quilt was crumpled where he had got out of bed, but it wasn't just this proof of his presence that assured her he had really been there. She could feel him; she could still feel his touch upon her. The heat of his body warmed her senses. The scent of his maleness was on the sheets.

She tried to think rationally. Her husband had changed; the accident had changed him. That was why she'd had that sense of alienation when they'd made love. He had been different; he had been gentle, and oh, so wonderfully passionate. Dear God, any woman would have responded to him no matter how disillusioned they had once been.

It was incredible, but from the moment he'd kissed her, she'd been incapable of resisting the inevitable. The revulsion he'd once inspired in her had all been gone, and she'd found herself responding to emotions she hadn't even known she possessed. Her lips, her tongue, her skin, had all been electrified by the needs he'd aroused in her, and she'd been desperate to feed his hunger, and in so doing assuage her own.

Her limbs tingled still with the remembrance of how it had felt to feel him upon her. Between her legs, a tiny pulse throbbed at the thought of his powerful invasion, and of how eagerly she had welcomed him into her sheath. Muscles, slick with her arousal, had contracted and clenched around him, much as her legs had circled his hips and held him urgently inside her.

A wave of heat enveloped her at the memory, and those same muscles ached with remembered need. With one tremulous hand, she traced a path from the erect tips of her breasts, down over her quivering midriff, to the warm nest of blonde curls that hid her womanhood. Oh, God, she thought, she wanted him. She had never wanted him—or any man—before.

It was time to get up, she told herself, not wanting to face the thought of how vulnerable it made her, particularly as there was still the problem of Lisa Abbott to deal with. All right. She accepted he didn't remember her, but that didn't alter the fact that she was there. Impatient enough to call him at Fairings, she acknowledged resentfully. How long would it be before the woman plucked up enough courage to come to the flat?

Caitlin threw back the covers and got determinedly out of bed. There was nothing she could do about that for the present, she decided firmly, and until her husband recovered his memory, there was little Lisa Abbott could do, either. For the moment, she had the advantage, and instead of worrying about the future, she should live for the present. Nathan wanted her; he had proved that conclusively last night. Her wisest course should be to try and profit from it. To prove to him she was not averse to his lovemaking, and hope that when his memory did come back, he'd still feel the same way.

She was momentarily arrested by the sight of her own nakedness. For so long, she had avoided the demands of the flesh, and seeing herself unclothed seemed vaguely indecent somehow. Yet her pale skin was not unpleasing, and the sight of faint bruising on her breasts and thighs didn't make her feel any sense of dismay. The memory of how those bruises came to be there was far too disturbing, and she wondered if her husband had realised she had never had such feelings before.

She dressed in suede trousers and a skinny-rib sweater, choosing the most attractive items she had brought with her. She hadn't expected to be in the position of wanting to attract her husband's interest, and apart from the dresses she'd worn for dinner, which she'd had for some time, most of the clothes she'd packed had been chosen for their warmth, rather than anything else.

It was after eleven by the time she appeared downstairs. A shower and a careful application of make-up had taken almost another hour, and she was not surprised to find her mother and father sharing a pot of morning coffee in the conservatory.

"You're late," remarked her mother, breaking out of the conversation she had been having with Caitlin's father to offer her daughter a cup. But she left Caitlin with the impression they had been talking about her and Nathan, and it wasn't easy to sit down and act as if nothing momentous had happened.

"I'm afraid I slept in," she admitted ruefully. "It must be the air down here." She glanced about her with what she hoped was casual interest. "Where's Nathan?"

"He and Marshall have gone for a walk," replied her father rather tersely, and Caitlin wondered if he objected to her husband monopolising his assistant's time. Or was it Nathan himself he resented? She wished she knew what the South American problem was all about.

"Yes, your husband was up very early," observed Daisy Webster with rather less tolerance than she usually showed. She tossed her head. "He had the nerve to ask Mrs Goddard whether the family went to church!" She sniffed. "I suppose he was hoping to see that Kendall woman again. I can't imagine any other reason why he might want to confess his sins."

Caitlin's tongue clung to her upper lip. "I—I don't think Nathan was interested in Nancy Kendall, Mummy," she declared at last, accepting the cup of coffee her mother had poured for her. "He was just being—polite, that's all. And you know how flirtatious she always is with men."

"Hmm." Mrs Webster didn't sound convinced, but Caitlin's father chose to use another tack.

"Has he said anything to you about why he went to the United States in the first place?" he demanded, clearly more concerned about her husband's business dealings than any dalliance he might or might not be having with the schoolteacher. "I can't believe he doesn't remember anything. He's so—so perceptive in other ways."

"Perceptive?"

Caitlin frowned, and this time her mother intervened. "We're just concerned about you, darling," she said, giving her husband a warning glance. "So—tell me—did you sleep well? Mrs Goddard told me you'd asked her to prepare another room."

Caitlin's face suffused with colour. She couldn't help it, and it annoyed her that at twenty-nine she was still so hopelessly immature. But she'd forgotten all about her instructions to the housekeeper, and it was too late to go and muss the covers on the spare bed, even if she'd wanted to.

"Oh—I slept very well," she mumbled, hoping her parents would think it was the heat of the coffee that had caused the redness in her cheeks. "As a matter of fact, I—I stayed in my old bedroom." She licked her lips. "Nathan had a dizzy spell—" that, at least, was true "—and I didn't like to leave him alone."

Her parents exchanged glances and then, to her relief, she heard the sound of approaching footsteps. Looking up with what she hoped appeared to be only casual interest, she encountered Marshall O'Brien's inquiring gaze, and she quickly looked away again, annoyed that the anticipation in her gaze had been directed at him.

Matthew Webster asked the question that hovered on her own lips. "Where is he?" he demanded, and no one had any doubt to whom he was referring.

"I believe he's gone upstairs," replied Marshall, waiting for Mrs Webster's invitation before sitting down. "I don't suppose he'll be long. D'you want me to fetch him back?"

"Not particularly," said Caitlin's father broodingly. "You didn't get anything more out of him, I suppose?"

"I'm afraid not," declared Marshall, accepting a cup of coffee from his hostess. "As a matter of fact, he asked me some questions. He was curious about—about what he used to do."

"Huh."

Mr Webster was impatient, but for her part, Caitlin was wishing she hadn't left their room. Had Nathan gone to look for her? Surely he must have expected her to be up by now. There was no way she could excuse herself without arousing curiosity. In consequence, she was compelled to remain and indulge in small talk with her mother until Mrs Goddard announced that lunch was ready.

"Would you let Mr Wolfe know that we're ready to eat?" Mrs Webster asked the housekeeper a little peevishly as they left the conservatory, and Caitlin took the opportunity to intervene.

"I will, Mrs Goddard," she said, already heading for the stairs, but before she could attain more than the bottom step, she saw her husband coming down the stairs towards her.

Her heart flipped a beat, and she hoped no one else was aware of the nervous flutter in her stomach. Her knees felt weak, and there was a disturbing quivering in her thighs. All she could think about was what they'd done the night before, and she knew a crazy urge to fling her arms around him and scandalise them all.

"Looking for me?" he asked of no one in particular, and Mrs Webster forgot her indignation in the enveloping warmth of his smile.

"Well, we were getting a little worried about you, darling," she admitted, usurping Caitlin's position by tucking her arm into the curve of his sleeve. "Though I must say, it seems unnecessary. I've never seen you looking fitter."

"Thanks."

He cast a rueful glance in his wife's direction as her mother insisted he escort her into the dining room. Caitlin supposed she should be grateful that he had evidently disarmed her mother, but the frustration she was feeling wouldn't go away.

It was compounded when they left in the late afternoon. Both her parents came to see them off, but as Marshall was driving back to town with them, Caitlin couldn't be sure her father was there for their benefit or his. Apparently, Marshall had ridden down to Fairings with his employer in Matthew Webster's chauffeur-driven limousine, and to Caitlin's irritation, her husband had been far too eager to offer the other man a lift.

She had been looking forward to the journey. It was going to be the first time they had been alone together since the night before. When she'd gone to do the packing, her husband had been talking to her father, and Marshall had insisted on carrying down their cases because, as he said, Nathan was still recuperating from the crash.

In consequence, Caitlin had anticipated the journey with some enthusiasm. She'd hoped they'd have a much more satisfying replay of the conversation they'd had on the way down. She'd been trembling with excitement ever since she'd caught his eye across the lunch table. She hadn't mistaken the dark anguish in his gaze, which she was sure indicated he was as impatient to be alone with her as she was with him.

Marshall's inclusion in the party had been a total anticlimax. She couldn't believe it when she heard her husband suggesting that he drive back with them. All right, so they had two spare seats, but what of it? Why couldn't he take the train from Princes Risborough? She was sure that's what he'd expected to have to do.

Still, there was nothing she could do about it. Politeness forbore any alternative being offered, and she reassured herself with the thought that she and Nathan would have the rest of the night to themselves. It was dark already, and the prospect of a cosy evening at the flat was something to treasure. And probably all the more exciting because their being alone together had been delayed.

They dropped Marshall at the nearest tube station. He insisted that he preferred to make his own way home, and Caitlin was in no mood to argue with him. On the contrary, as soon as Marshall got out of the car, she felt as if an enormous weight had been lifted from her shoulders, and with a certain amount of daring, she moved her hand from the gear lever and let it rest on her husband's knee.

His reaction was hardly flattering. "Be careful," he said as she skirted a parked car with only inches to spare. "Concentrate on the road," he added, moving his knee so that his intentions were obvious. "How much farther is it to Knightsbridge? I'm not so familiar with this place in the dark."

Caitlin pressed her lips together. Her fragile ego had just taken a small battering, and she was not confident enough to believe it was only because he was concerned about the other road users. She hoped he wasn't angry about what had happened between them. It would be ironic now if he regretted it instead of her.

He went with her to park the car, and they took the lift from the underground level to the tenth floor. Despite her protests, he insisted on handling the cases himself, carrying them into the living room and leaving them on the rug.

Caitlin wondered if he had left them there intentionally; whether it was his way of giving her the option of putting them into separate rooms. After all, she had been so adamant before they went away about them having separate bedrooms. Was it any wonder he was confused when she had changed the rules to suit herself?

It was after seven o'clock, and Caitlin put off the decision and went into the kitchen instead. "Are you hungry?" she called, trying to keep her tone light and casual. "We can have steaks if you like. It won't take long to make a vinaigrette."

Nathan came to the kitchen doorway, propping his shoulder against the jamb. He was wearing jeans again, as if in defiance of what she had told him, and the supple cloth followed every line of his lean body like a second skin. Her eyes were drawn downwards to the apex of his long legs, where the bulge of his sex thrust against his zip, and she tore her gaze away in sudden self-loathing. Dear God, she thought, what was happening to her? She'd never known what lust was until now.

"I'm not hungry," he said, his voice cool and detached, and she wondered what she'd done to inspire such unexpected prejudice. He was looking at her as if he was wary of what she might say to him, and impatience—and raw frustration—had their way.

"What's wrong?" she demanded, abandoning any attempt at preparing a meal, and facing him bravely. "Why are you looking at me as if I'd offended you in some way? For God's sake, I didn't realise it was a crime to touch you—

without your permission, of course," she added with some sarcasm.

"It's not a crime." He was impatient. "You were driving, and—"

"You were afraid I'd take my eyes off the road," finished Caitlin drily. "Yes, I know."

"Oh, shit!" He turned his head away, and Caitlin knew a moment's panic that she had gone too far. Then, as if controlling whatever emotion her words had aroused in him, he straightened away from the door. "I'm going to take a shower," he announced without looking at her. "D'you have a problem with that?"

"No." Caitlin took a steadying breath. She turned to face the cabinets, her fingers clenching over the rim of the counter. "I'll wait until you come back, then, shall I? You might know what you want then."

Nathan's oath was low, but audible. "I know what I want now," he told her between this teeth. "Only you wouldn't understand."

Caitlin's breathing was suspended. "Try me," she suggested, not sure what she was inviting, but knowing that anything was better than his indifference.

"No."

His fist balled against the door-frame for another pregnant moment, and then, without another word, he turned and walked across the living room, collecting his suitcase on the way.

Caitlin's body sagged in the aftermath of the tension she'd been feeling, but she was no longer feeling so downhearted. She understood now. It wasn't that her husband regretted what had happened between them. On the contrary, she was fairly sure he had been as devastated by the events of the night before as she had. But—and it was a big but—until last night, she had made it patently obvious that she wouldn't welcome a closer association between them, and he must now have doubts about where they went from here. It was up to her to show him that as far as she was concerned, she was quite prepared to continue their relationship in its present form, and if she was any judge of character, he wouldn't object.

She refused to consider the possible ramifications of that decision should he recover his memory. Until that happened, she intended to play the cards as they'd been dealt to her, and if Lisa Abbott found out, then so be it. Nathan was still her husband. She'd never expected that that fact would ever do her any favours. But it did, and she had to prove she was woman enough to take advantage of it.

All the same, it took an enormous amount of determination to open the door to Nathan's bedroom a few moments later. Particularly without knocking first. Her palm was moist as it gripped the knob, and although she had intended to saunter casually into the room, she found herself peering round the door as if she was afraid she'd chosen the wrong room.

She didn't know if she was disappointed or relieved to find the bedroom empty, and if her husband's case hadn't been tossed carelessly onto the ottoman at the foot of the bed, she might have doubted his occupation. But there it was, unzipped, its contents spilling haphazardly onto the quilted lid of the chest.

The sound of water running explained his absence. Evidently, he had not been lying when he'd said he was going to take a shower, and her tongue circled her dry lips as she considered what her next move should be. Twenty-four hours ago, she wouldn't have had a problem. She'd have simply turned round again and gone back to the kitchen to prepare the supper. But after last night, she was uncertain. There had to be something more she could do....

The idea to join him caused a ripple of anticipation in her stomach. Dare she? she wondered. Dare she strip off all her clothes and join him in the shower? The prospect of doing so was too nerve-racking to consider calmly, and so, before she could change her mind, she unbuttoned her trousers and slipped them off.

Naked, the idea seemed even more outrageous. She'd never done anything like this before, and she had the uneasy feeling that she really wasn't the type. In the light from the lamps beside the bed, her skin looked pale and feathered with goose bumps. She was sure she looked nothing like the seductress her senses were telling her she should be.

She trod barefoot across the carpet, pausing in the dressing area, ostensibly to get her bearings, when in actual fact she knew the way only too well. Nathan's bathrobe was hanging on the back of the door, and she was tempted to use it. It was chilly in the dressing room, and although the fanlight above the bathroom door was misted, the humidity didn't reach beyond its panels.

She bit her lip, considering her options, but the realisation that he might finish his shower any minute had her reaching for the door. With a quivering haste, she pressed the door inwards and peered round it. As she had hoped, he was still in the shower cubicle, and he had his back to her.

The heat in the bathroom warmed her blood, and before she could have second thoughts, she tiptoed across the tiles and stepped into the cubicle behind him. The first inkling he had of her presence was when she slipped her arms around him from behind, pressing her breasts against his back, warming her stomach against his wet, slick flesh.

"Christ, Caitlin," he swore harshly, jerking away from her, and she consoled herself with the thought that she'd given him a shock. "What the hell are you doing?" he demanded, staring at her through the lukewarm fall of water, and she could tell from his strained expression that he was on his guard.

"What do you think I'm doing?" she asked softly, aware that the anger he was exhibiting was forced. Her eyes moved irresistibly down his body, and his jaw clenched as she did so. "I thought you'd be glad to see me." Her tongue circled her lips. "Ah—I see you are."

He swore again, half-turning away from her, as if anything he did could disguise the immediate reaction of his sex. "Get out of here, Kate," he muttered. "This isn't a good idea."

"I think it is," she contradicted him huskily, and ignoring his attempts to avoid her, she slid her arms about his waist. "I'm cold. I thought you might like to warm me." Her tongue brushed his nipple. "Or we might warm each other...."

Her husband's hands around her upper arms put her back from him. "You don't know what you're doing."

"Oh, I think I do."

Caitlin refused to be put off even though her confidence was fading by the minute. Grasping the tablet of soap he had left on the gold-plated dish, she applied it generously to her hands, and then transferred the lather to her breasts, massaging herself with apparently sensual enjoyment. Her skin was soon tingling with awareness, as much from Nathan's narrow-eyed appraisal as from any satisfaction she was gaining from the exercise, and by the time her hands moved to her stomach and the slight swell of her abdomen, she could practically feel the emotion pulsing from him.

"Stop that!" he snarled, his eyes dark and savage, and she tilted her face up to his in innocent inquiry.

"What?" she asked, her fingers sliding down into the curls that clustered between her legs, leaving provocative pearls of soap on the silvery mat of hair. "I'm just bathing myself—"

"Like hell you are," he muttered, and then, as if unable to resist the sensuous pull of her body any longer, he reached for her.

The powerful shower beat down on their overheated bodies as he imprisoned her against the wall of the cubicle. With one hand behind her head, he angled her lips for his kiss, his tongue plunging deeply into the parted sweetness of her mouth.

She thought she heard him say, "This is crazy!" but if it was, it was the kind of craziness she wanted. With a sensuality she hadn't known she possessed, she wound one leg about his hip, bringing the pulsing heat of his erection to the threshold of her woman's core. His maleness nudged the moist place between her legs, causing her to arch herself against him, and with a muffled oath, his hand curved along her thigh, bringing both her legs about him.

His body slid into hers with satisfying slickness. It was like the night before, only better. Now her body welcomed his. She had no fears about what he might ask of her, and her muscles tightened about him with an eagerness over which she had no control. Instead, she wound her arms about his neck and hung on.

Meanwhile, he covered her face with kisses, biting at her lips and sucking her tongue into his mouth until the urgent thrust of his body had them both weak and gasping for breath. Caitlin's climax came only seconds before he uttered a hoarse cry and spilled his seed inside her, the friction of the water cooling bodies that only moments before had been inflamed to fever pitch.

The first awareness of her surroundings came when he eased himself away from her, and her knees almost buckled when he set her on her feet. But, although she was reluctant to release him, her husband's actions were almost robotic now. Her husky "Nathan?" met only a tight-lipped appraisal, and if she hadn't known better, she'd have said he was angrier than before.

"Is something wrong?" she asked at last, when she emerged from the cubicle to find him towelling himself down with controlled movements, and he gave her a hard-eyed stare.

"Like what?" he asked, wrapping the towel sarongwise about his waist. "You got what you wanted, didn't you? What could be wrong?"

Caitlin caught her breath as she snatched up a towel to conceal her nakedness. "Does that mean you didn't want it, too?" she demanded, finding it incredibly difficult not to show how upset his words had made her, and he shrugged.

"That's not the point."

"Then what is the point?" she exclaimed, unable to understand what she'd done wrong, and his lips twisted.

"Good question," he answered, striding through to his bedroom. "I wish to hell I had the answer."

19

"What it is to be young and in love!"

Janie's sardonic voice broke into Caitlin's reverie, and she turned, almost guiltily, to look at her friend.

"As if," she countered, hoping Janie wouldn't hear the lack of conviction in her voice. She glanced at her wristwatch before thrusting her empty coffee cup onto the drainer. "Isn't it time we were opening up? I heard ten o'clock chime a few minutes ago."

Janie regarded her with a sceptical expression. "Ten o'clock may well have chimed," she agreed, "but you didn't hear it. You were miles away, Caitlin. Am I allowed to ask what you were thinking about?"

Caitlin managed a fairly casual shrug. "Oh—this and that," she answered lightly, aware that Janie had been trying to get her to open up ever since she returned to the shop yesterday morning. "I forgot to ask. Were you busy on Saturday? I'm sorry I had to let you down again."

"Mmm." Janie acknowledged the rebuff with a wry grimace. Then, "We managed," she replied a little coolly. "Della's getting better all the time."

Caitlin knew that that was a deliberate attempt to rattle her. Della Parish was the sixth-former they employed on a part-time basis, and generally Janie didn't have a good word to say for her. But the girl meant well, and she was enthusiastic, and Caitlin had no doubt that she hoped one day to join them full-time. But the fact was, the business wouldn't support more than two people, and until recently it hadn't been a problem.

Now, as Janie put down her cup and made to go through to the shop, Caitlin caught her arm. "Wait."

Janie looked as if she might shake her hand off, but then she, too, seemed to relent. "What is it, Cat?" she exclaimed. "Ever since you got back, you've looked—dazed. Is something wrong, for God's sake? Has that bastard been beating you up again?"

"*No!*" Caitlin's denial was almost too vehement, and Janie waited with some impatience for her to explain. "It's just—well, if you must know, the weekend was brilliant."

"With Nathan?" Janie looked staggered.

"Yes."

"You're not telling me you—slept with him?" And at her friend's guilty expression, "My God, Cat, are you out of your mind?"

"No." Caitlin licked her lips. "Oh, Janie, I don't know how to explain it. It just—happened."

Janie snorted. "You mean you let the man who raped—"

"Please." Caitlin held up a hand to silence her. "I know what you're going to say, and don't think I haven't thought of it myself. But it wasn't like before. *He* wasn't like before. My God, if it wasn't so outrageous, I'd say he was a different man!"

"He must have been." Janie wasn't sympathetic. She shook her head. "I can't believe this, Cat. I thought you wanted a divorce."

"I do. At least, I did. That is..." Caitlin didn't know what she wanted any more. Despite the explanation she had given Janie, she hardly believed it herself.

Janie stared at her. "He's that different?"

"Yes."

"So, as far as you're concerned, you're hoping he doesn't get his memory back?"

"Yes. No. Oh, I don't know, Janie. Try and understand. This has been hard for me to comprehend."

"I'll bet." Janie was still sardonic. "God, I can't believe you're saying this after everything that's happened. Caitlin, men don't change. Not so completely. Are you sure he's not just acting the part? I mean, when you said you were going to spend the weekend with him, I wasn't enthusiastic, but I never expected this."

"Do you think I did?"

"But how did it happen? I thought you slept in separate rooms."

"We do." Caitlin felt a trace of colour enter her cheeks at the other woman's words, and thought how ridiculous it was that a woman of her age should still feel embarrassed when she spoke about sex. "But—my mother—well, Marshall was at Fairings, and she'd given him my old bedroom. In consequence, Nathan and I shared a room. There was nothing I could do about it."

"And you're saying it just happened?"

"Not like that." Caitlin didn't want Janie to think it had just been a case of proximity and nothing else. "We—we went for a walk on Saturday afternoon, and—and he kissed me. Then—then on Saturday night, when we went to bed—"

"Don't bother to elaborate." Janie's lips twisted scornfully. "Believe it or not, but I can guess what happened next. I just don't know why you went along with it. Weren't you afraid of what he might do?"

"Initially, perhaps." Caitlin remembered that Janie's opinion of Nathan was still coloured by what she had told her during the early days of their marriage. "But—he was so sensitive, so gentle. I just knew I didn't have to be afraid. Don't tell me I'm crazy. I sometimes think I must be going mad."

Janie shook her head. "We're talking about Nathan Wolfe here? Nathan Wolfe, your husband?"

"Yes." Caitlin swallowed. "I know what you must be thinking. But believe me—it's the truth."

"And what about Lisa Abbott?"

Janie was nothing if not candid, and Caitlin drew a painful breath. "She—telephoned," she said. "On Saturday evening. As a matter of fact, I answered the call."

Janie gasped. "And you still went to bed with him?"

Caitlin got up from the stool where she had been sitting and paced restlessly about the small storeroom. "It does sound unlikely, doesn't it?"

"Unlikely?" Janie scoffed. "It sounds downright unhealthy to me. How could you, Cat? How could you do it? My God, after everything you've said."

Caitlin could feel herself getting angry and tried to subdue her temper. Janie was only thinking of her after all, and goodness knows, she had been there for her when everything had looked so black.

"He didn't recognise her," she said now, carefully. "He didn't know who she was. She obviously called because he hadn't been in touch with her. If he was lying, do you think I wouldn't know?"

Janie gave her a level look. "So—what did she say?"

"I don't know, do I?"

"You mean, you let him take the call?"

Caitlin's nails dug into her palms. "Of course. What else could I do? And, fortunately, she didn't even tell him her name."

"Did you?"

"Did I what?"

"Tell him her name," exclaimed Janie impatiently. "For pity's sake, Cat, what are you saying? Just because he's apparently mellowed enough for you to allow him to fuck your brains out, have you completely taken leave of your senses?"

"You don't know anything about it." Caitlin was hurt, but she hid her anguish beneath a show of indignation. "I think you'd better not say any more. I don't want us to fall out."

"And I don't want you to throw yourself away on a man who doesn't know the meaning of the word honour," retorted Janie. "But you're right, he's not worth our quarrelling about it. I'll go and unlock the door."

It wasn't quite what Caitlin wanted to hear, but she realised it was hard for Janie to understand. If she hadn't seen it—experienced it—for herself, she would never have believed it, either. And she dared not voice what she was secretly thinking: that not only did Nathan appear to be different, he *was* a different man.

But that couldn't be true.

Yet, with every day that passed, her feelings became more and more confused. Oh, she was well aware that it must be infinitely harder for Nathan to cope with, but at least he had nothing to compare his present behaviour with. She did. She remembered the man he used to be, and this man was nothing like him, in character, word, or deed.

The only solution she could come up with was that the knock he had received to his head had been more serious than the doctors had imagined. She'd read of psychological disorders that were treated by removing or killing certain cells in the brain. What if the accident had altered Nathan's brain cells? What if the amnesia he was suffering had subdued the violent streak in his nature?

But that begged the question of what might happen if—
when—his memory returned. It followed, surely, that if he
regained all his faculties, he would regain his previous
character, also. She couldn't bear the thought of that happening. She had begun to care for the man he'd become.

Nevertheless, if she was honest, she would have to admit
that Nathan had changed again. Not substantially, perhaps, but there was no doubt that since he'd made love to
her, he had become far more silent and withdrawn.

She'd tried to make excuses for it, but since Sunday night,
she'd begun to have doubts about his feelings for her. On
Sunday morning, she had been so bemused by what had
happened, she hadn't considered that he might not feel the
same way about her, but subsequent events had forced her
to take another look at his behaviour.

There was no doubt that she could arouse him. She'd
known that right from the first time she went to see him in
the hospital. He'd made no secret of his attraction for her,
and it had been that, as much as anything, that had erased
her fears towards him.

But since Sunday—or perhaps even Saturday night—their
relationship had subtly altered. Now she was in the position of wanting his attention, while he...

She moistened her lips. What did he want? The trouble
was, she didn't really know. She'd thought he wanted her,
but after making love to her on Saturday night, he had allowed her to make all the running.

Such running as there'd been, she amended wryly. After
the way he'd behaved on Sunday night after their lovemaking in the shower, she hadn't had the confidence or the
courage to approach him again, and far from sharing her
bed, he'd slept in his own bedroom for the past two nights.

It might have been easier if she could have consoled herself with the thought that it was what Nathan—the *old* Na-

than—would have done. It wasn't. The Nathan she had known before the accident would have ravaged her body whenever he chose to do so. And he'd never really known her. He'd touched her body, but not her soul.

And that was the real reason she'd come back to work. She couldn't bear to stay in the flat with him. If he didn't say something soon, she was very much afraid she'd dissolve into tears.

She sighed, and deciding she couldn't remain closeted in the storeroom all day, she washed up the coffee cups and left them on the drainer to dry. Then, squaring her shoulders, she went out into the sales area, exchanging a tentative smile with her friend.

"Will you be leaving at lunchtime as usual?" asked Janie, adjusting the pointers on a rather beautiful grandmother clock that was inclined to lose several minutes every day, and Caitlin drew a shaky breath. She'd forgotten it was Tuesday. She only worked half days on Tuesdays. It wouldn't do to arouse Janie's suspicions again by saying no.

"If that's all right," she said, "although as I've been off so much lately—"

"Think nothing of it." Janie was offhand. "I was surprised you stayed all day yesterday. Weren't you worried about leaving him alone?"

Caitlin acknowledged the reproof. "He's not a child, Janie."

"Isn't he?" Janie didn't sound convinced. "Well, if you don't mind, I'd like to have a little free time myself this morning. I want to go to the bank. Will you be all right on your own?"

"Of course." Caitlin tried not to sound defensive. "And—well, I'm sorry if you think I'm making a muddle of my life. But it is my life, and I have to live it the way I see fit. It may not work out. It probably won't. But I have to give it a chance, don't you see?''

"I see that you don't want to face the realities of the situation," replied Janie flatly. "But, as you say, it's nothing to do with me. I just hope you won't live to regret it."

"So do I."

Caitlin forced a smile, but after Janie had left, she admitted how unlikely it was. She was probably just tilting at windmills, with something less than providence on her side.

The morning passed fairly quickly, and although Caitlin was busy, she still found plenty of time to think. Too much time, she reflected unhappily. And her thoughts didn't soothe her anxieties at all.

Had she instigated everything that had happened?

That was her greatest fear.

She knew she'd instigated what had happened on Sunday evening when they got back to the flat, but what about Saturday night, as well?

After all, she had known the dangers of confronting him in the bedroom. She'd known there was every chance he might get the wrong signal from her actions, and yet she'd stayed there long after any sane individual would have gone to bed.

She had been angry, of course. That was her only real defence. She'd been furious that Lisa Abbott should have felt confident enough to ring him at Fairings, and desperate to expunge some of that rage and frustration before trying to sleep.

Or was that just an excuse?

In any event, his weakness had neutralised her anger.

She supposed the real truth was, she'd been jealous. Blind jealous, or she'd never have had the nerve to go to his room. But did that mean she was to blame for everything that had happened? And if not, why was Nathan so distant now?

A customer came into the shop to price a pair of Meissen vases Janie had set on a Queen Anne writing desk in the window, and Caitlin took the opportunity to escape her fears with real enthusiasm. So much so, that the customer, an elderly gentleman, was persuaded the vases were a bargain, and she was putting his cheque away in the drawer when her friend returned.

Janie's attitude didn't appear to have changed in her absence, and afraid she was about to launch another attack on Nathan, Caitlin hurried into speech. "I've sold those two vases," she said. "The Meissen ones that represented autumn and winter." She smiled rather triumphantly. The vases had been around for some considerable time.

"Great." Janie's tone was hardly enthusiastic, and Caitlin stifled a sigh.

"Isn't it?" she said, refusing to be daunted. "I don't know how you've managed to keep going without me."

"Nor do I," averred Janie wryly, but she didn't return her smile. Then, "What did you say Nathan was doing this morning? Do you trust him on his own?"

"Of course."

Caitlin couldn't sustain her good humour any longer, and turning away, she went into the back room to plug in the electric kettle. It was nearly eleven, she saw ruefully. Another hour and a half to go. If Janie continued to criticise her behaviour, she might have to reconsider her involvement in the partnership.

"So where is he right now?" Janie inquired from the open doorway, and Caitlin didn't pretend not to understand whom she meant.

"At home. I suppose," she said. "Mrs Spriggs was coming this morning. As far as I know, he had no plans to go out."

"So how come I've just seen him in Regent Street?" asked the other woman tautly, and Caitlin turned to her, anxiety filling her face.

"Nathan?" she breathed, not wanting to believe it. And at Janie's nod, "Was he—running? I told you, he's become very health conscious all of a sudden."

"He wasn't running." Janie's tone was flat. "He was coming out of a travel agent's, actually. I walked right past him, and he cut me dead."

Caitlin moistened her lips. "Well, that's not surprising, is it?" she exclaimed, feeling some small measure of relief. "I don't know how many times I have to tell you, but he really doesn't remember a thing. Certainly not people he used to associate with. Even Daddy and Marshall have accepted that."

Janie's lips drew in. "So you say." It was obvious she was determined to remain sceptical. "But why do you think he's been visiting a travel agent? If what you say is true, where would he be planning to go?"

Caitlin turned back to the kettle. "I don't suppose he's planning to go anywhere," she said firmly. "Can't you try and be a little charitable, Janie? He feels—lost—without identity. Isn't it possible he was just looking at the travel brochures? Maybe he was hoping they would strike a chord."

"You really believe him, don't you?"

"Yes, I do." Caitlin spooned coffee into two mugs and added the boiling water. "For goodness' sake, Janie, he's not lying. Do you think I wouldn't know if he was?"

Janie shrugged and came forward to take her cup. "I don't know," she admitted ruefully. "You say Marshall and your father are convinced?"

"Yes." Though whether that was strictly true, Caitlin didn't choose to hazard. She had the feeling her father's second in command still had his doubts. But whether they were the simple ones about Nathan's condition, or the more troublesome variety concerning his identity, Caitlin preferred not to speculate. Yet the fact remained, Nathan had never been so friendly towards Marshall in the past.

But that exhumed all her own doubts yet again, and she couldn't allow that. Certainly not here, with Janie watching her like a hawk for any sign of weakness. And she still had to cope with what her friend had told her. What had Nathan been doing in the travel agency? Although she might appear untroubled by Janie's revelations, deep inside she could feel that increasingly familiar fear.

"Oh, well..."

At last, Janie seemed prepared to leave it, but her acquiescence had the opposite effect on Caitlin. Instead of relief, a tight feeling of tension was gripping her temples, and if it hadn't been for the risk of rekindling the other woman's suspicions, she would have begged the rest of the morning off and gone home.

But, having achieved her objective, she had no intention of rescinding it. So instead, when Janie wasn't looking, she popped a couple of aspirin into her mouth. There was a perfectly reasonable explanation for Nathan's actions, she told herself. As soon as she got back to the flat, she'd ask him what it was.

20

Marshall had never been to Caitlin's flat before.

He had never been given the opportunity and, even now, he was unsure how she would react to his appearance. Just because Nathan himself had invited him was no reason to expect Caitlin to welcome him with open arms. If the previous weekend was anything to go by, she still resented him bitterly for usurping her husband's position.

But what could he have said?

When Nathan had arrived in reception that afternoon, he had been hard-pressed to remember his own instructions. On no account was the other man to suspect that anything was amiss, Matthew had warned him. Until Nathan recovered his memory, they were to behave as if it was an unhappy accident, and nothing more. Which meant Marshall had had to spend the rest of the day pretending he had nothing to hide, discovering that, for all his amnesia, Nathan was suddenly disconcertingly astute.

Even so, this invitation to accompany him home for supper had caught Marshall unprepared. For the past two years, he had become accustomed to Nathan's snide comments, his sly innuendoes, his unveiled antagonism. In his place, Marshall had suspected he might possibly have felt the same—though he knew he wouldn't have attempted to defraud the company. He had far too many scruples for that.

Nevertheless, his position now was no more tenable. Either he'd accepted Nathan's invitation or he'd run the risk of his suspecting there was something going on. It had been an uneasy dilemma, and in the end, he'd taken the coward's way out.

He cast his eyes sideways, towards the man occupying the other half of the cab seat. If he didn't know better, he'd have said that Nathan was apprehensive, too. Was he having second thoughts about his invitation?

Marshall's lips tightened. It wasn't as if he'd wanted to accept the position Matthew Webster offered him, he reflected ruefully. After the way the old man had treated him and his mother in the past, his initial impulse had been to tell Matthew what he could do with his job. After all, he was already working for another company; he was secure, and he no longer needed assistance from anyone. Least of all from Matthew Webster, who had treated him so dismissively before.

It was his mother who had persuaded him otherwise. He was entitled, she said. Whatever Matthew had done previously, he was ready to make amends now, and Marshall should take advantage of it. She didn't ask him to be grateful; she didn't ask anything of him but that he should take this chance to assume his rightful place. Matthew Webster was his father; he couldn't afford to have scruples now.

And, despite his fears, he couldn't honestly say he had regretted the move. For all his assumed hostility towards the man who had got his mother pregnant and then refused to divorce his wife and marry her, he had eventually come to recognise the difficulties Matthew had faced. Caitlin had still been so young at that time, and for all his infidelity, he still loved his wife. Besides, Daisy Webster could not have managed without him, whereas Mary O'Brien had always been a survivor.

Of course, Matthew had supported them financially, and if Marshall's mother had chosen to put the money he'd given her into a bank and continued to work as a shop assistant, that was hardly his fault. The cash had mounted up, saved for the day when her son would go to college. She was determined he would have a better chance in life than she'd had. She hadn't really trusted Matthew to continue to pay his dues.

The fact that he had had proved irrelevant.

Marshall remembered he had been eighteen when his mother had told him who his father was. Until then, she'd let him believe he'd been the result of some casual alliance with a man who'd seduced her, and then refused to make an honest woman of her. His lips twisted now at the old-fashioned sentiment. As if a wedding ring proved a person's integrity. Nathan was married, and he showed no integrity at all.

At least, he hadn't....

Finding his previous thoughts less disturbing, Marshall returned to the past, recalling with some loathing his own behaviour when he'd discovered who his father was. He remembered he'd actually accused his mother of keeping Matthew's identity from him; of protecting her secret because he could do so much more for his son than she could.

He cringed now at the thought of that first interview with his father. Far from welcoming his son, Matthew had been polite, but nothing else. He'd assumed Marshall was looking for a hand-out, and when he explained that all he really wanted was a job, he'd told him to go away and finish his education.

He'd never gone back. Even though he'd used his father's money to go to university and graduated with a double first in maths and economics, he'd never approached Matthew Webster again. So far as he was concerned, he didn't have a father. And he'd done his best to give his mother a better life.

Then the old man had sent for him—a sick old man now, much different from the arrogant man who had turned him away all those years ago. And with his mother's encouragement, he'd accepted the job he'd offered him. He knew she felt a vicarious kind of satisfaction that he was working for his father at last. But he still had no illusions that one day he would step into his father's shoes. At no time had Matthew promised him that.

"Do you live in town?"

Nathan was speaking to him, and abandoning his introspection, Marshall nodded his head. "I—live in Fulham," he admitted, glancing out the window of the cab and guessing they were only a few minutes from their destination. Then, "Are you sure your wife won't mind me turning up like this, uninvited? I mean, you could have rung and warned her before we left."

"I could," agreed Nathan with a wry smile, and Marshall wondered why he had never noticed the humour in the other man's face before. He had always found Nathan completely humour*less*, and it was another point of contradiction to be stored away.

He sighed. In the past two years he had, reluctantly, come to respect his father's dedication to the business, and he shared Matthew's bitterness at Nathan's betrayal. Only the accident had saved him from certain prosecution. For the first time since she'd married Nathan, Matthew wasn't taking Caitlin's feelings into account.

But if there was one thing Matthew loved—more than either of his two children, Marshall acknowledged with some regret—it was the company and the integrity on which it was founded. Nathan had jeopardised that, therefore Nathan must be punished. But what could you do with a man who didn't remember who he was?

"How well do you know—my wife?" Nathan asked suddenly, and Marshall was once again compelled to look the other man's way.

"Not—well," he conceded, acknowledging the understatement. If it was up to Caitlin, he probably wouldn't have known her at all.

"You're not married?"

Marshall hesitated. He was supposed to be the one asking the questions, he thought ruefully, but it was easier to answer than demur. "No," he agreed. "I—share a house with my mother. It's convenient for both of us, and she'd miss me if I moved away."

"I'm sure."

Once again, Nathan absorbed what he had told him, and Marshall wondered what he was thinking now that the journey was almost over. He still didn't really know why Nathan had come to the office. According to Matthew, he had an appointment with a neurologist later in the week, and it would seem unwise to do anything without his approval.

Nevertheless, it was becoming harder and harder to dislike Nathan. He'd discovered that during the weekend at Fairings, and his opinion hadn't changed today. The man who had been shown into his office that afternoon had seemed almost diffident—and he'd demonstrated an unnerving ability to learn.

The cab braked, and glancing through the window again, Marshall saw the block of luxury flats towering above them. Wellsley Square was also the home of several media stars, and at least one Member of Parliament. In consequence, the security was efficient, but not noticeably overt.

Nathan paid the cab driver, and then the two men walked into the glass-walled foyer. Obviously, Nathan was known here, and no one questioned their progress as they walked towards the lifts. Then, in no time at all, they were at the door of the flat, and before Nathan could insert his key in the lock, it opened.

To say Caitlin looked surprised to see Marshall would have been an understatement. Shocked, perhaps; anxious, certainly. Her expression mirrored a wealth of emotion as she forced her gaze back to her husband's face.

"You're late," she said, her words clipped, her tone verging on the accusatory. "Where the—where have you been?"

"I went to the office," replied Nathan easily, stepping forward so that his wife was obliged to move out of his way. He glanced back reassuringly. "And I've invited Marshall to supper. I hope that isn't a problem."

Caitlin's response was hardly enthusiastic. "I—of course not," she answered eventually, inviting Marshall into the hall. She seemed to be struggling to find her manners. "It's just a casserole, I'm afraid. I—didn't know what was going on."

"It sounds delicious," said Marshall, pushing his glasses up his nose as he did in times of stress. God, he thought, what the hell am I doing here? When Matthew found out, he'd been livid. He'd always done his utmost to keep them apart.

Caitlin closed the door behind them, and then hurried ahead into an attractive living room. "If you'll excuse me," she said, giving her husband a speaking look. "I'm sure everything's going to be overdone."

"No sweat." Nathan was deliberately casual, and Marshall wondered again why he'd brought him here. It wasn't as if he hoped to gain anything by it, and in his experience,

Nathan had never done anything without having his own agenda. "Can I offer you a drink?"

Marshall hesitated, then decided it might ease his nerves. "Scotch would be nice," he agreed, forcing himself to relax a little. He looked about him. "What a beautiful room this is."

"You haven't seen it before?"

Nathan sounded surprised now, though looking into those dark eyes, Marshall had the feeling he already knew the answer. "No," he concurred, "I've never had that pleasure." He paused. "You and I weren't exactly—buddies in the past."

"No." Nathan seemed to accept this, though there was no trace of censure in his face. He handed Marshall his Scotch, and then smiled expansively. "Perhaps we can amend that in the present."

There was a table laid for two in a dining alcove, and as Marshall was trying to think of something to say in response, Caitlin reappeared from the kitchen. She was carrying another set of cutlery, and as he watched, she laid another place. But her movements were all sharp and staccato, and he guessed she wasn't pleased at all.

"If it's any inconvenience—" he began, but once again, Nathan forestalled him.

"It's not," he said. "Caitlin was just worried because I've been out all day." He looked at his wife. "Isn't that right, Kate? Did you have a good morning at the antique shop. I'm sorry I couldn't join you for lunch, but I had things to do."

"Like going to the office," suggested Caitlin shortly, her eyes flashing. "Forgive me, but don't they have phones at the office these days? You could have given me a call."

"I could," he agreed, his eyes gentling as they settled on her. "Forgive me, but I was tied up with your—with Marshall. I've been trying to get a handle on what's been going on."

Marshall realised that Caitlin accepted her husband's words at face value. The fact that he'd stumbled over Marshall's name meant nothing to her. But he was far too sensitive to the situation to ignore any flaw in the conversation, and Nathan's hesitation jarred his nerves.

Was that why he'd brought him here? Because Nathan had guessed who Matthew's right-hand man really was? Was all this *bonhomie* just a façade? Was he wrong about Nathan, in spite of everything? Did he intend to expose him to his wife?

"Oh, well . . ." said Caitlin now, retreating towards the kitchen. "I suppose you know what you're doing." She paused. "What did Daddy say? I suppose it was his idea to try and jog your memory. I told him it wouldn't work, but you know what he's like."

"Mr Webster wasn't there."

"Matt didn't come into the office today."

The two men answered her simultaneously, and Marshall thought it was just as well that a cooker timer began to ring at that moment. It gave him a moment to consider the fact that Nathan had called Matthew *Mr Webster*—which seemed to confirm his status—and enabled her, he hoped, to think about something else.

Not that he had forgotten Nathan's earlier error, and the look he exchanged with his host at that moment assured him that the other man was aware he'd noticed his *faux pas*. "Sorry," he said. "I didn't mean to embarrass you. A slip of the tongue. It won't happen again, I promise."

Marshall wondered. "How long have you known?"

Nathan's lips twitched. "Well, not long, obviously," he replied, and Marshall was forced to accept that this must be so. After all, if he'd suspected earlier, Caitlin would have known about it. The Nathan he was used to dealing with would have enjoyed putting Marshall on the spot.

So why was he guarding his tongue now? Marshall pondered frustratedly. It didn't make sense. Hell, none of it made sense, that was the truth. Nathan simply wasn't the man he used to be, and if it wasn't so outrageous, he might doubt that's who he was.

He frowned as he considered the situation. Could Nathan have a double? And what would be the advantage of that? Had he suspected they were onto him? Could he have persuaded someone else to take his place?

But he dismissed that idea almost before it had had time to germinate. To start with, Nathan didn't even have a brother, let alone an identical twin. Matthew had all his details on file. Nathan's father was Jacob Wolfe, and his mother, Iris Wolfe, was dead. She'd died when the boy was young, and Jacob Wolfe had never remarried.

He had to accept that apart from having somewhat thinner features—a result of the accident, no doubt—this man *was* Nathan. It was crazy to consider anything else. Dear God, Caitlin had accepted him as her *husband*. She had no doubts about him, so nor must he.

"Just out of interest, why haven't you told Caitlin?" Nathan asked suddenly, and Marshall's eyes widened in dismay.

"I don't think—her father would be very pleased if I did," he replied stiffly, and Nathan looked sardonic.

"He's your father, too, isn't he?" he countered. "You know, it just might be that Caitlin needs a brother. Her parents don't give her much support."

His wife's return with the casserole brought an end to any further private conversation, and Marshall told himself he was relieved. But he couldn't help wondering how Matthew would react when he discovered his son-in-law had found out about their relationship. Until now, he'd considered it a closely guarded secret; though Marshall suspected Daisy Webster wasn't the only one to guess the truth.

"Shall we eat?"

Caitlin's voice, inviting them to join her at the table, put an end to his troubled introspection. It was Matthew's problem, he told himself; Matthew's decision when—or indeed if—Caitlin should be told. But how long could they trust Nathan not to tell her? Particularly if his future was on the line?

Caitlin had prepared a green salad to start the meal, and there was a fine white Sauvignon to accompany it. The casserole that followed was piping hot and delicious, despite her worst fears, and a selection of rich cheeses provided a fitting finale.

Conversation became general as they consumed the food, the wine relaxing each of them in turn. Besides, so long as he could forget his previous dealings with Nathan, Marshall found they had a lot in common, and even Caitlin's attitude seemed to mellow as the evening wore on.

Despite his misgivings, Marshall ate everything that was put in front of him, and he knew that in other circumstances he would have welcomed them as friends. His position at Webster's was so nebulous that he found it difficult to find a niche, and he hoped Caitlin would think more charitably about him from now on.

"It was kind of you to put yourself out on my account," he remarked in a low voice, as he helped her carry the used plates into the kitchen. "I know you were only expecting Nathan, and it must have been a pain to be landed with an unexpected guest. I guess you won't believe me, but I did try to put him off."

Caitlin straightened from stowing some of the dirty dishes in the dishwasher, and gave him a strangely quizzical look.

"On the contrary," she said, "I do believe you. I don't suppose you wanted to come here, either."

"That's not true." Marshall spoke instinctively, and then meeting her satirical gaze, he pulled a face. "Okay," he said, "I was apprehensive. I knew we hadn't got along in the past. But that wasn't truly my fault, was it?"

"No." Caitlin seemed inclined to be generous. "I know I haven't exactly been polite. But you have to remember, Nathan used to share my father's confidence, whereas now you've kind of commandeered that role."

"Hmm." Marshall nodded. He could hardly tell her why her father had changed his allegiance. "Well—maybe we can work something out in future. Nathan seems more inclined to be conciliatory. For a man who's lost his memory, he's amazingly astute."

Caitlin frowned. "What are you implying?"

"I'm not implying anything." Marshall held up a calming hand. "On the contrary," he added in a hushed tone, "I'd be the first to admit that he doesn't remember a thing about the company. I mean—" he coloured slightly "—I'm sure he'd have given himself away if he had." He pulled a face. "He's just so—different. It's as if he's lost that aggressive edge."

"Do you think so?" Caitlin's hand trembled as she closed the dishwasher door.

"Yes." Marshall pretended not to notice her nervousness. He pushed his spectacles back up his nose. "I guess that blow to his head did more than addle his brain cells. What do you think?"

"What do I think?" Caitlin's voice had risen slightly, and Marshall, watching her, sensed there was more to this than even he had thought. "Tell me," she went on, "do you think he'll ever recover his memory? If this flat—and the office—aren't familiar, if *I'm* not familiar, what can we do?''

"I don't know."

"What don't you know?" Nathan spoke from the doorway behind them, a pair of empty wineglasses dangling from his hands. "You were taking so long in here, I thought I'd better come and help you." He handed the glasses over. "What's going on?"

"Why—nothing," exclaimed Marshall hurriedly, wondering with some misgivings how long the other man had been standing there listening to what was being said. What had been said? he wondered, taxing his brain. Nothing controversial, he was sure, but for all his disability, he still felt as if Nathan held the upper hand.

Excusing himself, he brushed past the other man and gained the comparative safety of the living room with some relief. But as he did so, he heard voices in the kitchen behind him, and although he didn't mean to eavesdrop, he couldn't help overhearing what Nathan said.

"Don't discuss me as if I'm not here," he muttered, and Caitlin made some inaudible denial. "You have no idea what I'm suggesting," he added in a bitter voice.

21

Marshall left at about half past nine.

Caitlin sensed he would have been quite happy to go sooner, but Nathan had kept him talking, making it difficult for him to get away.

They hadn't spoken about relevant things, like Nathan's loss of memory, or how soon he might be able to get back to work. Nathan had seemed more interested in Marshall's background, and they'd spent some time arguing the merits of nurture as opposed to nature.

She'd guessed what Nathan was doing, of course. So long as Marshall was here, they couldn't have a personal conversation. And after talking to Janie that morning, she'd wanted that. She'd been waiting for him to return all afternoon.

In actual fact, *waiting* was hardly an adequate term. By the time Nathan inserted his key in the lock, she'd been on the verge of calling the police. In all her wild imaginings, she'd never dreamed that he might go to the office. Or if he had, that someone might not inform her. It was the least they could have done.

Still, she could hardly blame Marshall or his secretary. They were not to know that she didn't know where Nathan was. Or that he'd been out since early this morning. According to Mrs Spriggs, he'd left the flat soon after she'd gone to the shop.

Consequently, she'd been in no mood to welcome visitors, particularly not Marshall O'Brien. Although, in the event, he'd proved rather likeable. And Nathan had evidently had second thoughts about him, too. The two men had behaved like old friends, not old enemies, and she'd found herself re-evaluating everything Nathan had said about him.

If it hadn't been for that niggling doubt as to why he should have been visiting a travel agent's, Caitlin thought she might have enjoyed the evening. Even knowing that Nathan was using Marshall to avoid any intimacy with her was not enough to spoil her mood. Her relief at knowing he was safe and well had tempered much of her resentment, and although she was still indignant, it could wait.

Nevertheless, she hadn't been able to prevent herself from watching Nathan across the table. She'd wondered what he was thinking as he picked at his food. Unlike Marshall, her husband had eaten little, and there was a strange kind of tension about his actions that she didn't remember noticing before.

But that didn't dissipate her feelings, or the taut reaction she felt every time he was near. She couldn't understand it, but that didn't make it any the less disturbing. She was falling in love with her husband. So what on earth could be wrong with that?

Still, on the rare occasions when he looked her way, she made sure her eyes were averted. She had no wish for him to see how he affected her until she knew how he really felt. Just because they'd slept together—made love together—was no reason to imagine she had any real claim to his affections. She might be inexperienced in some ways, but she knew sex didn't mean the same to a man.

In consequence, she had welcomed the opportunities she'd had to escape to the kitchen. When her hands were busy, it was easier to distract her mind. But she'd noticed she was trembling as she'd forked the various cheeses onto the board, and Nathan's face was waiting behind her lids when she closed her eyes in an effort to reinforce her will.

Nathan had had some cheese, and once again she'd found herself watching his hands as he'd put the cheese into his mouth. He had nice hands, very attractive hands, she'd thought uneasily, and when he'd opened his mouth, she'd been able to see his tongue. It had appeared to lick a crumb of Caerphilly from his lip, and her stomach had hollowed almost uncontrollably. Was it two nights since he'd pushed his tongue into her mouth? The memory was still potent enough to turn her knees to water.

Which was why she was sitting down when Nathan returned from seeing Marshall to the door. They'd phoned for a taxi to take him back to Fulham, and Nathan had offered to go down with him when the cab driver rang from the foyer. By this time, the two men were on easy terms, and she guessed Marshall must be as confused as herself. However, like her, he seemed prepared to welcome the change and deal with it accordingly.

She sighed. She didn't know why, but there was something reassuring about Marshall noticing the change in her husband. It reinforced her own opinion, made her feel as if she wasn't going mad after all. And, if nothing else, this evening had broken the ice between her and her father's assistant. She had been guilty of judging him by other people's standards. Her mother's fault, perhaps.

The door slammed, and her nerves tensed. As her husband walked back into the living room, it took an enormous effort of will to look as casual as he appeared. Her hair was mussed from where she had been slumped against the cushions, but that was hardly an advantage. And although she'd been determined to confront him with Janie's accusation as soon as they were alone, her mixed emotions had diminished her inner strength.

Meanwhile, Nathan looked infuriatingly confident. He had shed the jacket of his dark suit earlier, and loosened the knot of his tie. Now, with his sleeves rolled back over his forearms, and the waistcoat of the suit providing a contrast to the crisp whiteness of his shirt, he looked almost unwarrantably attractive, and Caitlin's resentment rallied at his obvious lack of remorse.

"Interesting guy," he said by way of an opening, and Caitlin felt her resentment growing at his conceit. Did he think that because he had decided Marshall wasn't such a bad guy, she should follow his lead regardless? What did he think she was? Some kind of clone? Didn't he think she had opinions of her own?

When she didn't answer, he seemed to realise that perhaps he had been rather insensitive, and halting in the middle of the floor, he hooked his thumbs into the pockets of his trousers. "I guess you didn't think so," he remarked. "Though I have to say you seemed to be getting along just fine in the kitchen earlier. What was he saying to you? Was he apologising for arriving unannounced?"

"You tell me," said Caitlin stiffly, realising she might be cutting off her nose to spite her face, but unable to do anything about it. She couldn't let him treat her as if her wishes were of no importance. She'd promised herself that would never happen again.

"What do you mean?" he asked now, and Caitlin pretended to examine her fingernails.

"Well, you were eavesdropping, weren't you?" she countered. "I believe you warned me about talking about you as if you weren't there. In any case, it's none of your business. If you bring people here without asking me first, you can't blame me if I take advantage of the fact."

Her husband's mouth compressed. "What's that supposed to mean?"

Caitlin shrugged. "Whatever you like."

He sighed. "All right, I'm sorry if I upset your plans—"

"Upset my plans?" Caitlin came up off the sofa then, stung by the weary tolerance in his voice. "You have no idea how I was feeling when you sauntered in here at seven o'clock. You'd been missing since early this morning. Were you out all day yesterday, as well? Or have you forgotten?"

This last was said with a sweet sarcasm, and he scowled. "Ten o'clock is not early morning," he retorted, and Caitlin arched a quizzical brow.

"It is when you're supposed to be convalescing. Or had you forgotten that, as well? Along with your much-quoted hatred of Marshall O'Brien!"

It was amazing how much stronger she felt, thought Caitlin as she threw the words at him. When Marshall left, she'd felt tired, listless, incapable of conducting an argument with anyone. But suddenly she was alert again—invigorated, ready to take him on. Sparring with Nathan was the next best thing to making love with him, she realised. She enjoyed sparking his interest, even if it was just a mental thing.

Her husband frowned. "Why would—I—hate Marshall?" he asked slowly, and Caitlin was aware that when he looked at her with those dark, expressive eyes, she felt as if every nerve in her body came vibrantly to life. But she couldn't afford to be sympathetic. That wouldn't win her any favours. She had to remember what Janie had said: leopards didn't change their spots.

"Why would you hate Marshall?" she demanded now, rekindling her impatience. "Why do you think, Nathan? Because he's doing the job you once considered yours."

"I see." He nodded his head in understanding, as if another piece of the jigsaw had fallen into place. "I was your father's deputy." He paused. "What was Marshall doing then?"

"You tell me." Caitlin sighed. "He didn't come to work for Daddy until about two years ago. Before that—well, I suppose you were acting as his deputy. But Daddy's never given up running the company, even though he knows he should."

"Because of his heart attack?"

"And his age," said Caitlin quickly. "He is almost sixty, you know. Lots of men have retired before then."

"So—why was N—I—demoted?" he asked. "What did I do to lose your father's confidence? Was I negligent, or what?"

Caitlin shrugged. "I don't know," she admitted, and seeing his frustration, she felt a reluctant sense of compassion. Despite all her efforts, he'd got under her skin again.

She sighed. The exhilaration she had felt earlier had all dispersed now, and she just felt tired. Too tired to broach the reasons why he had been visiting the travel agency, she realised wearily. She wasn't even sure she wanted to know.

She was about to leave the room when he stopped her. Almost involuntarily, it seemed, he had taken up a position beside the rosewood bureau that supported the row of decanters he liked to keep on show. He used to say they were for his friends, but so far as she knew, he had never invited anyone back to the flat—until tonight. Unless, her lips tightened, he had brought Lisa Abbott here, while she was safely out of the way.

"We need to talk," he said, indicating that he was offering her a drink, but Caitlin shook her head.

"I thought we had been talking," she said, trying not to feel apprehensive. Was he about to explain his reasons for not sleeping with her since they got back?

"We've been—fencing," he said quietly, pouring himself a small measure of Scotch and adding a squirt of soda. "I think I ought to tell you, I'm going back to the States."

Caitlin's lips parted. "You're going to America?" she said, hardly able to believe it. No need to ask what he had been doing in the travel agent's now. He'd been making arrangements to leave.

"Yes." He allowed a mouthful of the malt whisky to slide down his throat. "I think it's a good idea. Don't you?"

"But you don't know anyone there. How will you get about?" Caitlin was trying not to panic. "I'll come with you."

"No."

"What do you mean, no?" She moistened her lips. "You can't stop me. I—I'm your wife."

"We both know that's not true," he told her flatly, and her eyes widened disbelievingly. "I mean," he said, not without some discomfort, "that I *can* stop you. I don't want you to come with me, Kate. I—need to do this on my own."

"It's Marshall, isn't it?" she exclaimed recklessly. "He's the one who's put this crazy idea into your head. All that talk about children—and whether it matters who brings them up. You imagine if you go to Prescott, you're going to have a sudden revelation."

There was a hint of colour in his cheeks now, and she wondered what she had said to embarrass him. She was the one who was embarrassed; she was the one who wanted desperately to beg him to change his mind. Or if not, to let her accompany him. She was afraid that if she let him go, she'd never see him again.

"I'd made my decision before I went to the office," he said gently. "I'm not denying I was interested in what Marshall had to say, but I've known what I have to do ever since—well, ever since last weekend."

Caitlin's lips twitched. "Since you made love to me, I suppose," she said bitterly. "Since you realised I wasn't what you needed. That whatever you said, I wasn't sexy enough for your tastes!"

"Don't be a fool!"

He was angry now, and if she hadn't known better, she might have believed he meant it. As it was, she could only think he was an incredible actor. Either that, or he really didn't remember how it had been before.

In any case, Caitlin was too distrait to care what he might be thinking. She just knew all her hopes for the future were gradually turning to dust. Once again, she'd let him get too close, and this time he'd destroyed her. She hadn't cared before; she did care now.

And, because she wasn't thinking very clearly herself, her next words were even more of a betrayal. "I suppose you'd rather take the Abbott woman with you," she taunted, forgetting for a moment that Nathan didn't know who the other woman was. "*Lisa Abbott*," she prompted, feeling sick as she realised what she was doing. "The woman who rang you when you were at Fairings? Surely you remember that."

Nathan blinked. "Lisa Abbott," he said faintly. "But how—I mean—" He broke off and rephrased what he had been about to say. "So that's who it was."

Caitlin stared at him suspiciously. "You remember her, don't you?" she said accusingly. "When I mentioned her name, you remembered who she was."

"No—"

"Oh, don't bother to lie. I simply don't believe you." She sniffed. "Just tell me. Do you remember everything?"

"No." He spoke frustratedly at first, and then seemed to make a concerted effort to calm himself. "Look, Kate," he said evenly, "it's not easy for me to explain. Can't you accept—at least for the present—that I'm still probing in the dark? I promise I'll tell you everything as soon as I know what that is."

Caitlin held up her head. "I'm tired," she said flatly, not giving him the satisfaction of an answer. "It's been a long day. I think I'll go to bed."

"Kate—"

"No. I don't want to hear that you're innocent," she retorted painfully. "I expected nothing from you—I *wanted* nothing from you—before the accident, and I'm damned if I want anything now. Just get out of my life, Nathan. Do you hear me? I never want to see you again!"

He uttered a harsh cry. "That's not true."

"It is true," she told him unsteadily. "You wanted to know what manner of man you were, what kind of marriage we had. Well, I'll tell you. It was a marriage made in hell, do you hear that? And you were its maker. I swore then that I'd never let you near me again, and I wouldn't have, if you hadn't convinced me that you'd changed, that you didn't remember what a brute you'd been, that I couldn't judge a man who couldn't even remember his own name. But I was wrong, wasn't I? I don't know what you hoped to gain by it, whether you thought you could sustain the charade long enough to get back into my father's good books, or persuade me that your affair with Lisa Abbott was over. I can see it would be attractive to you—the thought of making a brand-new start. My God, you even—what's that very appropriate word you use in your country? Suckered? Yes, that's it, you even—suckered Marshall. He was actu-

ally opening up to you, wasn't he? Believing—just like me—
that the old you was gone for good."

"No—"

"Yes." She wouldn't let him say anything that might interfere with the very fine indictment she was making. She
couldn't allow him to interrupt her; to say anything in miti-
gation of her words. She was too afraid of what she might
do if he attempted to defend himself. For all she told herself she despised him, she couldn't forget what might have
been.

"You don't understand," he overrode her harshly, and
although she was sure he was still lying to her, there was anguish in his voice. "For pity's sake, Kate, don't say anything you might regret later. I don't like hurting you this
way, and if there were any other course open to me..." He
sighed. "I'd take it. Believe me, I have no choice."

"Don't you?"

The scepticism in her response was unmistakeable, and he
closed his eyes against the accusation in her face. He rocked
back on his heels, and just for a moment, she allowed herself to look at him, unaware that her heart and soul were in
her eyes.

"God, Kate..."

He opened his eyes before she could look away again, and
although she turned towards the door, he covered the space
between them in a couple of strides. With his hand on her
shoulder, he spun her round to face him, and his hand
grasped her chin as he crushed his mouth to hers.

Caitlin's head swam at the first touch of his lips. His kiss
was hard and passionate, his tongue plunging into her
mouth with all the knowing skill of an experienced lover.
She staggered backwards, her spine coming up against the
wall beside the door as he came after her, imprisoning her

between the wall and his body, his hands raised at either side of her head.

His jaw was rough against her cheek. He had shaved that morning, but already the dark stubble of his beard was beginning to show. She'd thought earlier that the slightly dishevelled look only added to his attractiveness, and for all his skin abraded hers as his mouth moved possessively over her face, she wouldn't have had it any other way.

Her hands came up almost instinctively to cup his face, her breasts rising against his chest and causing him to moan softly, low in his throat. It was so very reminiscent of when he had kissed her in the shower, and she remembered only too well where that had led.

She moved against him, feeling the instinctive pressure of his body. His hands sought her breasts, squeezing their swollen fullness, his thumbs running sensuously across the hard peaks. The need for him to touch her naked flesh became almost an obsession, and the desire to feel his flesh against hers throbbed hotly between her legs.

She was beyond thought, beyond reason, eager only to reiterate what had gone before. They were alone in the flat; he could have taken her there on the floor if he'd wanted to. She could feel his erection, thrusting forcefully against her stomach, and she could smell his arousal in the clean scent of his body.

He wanted her. That thought sang in her head. Whether he had recovered his memory or not, whether he remembered Lisa Abbott or not, he still wanted her. He might try and keep her away from him; he might try to deny it. But his body couldn't hide its reaction to her nearness. His breathing was harsh and laboured, and there was a greedy possession in his touch. He wanted her; he wanted to feel her heat around him. He was losing control, and she revelled in his submission.

With a trembling hand, she released the buttons on her shirt. Then, with a feeling of abandonment, she took one of his hands and drew it down to the hem of her skirt. And when he didn't resist, she took it between her legs.

"Christ!"

His response was not what she had expected. Whereas before, his feelings had sapped his will, this time he found the strength to break away. With a contorted expression that only afterwards she identified as self-disgust, he pulled away from her. And before she could do anything to change his mind, he wrenched open the door and left the room.

22

Jake decided to drive to Prescott.

It would have been easier to take a plane—less tiring, certainly—but he felt as if he needed a little time by himself to try and come to terms with what was going on. He knew now that for the past three weeks he'd been living his life as Nathan. But that was over now. He had remembered who he really was.

He still got a headache when he taxed his brain too heavily. But he was determined to put the events, as he knew them, into order before he got to his father's house. He didn't know if Jacob Wolfe had been a party to Nathan's plan, but he doubted it. Whatever private opinion he might hold of the man who had sired him, he had always believed he was honest, if nothing else.

The fact that Nathan had come looking for him should have warned him to be on his guard. In all the years they had known of one another's existence, Nathan had never shown any real friendship before. Jake had always known their paths would never have crossed at all if he hadn't gone looking for his twin.

Still, the story Nathan had told him in Casey's bar had evidently held some elements of truth. Nathan was weak; Jake had always known that. And although he hadn't even known Caitlin then, her vulnerability—and Jacob's—had compelled him to try and do something to help them.

Not that he really had anything to thank Jacob Wolfe for, he mused wryly. Although Jacob had made an effort to meet Jake after he got back from Vietnam, they had never become close. Jacob's assertion that he would have adopted both boys if he could didn't alter the fact that he had abandoned their mother. He had never had any intention of divorcing his wife and marrying Alice, even if she had been prepared to leave Fletch.

Nevertheless, that association was important now. There was no one else Jake could turn to for advice. He only hoped Jacob knew where Nathan was, and that there was some way they could resolve the situation. He couldn't bear to think he'd never see Caitlin again.

A groan welled inside him.

Dear God, this wasn't just a difficult situation, he thought grimly, remembering Caitlin's face when he'd told her he was returning to the States. As far as he was concerned, it was a matter of life or death. He couldn't leave the woman he had come to love to his brother. After what she had accused him of, believing he was Nathan, he felt almost murderous himself.

He remembered that after they'd left the bar, Nathan had transferred the suitcase from the trunk of the rental car to the trunk of the Blazer in the parking lot. The only hitch had been Nathan's plan to exchange passports. That had entailed driving out to Pine Bay, where Jake had unwillingly collected his own passport from the condo. He supposed he hadn't taken into account the fact that Nathan would need his passport. Nevertheless, he didn't want to alert his brother to the fact that he was having any trouble believing his story, so they had switched passports as planned, and Nathan had left.

But from the start, he'd had his suspicions. Nathan was scared of Walker, he believed that, but if the man was really as powerful as his brother would have him believe, would he risk his reputation by employing someone like his brother? And why would Nathan come to him for help when he'd always despised him? It didn't ring true. Nathan wouldn't ask for his help. He'd do nothing to give Jake that kind of advantage over him. No, the more he thought about it, the more convinced he became that he was being used.

But for what? *As what?*

He'd opened the suitcase Nathan had given him as soon as he'd gotten home from work that evening. It was only then that he'd realised that the suitcase was locked, and Nathan had forgotten—deliberately or otherwise—to give him the code. However, after a few false starts, he'd managed to open it. Their birth date had proved to be decisive, and he thought how typical it was of Nathan to use something so obvious as that.

However, when he'd lifted the lid of the case, that had been forgotten. The suitcase had appeared to hold nothing but clothes. He found no hidden cavities, no false base, nothing that Jake could see out of the ordinary. Just a couple of pairs of shoes, some shaving gear, and two paperback novels, stuffed carelessly down the side.

That was when he'd decided that Nathan might not have been lying after all. It seemed infinitely more credible that Walker might have arranged for him to carry an empty suitcase back from New York. A kind of dress rehearsal, perhaps—a dry run, to assess Nathan's willingness to walk through Customs carrying what he believed to be his passport to imprisonment if he was caught.

But that hadn't rung true, either: Nathan must have chosen the code that had locked the suitcase. It was simply not credible that someone else might have chosen those numbers instead of him. So what the hell was the point? Why was he being implicated? Jake had decided to use Nathan's passport after all, and go to London and find out for himself.

He wondered now if he hadn't hoped that he might see Caitlin while he was in England. A remote chance, perhaps, but she might have been able to give him something about what Nathan was up to. For all his brother had said he wanted to keep the affair a secret from his wife, Jake had been in no mood to accommodate him, and he'd decided he didn't owe Nathan any favours after the way he had been duped.

In the event, the accident had prevented any confrontation. Which he knew now Nathan would have wanted to avoid. No wonder he'd felt such a sense of alienation with both the name he'd been given and his background. He'd been trying to fit into Nathan's shoes, and they hadn't been just physically too tight.

He grimaced. It had taken a momentous event to shock him out of his inertia, and in the aftermath of discovering he had just made love to his brother's wife, he'd found it difficult to accept what had happened. Not just because he'd somehow gotten away with it, but for the first time since the accident, he hadn't wanted to remember who he was.

But after that amazing revelation, he had had no choice but to try and do something positive. During the following days, he'd been stunned by the amount of information his brain had managed to absorb. There'd been times when he'd been afraid his head might explode with the conflicting messages he was receiving. He'd still been living as Nathan, but all his reactions were Jake's.

Which was why he should have kept away from Caitlin. He knew now the kind of relationship she'd had with his brother, and he felt as if he'd taken advantage of her innocence. But what they had shared was as new to him as it was to her. Totally new, he reflected painfully, aware of the irony. After all the women he had known, he had had to go and fall in love with his brother's wife.

He knew he had hurt her by not allowing her to accompany him to Prescott. But, dear God! how could he allow her to go on believing he was her husband? Until he had spoken to Nathan and discovered where he was and what he was doing, he and Caitlin couldn't have a life together. Goddammit, he didn't even know if it was him she cared about or the man she'd married.

The afternoon he'd spent at Webster Development had been useful. During his conversations with Marshall O'Brien, he'd learned a lot of what Nathan had been covering up. Marshall had tried to be objective, but Jake had sensed there was more to the questions he and Matthew Webster had asked him at Fairings that weekend than they were saying. They were obviously onto something, but they weren't inclined to tell him what it was.

Jake had checked Nathan's passport, too, and discovered he had visited South America in April. He doubted it was a legitimate visit. After what he'd learned, he couldn't believe Matthew Webster would give his son-in-law any more responsibility than he absolutely had to. He'd guessed even then that it had to have had something to do with the contract Matthew and Marshall had spoken about, and judging from the way they'd grilled him, it was more than just a cause of concern to them. The irony was, they still thought he was Nathan. Did they imagine he'd developed a conscience at last?

For the present, he had to concentrate on dealing with his brother's treachery. Had there ever been any drugs and, if so, where were they now? It occurred to him that his brother might have double-crossed not just him, but Carl Walker. Had Nathan hoped the other man might demand his pound of flesh in kind?

Jake's fingers tightened on the wheel. He had the feeling that he was getting closer to the truth. But Walker hadn't contacted him, probably leaving it to Lisa Abbott. And thankfully, he still believed the drugs had been destroyed.

According to Caitlin, there had only been one phone call for him, and that had been from the woman he'd visited the day before. Lisa still believed that Nathan's intention had been to come back to London, as he'd said, although Jake guessed she was having second thoughts when he left Majestic Court. . . .

Majestic Court!

Jake looked up at the rather ugly block of apartments, wondering why developers thought that giving a building a fancy name might somehow improve its image. Nothing could change the stark lines of the sixties era, when building high had seemed the answer to the housing problem.

Lisa Abbott's apartment was on the fourth floor, and he was relieved to find the elevators worked. His strength was returning, and he didn't doubt he could have climbed the stairs if he'd had to; but he was impatient and he didn't want to arrive panting at her door.

All the same, he couldn't deny a certain sense of apprehension when he rang the bell. She was expecting Nathan after all, and he had the feeling that it was going to be harder to fool her than Nathan's wife.

Not that he wanted to think of Caitlin right now. It disturbed him that he found it difficult to get her out of his mind, because whatever kind of an opinion he was forming of his brother's behaviour, she was still married to Nathan and not him.

Not that he had respected that.

The door opened as he was remembering how good it had been to hold Caitlin in his arms. She was so warm and soft, so giving. He'd never known a woman who had affected him so strongly; never wanted to submerge his own identity before....

"My God! Nate!"

His treacherous thoughts were arrested by the cry from the woman who had opened the door. Not Caitlin this time, but a woman who much more closely resembled the kind of woman he'd expected his brother to admire. Or at least find appealing, he reflected drily, until something more attractive came along.

Briefly, it crossed his mind that Nathan might have left his wife—and his mistress—for another woman. But the thought barely claimed a second of his time. Nathan was not the kind of man to risk his reputation, his comfort, his *life*, for sexual gratification. He might use a woman, as he had apparently used Caitlin, but he wouldn't sacrifice himself for love.

"Where the hell have you been?"

The woman was gazing at him with a mixture of anger and indignation, and Jake realised she was older than he had at first thought. Perhaps Nathan's age—*his age*—or even older. It was difficult to tell in the shadowy hallway, and she hadn't yet invited him in.

"Bastard!" she added, sniffing, as if she was on the verge of bursting into tears. "Oh—come here, you idiot! Don't you know I've been half out of my mind with worry over you? Weren't there any phones in that fucking hospital, or was that prissy wife of yours always on your back?"

She lunged towards him, catching Jake unawares, and it was all he could do to prevent himself from recoiling from her eager embrace. Accustomed to Caitlin's delicate beauty, he found Lisa's ample breasts and sultry lips a distinct turn-off, and it was a relief when she uttered a disgusted cry and pushed him away.

"You're not Nate!"

"No."

Jake decided there was no point in trying to deny it, though the fist that connected with his midriff at that moment made him catch his breath. He had hoped he might learn something from her before she realised he wasn't his brother, but the way she was glaring at him now seemed to have put paid to that.

"I know who you are," she added, reaching for the door, and he automatically wedged his foot against the jamb to prevent her from slamming it in his face. "You're his brother," she declared. "The twin he thought I didn't know about. So why are you here pretending to be Nathan? Because he's too scared to come and see me himself?"

"No." Jake was thinking on his feet now, and it wasn't easy. Somehow, he'd got to convince her that Nathan knew what was going on. "There's been a hitch," he said. "Um—Nathan got held up in New York, so I was supposed to come to London in his place."

Lisa's expression was not encouraging. "Really?"

"Yes, really."

"So how come you didn't tell me who you were when I opened the door?"

That was a difficult one. "I guess—I guess I was hoping you wouldn't notice," offered Jake unctuously. He swallowed. "It's not every day a beautiful woman throws herself into my arms."

Lisa still looked uncertain, but he could tell that his words had mollified her. She was still sufficiently confident of her own charms to believe he might be telling the truth. "You'd better come in," she said, saving him the trouble of asking. "I'm not saying I forgive you, but I'm prepared to listen to what you have to say." They went along a narrow corridor into a lamplit living room. It wasn't yet dark outside, but the illumination helped to banish the gloom of the day. "English weather," she muttered, gesturing towards the windows, evidently expecting a fellow American to sympathise with her. "When Nate and I get enough money, we're getting out of here for good."

Jake made no comment. But he had the feeling Lisa was going to be disappointed about that, as well. He suspected that Nathan might well be bored with her. Could he have had yet another betrayal in mind?

"D'you want a drink?"

She gestured towards a tray containing a decanter of Scotch and two glasses, but although he was tempted, Jake shook his head. He needed to keep his wits about him, even if the idea of a shot of Scotch was attractive. For all she seemed gullible in some ways, she might well be leading him on.

"So why did Nate send you here?" she asked, giving him little time for consideration. "And why haven't you been in touch before now if Nate asked you to see me?"

Jake took a breath. "Because—well, because of the crash," he said. "And because I lost my memory."

"Say what?"

She looked disbelieving, and Jake hurried to reassure her. "It's true." He paused. "Even Caitlin didn't know who I was. As far as she's concerned, I'm Nathan. My memory's just come back in the past couple of days."

Lisa stared at him. "If this is Nate's idea of a—"

"It isn't." Jake was on firmer ground now, and he showed it. "Ask anyone at Webster's. They'll tell you I'm speaking the truth."

"That still doesn't explain why you were travelling to London." She hesitated. "Did Nate tell you why he'd gone to New York?"

Jake took a chance. "The drugs, you mean?" he asked, and her expression revealed all he'd needed to know. Lisa had known about the drugs; but did she know Nathan hadn't sent them? "I guess you're as gutted as he is about the crash."

Lisa's face cleared. "Christ, yes," she said fervently. "Carl isn't too happy about it, either. I thought at first that was why Nate had sent you to see me. He's pretty intimidated by my boss, you know."

"Your boss?"

The words just slipped out, but happily Lisa didn't regard them as anything significant. "Yeah, didn't he tell you I work for Carl at the club?" She grimaced. "I guess you could say I set up the deal in the first place. Well, it was my idea that Carl use Nate as a courier. I mean, who'd suspect a law-abiding businessman like him?"

Who indeed?

Jake knew a moment's uncertainty. For a moment there, he'd thought Lisa had been going to say she set him up. It was possible, of course, though not entirely credible. He knew Nathan of old, and he wouldn't make that kind of mistake.

Nevertheless, he was beginning to get another idea, one that he didn't like one little bit. "I guess it's something you get used to," he said. "I must say, I was a bit apprehensive. I haven't acquired Nathan's experience yet."

"Hey, Nate's only done it once before," said Lisa at once, confirming his suspicions. "Course, that time everything went as smooth as silk, just like Carl said. I don't think Nate was keen, but hey—the rewards are worth it. What other chance would he and I have of getting it together?"

"He—plans to get a divorce?" probed Jake, realising he was pushing it, but Lisa seemed happy to confide in him, now that he'd proved his credentials, so to speak.

"I guess," she said, although a frown creased her forehead. "I suppose it depends on what Carl will do now."

About the drugs, finished Jake silently. And if he hadn't carried them to London, where the hell were they? With his brother, he guessed, which seemed to prove he had been just a decoy. So what had Nathan hoped to gain by sending him there? *Nirvana*?

Unlikely, he opined impatiently. But he'd gotten his passport, which might have been his intention all along. But surely Nathan knew that as soon as Jake realised the deception, he'd have reported its loss to the authorities. Nathan must have known he wouldn't let him get away with that.

"I bet you're wondering how come I knew you were Nate's brother," remarked Lisa consideringly, and he hoped she wasn't going to take him up on his flattery now.

"Well—yes," he said, although that thought hadn't entered his head.

"I've known Nate for a long time," she said. "Since before he came to England. His old man might have kept it a secret, but my mother used to work for Nathan's mother, and Iris spilled the beans before she died."

Looking back now, Jake was amazed at how quickly she had accepted his story. In her place, he'd have wanted to know what Nathan was doing in New York, why his brother hadn't phoned. Her main concern was that Carl shouldn't find out that Nathan hadn't been carrying the drugs to London himself. Her opinion that Carl wouldn't like them involving anyone else was probably the truest thing she'd said.

In addition to which, she had her own future to think of. If she had arranged for Nathan to become involved, she was just as likely to be accused of double-dealing as Nathan. Jake had the feeling that, given time, she was going to feel very aggrieved towards his brother. Her own fears would stop her from betraying him to Walker, however.

It had been easier for him to do what he had to do, knowing the kind of humiliation Caitlin must have suffered at their hands. Besides, Lisa was just as guilty as Nathan. She'd been quite willing to assist Carl Walker in his dirty trade.

It had been Lisa's hatred for Caitlin that enabled him to find out where Nathan had obtained the money to buy the consignment. Lisa had confirmed that it was through the contract for the Magdalena dam that Nathan had defrauded the company, and Jake was appalled to discover the extent of his brother's guilt. Some he'd guessed; some he'd gleaned during his conversations with Marshall. Had Nathan really believed he could get away with it? Hadn't he realised that Marshall was watching his every move?

It must have all stemmed from Matthew Webster's illness. Nathan must have believed the gods were on his side then. How soon, Jake wondered, had he attempted to wrest control from the old man's failing hands? How soon had Matthew Webster become aware of his son-in-law's guilt?

He wondered how long it had taken him to realise why Nathan had married his daughter? Pretty quickly, was Jake's guess, as he drove south on the Garden State Parkway. New Jersey in the fall was one of nature's small miracles, but Jake took little interest in the changing colours of the trees. His mind was too intent on reaching Prescott and finding out from Jacob where his brother was hiding. Surely Jacob would know where Nathan was. It was the only lead he had.

He sighed, thinking about how peeved Nathan must have been when the old man got better. Particularly after Caitlin's father had appointed his own son. How had Matthew persuaded Marshall to join the company? he wondered.

Although Matthew depended on the younger man, there
were times when Jake had sensed a certain tension between
them. It was ironic that he should be prepared to put so
much trust in the son he had never acknowledged.

Nevertheless, it seemed obvious that Marshall's arrival
had precipitated Nathan into taking drastic action. He'd
been ripe for any scheme Walker had put before him, and
Jake knew enough about the Colombian deal now to make
an educated guess at what Nathan had planned to do. But
he'd taken an enormous risk when he'd double-crossed
Walker. If it hadn't been for the crash, what might Walker
have done to him?

Jake decided he owed none of them any favours, whereas
he owed it to himself to clear his name. He didn't like being
mixed up in any part of this filthy business, and he meant to
find out why Nathan had been lying from the start.

23

Caitlin was seated at the cash desk, trying to make sense of the column of figures on the page in front of her. Janie had gone shopping, and she was in charge of the shop at the moment. And, as it was quiet, she'd decided to try and get a little book-keeping done.

It was useless.

No matter how she tried, no matter how she concentrated on the entries Janie had made over the past three weeks, she kept coming up with a different total time after time. It wasn't as if she was attempting to add the figures up herself. She had an efficient little calculator beside her, but it didn't make any difference. She couldn't seem to key in the figures correctly, and the bottom of the the page was already half-worn away with her rubbings out.

If only she could stop thinking about Nathan, she might stand a chance of having some success, she thought frustratedly. But how was she supposed to get on with her life when the man she loved was more than three thousand miles away? If she knew he was all right, if she could believe that his journey was not just another wild-goose chase, she could try and put it all to the back of her mind. But her fears were so self-contradictory, she was living in a constant state of unease.

Her greatest fear was that if—when—he did come back, he might not be the same man who had gone away. It was a crazy thought, and not one she could share with anyone else, but the fact remained, there was always that possibility. He'd changed already before he'd left, and she wasn't entirely convinced he didn't remember some things at least.

Like Lisa Abbott.

She didn't want to think about the other woman, but she couldn't help it. There was no denying that Nathan had been interested to hear her confirm who his anonymous caller had been. She'd been a fool to mention her, to blurt out her name as she had, but she'd been jealous. And whether the name had rung any bells with him or not, she'd played right into the other woman's hands.

Still, Nathan wasn't with Lisa at that moment. He'd left for New York that morning, and she knew—because she'd rung the airline to check on it—that he had been travelling alone.

She'd been quite foolishly pleased at her ingenuity in finding out that Lisa wasn't travelling on the morning's Concorde. She knew airlines didn't give out information about their passengers, so she pretended she was Lisa Abbott and that she was ringing to confirm her booking on the flight. She'd had the foresight to make a provisional booking, also in Lisa's name, on the evening flight instead, so the clerk quite innocently informed her that she'd got the bookings crossed.

It was a small victory, but one which she had clung to in the hours since. She had to believe that Nathan was only going to the States, as he'd said, to try and find his roots. Not just his name, but his identity. And only his father could give him that.

For her part, Caitlin was afraid to think of what might happen in the future. She had the uneasy feeling that nothing was ever going to be the same again. Not that she wanted it to be the same as it was before the accident, she reminded herself unhappily, but she was finding it hard to believe that the man she loved was anything more than a dream.

The door of the shop opened, the bell breaking discordantly into her thoughts. She glanced up, half-hoping it was Janie, despite the other girl's attitude towards what had happened. Naturally, her friend expected the worst, and she was not averse to saying so.

But it wasn't Janie. It was a customer—a blonde woman, wearing decidedly too much make-up, and dressed rather too youthfully for her age. Caitlin estimated the woman must be nearing forty, yet the miniskirt and teetering high heels would not have looked out of place on a teenager.

Contrary to normal practice, the woman didn't seem at all interested in browsing about the shop. Instead of casting even a salutary glance at the merchandise on offer, she swayed purposefully towards the cash desk, halting in front of Caitlin, forcing her to rise politely to her feet.

"Can I help you?"

The woman surveyed her between mascaraed lids, her gaze sweeping down over Caitlin's tight-sleeved T-shirt and ankle-length pinafore with a jaundiced eye. "Maybe," she said at last. "Although I doubt it. My guess is, you're more inclined to help yourself."

Caitlin's jaw sagged. "I beg your pardon?"

"So polite." The woman's lips twisted. "And exactly as I imagined. All milk-and-water innocence and no fire!"

Caitlin blinked. "Look, Mrs—Miss—"

"*Ms* will do," the woman inserted contemptuously, glancing about her. "Ms—Abbott. Does that name mean anything? How about if I mention Nathan? Does that ring a bell?"

Caitlin's knees trembled. She'd been trying to identify the woman's accent, and now she knew. Lisa Abbott. As she lived and breathed, this was Nathan's mistress. The girlfriend he'd risked his marriage for. Why didn't she feel more impressed?

"Of course," she managed now. "Ms Abbott." She forced herself to be polite. "How nice of you to call." She hesitated. "Did you get tired of phoning Nathan? Well, I'm afraid he's not here, if that's what you thought."

"I didn't think he was," replied Lisa, with a sardonic expression. "As far as I know, the bastard's still in the States. What I want to know is what you're going to do about it. Or is sleeping with his brother just your way of keeping it in the family?"

Caitlin prayed her father wasn't at the office. The last thing she wanted right now was to have to explain her visit to him. She only hoped Marshall was there and not out on some assignment; or even down at Fairings, explaining the evening he'd spent at the flat to Matthew Webster.

The receptionist soon put her fears to rest.

"I'm afraid Mr Webster's not here," she exclaimed, naturally assuming Caitlin was there to see her father. "I'd ask if there was anyone else who could help you, but I expect it's a personal visit, isn't it?"

"I—well, perhaps," said Caitlin nervously, feeling the doubts she had had about what she was about to do surfacing once again. It was all very well telling herself that she had to talk over what had happened with someone, but why was she so convinced she could trust Marshall and no one else?

The truth was, she was still in a daze, and nothing she had done since Lisa Abbott departed seemed quite real. She had the distinct feeling that this was a dream—or perhaps a nightmare—and that everything the other woman had told her was just her imagination working overtime.

Yet, for all her ambivalence about her physical state, there was no doubt that Lisa's explanation had made an awful kind of sense. Caitlin had known Nathan was different—but how different even she found it hard to accept. That he might be another person—his twin brother, in fact—was the cruellest kind of irony. Had she conceivably fallen in love with another man?

If she allowed herself to think about it, alone, she was afraid for her own sanity. Not because she didn't believe Lisa, but because she was very much afraid that she did. But how long had Nathan—no, *Jake*; she must remember his name was Jake—known about the deception? Not long, she hoped painfully. She didn't want to believe he'd deliberately seduced his brother's wife.

The ramifications of the situation were almost too numerous to mention. Why had Jake been on the plane? Why had he been carrying his brother's passport? And where was Nathan? Why hadn't he come back and set the matter straight?

"Kate—Caitlin?"

The voice behind her seemed to solve her immediate problem. As she turned somewhat reluctantly from the desk, she saw Marshall walking towards her across the veined marble floor. He had evidently just entered the building, and she guessed he was just coming back from lunch. And as he walked towards her, she felt that disturbing ring of recognition she had once felt before.

But it disappeared as soon as he reached her. She was too aware of how incongruous her arrival must seem to him, particularly as until that evening at the apartment, they had hardly exchanged more than a couple of words. He must know she hadn't liked him, that she had resented his intervention in their lives. Consequently, he must be wondering what she was doing here; even more so, when he discovered it was him she'd come to see.

"Hello, Marshall," she responded now, aware of the receptionist's interested gaze behind her. And, because she suddenly found she hadn't the guts to speak directly, "I understand Daddy's not here."

"No." Marshall frowned. "Did you expect to see him?"

That was more difficult.

"Well—yes and no," she said, feeling awkward. Then, "Do you think you could give me a few minutes of your time?"

"My time?" Marshall was understandably taken aback. "I—why, of course," he exclaimed confusedly. "Um—do you want to come up to the office?"

Caitlin shrugged. "Anywhere would do," she murmured, and something in either her voice or her eyes warned him that this was no ordinary visit.

"How about the boardroom?" he suggested. "There'll be no one using it today. We can be—private there. If that's what you want."

"It is."

Caitlin was grateful he didn't ask her to explain there and then, and going up in the lift to the fourteenth floor, she was grateful also for his understanding. He spent the entire time making small talk about the weather, and Caitlin was able to calm the nerves that had flared up when he appeared downstairs.

The boardroom at Webster Development was an impressive room, with a long table made of solid teak, and a dozen matching chairs upholstered in crimson leather. There was a painting of Matthew Webster high on the wall above her father's chair, and a long row of windows overlooking the roofs of the city below.

It was imposing by any standards, but today Caitlin paid little attention to her surroundings. Even the niggling thought that she had once harboured the belief that this would all be hers someday didn't trouble her any more. Indeed, she no longer felt any great desire to control anything except her own life, a circumstance that at this moment seemed almost as remote.

Marshall closed the door behind them, and then asked if she would like some coffee. "Not right now," replied Caitlin, pressing her lips together. She loosened her long cashmere overcoat. "It's very warm in here."

"Is it?"

Marshall seemed surprised at her comment, and Caitlin guessed that she was generating her own heat. But since Lisa Abbott left the antique shop, she'd been unable to control her emotions, and her blood felt almost feverish as it raced along her veins.

Marshall himself looked much as he had done when he had come to the flat for supper. His dark suit was smart, without being obviously expensive, its double-breasted styling accentuating the impressive width of his shoulders. He wasn't as tall as Nathan, and she found herself in the unusual position of meeting him almost eye to eye, but his steel-rimmed spectacles made reading his expression less easy to achieve.

"Is something wrong?" he asked now, watching as she paced somewhat agitatedly about the boardroom. "Why don't you sit down? And take off your coat."

Caitlin hesitated, and then, realising she would feel cooler without the heavy coat, she slipped it off her shoulders and draped it over a chair. But although Marshall pulled out a chair, she didn't immediately take it, linking and unlinking her fingers as she sought to find a way to begin.

It seemed easiest to approach the subject by a less-than-direct route, and realising he would probably think she was crazy, she chose a circuitous path. "Um—did you know that—that Nathan had a—*has* a girlfriend?" she ventured offhandedly, and was not surprised when Marshall threw her a wary look.

"A girlfriend?"

"As in—another woman," agreed Caitlin uncomfortably. She paused. "A—mistress, or is that an old-fashioned term? In any case, it doesn't matter." She hesitated again. "Did you know?"

Instead of answering her question, Marshall offered one of his own. "Did you?"

Caitlin sighed. "All right. Yes. Yes, I did." She pressed her lips together. "It's just as well, in the circumstances."

"What circumstances?"

Caitlin licked her lips now. "She came to see me."

Marshall looked stunned. "When?"

"Just this morning, actually." Caitlin wished she could be more casual about it. "She—she apparently had a visitor yesterday."

"Nathan."

"Well, I thought so," said Caitlin, swallowing. And then, unable to withstand the pressure any longer, she collapsed into the chair and burst into tears. Sniffing, she sought the pockets of her coat, searching for a tissue, and then gulped when Marshal pressed a white handkerchief into her hand.

Marshall waited until she had calmed herself before attempting to find out what she was crying about. He had a great aptitude for calmness, she thought, aware that her embarrassment at breaking down had been greatly reduced by his patience. He made her feel secure, comforted, cared for. That he was a friend she could rely on. If nothing else, she had Nathan—*Jake*—to thank for that.

When she was in control of herself again, she wiped her eyes one last time with his handkerchief, half offered it back to him, and then, realising she couldn't return it in such a state, she crushed it between her palms. "I'll let you have it later," she said. Then, "I'm sorry. I don't usually make a fool of myself like this."

Marshall lifted his shoulders. "Think nothing of it," he assured her gently. "Now—are you sure you want to go on?"

"Oh, yes." Caitlin was fervent. "I have to talk to someone, or I'm afraid I'll go mad!" She swallowed. "That woman—Lisa Abbott—said Nathan wasn't Nathan after all. He'd apparently admitted to her that he was really Nathan's twin brother, Jake, and that they had changed places before he boarded the plane."

Marshall stared at her. "Are you saying he's recovered his memory?" he exclaimed, slipping into the seat next to her. "Or that he'd never lost it?"

"Recovered, I think." Though Caitlin didn't feel she could be absolutely sure of anything at this moment. "In any case, he knows who he is. Like us, she thought he was Nathan at first, but he apparently convinced her otherwise."

Marshall frowned. "And you believe her?"

"Well, I don't disbelieve her," murmured Caitlin obliquely. "Why would she lie?" She felt an unfamiliar feeling of panic stirring inside her. "Do you think it's possible? As far as I know, Nathan doesn't have a brother. He's always maintained he was an only child. Isn't that what he told you?"

Marshall gave her a curious look. "It's not something we'd ever discussed," he murmured drily. "But situations aren't always as cut and dried as they appear." He paused.

"I suppose it's not inconceivable. It would certainly explain a lot of things."

"Yes," said Caitlin unhappily, her nails digging into the ball of cotton in her hand. "She also said she believed Nathan was trying to double-cross her. I didn't know what she was talking about. Do you think Nathan has found someone else?"

"I don't know." Marshall was thoughtful now. "So where is Nathan? And why is this man denying his identity, when for the past three weeks he's let us think he was someone else?"

Caitlin shrugged. "Because he did believe he was Nathan," she said tremulously. "He must have. He couldn't have faked something like that. Dr Harper—that's the doctor who dealt with him in New York, when he was first admitted to the hospital—said he had a mild concussion. I don't believe he could have pretended not to know who he was at such a time."

"All right." Marshall nodded. "So we'll accept that he had lost his memory. Why didn't he tell us it had come back?"

"I don't know." Caitlin drew an uneven breath. "It's like a nightmare."

But, after what had happened between them, perhaps she did.

Marshall shook his head. "Let's start at the beginning, shall we?" he suggested. "Exactly why did this woman come to see you? Did she say?"

"Well..." Caitlin considered her words before speaking. "I think she was angry with Nathan, and she thought I might know where he was. She said he—Jake, that is—had gone to see her because Nathan had sent him. But she didn't believe that. Like I said before, she accused Nathan of selling her out."

"Did she know about—about the amnesia?"

"No. Until this—other man told her, she hadn't realised what had happened at all. She just thought Nathan was avoiding her because the crash had screwed up their deal."

"What deal?"

"The deal he's supposed to have cheated her on. She didn't go into details. She did tell me that she and Nathan had been planning to go away together after he got back. I think she thought I'd be devastated at the news."

"And you weren't?"

"No." Caitlin bent her head. "If she'd known how long I'd wanted a divorce—" She broke off abruptly. "Well, she wouldn't have accused me of trying to get him back."

"So, go on," Marshall prompted. "Did she say how Nathan planned to finance their elopement?"

"No." Caitlin grimaced. "I assume he intended to ask his father to help him. He said he was going to see Mr Wolfe when he left."

"Nathan told you he was going to see his father?"

"Yes."

"So—do you know if he did?"

Caitlin gasped. "I know he didn't," she said in sudden confusion, remembering Jacob Wolfe's surprise when she'd told him his son was in the New York hospital. She lifted her shoulders. "But he must have been hoping to get some money from somewhere. I don't think Daddy paid him enough for him to have saved an enormous amount."

"He didn't," said Marshall flatly. "Not that that troubled your husband," he added reluctantly. "I think you ought to know, Kate, the reason your father employed me was because Nathan had been embezzling from the firm."

Caitlin's jaw dropped. "But—but why didn't Daddy tell me?"

"Why didn't you tell him you wanted a divorce?" countered Marshall with a wry face. "It looks like you've both contributed to Nathan's success in defrauding Webster's. But rest assured, it won't be happening again."

Caitlin gasped. "But—how? How could he do it?"

"In various ways." Now that Marshall had started, he seemed prepared to tell it as it was. "It started when your father was ill, though I believe Matt had had some inkling of Nathan's dishonesty before that. But when your father was in hospital, and Nathan took control—well, let's just say he almost ran the company into the ground."

"Oh, God!"

"I don't think you want to know all the details. I'll just say that Nathan was awarding contracts to anyone who was prepared to make it worth his while. Which in simple terms means that our costs were not competitive. Your father had to drag himself from his sickbed to avoid a vote of no confidence by the board."

Caitlin's face was pale. "I knew there must be some reason why Nathan was replaced."

"By me," conceded Marshall ruefully. "Your father needed someone he could trust."

"And he trusted you?"

"For his sins."

"That's an odd expression."

"It was an odd situation."

Caitlin's brow furrowed. "But how did he know he could trust you any more than Nathan?"

"Let's say we made a deal. How about that?"

Caitlin frowned. "I don't understand. How did he find you? You hadn't worked for the company before."

Marshall looked as if he would have liked to explain everything, but instead, he returned to the matter in hand. "Whatever," he said, "I was supposed to monitor Nathan's behaviour. Matt thought he'd covered all the bases, but he was wrong.''

"And you found out?"

"Eventually." Marshall pulled a wry face. "I didn't realise what he was doing at first. We suspect he's diverted funds away from the Magdalena River project. It would explain why our estimates don't add up."

Caitlin looked confused, and Marshall continued. "You may have heard the project mentioned. It's the dam we bid successfully for in Colombia. It's one of our biggest undertakings, and the funds involved are enormous. No one initially questioned the extra materials Nathan had costed to the job. But, as I say, our suspicions were aroused, and after making inquiries, I'm afraid it looks as if Nathan has managed to convert at least some of these funds to his own ends."

"The South American contract," breathed Caitlin, and Marshall nodded.

"The South American contract," he repeated. "From preliminary investigations, we do know that a healthy sum of money was deposited in a numbered account in Bogotá." Marshall paused. "I know we shouldn't jump to conclusions until we have positive proof, but that's my opinion. Which might account for why he's disappeared."

Caitlin blinked. "You think he never intended to come back?"

"It's possible. It might explain why his brother was on that plane." He paused. "I wonder how he persuaded— Jake, did you say?—to help him. It seems a small amount to split two ways."

"How small?"

Marshall hesitated. "Half a million pounds, give or take."

Caitlin frowned. "Well, it is a fortune to some people."

Marshall tendered a reluctant smile. "So your father tells me. But I would have thought Nathan needed more than that to make it worth his while. Except that we don't know what he plans to do with it. That might provide an answer, if we knew."

"What he plans to do with it?" Caitlin was perplexed. "Why, he'll spend it, of course. Nathan was always short of money. I know that."

"Perhaps. But don't you think the fact that the money was deposited in a bank in the Colombian capital is significant?" Marshall paused. "Particularly as it just happens to be one of the biggest producers of illegal substances in the world."

Caitlin was stunned. "You can't suspect Nathan of smuggling drugs!" she exclaimed. She caught her breath. "I don't believe it. He wouldn't know how to do such a thing. He may be a thief, but he's not an addict." She shuddered. "After what happened to me with David Griffiths, doesn't Daddy think I'd know if he was?"

"No one's saying he's an addict, or that he intended to smuggle the drugs himself." Marshall sighed. "But he could have paid someone else to do it." He shook his head. "He could have bought the stuff in New York and arranged for someone else to take it to England."

Caitlin felt sick. "It's not possible."

"Why not?" Marshall warmed to his theme. "People are smuggling goods into the country every day. Some get caught. Some don't. Believe me, not every ounce—or kilo— of cocaine is discovered. Pushers are making a fortune selling the stuff on the street."

"But some get caught?"

"Yes. And the penalties are severe. You'd have to be pretty foolish, or pretty desperate, to take the chance. But you have to admit, it is a possibility. It's something I've been considering for a while.''

Caitlin sniffed. ''You mean, you and Daddy have been considering it, don't you?''

''He knows of my suspicions, yes.''

''Is that why you grilled Na—Jake—when we were staying at Fairings? Were you trying to find out then if he was lying or not?''

''Something like that.''

Caitlin shook her head. ''It's unbelievable.''

''But possible.'' Marshall grimaced. ''Though knowing Nathan as I do—the real Nathan, that is—I find the idea of him risking everything to buck the system almost beyond belief.'' He hesitated. ''But this—what you've just told me—might provide an answer. It could explain his brother's presence on the plane.''

''No!''

Caitlin couldn't bear it. Even the idea of her husband smuggling drugs was more acceptable than believing Jake had been involved. He wouldn't, she told herself desperately; he couldn't. Though the fact remained, he had been travelling on his brother's passport....

Marshall was regarding her a little sympathetically now, and Caitlin felt the hot colour invade her cheeks. What must he be thinking? she wondered unhappily. He'd seen them together on more than one occasion, and he must know they'd shared a room at her parents' house.

''You sound very positive,'' he remarked now, and Caitlin spread the damp handkerchief between her palms.

''Do I?'' she said, hoping he couldn't tell how she was really feeling. ''Well, perhaps I am. I can't believe—Jake would do something like this.''

''For what it's worth, nor can I,'' declared Marshall flatly. ''It's just difficult to come up with another alternative. One thing's certain. No one could have foreseen the accident. Which brings us back to the problem of where the real Nathan is now."

Caitlin got restlessly to her feet and paced across to the windows. "What would you say if I told you I didn't care?" She traced the line of the wood grain with a wistful finger. "I know it probably sounds crazy to you, but I wanted to believe *he* was Nathan. I suppose that was why I didn't question the way he behaved."

"I know what you mean." Marshall rose now and came to join her. "He seemed so eager to learn, I was completely taken in."

"But you knew he was different. You said as much that evening you came to the flat." Caitlin sighed. "I suppose I just blinded myself to the fact that it couldn't be him."

"So where do we go from here?" Marshall looked at her gently. "I guess we talk to—Jake. I gather you haven't spoken to him since this woman came to the shop."

"No." Caitlin looked up at him through her lashes. "I couldn't. He—left for New York this morning to find—his roots."

"Shit!"

For the first time in their short acquaintance, Marshall lost his temper. But she could hardly blame him for his impatience, or for the fact that he felt betrayed. She'd had the same feelings herself, ever since Lisa had dropped her bombshell. She'd been asking herself why, after all that had happened between them, she didn't have his trust.

"You do realise we might have seen the last of both of them," Marshall said at last, when he had recovered his composure. "I'm sorry if I was rude, but I can just imagine what your father's going to say when he hears this." He paused. "Did he tell you where he was going? Or is that a silly question? How can we trust a man who's spent the past three weeks masquerading as his brother to tell the truth?''

"Not three weeks." Caitlin wouldn't have that. "A few days at most, and he did tell Lisa his real name."

"Probably because she'd realised he wasn't Nathan," muttered Marshall dourly. "Oh, dammit, what the hell are we going to do?"

"I could go to Prescott," suggested Caitlin cautiously, the idea blossoming tentatively in her mind. "Prescott, New Jersey, that is. Where Nathan's father is living. He seemed a little confused when he saw Nathan—that is, Jake—in the hospital. If Jake is Nathan's twin brother, then he'd know who his son was, wouldn't you think?"

Marshall's expression brightened considerably. "That's a brilliant idea," he said, and even Caitlin felt her spirits lift a little at the unexpected praise. "But I'll go to Prescott, and you can go and tell your father what I'm doing. He might not cut off my—" he grimaced "—allowance, if he thinks I'm making progress."

Caitlin gave him an old-fashioned look. "You are joking, I trust," she stated tersely. "If anyone's following—Jake to Prescott, it's me. I am his wife—well, I thought I was, and he probably thinks I still believe it. How you explain what's happened to Daddy is your problem. Not mine."

24

The car stalled as Nathan was driving it into the storage shed, and he swore angrily, getting out to shove the heavy vehicle the rest of the way. He was loath to risk starting the engine again and maybe attracting the attention of a black and white out on patrol. In all honesty, he was relieved that the car hadn't let him down before he got back to the lumber yard.

It had been a hell of a journey, and a wasted journey at that. He'd have preferred to have gone by plane, but something—some sixth sense, perhaps—had warned him to use the car. And it was just as well he had, in the circumstances. At least that nosy janitor wouldn't know exactly when he'd left Jake's apartment.

It had been just his bad luck that Fletch Connor should have been there when he arrived. He'd actually been feeling pretty confident, having fooled the janitor and all. He'd had to get the man to let him into the condo, and he thought his story about leaving his keys back at his office had gone down rather well. The janitor had bought his story anyway, even asking him how he was and if he'd had a nice trip.

Jake must have told the guy he was going away for a few days. In any event, the janitor had noticed Jake hadn't been staying at the apartment for several weeks. He hadn't seemed suspicious, and Nathan had been fairly sure he'd gotten away with it. And he would have done, if Fletch Connor hadn't been waiting for him inside.

He wondered how the old man had gotten into the apartment. The janitor hadn't mentioned he was there, but perhaps that was because he was a regular visitor. Whatever, as soon as he'd seen Nathan, he'd become almost deranged, accusing him of impersonating Jake, instead of the other way about. He wouldn't listen to reason; he wouldn't listen to anything Nathan had to say. He'd been like a mad bull, ranting and raving, implying that Nathan had done away with his brother, or something ridiculous like that.

As if.

Nathan hunched his shoulders as he closed the shed doors. It had been a stupid idea to go to Pine Bay in the first place. But he'd had to get away. Jacob was driving him crazy, and although he didn't trust him, if the old man didn't know where he'd gone, there was nothing he could do.

He doubted Jacob would have expected him to go to North Carolina. After what he'd said about Fletch, he'd have assumed Nathan would be too scared. He scowled. He should have listened to him for once. Connor was enough to scare anyone. When he'd come at Nathan like the mad dog he was, he'd had to fight to hold the old fool off.

Of course, he hadn't meant to hurt him. Well, not seriously, at least, but Fletch had been too reckless to control. He'd forced Nathan to use his fists to defend himself, and then crumpled like a pack of cards instead of fighting back.

Nathan groaned. Well, it was all academic now. Fletch was dead—sprawled across that fancy carpet in Jake's living room. And when he was found, they'd probably indict Jake for his murder.

Once again, everything had gone wrong. Why couldn't the old guy have let him have his say before lunging at him like some razorback in heat? But he couldn't have let the old man call the cops. Nathan felt sweat break out all over his body at the thought.

He grimaced. He hadn't realised his fist could be so lethal. When it had connected with Fletch's jaw, he was sure he'd hurt himself more than the old man. Jake had told him the guy had quite a reputation for being a hard man, but it hadn't seemed that way when he went down.

Nevertheless, it had taken Nathan some time before he'd had the nerve to check that he wasn't breathing. Panic had set in then, and it had taken every ounce of will-power he possessed not to go charging out of the apartment there and then. His initial instinct had been to put as many miles between himself and Fletch's corpse as was humanly possible. He was terrified someone else might come and find him there.

But common sense had persuaded him that darkness was falling. If he waited another couple of hours, he might be able to slip away without anyone seeing him go. He'd been glad he'd had the foresight to park the rental car a couple of blocks from the apartment complex. In his original bid to hide his real identity, he hadn't wanted any strange car ruining his plans.

The hours between taking the decision to wait and actually leaving had dragged. Nathan had never seen a dead body before. He'd been too young when his mother—his stepmother—had died, and it wasn't an experience he wanted to repeat. Fetch hadn't smelt particularly good when he was alive, and the apartment had seemed permeated by his unwashed smell.

But he'd known he had to be practical, so he'd spent some of the time wiping the surfaces where he might have left his fingerprints, and avoided looking at the body as much as he could. He would have preferred to drag it into the bedroom, but that would have entailed touching it again. Besides, he didn't want to run the risk of leaving more evidence. At present, the janitor thought Jake had returned home, and he preferred to keep it that way.

He hadn't left by the main entrance, naturally. He'd had no compunction about opening the patio doors and making his escape across the grassy slope beyond. It had meant leaving the sliding door unlocked, but that was a simple thing for anyone to overlook. And if a thief broke into the apartment—well, so much the better. The cops would have another set of fingerprints to muddy the scene.

The air in Prescott was much colder than the air had been in Pine Bay. It struck through the fine wool of his Armani suit with an icy hand. But the cold he could feel was not just a result of the weather. He felt chilled to the bone and in desperate need of sleep.

It would be light soon, he noticed. He'd driven through the night, and already he could detect a slight diffusion in the darkness around him. What the hell was he going to do now? he thought, self-pity gnawing into his stomach. He just hoped his father wasn't dragged into the murder inquiry. Jacob would be bound to be suspicious of his whereabouts at the time of Fletch's death.

He reached the door of the house and pressed the bell insistently. Unlike the last time he'd come here, he had little hope that his father wouldn't be in bed. But, to his surprise, he heard the old man unlocking the door almost immediately, and as far as he could tell, Jacob hadn't had to draw the bolts. Perhaps he'd taken what he said to heart, reflected Nathan with a grimace. There was nothing in the house that anyone would want to steal.

But when the door swung open, it wasn't Jacob who was standing behind it. Almost before he had a chance to register the fact that his brother must have recovered his mem-

ory after all, Jake's hand snaked out and grabbed the front
of his shirt. He was hauled into the hall of the house and the
door slammed before he could make a protest. But, in any
case, Jake's expression warned him that any attempt to resist would be futile.

The hall was dim, as usual, but even in the poor light he
was aware of his brother's menace. They might be alike, but
Nathan was sure he had never looked as savage as Jake did
at that moment. It was obvious he couldn't wait to get his
hands on him again, and only a thin veneer of civilisation
was holding him back.

"Well, well," Jake greeted him coldly, his bulk successfully blocking Nathan's attempt to move to comparative
safety along the hall. "The prodigal returns." His lips
twisted. "How did I know you would? What happened? Did
Fletch throw you out?"

Fletch!

Nathan swallowed, a little of his fear subsiding. Jake
didn't know about Fletch. He didn't know his father—*so-
called* father—was dead. Well, how could he? he chided
himself impatiently. Jake hadn't gone to his apartment,
thank God! He must have come here straight from the airport.

"I don't know what you're talking about," he blustered
now, gaining strength from his secret knowledge. "Why
would I go looking for that old fool? Why would I go to
North Carolina at all? In any case, who are you to question
my movements? You haven't been hanging about here for
weeks, waiting for your dumb brother to come to his
senses."

"I didn't lose my senses," grated Jake angrily, his jaw
tightening at the deliberate slur on his character. "I could
have been killed in that crash, and you know it." His eyes
darkened. "I bet you wished I had. Then all your troubles

would have been over. Well—" his mouth twisted "—almost."

"Don't be a fool!"

"I'm not the fool," said Jake. "You are." He regarded the other man with contempt. "So where have you been? Disposing of the dope?"

Nathan blanched. Until that moment, he'd believed he was prepared for anything Jake might throw at him. He'd had plenty of time to prepare his excuses after all. But his brother's accusation was just too near the truth for his liking, and a look of consternation crossed his face. What had his father been saying? he wondered. Had the old man told Jake what he thought Nathan had planned? *No!* He took a couple of nervous breaths to calm his system. Jacob wasn't up as he surely would have been if they'd been conspiring against him. Jake was whistling in the dark, that was all.

But his silence had betrayed him as a denial might not. While he was still assuring himself that he had nothing to fear from his brother, Jake moved in and slammed him back against the wall.

"You shit!" he said harshly, his forearm beneath Nathan's jaw, forcing his head back at an impossible angle. Nathan could feel the bones in his neck grinding together as Jake's grip threatened to sever his air supply. "You bloody, selfish idiot! What have you done?"

"For Christ's sake, Jake," he gasped, raising his hands to try and dislodge his brother's arm from beneath his chin, but all Jake did was use his free hand to twist one of Nathan's arms up behind his back. The pain was excruciating, and the sweat broke out on his forehead. He almost screamed at the agony it induced.

"I should break your neck," Jake told him without sympathy. "You planned this, didn't you? You sent me on that plane to London, knowing there was no cocaine in that suitcase—''

''No—''

''What do you mean, no?''

Nathan gulped. ''You don't know that there was no cocaine in that suitcase. Unless my father was lying when he said all the baggage had been destroyed.''

''He wasn't lying.''

''Then, how—''

''You don't think I'd carry a suitcase on a plane not knowing what was in it, do you?'' Jake sneered. ''For all I knew, it could have contained a bomb. You're stupid enough—or irresponsible enough—not to care.''

''As if I'd give you a suitcase with a bomb inside.''

Nathan was incredulous, but his brother wasn't convinced. ''There are other ways of causing an explosion,'' he said grimly. ''Did you hope Walker would deal with me first, thinking I was you, and ask questions afterwards?''

''No, I...'' Nathan's brain was buzzing. He had evidently underestimated his brother, and he thanked God he'd hidden the cocaine in a safe place. But Jake wasn't aware of what had been inside, or that he'd intended to call the cops, he assured himself more confidently. ''It wasn't like that,'' he mumbled at last. ''Jake, let me breathe, for God's sake. I can't tell you anything while you're crushing my spine.''

''So speak.''

Jake eased up just enough to let him take a gulp of air, and Nathan struggled to find a convincing explanation. ''I—I gave you the wrong suitcase,'' he offered lamely. ''I've still got the drugs, like you said.''

If he'd hoped that news would win him a reprieve, he was mistaken. ''You're a liar,'' said Jake harshly, ''but you're not stupid. Well, not totally stupid anyway. If you've got any sense, you'll tell me the truth before I lose what little patience I've got left.''

Nathan expelled his breath on a frustrated sigh. ''And if I don't, what will you do? Kill me?'' A sob escaped him as Jake increased the pressure on his arm yet again. ''For pity's sake, Jake, I'm your brother. Your *twin* brother! Isn't there supposed to be some respect around here?''

''Did you respect me when you sent me on that trip to London?''

''Yes.'' Nathan swallowed with difficulty. ''I didn't know what was going to happen, did I?''

''That's what bothers me,'' said Jake, regarding him dourly. ''I keep asking myself what you had to gain.''

''To gain?''

''Yes.'' Jake gnawed at his lower lip. ''I wonder—could there have been some cocaine in that suitcase after all?''

''No...''

Nathan didn't want him to start thinking along those lines. Jake was too astute; he'd had too much experience dealing with traffickers. God, if he guessed what Nathan had planned, he might really break his neck.

''Then what?'' demanded Jake, thrusting his face close to his brother's. ''It wasn't the first time you'd carried drugs. You lied.''

''How do you know that?''

''I spoke to your—girlfriend,'' replied Jake, shocking him still further. ''She was pathetically open, actually. When I told her you'd arranged the whole deal, she believed me.''

Nathan was speechless, but Jake didn't give him time to absorb the implications of what he was saying. ''She told me about Walker. I guess he's looking for you, too. She also told me about the Colombian deal,'' Jake continued chillingly. ''You've really fucked up your life, and you tried to fuck up mine, as well.''

Nathan shook his head. "Lisa's a liar—"

"Not as big a liar as you." Jake's eyes bored into his.

Nathan's stomach contracted. He had always regarded his brother as such a pushover—someone who'd do anything to strengthen the bonds he thought there were between them. As if he really had anything in common with this thug, he thought disparagingly. He'd thought he could use Jake, but once again, he'd misjudged the situation.

"What's going on here?"

His father's voice restored Nathan's belief in miracles. The old man was coming slowly down the stairs, and Nathan managed to turn his head to watch his approach. Not that he expected the dressing-gowned figure in worn carpet slippers was likely to be any match for his brother, if Jake chose to ignore him. But he managed a pathetic cry for help as Jacob reached the hall.

"Let him go."

Jacob's voice was low and controlled, and Nathan felt a moment's contempt for his naïveté. As if Jake was likely to take any notice of him, he thought frustratedly. Dammit, why didn't he come across the hall and try and prise the bastard off him?

"I said, let him go, Jake."

Jake eased his hold slightly, and Nathan was able to take his first deep breath since his brother had slammed him against the wall. Jake turned towards the stooped, but composed, figure of their father almost too obediently, and Nathan had a chance to see what was going on.

Shit! The breath left his lungs in a rush. The old man was holding a gun. It looked like his old service pistol, but it was obvious that Jake thought it might still be in working order. The fool! Didn't he realise that old Colt hadn't been fired for years?

Still, he was grateful for small mercies. Jake wasn't likely to argue with his father in the present circumstances, and a moment later, Nathan found himself free. Christ! He flexed his aching arm, silently congratulating the old man on his achievement. He even allowed himself an inward chuckle. He'd been half-convinced that Jacob would take Jake's side as he'd done before.

"D'you want to tell me what's going on?"

Jacob looked at Nathan, and realising it wasn't over yet, Nathan ran a soothing hand over his raw throat. "Thank God you've come down, Pa," he said. "I think Jake's taken leave of his senses. He's practically accusing me of double-crossing him, when what he really wants is a cut."

"Why, you—"

Jake would have lunged for him then, but Jacob raised the gun warningly towards his older son. "Let him go on," he said, and somehow Jake obeyed him. "You'll have your chance to tell me your story when Nathan is done."

Nathan glanced at both of them then, disconcerted by his sudden change of status. What was going on here? he wondered. Why was his father defending him? He should be feeling peeved that he'd disappeared without telling him where he'd gone.

"It's true," he muttered now, keeping a weather eye on his brother as he spoke. "I warned you Jake wasn't the innocent bystander you seemed to think."

Jacob frowned. "You're saying Jake was a willing partner?"

Nathan shrugged. "Yes." And at Jake's growl of anger, "I don't expect you to believe me. Jake always was the apple of your eye."

"And that's why you've come back, is it?" Jacob prompted. "Because you knew Jake was here?"

"Well—I hoped he might be," lied Nathan, gaining confidence from his father's apparent willingness to believe him. He cast another glance at his brother's baleful face and adopted an indignant posture. "I was trying to tell him I always pay my debts."

"And so do I," said Jake, but once again Jacob intervened.

"So your story is that you planned the whole thing between you?" he asked, and Nathan gave a rueful sigh.

"Something like that," he said. "That's why I tried to keep it from you. I just wish you could get Jake to listen to reason."

Jacob's lips twisted. "Oh, Nathan," he said, and suddenly he looked very old. "When Jake told me what he believes you'd planned, I couldn't take it in. That a son of mine should sink so low as to try and destroy his own brother's life. No—" This as Nathan began to speak again. "I listened to you, boy, and now you'll listen to me. You're a liar, and I know it. And you've not come back here to help anyone but yourself."

Nathan stared at him. "Oh, I see. He's got to you, has he? He's poisoned your mind against me, and you're prepared to believe him before me. That's great, isn't it? My own father won't listen to me. You'd turn against me, the son you raised yourself."

"Yes, I raised you," said Jacob steadily. "And I'm ashamed to say it, Nathan. Deeply ashamed. Oh, I knew you were a selfish boy. I saw you turn into a selfish man. But you're right—I haven't been a good father or I'd have recognised you for what you are before now."

"And what am I?"

"Greedy, weak, irresponsible." Jacob's voice was cold. "What I find so hard to believe is that you could think you might get away with it. For pity's sake, Nathan, were you so desperate that you'd consign your own brother to jail to escape what you deserved?''

"To jail?"

"What do you mean?"

The two brothers spoke simultaneously, but Jacob fixed his gaze upon his younger son. "Since you went away, I've had time to think, Nathan. I'd already surmised that you must have stashed the drugs Jake was supposed to be carrying somewhere. Is that where you've been? To collect them?" He moved his hand dismissingly. "It doesn't matter now. Where the drugs are at this precise moment isn't important. What is important is how you hoped to implicate your brother, and I think I've come up with an explanation."

He paused, but before Nathan could attempt any defence, he continued, "Jake has told me there was no cocaine in the suitcase he was transporting, but I think there was."

"Are you sure?" That was Jake, and Nathan threw him a nervous look.

"Yes," their father went on. "It's the only explanation. It was hidden, of course, so that if the plan backfired, you wouldn't suspect Nathan had been trying to double-cross you. But there must have been enough cocaine in the case to ensure you at least being arrested at Heathrow."

Jake gasped. "I don't believe it."

"Nor do I," cried Nathan, looking to his brother for his support. "You're going senile, old man. What would be the point of that?"

"I couldn't work that out at first," said Jacob quietly. "And then it dawned on me that the authorities would find it hard to believe that Jake wasn't who his passport said he was. I mean, who's going to believe a drug smuggler? And when he did eventually succeed in convincing them that he was Jake Connor and not Nathan Wolfe, they'd think he was using your passport because of his own record."

"What record?" exclaimed Nathan contemptuously, but he already knew. It was one of the things he'd banked on. The fact that Jake had been a junkie when he got back from Vietnam.

"You bastard!"

They were both glaring at him now, and Nathan realised he wasn't going to gain any advantage by continuing to lie. "All right," he said, "I'd stashed a few ounces of cocaine in one of the paperbacks in the case. I'd hollowed it out."

"So, you had no intention of meeting me in London," Jake said accusingly. "You expected me to be detained in England and, under cover of this smokescreen, you'd escape from your mess of a life no matter what disasters you'd bring on me, or pain to your father—and wife."

"Pretty clever, huh? So what are you going to do about it? We're all in this together. We're family, remember?"

"You wish."

Jacob's response was harsh with loathing, and even Nathan felt a twinge of regret for the relationship they had once had. Okay, so they'd had their problems; so did lots of other people. But he'd always believed his father loved him, no matter what.

"I need a drink," he said, wiping his hand across his parched lips. He saw to his dismay that his hand was trembling, and he thrust it in his pocket. Then he looked at his brother. "You can join me if you like. It might help us all to think—"

"Stay where you are."

To his astonishment, Jacob had turned the gun on him now, and Nathan stared at him with disbelieving eyes. Christ, he thought, the old guy really was losing it. He might be able to intimidate Jake with that old gun, but as far as he was concerned, it was a joke.

To prove it, he pushed past the old man and sauntered along the hall towards his father's study. "Has he told you he doesn't drink?" he addressed Jake, aware that he didn't feel quite so confident with the gun pointing at his back. "Well, don't you believe it. He's got a bottle in his desk drawer. He's just an old hypocrite. I should know."

The bullet that whistled past his shoulder had him diving into the study doorway. The light was on, and as he groped to turn off the switch with sweating fingers, he found his father was right behind him, with Jake at his heels.

He thought Jake looked a little stunned that the old man had actually fired the gun in anger. Like him, he apparently hadn't expected the gun to be loaded, let alone that it was capable of firing a shot. The realisation of how close to death he'd come made Nathan reckless, and he stared at them both with wide, accusing eyes.

"Are you crazy?" he choked, forgetting for the moment that only seconds before he had been disparaging his father for being senile. "What the hell's got into you, old man? If you want some—some target practice, go aim someplace else."

Jacob didn't say anything. He simply raised the gun again and a bullet ricocheted harmlessly into the woodwork just inches from Nathan's ear. The noise it made was terrifying, splintering the wood and sending fragments flying in all directions. One dug into the back of Nathan's neck and he screamed, believing for one awful moment that he had been shot after all.

"You're mad!" he cried when a tentative exploration discovered the sliver of wood that had grazed his neck. But there was blood on his hands and on his collar, and he gazed at it with disbelieving eyes.

"I was just proving I don't need any target practice," replied his father evenly, showing no remorse for his behaviour. "You shouldn't have tried to make a fool of me, Nathan. I can be ruthless, too—if I have a mind."

"Jake, for God's sake!" Nathan appealed to his brother. "Do something, can't you? Or are you going to let him kill me? Is that what you want?"

Jake hesitated. Nathan could see the uncertainty in his brother's eyes. Christ, what more did he need? A written confession? The old man was crazy. Couldn't he see it? He'd totally flipped his lid.

"I think you ought to put the gun down," Jake conceded at last, not without some reluctance, and in the second it took for Jacob to turn and look at him, Nathan took his chance. He wasn't fit, but he was younger and stronger and heavier than the old man, and when he lunged at him, Jacob fell heavily to the floor.

But he didn't let go of the gun.

Although Nathan had no choice but to follow him down, Jacob hung on to the gun as if for grim death. His bony fingers were glued to the butt, his forefinger hooked relentlessly round the trigger.

Another shot rattled ominously into the smouldering grate behind him, and Nathan knew that the next one might be for him. But it was impossible to extricate himself without running the risk of taking a bullet, and he could only struggle to stay out of the line of fire.

Jake's arm coming between them was another small miracle. His sainted brother was actually risking his life for him, he realised, scrambling for cover. As Jake grasped his father's wrist, Nathan scuttled behind the desk, so that when the gun was fired again, he was safely out of harm's way.

The silence that followed was horribly ominous. For a moment, he wondered if he had been shot after all, and that the reason he couldn't hear anything was because he was dead. But then someone howled, a terrible sound that turned his blood to ice in his veins, and he heard his father sobbing his brother's name.

Panic gripped him again. Oh, God! The old man had killed Jake, he thought wildly. Jacob would kill him now, for sure. Christ, what was he going to do? The world had gone mad around him. Was he the only sane one in this fucking place?

Quivering with terror, aware that it wasn't just sweat that had dampened his trousers, Nathan risked a swift glance round the corner of the desk. He drew back almost at once, his worst fears realised. He was right: Jake had been shot. He was lying, motionless, on the floor, with Jacob on his knees beside him, keening like a banshee.

He swallowed, the dry convulsion of his throat muscles sounding loudly in his ears. His hands conversely were so wet he had to dry them on his jacket, the blood smearing his lapel, reminding him of what had so nearly happened before.

This couldn't be real, he told himself unsteadily. It was all just a crazy dream. If he pinched himself, he'd wake up in his own bed back in London. But when he squeezed an inch of the midriff that hid his waistband, he almost gagged with the pain.

The sobbing continued on and on, until Nathan had to put his hands over his ears to block out the awful sound his father was making. It's no good crying, old man, he thought, despising his father, even at this time, for his weakness. If you hadn't intended to shoot anyone, you shouldn't have been carrying a gun.

The gun.

Nathan pressed his shoulders back against the side of the desk. Where was the gun? That was what he ought to be thinking now. It had to be here somewhere. He sensed Jacob would have thrown it aside when he realised he'd shot Jake. Nathan hadn't heard it fall, but then, he'd hardly been in any state to listen for it. If he could find the gun, he'd be all right, he thought urgently. Jacob wouldn't touch him if he was armed.

Licking his dry lips, he inched his way along the back of the desk. He would look through the knee-hole, he decided. Just in case his father was still holding the gun. He wouldn't present such an obvious target from that angle. Jacob might not even know where he was.

His luck held. As he'd hoped, the gun was lying just inches beyond the edge of the desk. His father actually had his back to it as he leant over his innocent victim. If Nathan could just ease himself though the knee-hole, he'd reach it easily.

Every sound he made seemed magnified in the awful aftermath of the killing. Even though his father was still moaning over the body, Nathan's efforts to reach the gun seemed certain to reach his ears. Nathan wished he was thinner; he wished he'd paid more attention to his diet while he'd had the chance. He could smell the fear that soaked his body. He prayed that Jacob wouldn't smell it, too.

His fingers touched the barrel only seconds later. But for a few minutes, his hands were so slippery, he couldn't get a grip. Looping one finger inside the trigger guard, he drew the gun towards him. Then, after smoothing his damp palm against the carpet, he lifted the gun and cradled it against his chest.

He'd done it!

Relief washed over him, and not caring if he made any noise now, he scrambled to his feet. God, he needed a drink, he thought, remembering the whisky. He deserved one for what he'd suffered. Then he'd decide how he was going to deal with the old man.

It was the noise of the desk drawer being opened that alerted Jacob to his other son's sudden revival. But although Nathan expected him to reach for the weapon, the old man seemed incapable of coherent thought. Nathan was almost disappointed when all his father did was watch him remove the cap from the whisky and drink thirstily from the bottle, his expression pale and haggard, his eyes red-rimmed with grief.

Nathan wished he'd admit that he had defeated him. He wanted his father to beg him for his life. He didn't want to see this pathetic figure, staring at him as if he were a phantom. He wanted some animation; he wanted an excuse to use the gun.

He hadn't realised how powerful a gun could make you feel. Cowering behind the desk, all he'd felt was fear for his own safety, but now he felt almost invincible. The realisation that Jacob might have been experiencing these self-same feelings when he was holding the gun made him angry. He'd killed Jake; he deserved to die. But Nathan found he just couldn't pull the trigger. He couldn't kill his own father in cold blood.

So he had to do something, say something, to arouse some sort of reaction. Aggression, preferably. It would be easier if he was mad. The old man probably thought he wouldn't use the gun against him. A half-hysterical gulp rose in this throat. If he only knew.

Jacob was getting to his feet now, and for all his bravado, Nathan felt a return of the terror he had experienced earlier. His father straightened his back and looked at him, his eyes dull and unseeing. He was beaten, thought Nathan firmly, but he tightened his grip on the gun just the same.

"I—I guess I ought to say thanks," he taunted, his voice higher than he would have liked, but it wasn't easy keeping his cool. "You've done me a favour, getting rid of that bastard. Now that Jake's out of the way, it makes things so much simpler for me."

The roar that erupted from Jacob's throat as Nathan spoke was almost too primitive to have human origins. It seemed to well up from the depths of his father's being, and his whole face took on an unholy glow. It terrified his son, despite the gun, and his breathing quickened instinctively. The old man was mad; did he need any further proof? God, he breathed, give me the strength to fire the gun.

"Keep back," he warned as Jacob started towards him, but although he'd wanted this to happen, his finger still trembled over the pin. "I—I don't want to have to kill you," he added, aware that he was backing away and despising himself for it. "For Christ's sake, don't make me do it, Pa. I didn't mean what I said."

But Jacob didn't seem to be listening to him. He just came on like some lumbering beast, closing the space between them, until he was only the length of the desk away. Behind Nathan was a wall of bookcases, with no escape possible. Oh, God! He closed his eyes, and using both hands, pulled the trigger. It clicked once—twice—and then his father's body fell.

When he opened his eyes again, Jacob was lying face down on the hearth. A trickle of blood was coming from his head and pooling on the stone beneath. Nathan didn't know if he was dead. It certainly looked that way, but he couldn't be positive. Not without touching him at any rate, and for the moment he could only stare at the gun in disbelief.

A mirthless laugh escaped him, and after fiddling with it for a few seconds, he at last managed to pull the magazine out. It was empty. It had been empty since his father fired the shot that had killed Jake. There must have only been four bullets in it.

He hadn't shot his father, he thought unsteadily. The clicks he'd heard were just that—clicks—of the hammer hitting the firing pin. Proof that he hadn't gone suddenly deaf as he'd feared. No, ironically enough, his father had fallen headlong over the open drawer from which Nathan had removed the whisky. His thirst had saved him. Or, God knew, he could be dead.

Steeling his nerves, he put down the gun and approached his father's prone body. A shudder of revulsion ran through him, but he managed to lay two fingers beneath the old man's ear. He was warm from the embers of the fire, but there was no pulse, not even the faintest thread of a heartbeat. He shivered. Like Fletch, the fall must have killed him. Jacob was never going to threaten him again.

Nausea almost choked him, but he turned aside and took another mouthful of the whisky. Christ, he thought, wiping his mouth, who would ever believe he was the innocent party here? If he called the police, he could say goodbye to his freedom for good. They'd probably lock him up and throw away the key.

He permitted himself a brief glance in his brother's direction. But the sight of the blood issuing from the wound on his head turned his stomach, and he quickly looked away. God, he thought incredulously, Jake had survived the plane crash just to be killed by his own father. If that wasn't ironic, he didn't know what was.

He tried to think, but his brain felt as thick as leather. It felt as if it was swollen, enlarged, pressing against the walls of his skull, until he felt sure it was in danger of splitting his head apart. What the hell was he going to do? Who would believe his story? Not Carl; not the Websters; not Caitlin. That bitch wouldn't lift a hand to bail him out.

No one knew he was here.

The thought came out of nowhere, and the bottle fell from his nerveless fingers as he acknowledged something that until then had been little more than a niggling awareness in his mind. No one knew he had been staying with his father. As far as the people of Prescott were concerned, his father hadn't had any visitors. And when they found his body—and Jake's, too—they'd probably blame his brother for what had happened.

He frowned. It might not be that easy to arrange, he realised grimly. If they found the bodies right away, they'd probably be able to tell who had died first. Jake could hardly be accused of killing his father if he'd been already dead, could he? Nathan needed a way to complicate the evidence. To ensure no one knew exactly how they'd died.

It was almost light. If he wanted to get away from here without anybody knowing, he didn't have much time left. He had to think of some way to delay their examination. Then the sale of this old woodpile would be his inheritance.

Not that it was worth much, he conceded bitterly. If the old man had sold out years ago, he'd have been worth a hell of a lot more. The insurance was probably worth more than the sawmill. His eyes glittered. It would serve him right if the whole place went up in smoke....

25

It was the smell that brought Jake to his senses.

The acrid aroma of smoke and kerosene was all too reminiscent of the plane crash, and for a moment he felt as paralysed as he had been then. He had a vivid image of himself, lying on the edge of the runway, incapable of doing anything to help himself or anybody else. He could hear the crackling of the flames; he could feel the heat. But this time his memory was clear.

And he could move. His head hurt—pretty abominably, actually—but he didn't think he was seriously injured. The bullet must have grazed his temple, he decided, tentatively exploring the area where it hurt. And, as with all head wounds, it had bled profusely. He wondered if he'd lost a lot of blood.

But that didn't explain the fire, he realised dizzily. Although his head swam when he moved, and his limbs felt like jelly, he levered himself slowly to his knees.

For a moment, nausea assailed him. Despite the urgency he felt to get to his feet, he had to wait for the sickness to pass. That was when he saw his father's body. The old man was lying half over the hearth, and he looked ominously still.

All around him now he could see billows of smoke swirling. The old house was as dry as tinder, and it was a mercy this room hadn't yet been engulfed by the flames. He realised the noise he could hear was coming from the staircase, and it was only a matter of time before the fire leapt along the hall.

Panic gripped his stomach. The realisation that he was in a house that was rapidly being consumed by fire was terrifying. How the fire had started—*why* the fire had started—were questions that barely licked along the edges of his consciousness. His first task was to get himself and his father out of the building. If he could, he acknowledged unsteadily. Somehow he had to find the strength.

If only he didn't feel so helpless. The bullet, which he thought must have ploughed a shallow furrow along his hairline, had combined with the lingering effects of the accident to sap his will. Confronting Nathan earlier had robbed him of most of his resistance, and now the amount of blood he'd lost was adding to his fatigue.

The smoke was getting thicker, and pulling off his jacket, he used it to shield his nose and mouth. Then, ignoring his own pain, he crawled across the floor towards his father. There might be some way he could protect the old man.

There was a pool of blood beneath Jacob's head that was rapidly staining the stonework of the hearth. Jake uttered a groan as he leant over him, but he sensed before he touched his cold cheek that his father was dead. He didn't know how long he'd been lying there. Although his skin felt cold, that was no guarantee. This was a cold room; it had been a cold house; and he was no expert. And the old man's blood must have been thin for a long time.

A feeling of helplessness was his first reaction, followed swiftly by an almost numbing sense of disbelief. He hadn't realised Jacob's death would mean that much to him. But it did. The man had been his father, and neither time, nor distance, nor their years of estrangement could alter that.

With trembling hands, he turned him over, catching his breath at the ugly wound that split his temple. Blood had congealed around the wound, and the old man's face was deathly white. Dear God, he thought sickly, had Nathan done this? Was that why he could smell the kerosene?

A splintering sound came from above his head, and looking up, he saw an ominous crack appear in the ceiling. Evidently, the intense heat was buckling the floorboards. The wood was baking and tearing the beams apart.

He staggered, but he managed to get to his feet. For all he would have liked to spend more time mourning his father's passing, he knew he couldn't indulge in maudlin sentiment now. If he didn't get out of here soon, the whole building would collapse around him, and he'd never find out if Nathan was to blame.

But he couldn't leave the old man behind. For all he was sure Jacob was dead, there was always a chance he might be wrong. Just because he couldn't find a pulse didn't mean there wasn't one. He'd seen men in Vietnam who'd looked as bad and made a full recovery.

But they'd been young men, with youthful constitutions. His father had been old and far from well. Looking at him now, he felt a pang for his frailty. He wouldn't have had much resistance to the blow.

All the same, it took every ounce of strength he had to move the body. With an immense effort, he managed to lever his father's shoulders off the hearth and haul him unceremoniously across the floor. It was an undignified exit, but it was the best he could do in the circumstances. The old man would remember nothing about it, and it was better than leaving him behind.

He'd reached the doorway when he heard the sound of hurried footsteps. He'd expected Nathan to be long gone by now, and the realisation that he might have misjudged his brother caused him a moment's grief. What if Nathan hadn't started the fire? What if he'd just panicked when Jake was shot and run away? Could the old man have thought Jake was dead and lit the fire himself?

The smoke in the hall was so thick Jake couldn't immediately be sure it was Nathan. As he'd suspected, the stairs were burning, and sparks from the flames would soon have the hall alight. Already the worn ribbon of carpet was smouldering, and as he watched, the curtain at the foot of the stairs was swiftly consumed.

And, in that brief flare of illumination, he recognised his brother. The sudden conflagration had startled Nathan, so that when Jake reached out and touched his sleeve, he had no chance of hiding his reaction. "Christ," he gasped, staring at his brother's smoke-blackened face with undisguised horror. He took a shuddering breath. "I thought you were dead."

Caitlin was the first to see the pall of smoke that hung over the sawmill.

Although they'd flown over from England the previous day, Marshall had suggested it would be more appropriate to arrive at Jacob Wolfe's house in the morning. There was nothing spoiling, he said. Nothing that couldn't wait until the following day at any rate. And they couldn't be absolutely sure Jake had gone to see his father. Better to arrive at a respectable hour than late at night.

Reluctantly, Caitlin had agreed to wait until the next day. Marshall usually spoke good sense, she'd discovered, and she had no wish to antagonise him now. She was grateful he'd agreed to come with her. She wasn't sure she could have handled this on her own.

They'd spent the night at a hotel in Prescott. It wasn't a particularly salubrious establishment, and the receptionist had looked downright suspicious when they'd asked for two single rooms. Caitlin could only assume the couples she was used to dealing with shared a double. Or perhaps she resented having to make up two rooms for only one night.

Caitlin hadn't slept well. She'd been too aware of what might happen the next day, and the prospect of seeing Jake again made her feel weak. What if he had only been playing a game? What if he didn't care about her? Or, most disturbing of all, what if he'd only pretended to be attracted to her because he thought she was his wife?

She'd been up before it was light, showering in the tiny bathroom, disturbing Marshall deliberately in the room next door by banging cupboards and drawers. By the time she'd put a call through to his room, he was dressed and ready, and because he knew how apprehensive she was feeling, he'd agreed to drive her out to the sawmill before they had breakfast.

It was supposed to be a reconnoitring expedition. A chance for Marshall to see where they were going, that's all. Or, at least, that was the excuse she had given him. She'd known from his expression that he hadn't been deceived.

The sight of the smoke drove all thought of delaying their arrival out of Caitlin's head. "Can you see that?" she exclaimed as they negotiated a crossroads, and the smell of burning timber came to their nostrils. "Oh, God! What's going on? Do you think Jake's all right?"

Marshall shrugged, but she could see he was concerned. "Who knows?" he said. "I wonder if anyone has called the fire service. If there's still timber lying about, that place must be the biggest fire risk in town."

"But how could it happen?" cried Caitlin, unable to sit still in her agitation. "No, turn here," she directed impatiently. "Can't we go any faster than this?"

"I wonder where there's a phone," murmured Marshall, still concerned about the repercussions, and Caitlin cast him a frustrated look.

"There'll be a phone at the house," she exclaimed, and then realised how insane that sounded. "I mean—let's just get there, shall we? They might need some help."

"That's what I'm afraid of," said Marshall, but he obediently pressed his foot down harder on the accelerator. "How much farther is it? Do you know?"

"Not much farther," Caitlin assured him, praying she had remembered the way correctly. It was one thing to see a pall of smoke—quite another to actually reach it. She felt like a rat in one of those mazes, with the reward it was seeking always out of reach. "There it is," she said at last, as they turned a corner and saw the derelict trading estate ahead of them.

The sawmill was the last lot on the block. They could see the flames now, leaping greedily above the roof line of the house, and Caitlin realised it wasn't the sawmill itself that was on fire as she'd thought.

Her stomach plummeted. Panic was setting in now, and even though Marshall was tearing along the pitted track at more than seventy miles an hour, she felt as if she could have run faster than the speeding car. She was gripped by an awful feeling of apprehension. Jake was in that house. She knew it. She could feel it in her bones.

"Oh, God, I don't believe it!"

Marshall's groan of dismay brought her head round to look at him. "What? *What*?" she asked impatiently, and he cast a speaking look towards the rear view mirror. Caitlin swung round, unable to comprehend his trepidation, and saw the black-and-white police car racing up behind.

She supposed it must have been flashing its lights and using its siren for some time, but she had been so intent on them reaching their destination, she had neither seen nor heard it. But the signals it was giving off seemed to be all against them, and she put her hands over her head in a gesture of defeat.

"I've got to stop," said Marshall, slowing as the police car swept past them, but although he applied the brakes, the police car didn't. It zoomed on towards the burning building, and he realised, with some irritation, that he'd made a stupid mistake.

His foot found the accelerator again, and Caitlin, who had closed her eyes when she'd thought they were about to be reprimanded, opened them again in disbelief.

"The fire," said Marshall impatiently. "They're going to the fire. We're so involved with our own problems, we haven't considered that other people can see the blaze."

They reached the timber yard just as the two policemen were getting out of their car. The heat was oppressive here, and one of the men gestured to Marshall to park some way back.

"Keep out of the way," he yelled. "Leave it to people who know what they're doing. I know you think you can help, but believe me, you're only in the way."

Caitlin wasn't listening to him. Now that they were here, she had no intention of being driven away. She climbed out of the car, and wrapping her arms about herself, stared up at the burning building. Her instincts were screaming at her that Jake was in there, but what could she do to help him?

"Get back!"

Sparks from the main building were arcing now, spiralling into the yard next door and turning windswept piles of sawdust into smouldering heaps. One of the policemen attempted to take her arm and propel her back to the car, but she pulled away from him. Dear God, she thought, how could anybody still be alive in that inferno? The flames were already licking along the roof.

"The fire department's on its way," said the other policeman, moving closer and surveying the upper floor of the building. "Shit—sorry, miss—but I wonder if the old man was in bed when the fire started. These old guys, they get careless. The cigarette slips from their fingers, and—"

"He didn't—he *doesn't* smoke," said Caitlin quickly as Marshall came to join them. "When I first got to know Nathan, he once joked that it wasn't wise to smoke in a sawmill, and I know for a fact that Mr Wolfe didn't even like tobacco."

The first policeman gave her a startled look. "You know the old guy?"

"He's her father-in-law," said Marshall, also scanning the upper floor of the building. "And you don't know that he's dead. He might not even be at home."

"Hey, that's a point," said the second man, nodding his approval of this suggestion. "There might be nobody in there, as you say. Sure, the place is dropping to bits, isn't it? It could just be faulty wiring that's caused the fire."

"Yeah, that's right," said his colleague, evidently finding that hypothesis more to his liking. "If there was anyone in there, surely they'd have been trying to get out."

"Unless they were overcome by smoke," said Caitlin tersely, not convinced by that argument, but before she could say anything more, Marshall uttered a startled cry.

"There's someone in there," he exclaimed, pointing towards a room on the ground floor. "I'm sure I saw a movement." He glanced at the two policemen. "There must be something we can do."

"Not until the fire truck gets here," said the first policeman. "Aitken, try and raise them on the radio, will you? They should have been here by now." Then, "Hey—come back!'' This, as Caitlin darted towards the entrance to the building. ''You can't go in there, miss. It's too dangerous!''

But Caitlin wasn't listening to him. She, too, had seen a movement within the shadowy pall of smoke that filled the ground-floor rooms. She couldn't be sure it was Jake, but whoever it was, she had to try and help them. Why didn't they get out? If they could move around, it wasn't because they couldn't walk.

Marshall overtook her before she reached the smoke-blackened doorway. It was only then that she realised that the door was open. The smoke had been billowing about so much, it hadn't been immediately apparent that they could get inside. But now it added to her fears as to why the occupant—*occupants*?—of the house hadn't escaped.

''Stay back,'' Marshall yelled, pushing her towards the policeman who had followed him. ''Keep hold of her,'' he advised the man as he pulled out his handkerchief to protect his nose and mouth. Then, without another word, he plunged through the doorway, ignoring the heat and the sparks that were flying about.

''Is your old man crazy?'' demanded the policeman as his partner came running to join them. ''Shit—hold her, Aitken, I'm gonna have to go in.''

''He's not my old man,'' said Caitlin, fighting furiously to free herself. ''Let me go. I've got to help him, can't you see that?''

''Ain't nothin' you can do, little lady,'' said Aitken, taking over the job of restraining her from his colleague just as the shed nearest to the main building caught fire. ''See, it's dangerous,'' he added, pulling her back. ''You watch what you're doing, O'Hara. There's no sense in getting yourself killed and that's a fact.''

The wail of a siren caused both men to turn their heads instinctively. "Thank God," muttered the one called O'Hara, clearly relieved that he wouldn't have to prove himself by going in. "Now, if we let you go, will you leave this to those who know what they're doing? I know you're worried, but they'll have your father-in-law out before you know it."

Caitlin made no promises, but when they let her go, she didn't immediately rush towards the door. She knew that when the fire-fighters arrived, any interference could only be a nuisance. But her hands balled into fists as the huge scarlet truck thundered up the road.

Then, before anybody had time to do anything, she saw three figures emerging through the smoke. One of them was Marshall; she could see that from the handkerchief he was still clutching to his face. But the others were too blackened by smoke to identify immediately.

As they stumbled through the doorway, she realised that Marshall was trying to restrain one of the men from going back into the house. He was struggling against the hold Marshall had on his collar, but for all he was taller than Marshall, he didn't seem to have the strength to fight back.

The other man took off as soon as he emerged into the daylight, stumbling towards the shed that was already beginning to burn. But like the other man and Marshall, he was hampered by lungs already choked with smoke, and after running a few yards, he crumpled to the ground and lay still.

Caitlin started forward, but before she could move more than a few feet, several of the fire-fighters rushed past her carrying hoses. A couple of them peeled off in search of the hydrant, but some veered towards the man who had collapsed. The others surrounded the two men on the path, and she heard them asking if there was anyone else in the house.

"Yes," choked the man Marshall was restraining. His face was streaked with blood, and he seemed to have some difficulty articulating at all. "But I think he's dead," he added, at last succeeding in pushing Marshall away from him. "He's through the back. Do you think you can get him out?"

Caitlin caught her breath. She knew that voice. It was Nathan's. Or was it Jake's? In that moment, she wasn't sure, and the realisation that it could be the man she loved in that back room filled her with despair.

"In back, you say?" The fireman frowned, donning the breathing equipment another of the men had brought for him to wear.

"Yes." Marshall answered him as the man he'd rescued succumbed to a fit of coughing. "Come on," he added, putting his arm about the man's shoulders. "Let's get you away from all this smoke."

They came towards Caitlin absurdly slowly, stopping every now and then to allow the man to try and clear his lungs. But it was obvious he'd inhaled a lot of smoke, and the effort seemed to leave him dizzy. In any event, he obviously needed Marshall's assistance to move at all.

Caitlin watched them with varying degrees of apprehension. It wasn't that she wished Nathan dead, she told herself, but if this blackened figure was Nathan, who was that lying on the ground? He was being attended to by one of the other firemen, and she was anxious to go and speak to him. But she waited for Marshall to tell her what was going on.

"What's happened?" she asked, unable to restrain herself any longer, and Marshall, who hadn't inhaled as much smoke and who had obviously recovered that much quicker, allowed the man he was supporting to slide gently to the ground.

"God!" Marshall shook his head. "When I got into the house, Jake was trying to get Nathan—" he jerked his thumb towards the man farthest away from them "—to help him carry his father outside. But Nathan couldn't wait to get out of there. He said—Jake—had started the fire, but I don't think he could. For one thing, he's been shot. See..." He bent towards the man who had collapsed full-length on the gravelled forecourt, and pointed towards his temple. "He's very weak. He's lost a lot of blood."

Caitlin stared at the man on the ground. "How do you know this is Jake?" she asked unsteadily. "It could be either one of them beneath all that soot."

"Because Nathan was only interested in saving his own skin," replied Marshall in a low voice. "He couldn't wait to tell me that his father had shot Jake, but I don't know if that's true, either."

"Oh, God!"

Ignoring the other man now, Caitlin knelt beside Jake, touching his cheek and running helpless fingers along his jaw. At least he was alive, she thought, uncaring at that moment who was to blame for his injuries. If only he would open his eyes. She had to know that he was going to be all right.

A trickle of blood ran down his cheek, and she saw that the wound was still seeping. It created a vivid splash of colour against his smoke-blackened cheek. His clothes were filthy, too, and she could only imagine what he had been doing. Dear God, what might have happened if Marshall hadn't intervened?

His eyes opened as she was bending over him, and as if suddenly realising where he was, he struggled to sit up. "Are you all right?" she asked as an ambulance whined into the mêlée, and Jake closed his eyes for a moment before giving her a weary look.

"I guess so," he said at last. Then, "your husband's over there, you know. I'm not Nathan. I'm Jake. His twin brother."

"I know." Caitlin's response seemed to startle him, and she hurried into a garbled explanation. "We found out. Lisa Abbott came to see me. Marshall knows, as well. Oh, Jake..." She caught her breath. "I'm sorry."

"You're sorry?"

Jake was still staring at her with stunned eyes, when there was a protesting yell from across the yard. The man who had been left to attend to Nathan had evidently gone to meet the paramedics, and in his absence, his patient had staggered to his feet. Now they all watched in horror as Nathan stumbled towards the shed, and although several of the men started after him, it was obvious they weren't going to reach him in time.

"For God's sake, Nathan, leave it!"

Jake's hoarse cry must have reached his brother, but Nathan wasn't listening to him. Shaking his head as if to clear it, he disappeared inside, just seconds before a loud blast shook the ground round them. The shed exploded in a ball of flame, sending wood and metal flying in all directions. Then an ominous silence fell as the fire-fighters all stopped what they were doing to stare at the blaze.

"Shit," Caitlin heard someone say as if from a distance, "there must have been a vehicle in there."

"Yeah," said someone else. "He must have been trying to save it. Goddammit, he didn't stand a chance!"

26

Jake drove home in the warm twilight of a spring evening.

He was glad to be out of the office; glad to be away from his desk and able to pull his tie free of his collar and toss his suit jacket into the back of the car. He felt both tired and weary, which were not the same thing at all. Tired of the unending stream of flawed humanity that passed through his door, and weary, with a bone weariness, of trying to pretend he had a life.

This time of year used to be his favourite, with the dogwoods blooming and the first lush growth of the season turning the golf course next to the apartment complex a rich shade of green, and he usually felt expectant and optimistic. The winter was over—as much of a winter as they got in North Carolina anyway—and the sweltering heat of summer was still some distance away.

But this year was different. This year he felt no sense of expectancy, no air of optimism that his life was satisfactorily on track. Not even the unexpected offer of a partnership could lift his spirits—an opportunity to be his own master, with the option to accept a case or not, as he chose.

There was no doubt that Dane Meredith's proposition had come out of the blue. Because Jake worked mainly for the public defender's office, and Meredith spent his time representing the more affluent members of the community, they had never confronted one another across a courtroom. The idea that Jake's reputation for hard work and integrity might have come to the distinguished lawyer's ears was flattering. Meredith's name was a byword in Pine Bay and the surrounding area, and nine months ago, he knew, he'd have jumped at the chance. It was the kind of opportunity most young lawyers dreamed about: independence, and the support of an established firm behind him.

It was an offer he'd be a fool to reject, but the prospect of establishing himself here seemed to represent an acceptance of his present situation, and right at this moment, he didn't even know what he wanted to do.

Once, he would have said he was quite content to stay in Pine Bay. He was not without ambition, but the idea of using his talents, such as they were, for the benefit of his fellow citizens had seemed a fair compromise to him. He wasn't interested in earning fantastic sums of money, and he liked knowing the people he was dealing with.

It was true, he was ready for a change of direction, but he was no longer sure he wanted to stay here. Maybe a change of location would give him what his work could not: a rekindling of his own self-worth, of there being some purpose to his life—something he seemed to have lost in the six months since his father and his brother had died.

He sighed, refusing to acknowledge that there was more to his uncertainty than a lingering grief that the only male blood relations he had had in the world were dead. Any other regrets he had were just that: regrets. There was nothing he could do about them; no way he could change the past or undo the things that had been done. It was over now; they had all moved on, and he was only delaying the inevitable by pretending that anything more could come of it.

But when he reached the apartment complex, he didn't immediately get out of the car. Instead, he rested his forearms on the wheel and stared unseeingly towards the ocean.

The mournful cry of the sea birds scavenging among the sand-dunes suited his mood, and he felt an overwhelming sense of melancholy.

Caitlin, he groaned inwardly. God, Caitlin, tell me what I'm going to do.

He wished he didn't have to go into the apartment and face Fletch. It wasn't that he didn't want to meet the old devil, and he'd been glad enough to see him when he first got out of the hospital. Hell, he'd considered himself so lucky that the old man was well again, and the horror he'd experienced when he'd first heard that Fletch had had a stroke still had the power to chill his bones.

Fletch had told him how he had surprised Nathan by being at the apartment. He hadn't gone into details, but Jake could guess at the old man's fury at meeting his brother there. Particularly after Jacob had been to see him and told him he had been in the hospital in New York. Fletch had never trusted Nathan, and he was bound to have suspected Nathan's motives for coming to Pine Bay.

Nevertheless, Nathan had had no right to hit him, even if Fletch had admitted that he'd invited the punch that had brought on his seizure. His brother should have realised that Fletch was old and frail these days, and not half as robust as he'd like everyone to believe.

He grimaced. He never thought he'd ever have cause to be grateful to the old janitor. He used to think the old man was a pain, snooping round the complex, spying on everyone who came into the building. But without his ever-vigilant inspection, the unlocked door to Jake's condo would not have been noticed, and Fletch would undoubtedly have died if he hadn't had immediate attention.

Jake expelled a pained breath. Christ, he thought, not for the first time, no wonder Nathan had looked so shocked to see him. He must have been terrified that Jake had been to the apartment and found Fletch's body. For he had no doubt that Nathan had believed the old man was dead.

He wondered if Nathan would have called 911 if he'd thought Fletch was only unconscious. Jake preferred not to speculate about that. They'd never know what Nathan might have done if he'd realised Fletch was still alive. As far as Fletch was concerned, the incident was better forgotten.

For his part, Jake was simply grateful his father had survived. He still blamed himself for indirectly involving the old man in Nathan's activities in the first place, and although Fletch would have none of it, the fact remained he was lucky to be alive.

Jake's own problems had been a little less easy to cope with.

It was strange, really. He'd been shot; he'd found his father's dead body in a burning house; and he'd watched his brother blown to pieces in an explosion. Yet he'd been able to attend their funerals without turning a hair. He was sure someone must have commented on his coolness, his self-possession; and if it hadn't been for his concern for Fletch, people might have been forgiven for thinking he didn't have any feelings at all.

He'd attended to everything himself, declining Marshall's offer to help with a confidence that made him cringe now. It was what his father would have expected, he'd assured him, whether that was true or not. It was his place, as the only surviving member of the family. He didn't consider Caitlin's rights or otherwise. It was important for him to keep busy. He didn't remember sleeping at all until the funerals were over.

Caitlin's father and mother did not attend the ceremonies. They sent their condolences, but they had the perfect excuse for refusing to come. Matthew Webster's doctor had advised him to rest after the shock of learning of his son-in-law's death, and besides, the journey would have been too arduous for him.

A young couple came out of the building behind him and walked across the parking lot to their car. The woman recognised him and raised her hand in greeting as they passed, but Jake guessed they must both be wondering why he was sitting here instead of going inside.

Sighing, he propped his chin on his folded wrists.

What had Caitlin thought about his behaviour? he wondered. Like everyone else, she had obviously been horrified by the way her husband died. But when the shock was over, what had she thought of him, Jake, for betraying her? For deceiving her, and seducing her, and pretending they had a future?

He expelled an anguished breath.

At the time, he'd been glad Marshall was there to look after her. It had seemed important for him not to show any emotion, and he couldn't have coped with her grief and kept his own in check. In any case, from the moment the shed exploded, he'd known that any chance they might have had was over. That day would be printed indelibly on her mind.

He remembered Marshall had tried to talk to him after the services were over, but by then he'd been so inured in the role he'd chosen to play, there'd been no way to answer him rationally. He knew Marshall had guessed about the drugs, but he had had no intention of betraying his brother's intentions to him. Instead, he had let Nathan's dirty secret die with him. It was the only way he knew to protect his father's memory.

Marshall and Caitlin had returned to England the following day, and Jake had assured himself he felt better once they were gone. There was nothing he could do to change things; no way of defending his involvement. He regretted the past, but he regretted what he'd done to Caitlin most of all.

It was when he'd had a visit from the police that he'd finally gone to pieces.

Unbeknown to him, the authorities in Pine Bay had been trying to locate him for days. Loretta had been the first to receive the news that Fletch had been found unconscious in his son's apartment, and to begin with, despite her protests, Jake had been suspected of being involved. She'd insisted he'd been away, but the janitor was positive he had let Jake into his apartment just hours before the old man's body had been found. And until Fletch regained consciousness and was able to exonerate his son, a warrant had been issued for his arrest.

Of course, Jake had known none of this to begin with. He had still been in Prescott, trying to deal with all the details of his father's will. Jacob had left half of what he owned to each of his sons, and although Nathan's death had complicated matters, Jake was determined that Caitlin should get her husband's share.

For his part, he'd wanted nothing that was Jacob's. With the lawyer's help, he had prepared a document donating his small legacy to the town. It was up to the mayor and the sheriff to decide what they might do with it. Jake never wanted to see Prescott again.

Which was why he got such a shock when the police came to see him. It appeared Fletch had been able to tell the authorities that the father of the man they now wanted to question lived in Prescott, and when they'd contacted the police there, they'd been informed that both Nathan Wolfe and his father were dead.

But hearing that Fletch had been attacked—almost killed, in fact—had been the last straw as far as Jake was concerned. To his everlasting shame, he'd gone completely to pieces, and his much-vaunted self-control had simply collapsed.

He'd spent the next six weeks in various hospitals. As soon as possible, he'd been transferred to the facility in Pine Bay, to enable Fletch to come and visit with him. At that time, his old adversary had been a tower of strength—the only sane thing in a world gone mad.

They told him he'd experienced a brief return of the stress-related illness he'd suffered when he came back from Vietnam. Whatever it was, he remembered he'd felt pretty devastated. He'd also discovered he was no more immune to tragedy than anyone else.

Fletch had spent several weeks with him after Jake had got home from the hospital. Jake had become accustomed to finding beer bottles behind the couch and the constant scent of tobacco in the air. But what the hell, he thought, Fletch was the only person who cared a damn about him. If he felt able to make himself at home in the apartment, that had to be a plus.

There'd been no word from Caitlin, of course, but he hadn't expected any. She probably considered she was better off out of it. The short time they had had together was best forgotten. She certainly could have no fond memories of her husband or his family.

He'd returned to work after Christmas, and since then, he'd had to contend with Fletch calling him day and night. He knew the old man was still concerned about him; that, although he was supposed to have returned to his own home in Blackwater Fork, he still spent a couple of nights a week at the apartment because he was worried about him. Jake appreciated the sentiment, but he knew he had to make a life for himself, and perhaps this partnership with Dane Meredith was the first step.

Or was it?

Perhaps he ought to get right away from Pine Bay, North Carolina. With his qualifications, he knew he could find another job in another town. He could even move right across the country, to California or Oregon. The climate would be better. He'd heard they didn't have such a high level of humidity in L.A.

But he knew he wouldn't do it; not now, not while Fletch still needed him. He couldn't trust his four half-sisters to look after their father. They had always been more interested in their own lives and their own families than in taking care of an old man who they considered deserved everything he'd gotten.

Jake grimaced. Today had been a bad day, he reflected wearily. He was letting the problems he had faced in the courtroom accompany him home. Just because Winston Miller had gone to prison, he was feeling dejected. Dammit, the kid had been found with several bottles of amphetamines in his sport bag.

It hadn't helped to go back to the office and have Loretta bending his ear because Fletch had interrupted her schedule. The old man had been calling all afternoon, she said, and she'd eventually told him in no uncertain terms, if Jake knew his secretary, to get off her back. It wasn't that Jake didn't want to see the old devil, but tonight he would have appreciated a little privacy. When he was feeling as low as he was feeling at present, he just knew he wouldn't be good company.

Still . . .

Fletch was not to know that, and pushing open the car door, Jake gathered his jacket and an armful of files from the back seat. Then slamming the door again, he started towards the building.

To his relief, the janitor wasn't about as he let himself into the foyer. Shifting the weight of the files from one arm to the other, he walked purposefully down the corridor towards his apartment, mentally girding his wits for the evening ahead.

He had no desire to upset the old man, and if Fletch had even suspected he was still suffering the aftermath of what had happened, he would worry all the more. Fletch didn't know Caitlin; he'd never met her, and Jake could hardly admit he was in love with his brother's widow. Anything to do with the Wolfes was anathema to Fletch; he'd consigned them both, father and son, to the devil.

Jake was juggling with his keys when the door opened, and his father stepped into his line of vision. The old man was looking older, Jake thought, feeling a twinge of conscience. He hoped he wasn't responsible for the added lines of worry about his eyes.

Fletch had evidently been waiting for him, and Jake belatedly hoped he wasn't aware of how long he'd been sitting outside in the Blazer. He couldn't be, he consoled himself. The windows of the apartment overlooked the sound, not the parking lot. He must have rung the office again and discovered Jake was on his way. He'd probably been listening for his footsteps in the hall.

At least he looked cheerful, Jake mused, summoning a rueful grin as he eased past him into the apartment. "I'm sorry if Loretta chewed your balls off," he apologised, by way of a greeting. "But you know what she's like when she's got a lot to—"

He broke off abruptly. Fletch hadn't said anything, but across the split-level living room, a slim figure had risen from an armchair. A feminine figure, tall, with toffee-fair hair, and dark-lashed eyes, who was gazing at him almost tremulously.

Christ Almighty, he thought unsteadily, it was Caitlin!

Oh, God, what was she doing here?

27

Oh, God, oh, God, oh, God!

Caitlin's heart skipped at least half a dozen beats, but it was pounding so fast, she never even noticed it. It wasn't a hot day, but she was sweating. She could feel little rivulets of perspiration sliding down the hollow of her back.

She took a steadying breath. He was here, she told herself. She had to control herself. This was what she had been waiting for, and she didn't want to ruin everything now. She had to stop staring at him like a mesmerised rabbit. No matter how specious it seemed, she had to give a reason why she'd come.

The trouble was, she was so thrilled to see him again, she couldn't think straight. For weeks—*months*—she had thought of nothing else. And he was exactly as she remembered: so dark, and lean, and attractive. How she had ever mistaken him for Nathan, she didn't know.

Except that she hadn't known Nathan had a brother—a *twin* brother, moreover, who'd believed her when she said she was his wife. They'd both been caught in a trap of Nathan's making, and it was only good luck that they'd both come out alive.

"Hi," she got out now, awkwardly, and Mr Connor—Fletch, as he had insisted she call him—gave his son an impatient shove.

"You've got a visitor, Jake," he exclaimed. "Ain't you gonna say you're glad to see her? The way I hear it, the lady's come a helluva long way to see you."

Jake moved then, dropping his jacket and the armful of files he was carrying onto a chair in the entry, and approached the shallow steps that led down into the living room. "Of course," he said, though his voice was taut and wary. "This is an unexpected pleasure, Caitlin. You should have let us know you were coming."

Caitlin?

She moistened her dry lips. Was that an indication that he wanted to keep their association on a formal footing? And why had he said she should have let him know she was coming, when it seemed obvious he didn't want her here?

To warn her not to come, perhaps? she mused, trying not to let his aloofness upset her. After all, if he'd wanted to see her, he'd had only to get on a plane. And she had to remember he hadn't wanted to speak to her or Marshall after the funeral. He hadn't cared about her then, so why would she think he'd care about her now?

"I think I'll take myself off home," declared Fletch with remarkable discretion, but Jake turned back to look at him, and Caitlin was fairly sure there was anger in his eyes.

"No..." he began. Then, "you don't have to go, Fletch. Whatever—Mrs Wolfe—has to say won't take long, I'm sure. We can send out for a pizza later on."

"Nah." Fletch hooked his jacket off the peg by the door and offered Caitlin a wicked grin. "You don't want an old man like me horning in on your conversation. Now, you be good, boy, and I'll see you in the morning."

Caitlin saw the way Jake's jaw tightened as his father let himself out of the door, but short of collaring the old man and setting him down, there was nothing more he could do. Consequently, he turned back to her without his previous courtesy, coming slowly down the steps and facing her across the oriental rug.

Caitlin's throat constricted. Oh, Lord, she thought, why had she ever had the notion of coming here? Just because of what they'd once shared, she was risking her own self-respect and her reputation. If Jake turned her away, it was going to be so much worse.

"Did Fletch ask if you wanted a drink?" Jake inquired now. He had himself in control again, and his question was the usual one offered to any guest.

"I didn't want anything," she responded obliquely, without really answering him. She licked her lips. "I expect you're surprised to see me." She hesitated. "How are you?"

Jake's mouth compressed, and he started forward, but although she found herself closing her eyes in anxious anticipation, he merely passed her by on his way to the kitchen. He reached the fridge, and through the open doorway, she saw him take a bottle of beer from the cooler. Then he flipped the cap and drank deeply from the bottle.

Watching him, her stomach felt wobbly. With his head tipped back, and the muscles of his throat moving rhythmically as he swallowed, he presented a fascinating picture. Yet the knowledge that he could ignore her presence so completely was daunting. She knew she could never be so indifferent to him.

He finished the beer, saw her watching him, and deposited the empty bottle in the waste bin. Then, wiping his mouth on the back of his hand, he came towards her again, making her limbs feel so weak, she found herself groping for the chair behind her.

She sank down as Jake paused in the kitchen doorway, propping his shoulder indolently against the jamb. He looked so cool, she thought, regarding her with that narrow gaze that was blank and guarded. She had no idea what he was thinking. She wished she did.

"So," he said, and she was relieved to hear that she wasn't expected to carry the whole conversation. "Perhaps you'd better tell me why you've come. I mean, it's not that I'm not pleased to see you, but I don't think it's wise, your being here. And I'm sure your father wouldn't approve of it, if he knew."

"He knows," said Caitlin swiftly. "You don't imagine I could leave the country without telling him, do you? And—" she hesitated "—and as far as the advisability of my being here is concerned, well—I suppose that rather depends on you."

"On me?"

Jake pointed towards himself with a disbelieving finger, and Caitlin nodded before she lost her nerve. "Yes. If—if you don't want me here, I'll leave. You've only to say so. I don't want to interfere in your life again, without your permission."

Jake's mouth compressed. "I thought I interfered in your life," he said after a moment. "You could hardly be blamed for the plane crashing, or—or anything else Nathan had intended to do. It was a crazy plan, and only a fool would have expected it to work. You were his wife. That doesn't make you his keeper."

"All the same—"

"All the same—nothing." Jake's features hardened. "It's all over now, and if this is some belated attempt to explain your part in the proceedings, forget it. As far as I'm concerned, it's better left unsaid."

Caitlin quivered. This wasn't going at all the way she had hoped, and it was difficult to see how she could broach what she wanted to say without arousing the wrong response. Perhaps she ought to give him the excuse she'd trumped up to bring her here. Maybe if they talked about something else, she'd get a better understanding of how he really felt.

"As a matter of fact," she began, "I didn't—just—come to see you about—about what happened. Your father's solicitor—that is, *your* solicitor—wrote and told me Nathan was a half legatee in his father's will." She paused to gather her thoughts, and then continued, "He told me you'd given my name as Nathan's next of kin. He also told me where you lived. Until then I didn't know."

Jake's brows descended. "You didn't know?"

It was as if it had never occurred to him before, and she wondered if she was only imagining the effect it had had on him.

"No," she conceded now. "You didn't tell me." She stifled a half-hysterical laugh. "How could you? You thought you lived in Prescott."

Jake stared at her. "But that morning—the morning of the fire—you knew I'd recovered my memory?"

"Oh, yes. Lisa Abbott told me that. But she didn't tell me where you lived. I doubt if she even knows."

Jake shook his head. "Christ, and I thought—" He broke off abruptly and raked long fingers through his hair. "So, you don't know what happened? After the funeral, I mean..." He took a breath. "I never thought."

Caitlin pushed herself rather cautiously to her feet. "What don't I know?" she asked carefully. "I know about Nathan. I know what he was doing. Marshall went to see Lisa when we got back. I don't know what he said, but he managed to get the truth out of her somehow. He probably threatened to report her to the authorities if she didn't come clean. In any event, she was pretty cut up to hear that Nathan was dead, and all Daddy really cared about was finding out where the money had gone." She paused. "Oh, yes, and I know about the way Nathan was cheating the company when Daddy had his heart attack.'' She frowned. ''So you see, I'm not totally naïve.''

Jake's fingers had come to rest at the back of his neck, but although he was still looking at her, she had the feeling he wasn't really listening to her. ''You didn't know,'' he said again, and she almost stopped breathing when he dropped his hand and let his knuckles caress her cheek. ''Oh, God, Kate, is that the only reason you came to see me? Because you and I are joint legatees of my father's will?''

Caitlin's breath whistled in her throat. ''What...'' she whispered, and then, more positively, ''What else could there be?''

''Indeed,'' he conceded softly, but his hand had slid behind her head, and he was slowly but surely pulling her forward. ''What else?'' he breathed against her lips, before he found her mouth.

The flat, cool and shadowy, was heated by the hungry passion of his kiss. His lips devoured hers, eating urgently at the nourishment that had been long denied him. His tongue delved deeply into her mouth before tangling with the eager provocation of hers. His hands slid into her hair and turned her face up more fully to his urgent assault.

Caitlin's senses swam. There was something unashamedly carnal in his knowledge of her that she was either too weak or too desperate to restrain. She didn't care how long it lasted, so long as he made love to her. She'd been aching for the touch of him ever since he walked in the door.

But, evidently, Jake was not as swept away by his emotions as she had been by hers. Although briefly his hands had slid down her back to cup her rounded buttocks, and she'd felt the unmistakeable brush of his arousal, he was still in control. He bit her tongue and her lower lip, and then put her away from him, raking the back of his neck with a hand that revealed how fragile that control was.

"We have to talk," he said tautly, forcing himself to walk towards the darkening windows. "There are things you don't know about me, and I have to tell you what happened to Fletch."

"Fletch?"

The word came out faint and disbelieving. Caitlin couldn't believe he'd broken off making love to her because of that old man. Didn't he realise how fragile she was—how brittle? She felt as if she was in danger of falling apart.

"Yes, Fletch," said Jake now, keeping his back to her. His shoulders were broad, and in the pale light, she could see the shadow of sweat that outlined his spine. It was reassuring to know that he was not indifferent to his feelings. Though she desperately wanted to feel his arms around her again.

"What about Fletch?" she asked tremulously, sure that whatever he wanted to tell her, it could have waited until after they'd been to bed. It was frightening to think how much power this man had over her senses; she, who had always considered herself indifferent to sex in the past.

"Nathan nearly killed him," said Jake flatly, and Caitlin caught her breath. "He thought he had killed him, actually, except that the old devil is stronger than he thought."

"Oh, God!" Caitlin felt sick. "But when did Nathan see Fletch?"

"He'd come down here to get away from Jacob, I believe, and Fletch was in the apartment when he arrived. He accused Nathan of God knows what, and they had a fight."

"Fletch—and Nathan?" said Caitlin faintly, and Jake half turned, supporting himself against the frame, his expression sombre with reminiscence.

"Yeah." He grimaced. "But don't think it was a wholly unequal contest. Fletch used to be quite a hell-raiser in his time." His lips twisted. "I should know. He's laid his belt across my back more times than I care to remember."

Caitlin's lips parted. "You remembered that."

"It was hard to forget." Jake was rueful. "He never could forget what my mother had done."

"Your mother—she had an affair with—with Jacob Wolfe, your father?"

"Sort of." Jake shrugged. "As far as I can make out, it was never intended to go as far as it did. Hell, Nathan and I weren't planned for. She and Fletch couldn't afford the four they already had."

"Four?"

"My half sisters," agreed Jake wryly. "The youngest was already half-grown when we were born. That's why she let Jacob take Nathan. That—and the fact that he paid Fletch a hefty sum for the privilege."

"But Fletch didn't know you weren't—"

"His own kin? Hell, no. Not at first. He'd have kicked us both out if he had. Yet—" he was thoughtful "—when he did find out, and Alice—that's my mother—threatened to leave him if he threw me out, he let me stay. I think secretly he liked having a son, even if he pretended to hate my guts."

"But he doesn't hate you now."

"No." Jake shook his head. "I guess you could say Fletch and I have come to an understanding. He knows I love the old bastard, and I guess the feeling's reciprocated."

"I think so." Caitlin waited a beat. "It doesn't make any difference, you know." She took a breath. "Oh, Jake—why didn't you come to England? You must know I—"

"Wait." Jake straightened away from the window and thrust his hands into his trouser pockets. "You don't know everything yet. How and why Nathan and I came to live such separate lives isn't important. It may account for some of the differences in our characters, but that's all." He sighed. "No, what I have to tell you concerns me, and only me." He breathed deeply. "I guess no one's told you that I was once an addict myself."

Caitlin was stunned and looked it. "A drug addict?"

"Is there any other kind?"

Caitlin swallowed. "I don't know." She felt a little dizzy now. "Did—did Nathan know?"

"Oh, sure." Jake was sardonic. "My brother lost no opportunity to remind me of it."

Caitlin blinked. "I can't believe it."

"It disgusts you, doesn't it?" Jake was bitter. "Well, don't worry, it disgusts me, too."

"But—how...?" She moistened her lips. "If you told me, I might understand."

Jake stared at her. "Run that by me again."

"I just want to understand," said Caitlin unevenly. "Was it—Fletch? Was it the knowledge that Nathan—that your brother—had a better life?"

"Christ, no!" Jake was vehement. "I didn't get the habit here." He groaned. "Of course, that's something else you don't know about me. I was in Vietnam."

Caitlin's eyes widened. "But you were too young."

"Young, but not too young," Jake assured her flatly. "Except maybe for the brutality. Hell, yes, I found that pretty hard to take."

Caitlin moved forward. "Oh, Jake! Why didn't you tell me that before? I know—I know lots of young men grew old during the war in Southeast Asia. No one—no one could blame you for that."

"Couldn't they?" Jake was still not convinced she meant it. "You've got no idea of the state I was in when I got home. If it hadn't been for my mother and Fletch, I might still have been in the loony bin.''

"Don't sell yourself short," said Caitlin huskily, risking laying a hand on his arm. "You're not weak. You're strong. And I can help you."

"Help me?" A choking laugh escaped his throat. "Sweet Jesus, you think I'm still a user, don't you?" And at her colouring cheeks, "Kate, I kicked the habit years ago! Since then, I've been back to school and got my degree, and these days I make a living defending some of the poor punks who thought they could screw the system, too."

"You do?"

Caitlin was stunned, and Jake nodded. "I'm afraid so."

She lifted her shoulders. "I'm sorry. I just thought—"

"I know what you thought, and I love you for it," he said softly, causing a flutter of awareness to spiral down into her stomach. "And if I'd known how you'd feel, I might not have wasted all these months going out of my head wanting you."

"You—want—me?" Caitlin trembled, and as if sensing that sensitive quiver through the sleeve of his shirt, he covered her hand with his.

"Of course I want you," he told her roughly. "But how do you think it made me feel, falling in love with my brother's wife?"

"The same way I felt falling in love with my husband's brother, I suppose," said Caitlin unsteadily.

"You thought I was Nathan," he reminded her.

"I prayed you were," she admitted, licking her lips. "But my prayers have never been answered before."

"Oh, baby!"

Unable to prevent the inevitable any longer, Jake used his hand to draw her towards him, and then, resting his forearms on her shoulders, he covered her mouth with his.

Passion flared anew, more urgent this time, and they both knew that any further explanations would have to wait until they'd satisfied the hunger they were both feeling.

"Come on," Jake said thickly, when he could drag his lips away from hers, "I'll show you my bedroom. My real bedroom this time. Not just a poor imitation."

The room was almost dark, and Jake turned on the pair of lamps at either side of the king-sized divan. They illuminated a room that bore no resemblance to the room she had said was his at the flat in Wellsley Square, and although her surroundings were of little importance at this moment, she felt a sense of familiarity in the cream and green walls, and the rusty brown patterns on the quilt. A sense of homecoming, too, in the possessive light in Jake's eyes, and although she'd never done it in front of a man before, she couldn't wait to get her clothes off.

Jake had kicked off his shoes and was presently tugging off his tie and loosening the buttons on his shirt. His chest was as strongly masculine as she remembered, and realising she was wasting time watching him, she attacked the buttons on her thigh-length sweater.

Below the sweater, she was wearing an ankle-length skirt that buttoned to the knee and was split thereafter, and her fingers fumbled as she endeavoured to release the tiny buttons from their holes.

She removed the skirt first, aware that Jake's eyes went straight to her stockinged thighs and the three inches of flesh exposed by her stocking tops. There was something rather arousing about undressing in front of a man who admired you, she discovered, and almost without being aware of it, she started to enjoy the experience.

Her sweater followed her skirt onto the floor, and she stood before him, clad only in her low-cut bra and panties.

"Wait," he said hoarsely, stepping out of his trousers and coming round the end of the bed to reach her. His erection strained at the navy silk of his underwear, but his eyes were all for Caitlin. With a frankly sensual expression, he cupped the swollen globes of her breasts in his hands, and then, as if losing control completely, he pulled her down onto the bed. He swore softly as he found the catch of the bra and it opposed him, but eventually it gave way, and the tender nipples nudged his palms. "Beautiful," he said, bending his head to nibble at them. "Oh, Kate, I'm never going to let you go away from me again."

"Did I say I wanted to go?" she breathed, bestowing hot little kisses all over his chest and throat, and he sought her mouth again with undisguised need.

He was lying half over her now, one well-muscled leg wedged between her legs, his arousal throbbing insistently against her thigh. But although he had disposed of her panties, he was still wearing his underwear, and she allowed the hand that had been clutching his shoulder to slip sensuously beneath his waistband.

"Christ!" His reaction was every bit as violent as she had hoped, but although he yanked off the offending briefs, he wouldn't let her touch him again. "Give me a break," he groaned, his face hot against her throat. "I'm only human."

"So'm I," murmured Caitlin, shifting restlessly beneath him. "But I want you to touch me."

"How?" he asked huskily, drawing his finger up the inside of her thigh. "Like this? Or like this?" He allowed his finger to penetrate the moist honeycomb between her legs, and she clutched him tightly as a sudden spasm gripped her. "Or like this," he appended, spreading the blonde curls that protected her sex, and bending his head. "God—you taste good!"

"Jake!"

Her cry was plaintive now, and because he was already beyond the point of no return, Jake moved over her and allowed his aching body to find the relief it craved.

"Okay," he said, and she could see the sweat standing on his forehead. "Let's make love."

The first time was fast and furious. Jake tried to keep control of his emotions, but his need and hers were too great to allow for any restraint, and within minutes they were both panting and enjoying the delicious sense of relief that had followed their mating.

"You are one sexy woman," he said as the convulsions that had shaken his body began to subside. "And I am the luckiest man in the world."

"Do you think so?"

"I know so," he assured her softly. "Did I tell you I'm crazy about you?"

"You did. But I don't mind if you say it again," she whispered, allowing the sole of her foot to move sinuously against his calf. "Hmm, I see you like that. You are one greedy man, Mr Connor."

Epilogue

Hours later, Caitlin was awakened by Jake coming back into the bedroom carrying a bottle of wine and two glasses. He was naked, and her eyes moved over him with possessive thoroughness, until his body's response brought a smug little smile to her lips.

"What time is it?" she asked as he climbed onto the end of the bed, and Jake consulted the watch that was all he was wearing.

"About midnight, I think," he replied with a grin. "My watch has steamed up."

"I don't believe it," she exclaimed, scrambling onto her knees and facing him without shame. "Mmm, is that champagne?"

"The next best thing," said Jake drily. "Fletch got it when I came home from the hospital, but I wasn't in the mood for celebrating right then."

"The hospital?" Caitlin looked anxious. "You mean— the wound on your head was more serious than we thought?"

"The bullet wound?" Jake shook his head a little ruefully. "No, that was just a glancing wound. Nathan was trying to get my father's old service revolver away from him and it accidentally went off."

"Oh, Jake!"

"It sounds much worse than it actually was," he assured her gently. "But—well, I guess I wasn't as tough as I thought I was." He poured some of the sparkling wine into a glass and handed it to her. "After the funeral arrangements had been dealt with, the cops came to tell me that Fletch had been attacked and had a stroke, and I couldn't take it." He took a sip of his wine. "Stupid, hmm?"

Caitlin stared at him. "Not stupid at all," she exclaimed hotly. "Oh, God, I knew you were strange at the funeral. Marshall said he tried to talk to you, but you just put him off."

"I know."

"But why?"

Jake took another mouthful of wine. "I guess the simple answer is that I thought I'd never see you again."

"Jake!"

"It's true." He regarded her with rueful eyes. "Remember, you'd just seen your husband killed in an explosion, and so far as I was concerned, you'd thought I was Nathan, so—"

"So nothing." Caitlin was impatient. "If only you'd said something."

"I couldn't." He grimaced. "And then, later on, after I'd gotten my head together again, I convinced myself that if you'd been interested, you'd have written or called or something."

"I did!" Caitlin spoke urgently. "I tried to get in touch with you at Prescott about—oh, I don't know, maybe two weeks after the fire." She sighed. "But you weren't there, and someone called—Hank Grafton?—"

"He used to work for my father."

"Yes, well, he said you weren't there, and he didn't know where I could reach you."

"Jesus."

"I could only hope that you'd get in touch with me," she explained huskily. "But you never did."

"And now you know why," said Jake drily. "Are you sure you know what you're doing? Are you sure this is what you want?"

"I was never so sure of anything in my whole life," said Caitlin, and with a groan, Jake lunged towards her, carrying her back onto the bed. "The wine," she wailed as her glass went flying, but Jake wasn't interested.

"To hell with the wine," he said thickly, spreading her legs with one of his. "Hmm, that's better. I've got you exactly where I want you."

It was the following morning before Caitlin got around to telling Jake that she knew about Marshall.

"You knew, didn't you?" she asked, after she'd confessed that her mother had finally told her the truth. "He said you'd guessed almost at once. I must be awfully naïve."

"Just awfully sweet," Jake told her gently. "And you have to remember, I'd had a similar history myself."

"Hmm." Caitlin looked at him across the kitchen table. "What you don't know is that Daddy's had another heart attack, and he's been virtually forced to choose a successor."

"Marshall."

She nodded.

"And how do you feel about that?"

"Me?" She looked surprised that he was asking such question. "It doesn't make any difference to me. I told Marshall, when he asked, much the same thing. If Daddy had needed me, of course, that would be different. Nat rally, none of us want to run the risk of him being ill again. He's so frail since his last attack, we're all really grateful to Marshall. But I haven't been interested in running Webster's for years.''

Jake frowned. "Because you prefer your work at the antique shop?''

"Well..." Caitlin coloured. "As a matter of fact, I don't work there any more, either. Janie and I—Janie Spencer, that is—"

"I remember. The woman you worked with.''

"We agreed it wasn't working out. She's got a new assistant. Della Parish. She's the sixth former who used to fill in when I wasn't there.''

"I see.''

Jake was watching her intently now, and Caitlin wondered if she was as transparent to him as she seemed to be to herself. Didn't he realise yet that she wanted to stay with him? That she couldn't bear to live with so many miles between them?

"I—I was wondering if I might possibly get a job over here,'' she ventured at last, and Jake frowned. "Over here?'' His tone seemed deliberately expressionless. "As in Pine Bay, do you mean?''

"Why not?'' Caitlin tried to sound casual. "It would mean we could see one another on a regular basis. Get to know one another better, if you see what I mean.''

"No.''

Jake spoke matter-of-factly, and Caitlin winced. "No?'' She moistened her lips. "Why not?''

"Because I don't think we could know each other any better,'' replied Jake softly, and Caitlin's heart leapt wildly into her throat.

"So—you don't mind if I look for a job?''

Jake shrugged. "That's up to you. As my wife, I should think you'd stand a fairly good chance."

"As your wife?" Caitlin swallowed. "Do you mean it?"

"Well, it is what we both want, isn't it?" he teased her gently. "Leastways, it's what I want. How about you?"

By the bestselling author of *FORBIDDEN FRUIT*

FORTUNE
ERICA SPINDLER

Be careful what you wish for...

Skye Dearborn knew exactly what to wish for. To unlock the secrets of her past. To be reunited with her mother. To force the man who betrayed her to pay. To be loved.

One man could make it all happen. But will Skye's new life prove to be all that she dreamed of...or a nightmare she can't escape?

Be careful what you wish for...it may just come true.

Available in March 1997 at your favorite retail outlet.

Bestselling Author DEBBIE MACOMBER

Carla Walker thinks she's found paradise with Philip Garrison. Theirs promises to be much more than a casual holiday romance...until Carla learns he's a cop—just like her father. She's never forgotten what it had been like for her mother—always waiting for the phone call that would shatter her world. Carla knows she can't live that kind of life. But Philip won't let her go. He will convince her that their love can chase away the darkness of doubts and fears—putting an end to the...

SHADOW CHASING

Available this February at your favorite retail outlet.

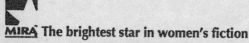

MIRA **The brightest star in women's fiction**

MDM6

From the bestselling author of *Scandalous*

Cam Monroe vowed revenge when
Angela Stanhope's family accused him
of a crime he didn't commit.

Fifteen years later he returns from exile, wealthy
and powerful, to demand Angela's hand in marriage.
It is then that the strange "accidents" begin. Are the
Stanhopes trying to remove him from their lives
one last time, or is there a more insidious,
mysterious explanation?

Available this March at your favorite retail outlet.

Cool warmth...fire and ice...

SNOW KISSES

by bestselling author

DIANA PALMER

Abby Shane has come home to Montana. It's to be a
healing period for Abby—a shelter from the nightmares of
Manhattan and the trauma that jeopardized her career.

She's also come back to Cade McLaren, and to the painful
memories of a long-over and far-too-brief love affair.

Maybe what they once shared was never really over....

Available in February 1997 at your favorite retail outlet.